THE PENTECOST PAPERS

THE PENTECOST PAPERS

A Novel

Ferdinand Mount

BLOOMSBURY PUBLISHING
LONDON • OXFORD • NEW YORK • NEW DELHI • SYDNEY

BLOOMSBURY PUBLISHING
Bloomsbury Publishing Plc
50 Bedford Square, London, WC1B 3DP, UK
Bloomsbury Publishing Ireland Limited,
29 Earlsfort Terrace, Dublin 2, D02 AY28, Ireland

BLOOMSBURY, BLOOMSBURY PUBLISHING and the Diana logo
are trademarks of Bloomsbury Publishing Plc

First published in Great Britain 2025

A catalogue record for this book is available from the British Library

ISBN: HB: 978-1-5266-8272-7;
EBOOK: 978-1-5266-8278-9; EPDF: 978-1-5266-8273-4

2 4 6 8 10 9 7 5 3 1

Typeset by Integra Software Services Pvt. Ltd.
Printed and bound in Great Britain by CPI Group (UK) Ltd, Croydon CR0 4YY

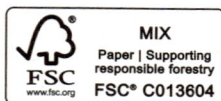

MIX
Paper | Supporting
responsible forestry
FSC
www.fsc.org
FSC® C013604

To find out more about our authors and books visit www.bloomsbury.com
and sign up for our newsletters.
For product safety related questions contact productsafety@bloomsbury.com

Contents

Q. Why can't you play cards in the jungle?
A. Too many cheetahs.

The Ha Ha Bonk Book

I thought when I started that I would be the sole narrator of this story. It was my property. Only I possessed the intimate connections with the characters and also, I flattered myself, the coolness to handle their erratic comings and goings. But then other narrators pressed into my head, protesting that there were bits that they and nobody else had the right to tell, and tell in their own voices. It was like one of those dreams when you have no control over who bursts in and takes over the dream – often some dim character from your past whom you never thought much of. First there was Timbo himself – the whole thing began with him, after all. In his peculiar blundering way, he turned out to be quite a storyteller, and as he was a stranger to embarrassment, he didn't seem to mind whenever he came out of it badly. Then Rowley Beavan hove into view, as he would have put it. There were a couple of scenes where he was the only one of us present, and he's a journo of course, one of the old school of City hacks, so he's used to telling a tale, and tickling it up a bit too. Finally – and this was the surprise to me because at the start I hadn't even heard of him – I found myself yielding the podium to Professor Luke Deverill, philosopher of the Oxford school, late-flowering computer wizard, semi-functioning alcoholic and notorious ladies' man, though 'ladies' man' is putting it delicately – he wouldn't have lasted a college term in the #MeToo era. This is an ill-starred odyssey through an incurably slippery world, and one recorded by several hands – most of them unsteady. But then wasn't Homer supposed to be four or five different people? Anyway, I needed their help. Collaborating is the only hope of getting into other people's heads. Philosophers like Luke Deverill knock themselves out over the problem of Other Minds. But they never ask themselves why on earth we should *expect* to know what other people are thinking. Trying to figure out what they are going to do next is part of being human. Everyone has to attempt it – investment advisers, politicians, therapists, parents and lovers, not to mention con artists who make a living out of it. Getting it wrong is what produces so many of the terrible things that happen to us – bankruptcies, break-ups and breakdowns, broken limbs and broken hearts. If you get it right, it's usually a lucky guess. This story is mostly about getting it wrong.

PART ONE

I

Back Magic

'Are you on your own?' The voice seemed to come from inside the big blackthorn at the side of the fairway. The blackthorn blossom was cold, dazzling white in the April sun, so white it was like a wonderful blank space, as if there was a hole in the view. A man's voice, heavy, insistent, arresting, even in that brief question suggesting discontent or resentment, as though I had somehow forced him to ask the question. Perhaps that was how the Lord God had sounded when He spoke to who was it – Moses? Adam? – out of a bush, a bit aggrieved to be caught in the thorns, wishing He had not come that way. Perhaps commandments always had that sort of resentful undertone – that you were putting the authorities to the trouble of spelling out things which you ought to have worked out for yourself.

The voice sounded sad too, plangent even. The mention of possible solitude was bound to sneak some sadness in. A mutual sadness, for he must be on his own as I was. Proust claimed that golf gave you a taste for solitary pleasures, but it wasn't supposed to. Proust was never on the committee of Beggar's Hill Golf Club, N23 2HN. The committee came down hard on lone golfers, denying them any rights on the course, allowing merry twosomes, loquacious threesomes and stately foursomes to play through them as though they were not there. A club member's duty was like a Victorian spinster's, to pick up a partner at all costs. A solitary golfer at Beggar's Hill was no more than a ghost.

I had been feeling a bit like a ghost myself the past few weeks, though you don't think of ghosts as battered creatures, and battered was also how I felt; battered and ghostly at the same time, as though there wasn't much left of me and all I had to convince me that I existed was this feeling of being knocked about. Not sleeping was part of it. The sleeplessness and the night sweats left me running on empty all day, the heart rattling and the eyes dry-socketed. Then there was the back, but we'll come to the back later in its proper place, which it currently wasn't. Anyway I was feeling decidedly suboptimal, to put it mildly, and I had come up here partly to catch a breath and soak up the view.

My spirits began to chirrup as soon as I passed through the rusty green gate next to the run-down Montessori school. Ragwort poked through the broken railings either side of the potholed lane. A kind of peace came over me, as it always did here. I loved it all, down to the soggy moss on the tiles of the clubhouse roof. Beggar's Hill was a refuge, not from despair but from any kind of expectation. The members were falling off, either through death or because they could no longer afford the sub, the club could barely raise a team for the North Middlesex League, the overdraft at Barclays didn't bear thinking about, and the catering was worse than ever, thanks to Slobo the surly Serb. All the same, for me at any rate, Beggar's Hill was where peace came dropping slow.

From the top of the fourth fairway you could see the towers of Colney Hatch, except it wasn't called Colney Hatch any more, though it was still a mental hospital. I toyed with the thought of spending a week or two inside. These days you could always slip out the gates the moment you had had enough. But it probably wouldn't be much of a rest cure. Institutions never were, you always had to join in with the rest of the group. It wasn't just the talk, it was the relentless company. A Trappist monastery would probably be a strain too. Who was Trapp anyway? Anything to do with the Von Trapps in *The Sound of Music*? My mind was wandering but then that was the point of coming up here: to let my wits have an outing, like taking a dog for a walk, not that I ever wanted a dog. Who was it said she could never love a man who didn't like dogs? Someone who there was no question of loving or being loved by, I remember that much, especially not after the dog pronouncement. But then love was not what I was in the market for, a bit of peace and quiet would be quite enough. Anyway I have a wife, Jane, who needs no replacing. She is a consultant oncologist, and in the time she can spare she looks at me with the same cool, inquisitive eye as I imagine she inspects her patients' tumours before she zaps them. I undergo a little zapping myself now and then, but I cannot complain. So I was not looking for a partner in life, I wasn't even looking for a partner on the golf course.

Which was why I did not welcome the voice calling for company from the middle of the blackthorn bush. Presumably he had a lost ball in there somewhere. But then why didn't he wait to call when he was back out on the fairway or at least the semi-rough? Then I realised that I had pushed my trolley on twenty yards or so past the blackthorn before I had taken in that the question was addressed to me. When I went back a little, there he was right out in the open and quite a distance from the bush. He hadn't been inside it at all, just a few yards the other side. He was a burly figure with his clubs slung across his back. He looked rather hot in his Pringle jersey, the old-fashioned sort in a diamond pattern of blue and beige, the sort people now would not be caught wearing, except as an ironic statement. Even from where I was standing, he did not look like someone who went in for ironic statements or for Marcel Proust either, which was nothing but a good thing. He came towards me, rubbing his spectacles with a handkerchief before replacing them. He had an ambling, rolling sort of gait, faintly ape-like except that he stamped each foot into the turf, as though pressing down invisible divots.

'Are you on your own?' he said again, thinking I had not heard him properly the first time.

'Yes,' I said. 'Yes I am.' I was flustered by having been so slow to reply. There were ways of fobbing off in this situation, like saying you were only playing a few holes or playing such rubbish that you would only spoil his game, but you had to be quick off the mark to have that sort of defence ready and he had caught me unprepared. So when he followed up with the inevitable 'Would you mind if I joined you?', I limply said, 'Yes, that would be great,' and forced myself to smile at the prospect.

'Timbo Smith,' he said, putting out a hand, a big meaty hand with the crunching grip that went with hands like that. 'Christened Timothy, but saddled with Timbo from the age of two.'

Now that I got a better look, what was most remarkable about him was his dark red hair, nearer the colour of dried blood than carrot.

I suppose it was the hair that gave him a miasma of menace, even though he was smiling back at me as we shook hands, or perhaps it was the smile that was menacing. I gave my name and he nodded as though he half-knew it already, or it was just the sort of name he expected me to have.

Which was strange, because my surname is Pentecost and people usually look a bit startled when they hear it. My father was a Greek from Asia Minor called Alexander Pentecostas. He was lucky to escape from the burning quayside at Smyrna in 1922, and when he got to England, was very keen to be British and not Greek which had so far brought him nothing but trouble, though of course he was always taken for Turkish when he said he'd been born in Smyrna and he liked that even less. He was relieved to discover that there were English Pentecosts too, in East Anglia I think, and it was no trouble to drop the final syllable. All the same, he had me christened Domenicos Kyril like his father, so I was D. K. Pentecost and always known as Dickie. So Timbo just repeated 'Dickie Pentecost' after me as we shook hands and smiled his menacing smile; I say menacing but I don't mean that he looked as if he might turn nasty, more that he might bring me trouble in a way I could not begin to guess. As he spoke, he shifted from foot to foot in a strangely emphatic fashion, as though further divots, possibly even molehills, needed pressing down.

'And what's your line of country?'

'I'm a diplomatic correspondent. I write as D. K. Pentecost.'

'Yes,' he said, again as if this was the sort of information he had expected, though not giving any clue whether he knew my byline. Not surprising if he didn't, the paper's been losing sales for years, and these days I don't often get a piece into it. We're a dwindling and forgotten crew, those of us who still call ourselves Dip. Corrs rather than foreign reporters. We gather in the stale old briefing room in Carlton House Terrace and dutifully take down the banalities dispensed by the press officer, misleadingly called the Head of the News Department, whose mission is to tell us nothing of the slightest interest. Now and then I lunch with an attaché from some embassy (these days he usually pays because our exes have been shrivelled), and I flatter him by pretending that he's a spy and he returns the flattery by pretending that he's telling me something exclusive.

A pointless existence, I don't deny it, which is why golf, being the most pointless activity in the solar system, gives me a purpose in life.

He knocked his ball across to where mine was and with a wave of the meaty hand invited me to play first. I hit an awkward little shot with a mid-iron, a five perhaps, and it bobbled down the hill and into the reedy stream that guarded the plateau green, more of a ditch really, a dismal place to be.

What people would normally say, especially after just meeting you, was 'bad luck' or 'I'm sorry, I put you off barging in like that'. But what Timbo said was 'You looked a little stiff there. You haven't been having back trouble by any chance? A little dicky in the dorsal department, no pun intended?'

'Well, yes, a bit,' I said, my hastily mustered bonhomie draining away already. 'One man said it was a disc but another said it wasn't, so I haven't done anything about it.'

I had no time for people who talked about their back pain and I resented becoming one of them myself. But the truth is that the non-sleeping and the being wrung-out were not really symptoms of any early midlife crisis. No, the problem was, quite simply, the Back. Without that, life would be much like it had always been, a few points up or down but well within the familiar range. It was the long wrenching ache as I shifted my hip in bed, the sudden stab between the vertebrae as I tried to sit up, then the unfurling carpet of pain as I tried to lie down again. Then with luck I would find a little pain-free ledge to cling on to until a minute movement toppled me off it into a new position of unmitigated agony which I had no idea how to escape from. Alcohol and paracetamol and codeine could numb the pain, all three together preferably, but numbing was really no great improvement because when the pain was so sharp that you wanted to yelp, you couldn't think of anything else, but when it was a little dulled, there was room for despair. So, yes, as you see, I too can talk about back pain and be as unendurable on the subject as anyone else.

Jane had banned the subject at home. Fair enough, she's an oncologist and spends a lot of her time handing out death sentences, so her reserves of sympathy are running low by the time she gets back from the Marsden. I rather worship her, and I cannot help feeling how futile my work is compared with hers. But I must admit that she is not abounding in instant warmth. Even her small talk sounds like a second opinion. We are a cool couple, but not in the modern sense.

In fact I'm not like most people's idea of a Greek at all, partly because I'm fairish like my mother who came from Norfolk, but also because I'm like my father Sandy who worked for the World Service most of his life. And if his life had a mission, it was turning himself into an Englishman and he managed it perfectly – the tweed jacket with leather patches at the elbows, the hesitation on first meeting, the distracted courtesy, the absence of passion at all times. Perhaps he was suppressing stuff. If so, I never noticed. Anyway, I inherited all his mannerisms. The difference was that I did it naturally. At least I did, until I had the bad back and I began to discover my inner Greek.

'Would you mind if I had a little go at it?' Timbo asked.

'How do you mean?'

'It's one of my few talents, backs especially.'

'You mean you do massage?'

'No, no, I don't even touch you. I'm, well, like a healer – I don't fancy the word much, it sounds so pretentious. I haven't had any training. It's just a gift, you see, goes with the red hair apparently. The ginger gene, you can't escape it.' He dragged his fingers through his rufous thatch, as though he was charging it up for action.

'You want to do it out here?' I said, looking around me, seized by panic that a foursome of the Greens Committee might be bearing down on us. Among other things, it was an iron rule that no business might be transacted on club premises, which would surely apply to this sort of funny business. If this dubious therapy had any place at all, it was in a proper surgery and carried out by a registered practitioner, not a self-confessed amateur I had only just met. It shows how desperate I was that I should even think of placing myself in the hands of the least plausible entrant in a field which was already crowded.

'You don't have to do anything. Don't worry, it might even improve your golf score. All I want you to do is just stand there and hold on to your trolley with both hands and relax as though you're just enjoying the sunshine while waiting for the people in front to clear the green.'

It seemed easier to do as he said rather than go through all the reasons why I didn't like any of this at all. Besides, I could see a couple of players coming up to the green at the previous hole and the sooner we got it over with the better.

So I said, all right.

'Brilliant,' he said. 'It won't take a minute, and if it doesn't have much effect first time, we can try again when we're back in the clubhouse. It sometimes takes more than one go.'

'Do I need to, um, *believe*? I don't mean believe in God or anything, but, you know, well, believe in you?'

'Christ, no. In fact, it's often better to be a bit sceptical. Believing can get in the way.'

'Ah,' I said, not wanting to pursue this line of questioning.

I stood behind my trolley, gently holding on to the handle as instructed and letting my body go as slack as I could manage, though the embarrassment was still throbbing through me.

He was standing close behind me, so close that I could feel his minty breath on my cheek. I was somehow aware of his hands travelling down my back but not touching it, perhaps a couple of inches away. I tried not to flinch, but then I began to find I did not feel like flinching at all, because a sensation of heat began to travel down my back, starting from somewhere between the shoulder blades. Not a powerful or jabbing sensation, rather a steady, downward-trickling warmth, like a can of not too hot water being emptied over me but travelling slower than water would. As it reached the small of my back, the sensation faded, a slow, pleasant fade. When it was over, I felt drained in a sweet, languorous sort of way. He stepped away and came round to face me.

'Feel anything?'

'Oh, yes, I did. It was rather wonderful.'

'And how do you feel now, Dickie? A bit like after you've had a good wank?'

'Mm, yes, I suppose so, a bit.' This was in fact just what I had thought but had not thought of putting it into those words, or words at all, and wished he hadn't either. You have to know someone quite well to talk in those terms and not presume on the universal camaraderie of men out together which is not a camaraderie I am a member of.

'That's pretty much par for the course, although it only works for about one in three people. For some reason, it seems to work better when people aren't expecting it. Doesn't give the body time to stiffen up, I suppose. How's the back now?'

'Well, yes, it is definitely much easier.'

He grinned at me, an unholy, conspiratorial grin, as if we had just brought off some dodgy trick together, which I suppose we had. As for me, along with the relief which was a real blessing, there was a trickle of shame, because I didn't think that I was susceptible to that sort of thing.

'My shot.'

He addressed his ball with exaggerated concentration, clenching his eyebrows and pressing his lips tightly together, then with an abrupt heave sent the ball on an enormous parabola deep into the still leafless sycamores on the right.

'Too much right hand,' he said in a curiously cool way as though the shot had been a deliberate experiment.

It ought to have been a relief that he was no better than I was, though it seemed odd that his physical gifts did not extend to playing golf. The only difference between us was that he tended to slice the ball off to the right while I was pulling my shots round to the left in a J-shaped curve which was especially disheartening because the ball started off looking as if it was going straight. There was another difference, though, in the way we reacted to these misfortunes. I was surfing on a boiling tide of anger with patches of sullen despair in between. Timbo, by contrast, appeared unmoved. He issued reproofs to himself in a calm, detached voice as if he were a coach walking round at his side: 'Not enough torque on the backswing there, Timothy.'

What he mostly did in between shots, though, was ask questions. He had something to ask me in an easy but unrelenting way every time we were reunited on the green after our wayward journeys through the gorse and heather, his more wayward than mine. In fact, he several times disappeared into the thick shrubbery. The odd thing was on one occasion that I could see his ball lying perfectly visible in the semi-rough. There was something purposeful about the way he strode into the blackthorn thicket, as though he was going to pick up a message left by an unseen contact or himself drop one in some hollow tree or disused water butt. Perhaps he was only taking a leak, but the fantasy flitted though my head that he had some kind of hideout in there, where he would lurk until he caught sight of an unfriended golfer like me coming up the fairway. Was his hidden shack or burrow a tacitly acknowledged peculiarity of the course, tolerated by the committee, perhaps even boasted of with a chuckle to their intimates?

Then he would come out again and throw me another question, almost as though prompted by his unseen contact. By the time we had played the first nine, he had all the information about me you would need to fill a census form. But these were only the preliminaries before he went in-depth. What did I think about the invasion of Crimea? Was Putin going to be a real threat? Yes, I thought he was, I said. And Brexit? Not a good idea, I said, we'd regret it. But he did not react to any of my answers, or offer his own opinion, just asked another question, usually quite unrelated. And Pope Francis? Had I heard that he was dying? How long did I think it would be before the Vatican allowed woman priests?

It would have been less disconcerting if he had shown any visible interest in the answers I gave, but he simply moved on to the next question, like a market researcher going through his list. I wondered if he himself had been in some type of therapy, a type which had told him to show more interest in other people by asking them questions but which had not as yet managed to teach him to take an interest in the answers. There was certainly something missing in our exchanges. For a man with hair the colour of dried blood, his calm was eerie.

Over the next few minutes I must have missed three or four of his questions, because the long tenth at Beggar's Hill runs along the side of a railway cutting, and only a thin straggle of blackthorn and bramble separated us from the whoosh and rattle of the trains at this mid-morning hour, carrying shoppers in from Metroland to Marylebone, and so I couldn't hear a word he said. I nodded and smiled back at him, to indicate my eagerness to catch what he said as soon as the trains had passed. He must be hearing the trains too, but there seemed no question of his suspending operations. I wondered how long it would have taken him to catch on if I had been deaf and/or dumb.

'How old would you say I was?' he asked suddenly when the trains had gone and I was clearing some withered leaves from my ball on the edge of the gorse.

'Oh, I really haven't a clue, I'm no good at guessing ages.'

'No, go on, have a guess.'

'Well, um, thirty-nine.'

'Thirty-four,' he said, looking downcast.

'I said I was rubbish at guessing ages.'

'I used to think I looked younger than I was, but obviously I don't. Girls are always amazed when I tell them I'm only thirty-four. Aurore, that's my girlfriend at the moment, couldn't believe it. She's in the Congo right now. Médecins sans Frontières.'

'Fantastic,' I said, for want of anything better, giving him what I meant to be a sympathetic look to indicate admiration for the work of Médecins sans Frontières and for him having a girlfriend in it. I rather expected him to develop the subject, saying perhaps how anxious he was about her safety or how difficult for them it was being separated for such long periods. But he said nothing more about her, and when we met on the next green, he began asking for my views on the use of drugs in sport and whether it was fair to ban substances that occurred naturally in the human body.

I tried to vary the relentless interrogation by making a feeble joke about my swing needing a shot of nandrolone. He looked back at me with a blank, not unpleasant expression before responding that there was no evidence to suggest that steroids could improve a golf swing.

'Well, mine's beyond hope anyway, I'm afraid.'

'Oh, I wouldn't say that, you just need to pivot a bit more.'

I failed to conceal how much this piece of unasked advice annoyed me.

'You probably think I haven't got much sense of humour. Aurore said I was the first Englishman she had met who had no sense of humour at all.'

'Did she?'

'The strange thing is, you wouldn't believe it but I used to do stand-up at university. I did a gig at Edinburgh one year. Nobody much came, one night I had an audience of three, but they seemed to enjoy it.'

'Where did you get the jokes from?'

'I didn't tell jokes exactly. It was more situation comedy, you know, when you describe how you got stuck on the train or you mishear what somebody says to you.'

'Can be very funny, that sort of thing.'

'Do you really think so?'

Timbo laughed suddenly, a not unpleasing baritone gurgling sort of chuckle but rather unnerving because of its lack of obvious connection to anything that either of us had said. Then I noticed that, as we went on playing, he would usually laugh at least once when we met on the green, again not because he or I had made anything resembling a joke. He did not seem like one of those people who corpses at his own jokes and keeps a straight face at anyone else's. In fact, he showed no signs of wishing to crack what could be classified as a joke at all. Perhaps Aurore had put him off trying. His restraint in this department might be merely showing consideration for others, just as some polite people who have been told they are tone-deaf will refrain from joining in the singing. The baritone chuckle seemed less connected with mirth, more in the nature of a release required at regular intervals, like the periodic draining of a washing machine during its cycle, a sound to which his rich gurgling bore some resemblance.

'That was really great,' he said as we packed our gloves and tees away at the side of the final green. 'I'm so glad we met up, we've had such a fantastic natter.'

As we came into the clubhouse under the little Dutch-style tiled porch, Timbo turned aside to use the new airjet machine for blasting mud off golf shoes. As he bent forward to offer first one sole, then the other to the hissing nozzle, like a horse offering its hooves to be shod, I was overcome by an unaccountable feeling that the whole healing episode had been a daydream. Timbo was no more peculiar than anyone else you were liable to pick up on a golf course. The last man I had played with had once been an airline pilot but had switched to working in an abattoir because he liked working with animals. Yet the time Timbo and I had spent together, only a couple of hours, seemed somehow out of time, or out of my own time. It was like being in a stationary train and looking out of the window and seeing yourself suddenly appear in the window of the train stopped alongside you.

'Let me buy you a drink,' Timbo said, swinging open the door to the bar. 'I could kill for an all-day breakfast.' And he gave his inappropriate laugh.

The first drink at the Beggar's Hill bar was in fact free if you produced your green-fee tag. This did not deter Timbo from depositing my pint of shandy in front of me with a flourish suggesting generosity beyond the norm. He came back again with his plate piled high with egg, sausage, tomato, bacon, mushrooms, hash browns and black pudding. He needed a separate plate for his side order of baked beans on toast.

'The first thing I look for anywhere in the world is a place where they can do you a full English.'

He paused between mouthfuls for one of the baritone chuckles. It was clear to me now that he did not use laughter like most other humans, as a celebration of irony, wit, mockery or the general absurdity of things. That made his laughter hard to read, like the grin of a chimpanzee.

'You been a member here long? I don't think I've seen you around before,' I asked, for want of anything better.

'A couple of years,' he replied, spreading out his meaty hands, as though to indicate an uncertain stretch of time. 'I don't get up here as often as I'd like, because of the travelling.'

'You travel a lot, do you?' I asked, cautiously assailing the edge of my club sandwich.

'A fair bit, mostly for work, if you mean foreign travel. When I'm on leave, what I do is try to get to know this old island better, walk the Pennine Way, chug through the Broads, that sort of thing.'

'What is your line of work exactly?'

'Well, it's rather hard to describe, partly because of security, to be honest.'

'Security?'

'We're in the risk management business, I suppose you could say.'

A look of blissful satisfaction passed over his face. I wondered if he was going to do the gurgle, but the moment seemed too holy.

'What sort of risk?' I began to see the charm of asking the questions. They were usually easier to think of than answers. Anyway, I really did want to know more about this mysterious vocation, which had just broken the surface without explaining itself properly.

'We're sort of on the cusp of the business–politics interface. We find out the stuff that the decision makers need to know before they go in but which isn't officially available.'

'Sounds thrilling,' I said, wiping the mayo off my mouth.

'It's quite rewarding in every sense.' Again the bliss bathed his sturdy features, but this time the baritone chuckle did follow the bliss, gurgling up from the depths of his diaphragm, the way an opera singer does it. 'Let me show you round the office sometime, I think it might interest you.'

'Wouldn't I be a security risk?'

'We like to make new friends. We need to seek as well as to keep.'

'Is that your firm's motto?'

'You ask too many questions, my friend,' he said, putting on a movie villain's accent, which I would not have thought him capable of. But then who knew what anyone was capable of? 'Now, it's time for your next treatment.'

'Not here,' I said, unable to stifle my panic as I stared round at the Beggar's Hill regulars quietly supping their lagers.

'We'll go into the changing room,' which, thank God, turned out to be empty. With only two small high-up windows above the lockers, the place had a cavernous gloom and an abandoned feeling; shoes and sweaters littered about as though their owners had had to get out in a hurry, leaving behind only the smell of their dried sweat and their aftershaves. There was nobody else about, but I was still trembling with nerves as I stood with the palms of my hands pressed against the grubby wooden lockers. Again, I could feel Timbo's breath on my cheek, no longer minty but carrying a deranging aroma of bacon and baked beans. The sensations of heat were fainter this time, and travelled slower and more uncertainly down my spine, but they were real enough.

At that moment it struck me with fresh horror what any club member who came in and saw us together would think, me pressed against the lockers and Timbo's meaty hands travelling down my back. Saying it was only a massage would make the whole thing worse. Then in the same instant I wondered with even fresher horror whether something like that was really Timbo's ultimate goal and the healing was only a warm-up. Yet I didn't really think this, he seemed too detached to have any more intimate intent. Now I just desperately wanted him to finish.

'Not so good this time?' Timbo asked. 'Probably not the right venue. Plus you're still sweating a bit after the game which doesn't help.'

Even so, as I straightened up, there was a sense of well-being running through me, not just an absence of backache but a feeling that I was in fettle.

Timbo was standing in front of me now, gently massaging his hands as though rubbing the electricity out of them. He looked sad and depleted, as if the business had taken a lot out of him. Or perhaps it was the dusty sunbeams now slanting through the high-up windows that made him look drained.

'You must come to the office and I'll give you a session there. It's a good place, quiet and cool, it'll help you to relax.'

In that dusty half-light, there was, for the first time, something sage about him. For a moment he seemed hallowed, like one of those children who is picked apparently at random out of an ordinary family to become a lama. The half-light sharpened his features and the dried-blood hair looked nearer black, so that just for that moment you could have thought him almost handsome.

'Here's my card,' he said. 'Ring me any time.'

'Timothy L. Smith, Senior Associate Director, Ophion Research, 38 Audley Lane, W1,' I read. 'Oaf-eye-on, is that the right way to say it?'

'Spot on. We call ourselves the Ophites.'

'Sounds like some tribe of ancient Israel, one of the more ungodly ones who were always smiting.'

'Actually it's Greek. They were a mysterious sect who had access to knowledge nobody else possessed. They were Gnostics, if that means anything to you. Ophis means serpent, see our logo.' He pointed to the wiggly snake above his name on the card.

'Speaks with forked tongue, I expect.'

'Totally forked.'

'I'll think of you when I need to phone a friend.'

'I must run or I'll miss the bus.'

We parted as strangers who have been playing golf together usually do, with a mixture of unexpected intimacy and relief. After he opened the side door into the lane, waving to me awkwardly as though beckoning for assistance, I thought that, no, I would not see him again and that this was a good thing. Yet my thinking this somehow seemed to presuppose the opposite.

It was two, perhaps three, weeks later that I bent over sideways to retrieve a couple of sheets of paper that had fluttered off the desk, and in a flash I was locked in a gridiron of pain, unable to move without doubling the agony. I lowered myself gingerly out of the chair and crouched immobile hanging on to its arm, feeling like one of those bent old men who stand motionless in a deserted lane in one of the later poems of Thomas Hardy. After a small eternity, Gil Goulthwaite caught sight of me over the half-partition between his office and mine and came round to shepherd me gently onto the little sofa at the end of our pod. At other times, his oily solic-itude tended to put me off, but this was the sort of moment he was born for. In no time, he had diverted my calls, ordered up a cappuccino and was starting to fix up an appointment with his own back wizard.

'No,' I protested pluckily through the pain, 'I've got a new man.'

'Brilliant,' Gil said. 'An osteopath, is he?'

'Not exactly,' I said, 'but he's first-rate.'

I had not intended to confide in Gil, because in retrospect the whole episode seemed more embarrassing than anything else, the kind of experience that only a gullible person would let himself in for, but Gil always knew the best place to go for anything and I felt the need to keep my end up.

Which was how I found myself crawling through Mayfair, winc-ing at every step, looking for the turning to Audley Lane.

Number 38 was a tall cream-stucco house, just like the others. There was nothing to tell you that this was the Ophion office except the wiggly snake on the brass plate with the house number. No doubt this was the secrecy that was designed to attract attention, the Gnostic style. The long wait after I rang the bell was proba-bly programmed in too. To my surprise, considering the grandeur of the premises, the voice that answered was the inimitable gurgly baritone of Timbo himself and it was he who opened the door.

'Where are the security men and the AK-47s?'

'Oh, they're all in Brindisi.'

'Brindisi?'

'It's an entrepôt.' He pronounced the final 't', which I thought was meant to be silent, but these people must speak their own lingo.

'Entrepôt for what?'

'All sorts of kit. God, you look terrible.'

'I feel terrible.'

'Come on in. We'd better have a session right here and put you out of your misery.'

He led me into a high white hall with a black-and-white floor. The weather outside was warm enough, but the hall was searchingly chilly, perhaps partly because it was so empty: no board with notices of forthcoming events or information about fire assembly points, no coffee table with back numbers of *London Property* or *Tatler*, not even a chair. Timbo had to fetch one out of the little glass box to the left of the door where you would have expected to see a porter or receptionist, and he sat me down sideways on it, so he could get at my back.

His hands had only just begun and I could not tell yet whether it was working or not when a skinny little man carrying a kitbag over his shoulder skipped down the stairs at the back of the hall, taking the steps two at a time.

'Hail, O thou great healer.'

'Where is it this time?'

'Baku, then Rawalpindi if they need me. You want to watch out, sir, Stoke Mandeville is full of his old patients.'

'Fuck off, Jonty.'

Timbo paused in his operations until the skinny little man had slammed the front door behind him.

'He's our best man. You remember that Greenpeace ship that never left harbour for some mysterious reason. That was one of Jonty's. The Colonel thinks the world of him.'

The brief appearance of Jonty seemed to have left Timbo in a daze of pleasure. I wondered whether this would interfere with his magic powers. Healing seemed too serious a business to be mixed up with badinage. But then he set to work, and it turned out that the chilly hall with its black-and-white stone floor and high ceiling was perfect for reception, if that was the right word to describe the process. The heat from Timbo's hands, combined with the surrounding chill, made me shiver as it passed down my spine and the flush of well-being was almost instantaneous. I felt wonderfully refreshed as I stood up straight, taking it slowly but at the same time confident that I would be all right now.

'That's marvellous,' I said. 'Timbo, I was wondering – I mean I'm so grateful and if I could possibly make some contribution …'

'Don't even think of it, old boy, it would only break the spell.'

'But I really do feel—'

'Well, if you're going to be boring, I never object to the odd bottle of vino.'

So we fell into a routine. About once a fortnight at midday I would take the Tube to Green Park and walk up Audley Lane for Timbo to give me a going-over. On the way I would stop at Justerini's to buy a couple of overpriced bottles of red wine; nothing too fancy, he liked Rioja. The second time I went, he took me to his office, a little room at the back of the mezzanine floor which he said was handy for keeping an eye on things, though all he had in there was an old Mac and I did not see him pick up any emails.

Another time, he took me up to the top floor of the building and flung open the door into a long attic room with three or four screens in it. At the far end of the room a youth in scarlet braces was throwing a miniature basketball at a small metal hoop fixed to the wall.

'This is our little dealing room. It's handy for clients who've got moolah they don't want to put through their regular brokers. That's Adrian, used to be with HSBC. How's the market, Ades?'

'Flat as a kipper,' the young man replied moodily, bending down to retrieve the little plastic ball from underneath the bank of computers.

These were the only people I ever saw in Ophion House on those first visits: Jonty (just that one time), and Adrian the broker. It was a quiet place, arctic-chilly to begin with, then when the weather warmed up properly – not until the end of May that year – it became stuffy and Timbo opened one of the tall windows to let in some air. There was no noise from the street, which was unsettling, almost as though life on the planet had ceased without warning. It made you realise how tranquil a backwater this was, one of those bits of Mayfair that had become too expensive for human beings. There was no sign of the mysterious Colonel whose name was so often on Timbo's lips.

'Does the Colonel come in much?'

'Not a lot. He always puts his head round the door at Christmas, brings some amazing prezzies, but otherwise not, unless there's a flap on and he needs storage.'

'Storage?'

'When somebody needs to be kept out of harm's way for a bit. He always likes to say hullo to our guests if he doesn't know them already. In the final reel it's the personal contact that makes the difference. Ultimately, loyalty is the secret ingredient of this business.'

'But surely, I mean I don't know exactly what we're on about here, but don't you, well, have to buy people's loyalty quite a bit in your business, whatever it is?'

'Absolutely right.' He looked at me with a delighted expression as at a pet who has after long training finally managed to perform a simple trick. 'But you wouldn't call that loyalty exactly, would you? More a question of payment for services rendered or about to be rendered. The deal ends when the contract's fulfilled.'

'That's just what I mean.'

'What you're talking about are civilians, the blokes we pull in to do a job. I'm talking about soldiers, the guys who take the oath.'

'And they invariably stay loyal?'

'Loyalty is what we're all about, Dickie. Without loyalty you're a dead man walking.'

Timbo spoke with a kind of confident vehemence. He didn't seem angry that I had raised the subject. It was more as if I had given him the opportunity to declare his faith and this pleased him.

'You mean you never come across people, for example, people of mixed race or people who have two passports, who say quite sincerely that they feel no loyalty to any country, even the one they were born in?'

He looked at me with a kind of mulish bafflement.

'They're not being straight with you. Everyone belongs some-where. If there's nowhere you really care about, Dickie, then in my book you aren't a genuine person at all.'

He paused and rubbed his hands together, the way he often did before treating me, but now it seemed as though he was doing it to charge up his thought processes. After the pause, he said very earnestly:

'You don't really care for the P-word, I expect, Dickie?'

'The P-word?'

'Patriotism, that's not quite your thing, is it?'

I found this a hard one to answer. As Greek immigrants, we Pentecosts have to try harder. On the other hand, we are under the impression, my father and I, that in this country part of being patriotic is not boasting how patriotic you are. I tried to convey something of this, but Timbo ignored the subtleties.

'Greek, that's interesting. You don't look Greek.'

'I know. I take after my mother. She came from Norfolk.'

'Do you ever long to go back?'

'I've only ever been there twice, on holiday. So it wouldn't be going back exactly.'

'Greek, well,' he said, half to himself, with a hint of satisfaction as though he had extracted this information by cunning interrogation.

I was annoyed by Timbo's declaration of loyalty, impressed by it too, though I didn't care to admit it. But it brought me no closer to understanding what his precise role in the whole operation might be. He did not appear to be someone you could describe as a courier because he was there in Audley Lane most of the time. He could have been some sort of intelligence analyst or researcher, except he never seemed to have a file or a briefcase with him and there was no sign of papers in his little office or any beeps from his computer. All that might be kept hidden away for reasons of security. Even so, he didn't strike me as having the temperament of a research analyst, even if he had the intellectual firepower, which did not seem likely either. His talk of soldiers and loyalty suggested that he might lend a hand with the physical side of operations, as an escort for the Colonel's guests perhaps. His muscular build might come in handy if there was any trouble. Obviously he relished, perhaps cultivated, a certain air of mystery. At the same time, I felt that he would tell me the truth soon enough if he wanted to. Was his keeping me in the dark a sign that his job description did not quite measure up to his expectations? It might be preferable to wrap himself in the shimmering aura of Ophion House rather than spell out exactly what he did there. I googled Ophion House and the Ophites. Nothing, not a sniff. If they were looking for business, surely they would need a web presence. True, Timbo had said they preferred to operate below the radar, but wouldn't they need some kind of public face – a front, to put it in crude terms?

One time, though, I should say it must have been about my sixth visit, I noticed that there was a little door half-open at the back of his office and I had a glimpse of an unmade bed in the room beyond. He followed my furtive glances.

'It's a bit poky, but it comes in handy when I'm kept late,' he said.

I realised that he had never given me a clue where he lived, and it came to me in the same moment that this must be where. So perhaps he was really the office manager, or not even that, something more like a night porter, which would explain why he was so cagey about his duties. When the Colonel's operatives were all out on mission, Timbo would be always there at Ophion House, minding the shop. Essential no doubt, but not the glamour end of the show.

'Very central too,' he added, 'when you've been out with a girl.'

'Brilliant,' I said vaguely, not wishing to speculate too hard in that direction.

'When you think what a pad round here would cost.'

'Absolutely. By the way, any sign of Aurore coming back soon?'

'Come again?'

'From the Congo. Aurore. Your girlfriend.'

'No, not for a bit. Not as far as I know.'

He spoke in a curious absent tone, as though the whereabouts of Aurore was too remote a question for him to be qualified to answer. In my mind I pictured Aurore, delectably slender in her white coat, brushing her silky chestnut hair out of her dark eyes as she bent over to change the dressing on a sick Congolese child. I could not imagine her having a lot of time to think about Timbo. On the other hand, his vagueness might not be connected with whatever their relationship was or wasn't. I noticed that he became distracted in this fashion whenever I happened to ask him anything at all personal. Not that I was trying to be intrusive, but if you go on chatting to someone for long enough, it's hard not to stray on to more intimate things.

Besides, I had become fond of him as well as being grateful, and this naturally meant wanting to know more about him. His friendly blundering manner relaxed me even before he ran his hands down my back: never touching, always two inches away, never more, never less, he said. I would have been just as grateful, I suppose, if he had been someone quite different, a fey, otherworldly type who made a great exhibition of his supernatural powers, if supernatural is what his powers were. But then the experience would have been weird and creepy, which it wasn't a bit with Timbo. The outings to Ophion House were more like popping over to a friend's place for a regular game of, not chess, something less demanding, Scrabble perhaps.

So I was saddened when he told me one week towards the end of July that he would not be able to see me for a bit because he was going away.

'You really deserve a break after all your exertions with me,' I said. 'Going somewhere nice?'

'No, it's not a holiday. It's more in the nature of a mission.'

'For the Colonel?'

'No, nothing like that. It's not for the office at all in fact. It's more a personal mission.'

'But secret just the same?'

'Yes, I'd prefer to keep it to myself, for now anyway.'

'Fine. Well, the very best of luck. You know how much my vertebrae will miss you.'

He had been looking anxious as he spoke, and my pathetic quip did not dispel his anxiety. But he looked excited too, as though the mission might be as rewarding as it was nerve-racking. I got the impression that he had been waiting some time, perhaps a long time, for this moment.

'How long do you reckon you'll be away?'

'Hard to say, could be a week, could be more, might be as much as a month.'

'Depends how it goes?'

'Yes, depends how it goes.'

'Come and have a meal with us before you go. My wife is longing to meet my miracle worker.'

That wasn't exactly true. As I might have expected, Jane had the darkest suspicions about 'your quack' as she called him. All the same, she did want to check him out.

'I wouldn't want to upset your wife, Dickie. Anyway, I'm not much good in respectable company.'

'Well, you must come for a drink at least.'

Timbo's visit did not go well, in fact it went worse than I had expected and I hadn't expected much. It was a hot evening and the three of us stood out in the back garden, Jane still in the smart shirt and skirt she wore to work, and she was too tired to bother to conceal how she wasn't taking to Timbo. Though he was no taller than I am, he somehow bulked too large for our little terrace. To be fair, he asked the sort of questions ordinary people ask – how long had we lived there, which of us was the gardener, what our daughters were doing just now – but coming from him the questions sounded intrusive, almost impertinent. Jane reacted by giving answers that were brief to the edge of rudeness. She may have hoped to shut him up, but I could have told her that she would only egg him on.

Soon enough, he was asking her what it was like to tell someone that their cancer was inoperable and whether she told them how many months they had to live, or only if they insisted on knowing. Out of nerves, I filled his glass too often, gin and tonic with not much tonic. He didn't become incoherent, just more insistent in his questioning. Then he started to go round the garden. Not that there's much to go round, 30 ft by 35 ft to be exact. But he made a performance of it.

'Those are great hollyhocks, Jane,' he said.

'Hydrangeas,' she said, more annoyed by him calling her Jane than by getting the flowers wrong.

The sun was setting now over the heights of Hampstead and it cast a fiery light on Timbo's hair, so that he looked like a blazing angel in a William Blake illustration, and I just wished he would go.

'I'm so sorry,' I said, as I finally closed the door behind him at 8.40.

'He's feral, that man, really feral. I'm just glad the girls weren't here, they'd have been so embarrassed.' Jane spoke with a violence that startled me because it was so unlike her.

24

'Well, he did say he wasn't fit for respectable company.'

'He was right there,' Jane said grimly. He seemed to draw the fierceness out of her as though sucking a sting, and I felt grateful, I don't know why. In fact, Jane taking against him so violently somehow attached me closer to him and only confirmed my belief in his powers.

Typically, Timbo himself lost no time in bringing up the subject when we met for my final session before he went away.

'I didn't go down well at all, did I? I told you I wasn't much good in company.'

'Jane was very pleased to meet you.'

'No, she could see right through me. She's a formidable lady, your Jane.'

So she is, but I didn't much care for the way he said it. All the same, I thought I would miss him when he went away, and not only because of the healing. I had to admit that he conferred a weird sort of calm on me. I was sleeping better, not just for longer, but sleeping the sort of sleep you wake from clear-headed and washed clean. Which was odd, because you could not call his company restful, nor could you say that he seemed at ease with himself. It was as though he was somehow hoovering up my worries. I never thought I would be saying this, and I would not have dreamed of saying it to Jane, but I needed him.

So I was pleased when he rang a couple of days later.

'Mayday, Mayday. The old GTi has packed up and I need wheels. You couldn't possibly—'

'I'm afraid the Corsa's only insured for—'

'No, no, Dickie, I wanted the pleasure of your company. Could you possibly spare a couple of days to be my chauffeur, peaked cap not required?'

'Um, I've got a couple of days' holiday owing, but what exactly ...'

'It'll be like one of those spa holidays, treatment thrown in at no extra cost.'

'But I thought it was a secret mission you were off on.'

'I have no secrets from you, Dickie.'

II

Scrivenham Barracks

Jane was off to a conference of oncologists in Perugia and the girls were staying with her sister in Bridport, so I was a free agent. All the same, I had expected a greater show of gratitude from Timbo when I told him I'd be happy to drive him around for a couple of days as he asked. In his world, it seemed, people were always *en disponibilité*, as we dip.corrs say. Perhaps he already thought of me as a soldier in his private army.

'Rendezvous OH 0900. Should take us a couple of hours to make it to Scrivenham.'

'What's Scrivenham?'

'It's the barracks where Moth did his basic training and met his best wartime friend Derek Deverill. They reported there for embarkation before D-Day too.'

'Moth?'

'Moth was my grandfather, he sort of brought me up after my dad …' Timbo mimicked someone draining a glass. 'He was only just forty when he died.'

'What about your mother?'

'Oh, she sugared off with a merchant banker, at least he said he was a merchant banker. They lived in Lausanne, so I scarcely ever saw her. Moth was my real dad. He was christened Timothy like me, but he was always called Moth, though there was nothing moth-like about him; he was sixteen stone when he grew up, but he had this speech impediment as a child, which made him splutter on his th's – Ti*moth*y. He used to sign his letters with a floppy sort of moth, he was crap at drawing.'

'He sounds a nice sort of grandfather to have.'

'Well, he wasn't, really. He was so restless, you could never tell which way he would jump. He had opinions on everything but you couldn't guess what they were going to be. He hated strawberries and moustaches, and cardigans, and he loved the ballet and the seaside – amazing that he loved the ballet, he was so clumsy, like me. Oh, and he approved of homosexuals. "I've got a lot of time for poofs," he would say, don't know why, perhaps he was a bit that way himself. But he was angry such a lot of the time, angry or in tears.'

'In tears?'

'After the war, he was never quite the same, not of course that I knew him before. He was so embarrassing to be with, he had this loud and frothy voice, like an old coffee machine, and he was so much older than other boys' fathers, over sixty when I was born. My stepgran, Mia, was his second wife. The first wife was called Gaye, and she died way back in the fifties.'

'Did you tell them about your healing powers?'

'Christ, no. Mia would have been terrified that it would get me into trouble, she worried about everything, and Moth would have thought it all a load of rubbish. Anyway, he died before I started the healing, and she passed away too, two months ago, which is why we're going to Scrivenham, as a sort of pilgrimage.'

'Was it sudden, his dying?'

'He was a fair old age, and he had a lot wrong with him, prostate cancer, macular degeneration, you name it, but what killed him off was the argument we had about the Iraq War.'

'I never heard of that killing anyone before, an argument I mean, not the war.'

'It actually started with him refusing to go into a nursing home, because he wanted to be there when they redecorated the bathroom. Then it segued into this row. I said I could see Tony Blair's point of view and he said Blair was a prancing imbecile. Then he exploded with a sort of purple gurgle and collapsed on the doormat – I was just leaving to go back to college. Funny that he should be a casualty of the Iraq War when he came through the whole of World War Two with only a twisted knee.

'Anyway he left everything to Mia, and when she died, they sent me all his stuff, and I started trying to make sense of his correspondence. The dates were so hard to read, well, all the letters were hard to read because his handwriting was so bad. Quite often it was hard to tell which of the two wives he was writing to, but there was one letter dated quite clearly 12 July '44. I'll read it to you if I may. It's to my grandmother Gaye, the one who died years before I was born.'

We were driving down the M3 in thickening drizzle and the wipers were screeching, so Timbo's reading was hard to hear, also because the reading of it made him hoarse, so that the words sounded as if they came from far away, from beyond the grave even, which of course they did.

Gaye, my darling,

Well, I really can promise you now that if something happens to me you'll be properly looked after in a funny sort of way. Derek and I got talking last night in the village, fearful hole but there's a café still open or reopened with a big barrel of cider and all the Calvados you could want to drink. We were saying to each other that we thought tomorrow looked like being uphill work. He's a dry stick Derek as you would expect being a maths prof but the men adore him for some reason and he does come out with things that can surprise you. I'd almost rather stop a bullet myself tomorrow, he said, than have to write another letter saying what a wonderful chap Private So-and-so was and how much everyone in the battalion would miss him when in fact everyone hated his guts and thought he was a useless sod. Promise me, Moth, he said, you won't write a slushy letter to Jacquetta about me. Well, he looked so down in the mouth that I said I wouldn't but if anything happened to him, I would promise to see that Jacquetta and little Luke were OK and keep an eye on them for him. And he said in that dry way of his, 'oh that is most kind and I solemnly undertake to do the same for Gaye and Sarah-Caroline'.

'Sarah-Caroline's my aunt,' Timbo interjected, 'she lives in New Zealand, we don't really get on.'

I was surprised that he even knew your name, let alone S-C's because he's not the sort of chap who encourages you to gas about your family or appears to be listening if you do. So we shook hands on it as if it was a sacred oath, we were both a bit squiffy from the Calva I expect. So there you are, my darling, if the Moth flies too near the flame, you have a protector five foot eight in his socks but with a brain as big as the Eiffel Tower. At least he'll be able to help S-C with her maths homework. We move off at first light. Wish me luck and I wish I was in your arms.

Your own Tiger Moth

'And there's the moth.' Timbo leant across me and briefly flattened the letter out on the steering wheel.

'It's a lovely letter,' I said. 'But I see what you mean about the moth.'

'The sad thing was, Moth really liked drawing. He took his black tin box of watercolours on holiday and did sketches of bridges and churches – anything that had a nice sharp shape – and would pass them round for inspection over lunch at the local bistro or trattoria – "There's a touch of the Monets about this one, don't you think?" Even I could see he had no gift at all. The sketches always had a collapsed look to them, as if they had been left out in the rain. But the sight of the moth always made my heart thump. When I saw pictures of ancient Egyptian tombs with the soul escaping in the form of a bird, I thought of Moth's moth. It was more than a signature, it somehow contained my grandfather's soul.'

Timbo pretended to blow his nose and wiped his face free of tears, and sweat too; he seemed to sweat a lot when he cried.

'And his friend, Derek Deverill was it, what happened to him?'

'He copped it the next day in the big push through the corn-fields beyond Les Aunes. We went camping in the Black Mountains when I was eleven, and we were struggling through a sodden field with waist-high rushes, and Moth said this was the wettest field he had ever slogged through since that sodding cornfield before dawn beyond Les Aunes. Dew up to your armpits, he said, and then he began to cry, sort of slow gurgling tears while he was standing there on the side of the hill, and that was when I realised that Moth was still a war casualty, because grandfathers didn't cry on camping holi-days at eleven in the morning. But I don't know exactly how Derek died, that's what I hope to find out in the Regimental Museum.'

It seemed a strange quest, but it obviously meant a lot to Timbo. Yet on second thoughts, perhaps not so strange, given that his grandfather had been such a pivotal figure in his life, perhaps the only thing resembling a pivot. I found myself sharing something of his tingle of anticipation as we came down the lane and saw the camp sign.

The camp was on the edge of the market town, and there was an old Churchill tank reared up on a mound outside the perimeter fence. The museum was little more than a long hut beyond the visitors' car park. I had expected more – tattered banners, ancient rifles, dented helmets, perhaps even a wax figure of a soldier in the uniform they wore in the Crimea – but there were only a case of medals, two campaign relief maps and a couple of bookshelves, and a single Union Jack which looked new and rather cheap. The duty orderly sat us down at a trestle table and gave Timbo a copy of *The Chalkies: A History of the 3rd Battalion the South Wessex Regiment in Europe 1944–45*, by Lt-Col. G. F. Balderstone MC and Maj. A. S. F. Clerk. Unusually for a regimental history, Timbo told me, it had never got into print because the regiment was amalgamated, which was why we had to come down here to read it. But the copies had nice green boards and on the front a cut-out silhouette of the regimental emblem, the White Horse of Longdown. The typed pages were beginning to fade a little but were still easy enough to read. Timbo released the clips on the boards and passed each page to me after he had finished reading it.

The tanks stuck up out of the waist-high corn like ships riding on the high seas. The 3rd Battalion had orders to dig in along the ridge above the Caen–Villers line. It was only a temporary position but the drill of digging-in had become automatic and the whole battalion was well underground within half an hour. 'A' Company pushed on to occupy the area of the watermill which the enemy had only just evacuated. But the French locals were soon out in force and gave us a warm welcome and much cider and Calvados. It was a perfect summer's evening although the shelling and mortaring never stopped and the sound of bursting shells echoed and re-echoed from the cliff face across the river. As the Company moved up, the great Lancaster raid on Caen took place before our eyes. It was a most wonderful spectacle in the light of the setting sun. The cloud of bombers hardly seemed to move, with the fighter escort weaving above and around them through what looked like an impenetrable curtain of flak shells. When darkness fell, the assault troops of 'E' Company moved to their forming-up point. They then crawled in open formation some three hundred yards through corn and roots until they reached the village.

I looked across the table at Timbo. He was blowing his nose and wiping his specs again. There was one other table in the room and the elderly man sitting at it was also blowing his nose, only more vigorously than Timbo. He had a bulbous nose which almost disappeared into his dirty blue handkerchief. I wondered whether he too was overcome with grief at some shared memory of combat, but I could just see that he was reading a big picture book full of flags and medals, and he had started copying the White Horse with a crayon in a small sketchbook. Timbo noticed that I had stopped reading.

'Moth was invited to contribute to the book,' he said proudly, 'but he didn't like Baldy and said he didn't want to have anything to do with that parcel of rogues, though I expect he was secretly pleased to be asked. But he was like that, never went out of his way to be helpful.'

On 10 July the Battalion was relieved by the 3rd Brecons and left Les Aunes to regroup in the area west of Lafontaine in preparation for the full-scale attack 'Operation Westbury'. The first phase of Westbury was the capture of Hill 92. The Chalkies were to sweep the cornfields to the west, supported by Churchill tanks from the 33rd Tank Brigade. H Hour was 0500 and the start line was the crossroads on the Lafontaine–Les Aunes road.

The growing corn was red with poppies and it concealed numerous carefully dug enemy positions. Some of these were single narrow slits or round holes containing a sniper who was ready to hide until several hours after our attack had passed over him and then begin firing. Others were deep dugouts within a web of roofed-over crawl tunnels leading to weapon pits manned by Spandau teams. When the battle was at its height the bullets were coming from every direction and whichever way you dodged, you ran into more of it. It was a confused battle, very much a soldier's battle.

Lieutenant D. G. Deverill went on ahead to knock out the Spandau which had been making a nuisance of itself. The platoon was then ordered to withdraw, but Lt Deverill stayed behind to evacuate a mortally wounded member of his company. He had almost reached the shelter of the cornfield when a German who had been lying in a culvert opened fire and killed him instantly. Both in training in England and our first few days in action Lt Deverill had been an inspiration to his Company and his death was keenly felt.

'I'll be locking up now, gentlemen.'

'Locking up? But it's only …' We had been so immersed in *The Chalkies* that neither of us had noticed the orderly standing at Timbo's elbow.

'If there's anything else you'd like to look at tomorrow, I could have it ready for you, but we close early on Wednesdays.'

We got up and filed out of the hut behind the man with the bulbous nose who was clutching his sketchbook. On the way back to the car park, we passed a flagstaff with the Chalkies banner drooping in the damp air, the White Horse crumpled in its folds. In front of the flagstaff there was a bench and a small flower bed of white pansies, floppy-petalled in the chalky earth. We sat down on the bench to review the experience. The other side of the parade ground some soldiers were loading up a lorry. You could just hear the noise of the traffic beyond the perimeter fence.

'So did he help her out, what was she called, Jacquetta, and the baby?'

'Moth? Never lifted a finger so far as I'm aware. If he'd done the slightest thing to help, he would never have stopped telling us about it. "I've just had a word with the headmaster at the Hawthorns about little Luke and he thinks he can squeeze him in", that sort of thing. But not a word, ever. Silence speaks inaction, as the Colonel puts it. So that leaves it all on me.'

'How do you mean?'

'It's up to me to make good the promise.'

'It's a bit late for that surely. Little Luke must be pushing sixty, no, seventy by now. In any case, if his dad was killed the next day, his mother probably never knew about the sacred pact. Even if Derek did leave a letter behind like Moth, she might not have told the boy, particularly when Moth never showed up.'

'No, no, you don't understand, you don't see at all.' Timbo was agitated now. 'The passage of time only makes it more important to remember. It's like in the sagas or the *Odyssey* when the warrior voyages for years across stormy seas to honour his father's ghost. In fact, the man we're after is Luke Junior. His dad died of cancer when he was only just a bit older than my dad.'

'Supposing Luke Junior doesn't want to honour his grandfather's ghost, or your grandfather's, come to that.'

'I did think he might be a bit taken aback. That's why we're going to see him without warning him first. Nothing to beat the old foot in the door. The formal approach is much more likely to get the brush-off.'

'We?'

'You are my trusty – what's the ancient Greek for chauffeur?'

'So how on earth are you going to discover where Luke Deverill hangs out?'

'I've tracked him down. He's got a cottage in the Fens.' Timbo looked happy again at the thought of the tracking down.

'So we'll be braving the stormy seas of the M25.'

'I knew you wouldn't fail me. *Fidus Achates*, that's the name of the faithful companion.'

'Fido for short.'

'Besides,' Timbo said, 'I've got something to give him.' Out of the deep pocket of his Barbour, he took a flat rectangular tin, about four inches long, and tapped it gently with his index finger.

III

Dewpond Cottage

There was a muddy scrape at the side of the ditch, just wide enough to park the Corsa on. The ditch went on for miles till it met the sullen sky. A shivery little breeze tickled the standing corn, huge flat fields of it all the way to the horizon with nothing but the dykes dividing them. Even now, late June, it was a cheerless landscape. I had thought I might like the Fens, but so far I didn't.

Timbo said we should leave the Corsa at the top of the lane which led straight down to the cottage. He wanted to have a look around before he moved in on the target.

'The Colonel's Rule One on Operations is, Time spent in reconnaissance is never wasted.'

Though it was a damp day, I didn't mind lingering there at the top of the lane for a few minutes. Even the hawthorns in the hedge prickling my chest was a pleasure.

It had not been difficult to track Luke down. Never was these days, Timbo said. All you needed to find anyone anywhere in the world now was Internet access and a little imagination. He took it as given that Luke would follow more or less in his grandfather's footsteps, as a teacher or academic of some kind, perhaps a doctor. No luck with the List of Registered Medical Practitioners, or the General Teaching Council's online register, but five minutes with the Commonwealth Universities Yearbook and he was sure he had his man. 'East Midlands University, Philosophy Dept: Senior Lecturer in Philosophy and Computer Science, Dr L. D. Deverill, MA Cantab, PhD.'

Timbo crouched behind the hawthorn hedge and got out his binoculars.

'Office-issue bins, Zeiss Conquest 15x45, seen a fair bit of service but still the best.'

Over the top of the hedge we could see the ridged red tiles of the cottage. Two up and two down, no more than that unless there was an extension at the back which we couldn't see. Behind the cottage there was an old farm windmill with rusty sails and a vegetable garden – I could just make out the runner beans halfway up their sticks and the raspberry canes. To one side below that garden, I could also see the top half of the dewpond which gave the cottage its name. There were cornfields all around. The lane was the only way to get to and from the cottage.

Dewpond Cottage had not been too hard to track down either. 'Urgent package for Dr Deverill,' Timbo had said, waving a package covered in red sticky tape – and containing nothing more urgent than that morning's newspapers – at the porter's lodge of Emu (the man at the station had told him that what was everyone called it when Timbo asked the way to the East Midlands University). 'Sorry, sir, they're all away for the summer vacation.' 'Do you have a vac address for Dr Deverill?' 'I'm sorry, sir, but we aren't allowed to give out …' 'I quite understand but this is from the Vice-Chancellor and he's most anxious that it should reach him within twenty-four hours. Dr Butterwick said he knew you would be most helpful, George, isn't it?' (Timbo had sneaked a look at the duty roster on the wall behind.) 'Oh, well, sir, if you're sure …' Authority was easy to assume if you were wearing a jacket and tie.

'That'll do,' Timbo said. 'Time to move in. The Colonel's Rule Two is, Reconnaissance is not an excuse for inaction. As soon as you've got your bearings, move in fast and hard on the target.'

Strange to think of Luke Deverill as a target. We had only come here to salute the memory of their grandfathers. But perhaps Timbo thought of most people like that, me too possibly.

I opened the passenger door to allow Timbo to put the bins back in the glove compartment. As he twisted his upper body out of the passenger side, he felt a fierce clutching at his shoulder.

'Can you give me a lift out of this fucking place?'

He turned to face a woman in a long flappy raincoat. She must have come up the lane while we had our backs turned. She had silvery-blonde hair which straggled round her handsome bony face.

Even though she was almost shouting at him, she looked fiercely intelligent. Timbo became aware that she was still clutching the shoulder of his Barbour and he tried to shake himself free of her, but gently so as not to annoy her further.

'You have to give me a fucking lift,' she snarled at him before he had managed to reply.

'We were actually going down the lane, to the cottage.'

'Down there? You must be mad.'

'We were going to call on Dr Deverill.'

'Well, you won't find anyone else down there. Nobody in their right mind would go anywhere near that prick.'

'Forgive me, you are?'

'His wife, of course. Ex-wife as soon as I can afford a lawyer which I can't. Are you a lawyer? Perhaps you're his lawyer. Or this man here? Is he a lawyer?'

She glared at me, giving the clear impression that she didn't think much of what she saw.

'No, neither of us is a lawyer but we can give you a lift.'

'Take me to Deeping Junction, I might just catch the 4.23.'

He opened the door without a word and she swung her shoulder bag onto the back seat. She was already sitting in the passenger seat by the time we got in. I was impressed by Timbo's readiness to change plans to meet this new situation – probably another of the Colonel's rules. She twisted round to harangue Timbo in the back seat, as I started the car.

'Why do you want to see him? Does he owe you money? I bet he does, he's always owing people money. You haven't a hope of getting it back, I can tell you that.'

'Why do you hate him so much?'

'Hate – he's not worth hating. I despise him, except I hate him too. Perhaps it's despising he's not worth.'

'Well, you must have rated him to begin with, to marry him, I mean.'

'What the fuck do you know? You probably don't even know the way to bloody Deeping.'

'As it happens, I do,' I interjected, 'because we came through it on the way here.'

She looked at me with a sudden flicker of interest.

'Christ, you're a pushover, aren't you, Chauffeur? I could probably ask you to take me to Glasgow.'

'We aim to please.'

She twisted round to concentrate her fire on Timbo again. 'Anyway, you didn't say why you wanted to see little Lukey.'

'Well, it's kind of a mission. It'll probably sound a bit crazy but my grandad was in the war with his grandad, and they promised each other that if anything happened to either of them—'

'*Anything happened!* That's so fucking British. He got blown up in his tank, what else do you expect? It was a fucking war.'

'Actually he got picked off by a sniper. Anyway, they promised each other the other one would do what he could to look after his family. Well, my grandad's second wife has just died and they sent me the letters telling the story, so I thought it was up to me to ... to ... come and, well, say Hi.' His voice trailed away as he wilted under her scorn.

'I never heard anything so freakish in all my life. You are a really weird person. Luke is forty-nine years old. What makes you think he wants some unknown weirdo coming a hundred miles to *look after him*?'

'I know it does sound odd. But I have to say that I found the letters, well, rather moving.'

'Did you? You were rather moved, were you?'

She spoke more quietly now, like a naturalist who has come upon some rare creature and doesn't want to frighten it away.

'Yes, I was actually, so I thought—'

'You thought Lukey might like to read the letters and he might be rather moved too.'

'Well, I thought it was worth a try.'

'Shall I tell you why it wasn't worth a try, not remotely worth a try in a million fucking years? Because little Lukey is incapable of being moved by a single normal human emotion, or an abnormal one come to that, and your little mission is so abnormal it's off the bloody scale.'

'Oh,' Timbo said. 'Why do you think he's like that?'

'Because he's a philosopher, a Kantian if you're interested, which I don't expect you will be. And philosophers only care about two things in the world: philosophy and fucking. Some of them care a bit more about philosophy than fucking but most of them care more about fucking. And none of them cares about anything else. That's the first thing you need to understand about them, what's your name?'

'Timbo.'

'In fact it's the only thing you need to understand. Have you got a light, Bimbo?'

'Timbo actually.'

'Timbo or Bimbo, have you got a fucking light?'

He flicked the lighter and she leant across to him and I hauled in a rich mix of scent and whisky. This was the first moment when I realised just how drunk she was, giddy fighting drunk, probably only one drink short of falling-down drunk.

'That's a wonderful perfume you're wearing. It's Calvin Klein's Destruction, isn't it? You can tell by that unusual hint of tamarisk.'

'*Bimbo*, you have hidden talents.'

'Can I ask your first name, Mrs Deverill?'

'My name is Lee Thorold. Did nobody tell you we don't take men's surnames any more? My friends call me Lethal – well, my enemies started it but my friends caught on rather quickly.'

'Lethal, that's fantastic.'

'Do you think so?' She turned back to me and clutched my shoulder with her fierce grip as though this was the only way to get anyone's attention. 'The station's just up here but you know that already. Just drop me off anywhere. You carry on with your mission impossible. I can't wait to hear how you get on.'

She was still chuckling her savage chuckle as she swung her bag off the back seat and stalked off up the tarmac path, swaying only a little so you would hardly know how far gone she was.

The car was full of cigarette smoke and scent and alcohol. We sat in a mesmerised haze, watching her long legs stalking up the path until she disappeared through the tubular arch at the top. Like willow leaves her legs were, I thought because I couldn't think of anything shapelier. Odd that she was wearing a skirt in the country. For some reason I felt that she was really a rather old-fashioned person although that was probably the last thing she would think she was.

The car behind hooted at me. I let in the clutch with a jolt like a learner driver and we shot forward into some suburbs without a clue where I was heading until we came to a roundabout, and I saw a sign telling me to go back past the station again.

It was raining hard when we got back to the muddy scrape at the top of the lane. Timbo didn't bother with the bins this time but shrugged on his Barbour and laced up his Gore-tex Eiger boots (I know that's what they were, because he told me), and we headed off down the lane. Timbo seemed a bit out of breath when we reached the cottage and he hammered on the door with his wet fist because there didn't appear to be a bell.

'Don't be so fucking melodramatic. You know it's not locked and anyway you took your keys.'

The voice was precise, a little reedy even, but with a confident edge to it. As the man inside pulled open the door with obvious impatience, he also took a step backwards as if expecting to be pushed in the chest.

'Who the hell are *you*?' he said, staring at us in amazement, well, mostly at Timbo because I was standing behind him, being inconspicuous. He was neat, rather stocky and had the look of being light on his feet. His face had an alert expression. You would not have put him down as being young, but you would not have thought of him as being forty-nine years old. He wore a white T-shirt and creamy chinos tucked into orange cowboy boots, which made him look like someone in a circus, a lion-tamer's assistant perhaps.

'My name is Timothy Smith. We've just taken your wife to the station.'

'And you've come back to accept my congratulations? No, of course, you need to be paid. Would ten quid do? Cheap at the price from my point of view.'

Now that he had spoken a bit, it was easy to see that lecturing was his trade. It was also easy to see that he too had had a few.

'No, that's not it exactly.'

'What is it, inexactly?'

'In fact it's you I've come to see.'

'And you took my wife to the station first as, what, a gesture of goodwill? How peculiar. And what role is your accomplice playing in this escapade?' he enquired, peering round Timbo to get a better look at me.

'This is my friend Dickie. He's driving me around because my car's out of action. I'm awfully sorry about the ... the circumstances.'

'She told you about those, did she? She's not one for holding back. But the circumstances can scarcely be said to be your fault. You cannot seriously claim to be awfully sorry that one person whom you do not know has left another person whom you do not know.'

'No, that's just it. I feel I do know you. We're sort of connected.'

'That I fear I cannot accept. It takes two to make a connection and I've never seen you before in my life. So if you'll excuse me, it has been a somewhat distressing day as you are by now aware ...'

He was still holding the door and now he began to shut it.

'No, please, you don't understand.'

'I don't know what your game is, but I do not feel like playing it just now.'

'Please, if you could just listen for—'

'Would fuck off help as a way of making myself clear? And that goes for your friend Dickie too.'

'It'll only take a minute.'

'They all say that.'

'Your grandfather, your paternal grandfather—'

'What about my grandfather? As it happens, he was killed in the war years before I was born, so I don't know a fucking thing about him and nor, I suspect, do you.'

'He and my grandfather were together in the war.'

'Oh, that old chestnut. As I said before, would ten quid do?'

'No, no, it's not a question of money. They had this pact, to look after each other's families if either of them was killed.'

'Did they now? And what exactly did your grandfather do about this sacred pact? I can't say I remember a Mr, ah, Smith — is that really your name? — doing anything for us when I was young.'

'He was known as Moth.'

'Was he? Well, there were no moths flying round my cradle that I noticed.'

'No, that's just the point. As far as I know, he didn't do anything at all to help you or your father. But his second wife died a couple of months ago, and she left me his letters, and I was going through them and ...'

'And so you thought you'd come instead and, what was the phrase, "look after me"? You don't think it's a bit late for that?'

Deverill spread out his arms in a gesture to demonstrate the hopeless absurdity of the idea. He was pretty far gone too, I realised, not as obviously drunk as his wife but sodden enough. With him too it wasn't something you noticed straight away, perhaps because both of them were quite used to swilling around in this condition.

'I know it's not a good time, but I just wanted to drop by and say hullo,' Timbo said lamely, half-holding out his hand towards Deverill who did not take it but just stood there staring at him.

'You're crazy,' Deverill said. 'You know that, don't you? And not in a good way either, if there is a good way to be crazy in, which I rather doubt. I'm beginning to wonder whether your chauffeur isn't a male nurse in disguise.'

'A lot of my friends think I'm pretty bonkers too.' Timbo tried an ingratiating smile.

'I'm not surprised.'

'I just thought you might feel a little bit like I do about my grandfather – about your grandfather, I mean?'

'And what sort of feeling would that be?'

'Loyal to his memory, I suppose.'

'Since I can have no memory of him at all for the reason already given, there can be nothing for me to be loyal to.' Although he still formed his words in academic tones, he spoke in a draggy way, suggesting that the drink was getting to him. His diction now had the forced precision of a drunken motorist talking to the police.

'You might want to know more about him, though.'

'I might, but I don't. So I think that we should call it a day, don't you, since we have nothing to discuss.'

He turned to me, passing his hand over his brow in a weary fashion: 'My dear Chauffeur, would you care to return your patient back to whatever institution he's on day release from?'

'You don't think it's a bit unnatural, not to be interested in your grandpa at all?'

Deverill suddenly came alive, as though a bucket of water had been poured over him.

'*Unnatural*? What makes you think that you might be a reliable judge of what is or is not natural to me?'

Timbo gave one of his inappropriate laughs.

'Well, for example, you've got a lot of his genes in you.'

'There are many persons whose genes have been transmitted to me in varying proportions for better or worse. I cannot be expected to take an interest in all, or indeed any, of them.'

'But you wouldn't be the same you if it wasn't for him.'

'I am not the same me that I was before you knocked on my door, but this does not entail that I have to be interested in you. I should add that it is not merely my grandfather's past that I am not interested in. I am not greatly interested in my own past either, or in my future either, whatever there may remain of it.'

'Yes, you are.'

'Yes, I am what?'

'The same you you were before I knocked on your front door.'

'That is surely for me to judge. You see, my dear Smith—'

'My friends call me Timbo.'

'Do they? I am not sure that I can quite manage that. You see, I fear that I am not a believer in the Continuous Self. I am what we philosophers call an Episodic Personality, a follower of Strawson the Younger rather than of Daniel Dennett, if those names mean anything to you.'

'I'm afraid they don't. I say, we're getting a bit wet standing on this doorstep, would you mind if—'

'Of course. Company on a wet afternoon in the Fens is not so plentiful that one can afford to turn it away.'

Luke Deverill stood aside with a humorous heel click of his orange boots to let us into the small hall. The air felt almost as damp inside as out. The hall was empty except for a couple of anoraks hanging on the wall. After having spent the first ten minutes trying to get rid of us, he now seemed entirely reconciled to our presence. It was as though we had just turned up, a little late perhaps, to a prearranged tutorial.

'I don't follow what you're saying at all, I must admit,' Timbo said, shaking the rain off himself.

'You probably think of your life as an unfolding story.'

'Well, I wouldn't claim it's much of a story, but—'

'You like to believe that it has a certain narrative thread to it.'

'Yes, I suppose I do.'

43

'And you believe furthermore that most people's lives are like that, that they can be described in terms of an ongoing story?'

'They have to be, don't they?' There was a hunted look in Timbo's eyes in so far as they could be examined behind his steamed-up glasses.

'Do they? I don't see it myself. If you show me a photograph of myself as a child, I do not recognise that as being the Me I am today at this moment. As far as I am concerned, that is somebody else entirely.'

'But he isn't somebody else. In fact you just admitted it, you said it was a photograph of yourself.'

'Yes, it is certainly a photograph of the L. D. Deverill who lived at Holly Lodge Cottage, Little Shawford at that time ...'

'And that L. D. Deverill must be exactly the same chap as the L. D. Deverill who I'm standing with now, mustn't he?' Timbo was warming to the discussion and risked jabbing a finger in the direction of the disputed Self.

'Not to me he isn't. Not merely is he not the same shape or size as I am now, but I do not share his feelings or desires or memories. I have no recollection of what he thought. I do not experience him as me.'

'Would you mind me asking,' I asked, not wanting to be left out, 'where does the cut-off point come? When exactly did you become you, when you passed puberty or when you did your GCSEs, say?'

'Aha, the chauffeur has decided to join the seminar. The answer is of course that there can be no such caesura, for the post-caesura self would have to be recognised as identical with my present self which is precisely what I do not recognise. So if I may repeat myself, I am not the same self as I was before you knocked on my front door. That's the way I experience life, episodically, like a series of film frames which will end only with my death.'

'So if you're not the you you were ten minutes ago, I suppose you cannot be held responsible for what you did ten minutes ago,' I hazarded. 'You can say, "It wasn't me, guv.'"

'I did not assert anything so audacious. I said merely that I am no longer experiencing life as that earlier self experienced it. Of course that would not prevent the police from arresting me for something I did ten minutes, or indeed ten years, ago nor should it.'

'But your new self would no longer feel guilty about it.'

'It might or it might not, my dear Chauffeur.' Odd that they should both call me Chauffeur, although Deverill had been told my name and Lethal hadn't bothered to ask for it. That was probably something they did have in common: nicknaming a person as a put-down.

'I've never heard anything so strange,' Timbo said.

'You think that I am odd?'

'Well, I've never met another, what do you call it, Episodic Personality.'

'There are quite a few of us, you know, Smith. Henry James, for example. You know Henry James?'

'Not very well.'

'He once said that one of his early books must be the work of quite another person than himself, a rich relation, say, who allowed him to claim that he was his fourth cousin. Or again,' Deverill continued, accepting that for the moment he had the floor to himself, 'take Montaigne. You could not accuse Montaigne of not having a self, but he said he doubted whether anyone else had a memory as grotesquely faulty as he had. He loved his friends, not for what he could remember about the past experiences he had shared with them, but because of how they were in the present. He was a Now Man too.'

'Montaigne, the one who wrote the essays?'

Deverill was startled.

'You know Montaigne?'

'A little bit,' Timbo said cautiously. 'I wouldn't call myself an expert.'

'Well, well, common ground at last, I think? We could drink a toast to the memory of Michel de Montaigne.'

'And to—'

'No, not to my grandfather. As I have already said ad nauseam, I have no memory of him.'

'A drink would be nice anyway,' Timbo said pacifically. 'We need something to keep the damp out.'

Deverill led us through a door at the back of the little hall. Timbo's wet boots skidded on the greasy flagstones. The sitting room at least had a square of old carpet covering the middle of it, but not much else in the way of décor. Books were piled everywhere in shaky heaps. The only picture, which hung over the fireplace, was a big swirly charcoal drawing of a female nude which was hard not to look at but was somehow discomforting.

'Lethal when young. She told you she was called Lethal?'

'Yes, she did.'

'It's the first thing she says to someone new. I don't know why. I'd keep it dark if I were her. But then she enjoys her reputation for fatality. Vodka do you all right?'

'Oh, fine. Does she deserve it?'

'The reputation? God, yes. One and a half suicides so far, the second man botched it. And me of course.'

Either the prospect of the vodka or the thought of his wife's track record seemed to cheer Deverill up. He patted the broken springs of the sofa to invite us to take a seat in a way that verged on the convivial. Behind the dry academic talk he had a kind of indolent charm which might work all the better because he only turned it on now and then.

He had grey-green eyes which had a sparkle that came and went as though controlled by a dimmer switch. I could see even more how women could be stirred. So perhaps all the action his wife talked about just dropped into his lap. What sort of women did he go for or went for him, I wondered: students (but that would count as harassment), wives of colleagues (worse in one sense if not technically an offence against college rules) or just intellectual women he met in drinking clubs, I imagined them with long straight hair and black jerseys.

'So how did you come, as it were, to Montaigne?' Deverill persisted, looking at Timbo with fresh interest. 'I wouldn't have thought – you'll forgive me for saying this – that you would be much of a one for sixteenth-century French essayists.'

'Well, no, the truth is it's a bit of a coincidence because that was part of the reason for me coming here in the first place. I'm sorry to return to the subject we first spoke of but I can't leave without handing this over to you because it's yours by rights.'

Timbo tugged out of his pocket the battered old flat tin box he had shown me the day before. He placed it in Deverill's hands, cupping the tin in his hands as though tenderly transferring a trapped bird.

'Ogden's St Bruno Flake. Why are you giving me this?'

'It belonged to your grandpa. I found it in among my gran-dad's stuff with a note saying property of Lieutenant L. D. Deverill, Normandy, 11 July 1944.'

Deverill handled the grubby buff-and-white tin with something approaching distaste.

'Why isn't it burnt, if it was in the tank with him?'

'He wasn't in a tank. That's what your wife thought too, but in fact he was killed by a sniper out in the cornfield. He was bringing in a mortally wounded comrade.' It was Timbo's turn to stare. I could see he was unable to believe that Deverill was so hopelessly ignorant of the manner of his grandfather's dying.

'Funny, I was under the impression he was in a tank. I imagined it exploding zerplat like in the comics. A glorious blaze except for those who happened to be inside.'

'No, he was in the infantry. The Chalkies didn't have tanks, not then anyway. I can't be sure whether he had actually had the tin on him when he was killed. He might have left it with his other valu-ables at the Battalion's forward HQ. Go on, open it.'

With some difficulty Deverill prised open the lid. Inside there was a little red book which fitted snugly into the tin. As he took out the book, a small black-and-white photograph fell from its pages.

'Michel de Montaigne, *Essays*. And that, I suppose, has to be my grandmother although it is difficult to tell because she's squinting into the camera. It must be a wedding photograph, I never saw her wear anything so smart.'

There was a long silence, two minutes long I thought, but then silences always felt longer than they were.

'Well, you win. I confess that this dirty old thing does move me. I imagine you're going to say that the reason I'm moved is because it's part of my life story.'

'I wasn't going to say anything,' Timbo said. 'I just wanted you to have it.'

'They probably produced these pocket editions specially for the troops, to give them something to occupy their minds while they were waiting to be killed.'

'Yes, it's part of a series. I looked it up on Amazon.'

47

'Funny to think of a taste for Montaigne lurking in the genes.' The grey-green eyes dimmed. I looked across at Timbo and I could see that he was feeling a little surge of triumph.

'Well, thank you, you know, for bringing this.' Deverill waved the tobacco tin as though words were now running out on him.

IV

Dilkusha

'I thought they were a desperate couple,' I said.

'No, they are really interesting people, definitely original types.' Timbo sounded defensive.

'Is that always such a good thing, being original?'

'I'm learning a lot from them. In fact we've become good friends, spending a fair bit of time together. I'm thinking of suggesting we go over to Normandy to look at the battlefield where Luke's grand-dad copped it. Could you straighten your back – it does help if the hands can move straight down – you seem to be a bit round-shoul-dered this morning. But you're right to call them a couple.'

'Am I? She sounded as if she never wanted to see him again, and vice versa.'

'At the particular moment we first met them, yes, absolutely, that was the position. But I've been talking to them quite a bit about their marriage. I thought from the start that it wouldn't take much to bring them back together.'

'You talked to them about their marriage?' I was incredulous at the thought of Timbo as a freelance counsellor for Relate.

'Yes, and about their drinking. They seemed quite interested in what I had to tell them.'

'And what did you have to tell them?'

'I think that had better stay confidential between the three of us.'

All this was too bewildering to get a grip on. I felt we had to go back to the beginning or somewhere near it.

'How did you get hold of each other for starters? She hadn't a clue who you were.'

'I popped my card in her shoulder bag as she was getting her case out of the car. She rang to thank me for the lift.'

'Do you often do that, slip your card into the bags of strange women without being asked?'

'Quite often,' Timbo said, with a curl of self-satisfaction in his voice. 'It's a good way to stay in touch.'

'And they are eager to stay in touch, these women?'

'Quite a lot of them seem to be, and not just women by the way. I think they find the card quite intriguing because they hadn't expected it.'

'Perhaps she was also excited by your guessing what perfume she was wearing.'

'Could be.'

'That was a guess, wasn't it?'

'Not really. I've had a fair bit of training. A couple of years ago we had this East German woman to look after. She was supposed to have been a Stasi agent – well, everyone in the DDR was a Stasi agent, so she probably was. But what the Colonel was asked to find out was whether she had been a double agent which she also claimed to be. Her cover in Bonn had been working as an expert parfumier in Rottluffs and she got to know all the politicians and diplomats and their wives. So the Colonel suggested she should make herself useful while she was with us by teaching us the rudiments. And she said at the end of the course that I had the best nose she had ever come across. In fact she said I was the nearest thing she knew to the chap in the famous German novel, which of course I hadn't read, it's called *Perfume* actually. Anyway I bought a copy and I really identified with the hero Jean-Baptiste Grenouille who was born without a personal odour, but to make up for it he has this brilliant ability to identify every element of any fragrance he encounters. He's a bit of a bastard really but I rather liked him.'

'Did she tell you that you didn't have any personal odour yourself?'

'Well, I must admit that's where the resemblance ends. She told me that I give out a sort of foxy smell when I'm agitated. You may have noticed it, although I'm not aware of it myself, which is often the case, she said.'

'No, never noticed anything like that,' I said, although as I said it I did recall sniffing a faint tang of urine about him when he had sweated up for one reason or another.

'It's a thing about redheads apparently,' he said. 'Nothing I can do about it.'

'It's probably the secret of your magic powers.'

'Do you think so? There, that'll do.' He moved away from me and let his arms hang limp as he always did at the end.

Then he said, 'Excuse me,' and waddled off with that stamping-down walk to the little toilet at the end of the passage. I treated myself to that languorous back-stretch that I always did at the end of our sessions and then strolled round the room to stretch my legs too. There was a little table in the corner where he piled his mail. There was usually only a couple of items on it but today there quite a heap, only just opened by the look of it which was unusual, because normally everything was meticulously filed away. On the top there was a card headed Driver and Vehicle Standards Agency and by casually brushing against it, I could see that it said: 'We regret to have to postpone the date of your driving test.'

I suppose it had been a harmless fib about the GTi being out of action. He obviously didn't even have a car. Most men over thirty don't like to admit that they can't drive. Curiously, I found that I didn't really mind. For me Timbo wasn't subject to the usual rules, I don't quite know why.

Summer started late that year and this was how I remember the start of it, Timbo talking about his amazing gift of smell and the problems of being a redhead and his arms hanging limp at his sides and my finding out about his not having passed his driving test. We must have reached mid-August already but only now did the city begin to smell of summer, the dust and the acacia blossom sticky on the pavement and the duvet thrown back at night and the warm air coming through the open window.

That last session with Timbo was the best I ever had. The effects were lasting. I felt cured, properly cured. For the first time in years, I could turn my body sharply without a twinge, bend down to do up my laces — but no, there is nothing more boring than someone describing how their back was cured, nothing except someone telling you how the pain started and exactly where it gets you.

We went on a canal holiday in France to celebrate and I swam along behind the barge letting its wake spill over my shoulders. Jane sat on the boat, her bare arm draped over the rudder to keep us straight. Flo and Lucy came too, protesting a little, in their mid-teens and beginning to think (or think they ought to think) that they were too old to go on holiday with us, but they enjoyed lying on the top of the boat in their bikinis, listening to sixties hits which they had taken a retro fancy to. The barge was slow but my breaststroke was slower and often the boat puttered on ahead of me out of sight round the gentle bend in the canal. As the chugging faded, I was alone. The tall banks of rosebay willowherb and Himalayan balsam muffled the sights and sounds of the outside world, although the main road to Toulouse was only a hundred metres away. It was so long since I had been able to live in the moment like this, that delicious moment of physical freedom and well-being which is completely absorbing. And when I curled up in our little cabin at night, I dropped off to sleep like a dewdrop falling off a leaf. I woke early with the sun squinting in under the faded blue curtains and listened to the slop of the water and the clucking of the moorhens and could not deny that being alive had its pluses. I owed Timbo a lot and I reminded myself to send him a thank-you postcard, but I didn't.

'You didn't send me a postcard.'

'Yes, I did,' I lied. The odd thing was that I don't normally find it easy to tell lies, even small ones, but with Timbo it came quite naturally, which can't have been much help when he was trying to extract reliable information from people, if other people felt the same as I did. The truth was, though, that Jane and I had sent quite a few postcards to our friends: hers dating back to university and the clinic of course, mine mostly to fellow journos, even the annoying Gil Goulthwaite, for example. But somehow I kept on forgetting to send one to Timbo. Our friendship, if that's what it was, belonged in another category, though I wasn't sure what.

'Well, I didn't get it.'

'I'm really sorry. We had a wonderful time. It's been such a great summer.'

'You must come for a picnic while the weather's still like this.'

'A picnic?' Somehow I had not thought of Timbo and picnics.

'You must, there's an amazing view.'

'View? Where from?'

'How about next Saturday? I'll email you the address.'

'That would be great,' I said, not meaning it. For some reason, the idea did not appeal to me. Timbo did not seem to have the gifts you needed for laying on a *fête champêtre*. But then I regretted my churlish reaction and asked whether I could bring a bottle.

'Bring a bottle?' He repeated my words as if this was a bizarre suggestion unheard of in the history of picnics. 'Yes,' he said, after a pause for reflection, 'yes, that would be a good idea, in the circumstances.'

It was well into September now but the sun still shimmered through the blowsy leaves as I pedalled up the wooded slopes with a bottle of Prosecco in my saddlebag. The address was in Highgate or Upper Holloway, I wasn't quite sure which, the postcode began N19. I couldn't find 33 Durbar Lane at first, because it was out of sync with the other numbers and turned out to have its own separate driveway with a broken-down garage made of asbestos boards at the end. I went along a narrow cinder path at the side of the garage and there was a smallish red-brick house, Edwardian I would guess, with a slate-roofed porch and Michaelmas daisies growing out of the tarmac in front of it. From the outside, the house looked unlived-in, as if it had been on the market for some time and nobody had fancied it. Timbo was standing in the porch making hostly gestures.

'Welcome to Dilkusha.'

'Dil – what?'

'Dilkusha,' he said, pointing to the rusty sign swinging under the porch. 'It means Heart's Delight in Hindi. The chap who developed the lane had spent a lot of time in India. This was the house he kept for himself.'

Inside, the house did not look much like anyone's delight. The hall had brown lino on the floor and a bulbous, rather grimy clock on the wall which might have come from an old railway waiting room. The sitting room at least had a new-looking oatmeal sofa and two matching armchairs and an oatmeal carpet which also looked new-laid. At the far end there was a big picture window with a side door out onto the terrace.

'There, you see what I mean.'

The whole of the city was spread out before us in a blue September haze. In the distance you could see the Surrey hills.

'Well, I guess you've met these two guys before, but not together. Dr Luke Deverill, and his wife Lee Thorold, also known as Lethal.'

'You're such a plonker, Bimbo. Hullo, Chauffeur,' looking at me with a smile that lit up her face.

The couple who had come in from the terrace looked quite different from what I remembered of my first meeting them.

'You look fantastic, Lethal,' Timbo said.

And she did. She was wearing the sort of casuals that models wear for picnics in the glossies: designer jeans, loose peasanty shirt of the type not worn by peasants and hair gleaming in the morning light from the terrace. Luke too had a gloss on him. His hair had just been cut and his chinos newly ironed. And there was nothing bleary about the look in their eyes either. They looked fresh and up for it. I could not recognise the untethered, frantic, drink-sodden characters at Dewpond Cottage. Yet how long was it since we had first met them in that decrepit state, more than a month perhaps but no more than two?

'Luke hasn't started the barbecue yet, so you'll have to wait for your burnt sausages.'

'I've been on this RSA thing all morning. It really is a bugger.'

'What's that? Something to do with the arts?'

'Luke has been on an intensive refresher course in public-key encryption,' Timbo put in. 'The GCHQ people in London say he's one of the best pupils they have had for years. It was an amazing piece of luck for us that cryptography was his special subject at Emu. We had been looking for ages for a top-notch code cracker and they don't grow on trees. Extraordinary that our grandads should have been such mates.'

'What does RSA stand for?' I asked, groping for a toehold.

'It's the acronym for Rivest, Shamir and Adleman, the three Jewish guys who invented it,' Luke explained in that dry didactic manner which appeared to come naturally to him, whether drunk or sober. 'I see you looking askance at my referring to their Jewishness, but the point is the three men were all at MIT together and they had this breakthrough, the Eureka Moment you might say, after they had all enjoyed a Seder together. That's when they, well, Ron Rivest principally, discovered the secret of deep encryption.'

'But I thought that ordinary hackers could now crack anything.'

'Most of the time they are tackling relatively cheap, low-complexity systems, that is, when they haven't bribed someone on the inside or purloined a memory stick. Professional deep encryption as practised by governments and public authorities, in the nuclear industry for example, is a much tougher nut.'

Timbo watched Deverill doing his spiel with a proud smile on his face, a proprietor's smile. I was more curious to know what Luke and Lethal were doing here. Something about the way they shifted the furniture to clear our way out into the garden suggested that they knew the place pretty well if they were not actually staying here.

The slope outside the windows was steep and the garden ended twenty yards below in some ragged laurels. The grass was scrubby and unmown. Two artificial stone vases at either end of the terrace had straggly plants which might have been geraniums lolling over their edge. The whole garden seemed utterly neglected.

'We ought to do something about the garden,' Timbo said.

'Don't look at me,' Lethal said. 'I've only just got my nails looking halfway decent.'

'Lethal, henceforward Lee once again, is just starting work as an events manager.'

'Events manager.' I dumbly repeated the words, finding them hard to credit. From what I had seen of her so far the only event connected to Lethal was herself, and it was not an event she had looked like having much hope of managing.

'For the big new charity which some of the major hedge funders and their partners are putting together. The initial endowment is massive.' Timbo's awestruck tones suggested an almost holy quality about the size of the sum, rather as worshippers used to hush as the sacred relics passed by. I was more awestruck by the thought of Lethal landing such a job, which I imagined demanded all kinds of patience and sycophancy, not to mention organising skills.

'Well,' I said, 'we ought to celebrate,' and I fumbled for the bottle of Prosecco in my bike bag.

'Ah, the fizzy poison,' Luke said. 'Not for us, I'm afraid.' He gestured towards the table at the end of the terrace which, I now noticed, had several family-sized bottles of Diet Coke on it and a large ice bucket.

'Yes,' he said, following my startled gaze. 'We are all on the wagon, I'm afraid. Lethal and I are formally enrolled in Alcoholics Anonymous, while Timbo is just coming along for the ride.' He pronounced Alcoholics Anonymous with exaggerated precision as if it was the name of an obscure foreign artist which it was easy to get wrong.

'I wouldn't have thought that you would be, well, into that kind of thing.'

'The mumbo-jumbo, you mean? It is of course wholly nonsensical but I find it curiously relaxing. In any case, I have always been interested in the role of performative utterances, in which one's words constitute not a proposition about how the world is but rather an action or intervention within the world. The pledges one takes and the self-descriptions one is obliged to make at AA meetings are performative in precisely this important way. When I solemnly say "My name is Luke and I am an alcoholic", I am not merely describing my condition. My statement is intended as the first step on the road to altering that condition. The recognition is not simply a perception; it is in itself an action.'

'Oh, stop being so pompous, Lukey, and give us all a drink.'

Now at least I had an accredited explanation of their bright eyes. It was remarkable what their abstention from the poison, whether fizzy or still, had done for their complexions and their general well-being. Which did not explain what they were doing here.

The barbecue was smouldering now and Timbo began poking the charcoal to level the grey ash, while Luke strung out the sausages on the griddle, playing the role of chef with an ironic brio.

'Do you happen to know,' I asked, 'who actually owns this house?'

'Not a clue, darling. We needed a place when we got back together and Timbo told us we could have it for a few months. It's a bit spartan at the moment but we're getting the rest of the stuff from Dewpond sent up, not that that ghastly hovel was exactly fully furnished at the best of times.'

She stressed the 'we' a little, as though she was trying to convince herself. But they certainly looked comfortable together, even sunny in one another's company.

'What made you think of events management?'

'I didn't. It was Timbo's idea. He thinks I have people skills, but I can't imagine why, as the only people he'd seen me with is Luke and it wasn't exactly a brilliant event, as you may recall.'

'It certainly wasn't,' Luke confirmed from the barbie, with a chuckle that was more rueful than sardonic.

Timbo returned from the house, carrying a box marked Waitrose and began unpacking some sandwiches, not troubling to remove the wrapping as he laid them out on a paper plate.

'Bimbo, Chauffeur was asking who owns this house of mystery.'

'It's just a place we use to put up our friends, somewhere quiet where they won't be bothered.'

'Oh,' I said in a light-dawning sort of way, 'you mean it's a *safe house.*'

'Well, we certainly hope our guests will be OK here. It's off the beaten track, as you can see.' Timbo acted as if the phrase 'safe house' meant nothing to him.

But why had he installed this couple whom he had only just met? How had he brought them back together? Even if their splitting might have been a temporary flare-up, he had surely had some hand in their swift reunion. Perhaps they were grateful to him and regarded him as a saviour or a lucky mascot and tagged along with him partly in the hope that this might help to restore their relationship. Even this much seemed hard to credit. How could someone who seemed so awkward when you first met him be anyone's choice as a relationship counsellor?

Timbo brought out some rickety deckchairs, the old-fashioned sort with stripy canvas seats, and a green fold-up metal table which had flakes of rust coming off it. We sat down and began unpacking the sandwiches. To any passing helicopter we might have looked like four ordinary picnickers enjoying the last of summer and the amazing view. From the air, you would not see how the garden had run wild or how neglected the house was. You would have thought, what lucky people to have a house with a view like that, and you would not have thought it odd that the house should be called Heart's Delight.

Yet we were not relaxed. This wasn't because Timbo started firing questions at us and not listening to the answers in his usual off-putting way. On the contrary, he was rather quiet. Luke and Lethal were curiously respectful towards him. Even when Lethal said, 'Oh, Bimbo, you are impossible,' she said it like a junior employee flirting with the managing director. In fact the whole picnic had a little of the uneasiness of a staff outing. There were moments of geniality but they had to be forced a little, like toothpaste out of the tube.

'Bimbo, I do have a couple of questions. Is it all right if I—'

'You mean, in front of Dickie? Fire away. He's like the three monkeys, hears no evil etcetera.'

'Dear Chauffeur, he's such a treasure.'

This rough pigeonholing nonplussed me and I didn't take in all that much of what he said to start with. But then I did begin to listen, not least because I had a sneaking feeling that some of it was being rehearsed for my benefit, though I could not see why. It was almost as if they had been through it all before and the little dialogue was being staged. But why?

'Look, the point is,' Timbo was saying, 'you're saving them trouble. And that's what they really like, because they're basically pig-lazy, these hedgies' wives. They want to save the world by doing good works, but they want you to do all the actual work. So you arrive fully equipped with your target list of potential donors, complete with names and addresses, and it has to be a genuine A-list – the Colonel has someone who can help you with that, in fact the same woman who got you the job in the first place. Then you say to them, if you just give me five minutes with your computer, I can integrate my list with your database. Of course they won't know you could perfectly well do that without going near their Mac; they probably hardly know how to switch the bloody thing on. Luke will show you how to do the business. A cup of tea and a cupcake and you're away out of there.'

I did want to know why Lethal was being taught how to bug the computers of the hedge funders' wives, but I was not going to give them the satisfaction of exposing my curiosity. What was clear was that Timbo had deliberately allowed me a glimpse of what they were up to, which sounded illegal and certainly immoral. Was this just a tease, or a show-off manoeuvre to impress me? Or did he somehow wish to draw me in, to implicate me as a co-conspirator or at least a witness? He was obviously keeping them on the wagon for strictly professional reasons. He, or the Colonel, needed them bright-eyed and bushy-tailed for whatever it was they were plotting.

I was not sorry when, just after half past two, Timbo said he had to get back down to town to meet someone and did anyone want to walk to the Tube with him. I said I had the bike. The two of us waved goodbye to what could now be called the Deverills again. From the decrepit porch Luke and Lethal waved us goodbye back, for all the world like a married couple who had lived there for ever and let the place go to seed a bit. I freewheeled down the hill, glad to feel the wind in my hair. Dilkusha did not give me the creeps exactly, but it certainly was not my heart's delight.

The sensible thing would have been to forget about the uneasy picnic and about the loose ends that trailed from it. But there were too many of them, and I found myself lying awake at three in the morning trying to work out exactly what the three of them were up to. And the more I thought about the whole thing, the more I was touched by the way Timbo had given this washed-up couple a break. Whatever I thought about the Ophion Group's latest murky project, there was no doubt that being part of it had helped the Deverills to get a grip on life and to get back together.

So in the end I gave in, out of curiosity as much as a sense of friendship, and used my ever-handy pretext for getting in touch with Timbo. In reality, my back was still behaving itself nicely, but I pretended, to myself as much as to him, that I was having twinges again, or at least the intimation of them, and it might be better to nip the trouble in the bud before it nipped me.

'Ophion House is not operational at the moment. We have to do a total refurb, because it's a repairing lease. But there's a little place round the corner where they let me use a room when I need one.'

'Are you sure? I don't want to be a bother.'

'Nothing easier. It's called the Brindisi Club, 28 Shepherd Market Mews, second floor. Fredo will show you up. Our usual time all right?'

The Brindisi Bar and Club, Members Only, was in one of the alleys which had not yet been done up and still had a sleazy feel. The barman or receptionist looked at me with minimal interest and managed to give an upward nod without raising his head from the sports pages. Timbo had a chair ready for me in the upper room which was bare except for a dusty table and another chair.

'So what did you think of my two little helpers? Quite a change there after our first meeting, don't you think?'

'It certainly was. How on earth—'

'No questions till we've finished, if you don't mind.'

His hands began the familiar descent. Then he paused.

'You seem really quite loose this morning. I'm surprised you're having trouble again.'

'Well, as I told you, it's not too bad but I thought it might be better to get in early.'

'Fine, fine, you're the patient,' Timbo said. He sounded unconvinced. And for the first time ever there was no sensation of heat as his hands travelled down my back, not the faintest. The connection, the circuit, whatever it was, seemed to have broken.

'No good? I thought not. I can always tell. Sometimes after a lay-off it takes a couple of sessions to re-establish contact but then it can work the other way too, like after a long lay-off from the golf course when you suddenly play better than you have for years. No point flogging a dead horse anyway,' he concluded patting my shoulder to dismiss me. 'Fredo should be up with the coffee in a few minutes. His real name's Jason but he thinks he looks like Fredo in *The Godfather.*'

He sat down in the other chair and stared at me. In the half-light of the dusty little room, he looked oddly severe.

'But that's not why you made the appointment, was it? You didn't come here for your back, did you?'

'Well, I—'

'You wanted to hear the rest of the story, didn't you? I thought if we let you hear a little bit, you might become curious, not immediately perhaps but when you thought it over. Whereas if we gave you the whole scenario straight off, you might run a mile.'

'I might still run a mile.'

'That's true, you might. But once you have, as they say, expressed interest, you are that little bit less likely to dismiss the whole project out of hand. You have made a tiny investment of your time, and it's up to us to convince you that you haven't wasted it.'

'So?'

'I don't expect you've heard of Elcatron, it's not exactly a household name. You might perhaps have heard of Parson Rowe which is what it used to be called in the pre-electronic age. It was a less successful rival of Marconi, had factories mostly in the same part of Lancashire and in the same sort of business: navigational and weapons delivery systems for warships and fighters, other stuff too but largely military software. Unlike Marconi it didn't get too big for its boots, which was its salvation but also its weakness because it was desperately short of working capital for big projects. So when the chance came to bid for the electronic kit in the new generation of diesel submarines, it didn't have the cash in hand or the political contacts to persuade the government that it deserved a soft loan. They had to move quickly because the Brazilian Navy was due to make a decision within weeks, and although they were only in for six boats, it would be a huge order for Elks and other governments would probably follow. So they needed to prove that they were in good enough shape financially to carry the project through to completion. The banks refused to come up with the money, so the only hope was to raise it from the markets by a rights issue. And that was when they became aware, almost simultaneously, of two unpleasant developments.'

The door opened and Fredo came in with two cups of coffee.

'Plotting to blow up the Stock Exchange, are we?'

'That's next week, Fredo.'

As I gulped down the coffee, I reflected that all this stuff seemed miles out of Timbo's league. He must have had some intense briefing from the Colonel or some expert in the field.

'The first thing was – and this wasn't a surprise, it's par for the course – that Elks became aware that their internal systems were being hacked into. It wasn't immediately clear, it usually isn't, whether the hackers were after something specific or whether they were just on a fishing trip. Elcatron, being in the business themselves, prided themselves on having some pretty robust encryption systems, but the hackers were clearly serious operators, which was disquieting because if they didn't get what they wanted by hacking, they would be likely to resort to other methods.'

'Such as?'

'Plain old theft or bribery, paying employees to pass over crypto keys or memory sticks. There's so much money around in these deals, it's hard for a low-level cipher clerk to resist.'

'But how do the hedge funders' wives come into it, if they do? I can't see them loosing off the latest torpedoes, let alone having a clue how they work.'

'Ah,' said Timbo. 'That was the much more disquieting thing. At almost exactly the same time Elks became aware of the hackers, their brokers who were preparing the prospectus for the rights issue suddenly told them that it was hopeless because the shares were being shorted on a massive scale and were tanking at a rate of knots. And as far as they could tell, it wasn't just one hedgie doing it, there was a concerted short going on, as if the word had gone out that Elks was going belly-up. There was blood in the water and the sharks were circling. If the shares became virtually worthless, they wouldn't be able to raise a penny on the markets and the banks would be even more reluctant to lend, so they'd be totally buggered.'

'But that's what hedge funders always do, isn't it? They depress the shares by selling loads of them, then they can buy them back for practically nothing.'

'That's the general idea.'

'So why can't they do that all the time to any old company?'

'Because if the business is sound other investors will have faith and go long on it, i.e. bet that the shares will go up, which of course makes them go up, leaving hedgies with massive losses. This happens quite often, I'm glad to say.'

'And you hope that the hedgies' wives will reveal all? I mean, would they even know what the whole thing was about?'

'Even the birdbrains have laptops with all sorts of links to their husbands' systems. That's the soft way in, they call it the Silk Road in the trade.'

'So Lethal plants the bug and Luke does the hacking.'

'That's the general idea. You don't sound very interested. It doesn't grab you, the story?'

'Frankly, no.'

'Not even if I told you that thousands of British jobs depend on the deal going through. If Elks don't get the business, there's virtually zero chance of them surviving. A whole town will close down. But the town happens to be somewhere north of Preston, so you probably don't give a damn.'

I didn't like his sharp tone and said so.

'But basically you think it's nothing to do with you?'

'I think there's nothing I can do about it.'

'You're a journo, Dickie. Aren't you interested in exposing corruption?'

'I'm not that sort of journo. I don't expose things. I just report what the ministers are saying.'

'You have political contacts though, people who could ask questions and publicise the bit we need to have out in the open.'

'Not that type of contacts.'

'You really could be a great help to us, you know.'

'Timbo, I'm no use to you. By some miracle which I don't begin to understand, you have managed to turn Luke and Lethal into a passable imitation of human beings by turning them into secret agents. Even if I wanted to get mixed up in this business, which I one hundred per cent don't, I'd only get in your way.'

'Well, at least you can think about it.'

'I am still not sure just what it is I'm supposed to be thinking about but I'm sure what the answer is, which is no.'

'I am very sorry to hear that, Dickie.'

The sharpness had gone out of his voice. He just sounded sad and disillusioned. 'You won't say anything about all this to anyone. Can I ask that of you at least?'

'Of course. In any case, I don't think I know anyone who'd be interested.'

'We probably won't meet again after this,' he said mournfully. 'I don't expect you'll want me messing around with your back any more. In any case I'm off to Brazil for a couple of weeks to see if I can pick up any leads that end.'

'Who knows? My back may always start playing up again.'

'To be honest with you, Dickie,' Timbo said, 'I don't really want to carry on with the healing. It takes too much out of me. I need to concentrate my energies on this thing if I'm going to make a success of it. I'm only sorry that you won't be coming in with us.'

'I'm sorry to hear that. I'll miss our sessions and I can only say how grateful I am, but in the circumstances I suppose we had better say goodbye for now.'

We said goodbye in a gentlemanly style, neither of us letting the anger spill out. As I went away through Shepherd Market, I was still furious that he had made me look so bad. I had to admit that I had cut a poor figure. It was not only the lack of personal loyalty which Timbo had taken so hard (loyalty was, after all, his big thing). It was my refusal to be stirred, my lack of curiosity, my total blank in the adventure department. Of course I was right too, I had nothing to contribute to this crackbrained enterprise. But being right is not always enough. Besides, I was nettled that he had only kept up with me in the hope of bringing me into his machinations. I had fondly assumed that he was helping me purely out of charity, and his using his gifts in this way struck me as a betrayal of them.

You must never offer an untrue excuse which would be a calamity if it were true, such as saying that your child is ill or that you have to go to your father's funeral. Such untruths have a way of returning to haunt you. Nothing like so serious of course, but I should never have pretended to Timbo that my back was agony again, because a few weeks later it really did start playing me up worse than ever.

I endured the nagging, yanking ache for two days, then decided that my pride had to be swallowed. Not that there was so much to swallow. I had concealed most of my annoyance, just as he had concealed his. He had put a proposal to me and I had said no. That was all there was to it. I had not exposed what I really thought of the scheme, which was that I could not begin to see how it would work. Even if Luke and Lethal did track down who was doing the hedging, the hedgers still might be doing it for an entirely legitimate reason, viz. that they believed, perhaps rightly, that Elcatron had little or no hope of getting the order from the Brazilians or anyone else. And in any case it would probably be too late to reverse the process and save the firm. Still, aagh, there it was again.

Timbo must be back from Brazil by now and I had to go and see him and plead for his healing hands again. There was no answer from his mobile, which was surprising because he usually answered on the first or second beep. There was a landline number too for Ophion

House which he had given me, though he said nobody much used it except the Colonel who occasionally rang Ladbrokes from it. There was no answer from the landline. I rang the mobile again, in case I had put in the wrong number. Nothing, not even a text message. In my inflamed state I immediately thought that something must be wrong.

Just before the time he usually applied his healer's hands – 12.15, now for me a magical moment in the day – I walked, rather fast, through the Park into the quiet streets of Mayfair. It was a still, damp day with a feeble sun coming through now and then. As I came up Audley Lane from the Park end, I expected to see Ophion House still showing some symptom of being refurbished, scaffolding perhaps or a builder's board outside, but there was nothing. Nor did it look as if the refurb had been finished or even started, because the cream-stucco on the portico was peeling and when I looked closer, I saw that the window frames could do with repainting too.

Then I looked for the brass plate which said '38' with the snake above the number. It was not there any more. Only four small screw holes remained to show where it had been. I also noticed that the colour of the stucco between the small holes was the same as the rest of the wall, which suggested that the brass plate had not been fixed there long.

I recalled the minimal furnishing inside, the untenanted porter's desk, Timbo's own room with its lack of papers and filing cabinets, the absence of people coming up and down the stairs, the cameo appearance of the skinny man bounding down the stairs two at a time – what was he called? – Jonty. Now that I thought about it, there was something transitory, impermanent about it all. Certainly, if they had had to get out quickly, they could have closed the whole show down in a couple of hours.

Perhaps I had got the wrong house. There was not much differ-ence between these cliff-like stucco mansions. But no, there was No. 40 to the right, and No. 36 to the left, the consulate of one of those new ex-USSR Islamic republics. Ophion House had vanished, or at best silently decamped to another address. I stood on the pavement taking asthmatic gulps of the damp air, which was doing my back no good at all. It was hard to put my thoughts into any kind of order. Had the place ever really existed? Timbo had seemed such a simple soul. What he said might sometimes sound clumsy or absurd, quite often did in fact. But his healing powers seemed a guarantee of his simplicity, his truthfulness, even — I used the word to myself for the first time — even his goodness. Perhaps he had been the victim of some cruel trick, but why and who would have wanted to play it on him?

It wasn't much of a hope, but as it was only a few hundred yards away, I thought it might be worth trying the Brindisi Club, in case he had decided to make that a more permanent, and presumably much, cheaper base. At first I lost my way in Shepherd Market and began to think that the twisty back alley the Brindisi was in might also turn out to be a mirage, but then I doubled back on my tracks and cast about and found the place. The door was locked and nobody answered the bell. As I was turning away to ponder my next move, I looked up at the blue sign. The sun had made one of its fleeting breakthroughs and in the sunlight I could see how dusty and cracked the sign was, with the corner of the 'B' broken off. It looked like the sign on a place that had closed years ago.

As I turned away from the Brindisi, a sharp stab across my lumbar region reminded me how much I owed to Timbo. It was not, I reflected, just the relief, though that had been wonderful enough. Our sessions together had taken me out of myself like no other experience, no recent experience anyway. Ecstasy, literally.

I stared down the dingy lane and realised that there was another place that might offer some kind of hope. I rang the office and told them that I would not be back till late afternoon and took a cab up to Highgate or Holloway, whichever it was, N19 anyway. Just conceivably it was not the Brindisi Club but Dilkusha that was Timbo's new base. It was at least out of the way and you could instal a bank of old computers anywhere.

The broken-down asbestos garage looked just the same, but as I shouldered my way along the cinder path beside it, brushing aside the dripping brambles, I saw that there was a To Let board nailed across the porch, obliterating the Dilkusha hanging sign. I looked in through the dusty windows, but there was no sign of life. I wrote down the name of the agent in my diary, more for the sake of doing something than in any serious expectation that it might provide a lead, which it turned out not to. The woman at the front desk in the

High Street office was, as it happened, the one who dealt with the Lettings and she remembered Timbo quite well because of his red hair: a strange shade of red, wasn't it, would you call it Titian (not exactly, I said, more the colour of dried blood). He had paid the rent in cash up front, so she had no bank details, not that she would have confided them to me if she had, she said proudly.

That uneasy picnic floating above the city was hard to get out of my head. Was there some subtle coded indication to be gained from it, something that at the same time might be quite easy to decode if I let it come to me? The thought of codes and ciphers brought up Luke's name on the screen. His university post did at least have a concrete, tangible link to the ordinary real world.

'Could I speak to Dr Deverill, please? I'm an old friend of his.'

'I'm afraid not, sir. He's left us.'

'Left the university?'

'Yes, in the middle of term, just like that. There was quite a to-do about it.'

'Why would he do that, do you think?'

'Well, I understand he was offered early retirement and he didn't like the sound of it.'

'So he took even earlier retirement. Not very logical.'

'People don't always behave very logically when they're in a state, do they, sir?'

'No, I suppose they don't. You don't happen to know where I could find him, do you?'

'No, we don't. In fact I was hoping, you being a friend of his, that you might have an address for him, because there's a whole lot of mail for him here and there's some stuff out at Dewdrop Cottage which the college is anxious to have taken away, because there's a new senior lecturer in the Business School who's waiting to move in.'

'I'm sorry, I can't help you.'

'He did tell me when he popped in to say goodbye that he had a brilliant job in computers lined up, at twice the money. But I didn't put much faith in that, because when they're leaving Emu, they all say they're going to a better place.'

At least that might explain Luke's desperate state when Timbo first met him. He must have just been told about the early retirement, which probably didn't have much voluntary about it, and he had drunk himself into a berserk rage and Lethal had done the same to keep him company. Their prospects, together or apart, would have been bleak. Which would also explain why he seized on the offer that Timbo made him. He was a sitting target. All his normal sceptical instincts would have been suspended. And when they both sobered up, it would not be that surprising if they got back together again. They had probably had bust-ups like this before. No, the behaviour of Luke and Lethal was easy enough to imagine. But Timbo? Where was he and what was he up to? Still in Brazil, if he ever went there at all, that is? I had run out of ideas where to look for him. Only now did I realise how little I knew of him, nothing at all really except what he had chosen to tell me. That perhaps was why he had so taken me out of myself. There were no strings attached to him. Being in his company was like being with one of the first men on the moon, taking those clumsy, weightless strides together. And now he had gone as though he had never been in my life. And I was overcome by a bitter sort of sadness which I could neither shake off nor explain.

Then an even more unsettling thought trickled into my head. Had our first meeting really been so accidental? Or, unlikely as it might seem, had I had been some sort of target from the start? Which would at least explain why he reacted so little whenever I told him anything about myself, as if it was stuff he already knew.

I could think of nothing better than to adopt a strategy of masterly inaction and wait to see if he or something turned up, just as unasked for and unexpected as he had originally on the fourth fairway at Beggar's Hill. There was probably some rule in the Colonel's Ops Book which said something along the lines of, When in doubt, sit still.

V

Arc Sunday

Through the windows of Rowley Beavan's hired Lexus, I could see the trees in the Bois beginning to turn, the spinach green of the leaves lighter now, and here and there the chestnut leaves going a rusty yellow. The Allée de la Reine Marguerite was jammed to a standstill with black and silver limos. Under the trees other racego-ers were lying on rugs with their picnics. Beside the cars the ladies were picking their way towards the gates, their high heels sinking into the giving turf of early October. Even today on Arc Sunday, Longchamp had an unperturbed grace.

In the front passenger seat, Rowley was busying himself, his curly grey head bent forward as he struggled with the wire that held the cork in. When the pop came, it sounded unnerving in the packed motor. Squashed next to me in the back I had Fergus McAteer who was something high up in HSBC and his wife Alison who was on the board of the Royal Opera House, both of them broad as haystacks. In the car behind, another Lexus hired by Rowley, was the head of Britain's second largest construction company and his wife and a handsome horse-faced woman who ran one of Philip Green's companies, or was it Michael Green's.

These were the sort of people Rowley collected. When I had first got to know him, years earlier, I imagined that all City editors lived on similar terms of intimacy with the people they wrote about. It was some time before I discovered that the more normal relationship was one of forced politeness or frosty suspicion. Rowley was a one-off. He made the tycoons feel comfortable with themselves and proud of what they had achieved. When he lunched and dined them or vice versa, they went away with a light step and a singing confidence.

Rowley's rivals said that he was not as innocent as he seemed, that he gave his friends' companies write-ups they did not merit and in return they let him have blocks of shares on insider terms or tipped him the wink about deals that were in the offing so he could get in on the ground floor. I knew nothing about all that. All I knew was that my spirits rose whenever I saw his chunky figure roll into view along the corridor, uttering, always from some distance off, his Wodehousian 'What Ho!' He dressed the old-style City slicker: three-piece suit with lapels on the waistcoat, silver curls straying over the collar. But he had no particle of snobbishness, being conspicuously proud of his forebears, Monmouthshire colliers to a man – his father had worked down Bargoed Pit all his life until he died of miner's lung, aged forty-seven – and of the place he came from: 'largest coal mine in the whole bloody valley, broke the world record for coal production for a single shift, then broke it again a year later, poor buggers. Nothing else to do, you see, except dig and sing, and there are only so many times you can reprise "Cwm Rhondda". I went to school with The Man Who Never Was, did you know that? Little Glyndwr Michael, runt of a fellow, Mam said he'd never amount to anything, took to the bottle, Glyn not my mam, did himself in with rat poison, then rose from the dead and won the bloody war. Only man I knew to be bodily resurrected, knew personally, that is.'

I was a late addition to this expedition, or substitution rather because Rowley's dear old friend and fellow Monmouthshire exile, Gerard White-Jones, the ENO tenor who was also a racing man, had had to go into hospital for an operation on his vocal cords, and I was drafted in, because Rowley knew I followed the horses. Jane didn't come, though she was warmly bidden, wouldn't have come in a million years, hated racing and didn't much care for Rowley the only time she met him. Too flashy, she thought, which was just the reason I liked him.

As he passed us our glasses of champagne, he reassured us, 'I'm really rather relieved that we're moving at this snail's pace. This chap drove me from the station last night, he's an absolute terror with a clear road in front of him, must have been to the Henri Paul School of Motoring.'

Ahead of us now I could see the white rails and the green lawns of the racecourse and the little toy windmill beyond. An immense feeling of well-being came over me. Life with Rowley often had that effect. *Bienséance*, I said under my breath, remembering the French word and liking the sound of it.

'What did you say?' asked Mrs McAteer.

'I'm looking forward to this,' I said.

'Ooh, so am I,' she said, as she levered herself out of the limo.

If Rowley had a fault, it was that in crowds his eyes began to wander. A crowd that contained nobody he knew was hostile terrain to him. As soon as he had clocked a single acquaintance, though, he would relax as if he had found the key to life and would then recognise half a dozen other people there, and in no time he would be at the centre of the party. You could hear the relief in his voice as he said, 'My God, there's George Furcht, wouldn't have thought he was a racing man. Hates crowds, hates publicity of any sort in fact.'

'Which one is he?'

'The big chap over there with the scowling look. Originally German of course, but his people landed up in Rio after the war, well, we won't go into that. He's an American citizen now, but his major interests are still in South America.'

I looked across in the direction Rowley was nodding. From what I could see, the man was not as big as all that, but strong-built with a carved sort of head, as though he had started out as a statue and had only imperfectly come to life. Perhaps scowl was not exactly the right word to describe his expression. It was more the grim look of someone who expects things to go his way and is beginning to suspect that they aren't.

'George.'

'Rowland.'

I had never heard Rowley addressed by his full name before, but he seemed to like it, as though this was a more intimate form of address.

George Furcht was carrying the usual racing stuff in his hands, racecard, form book and binoculars, but carrying them in a half-out-stretched hand as if he expected someone to relieve him of them, which someone immediately did, so that he was able to shake hands with Rowley in a warm double handshake which seemed somehow effortful. The hand clasping might have been part of a programme of therapy which he was finding it hard to get the hang of. But I wasn't really looking at the hand clasp because what caught my attention was the someone who had relieved Furcht of his stuff.

'Miss Thorold, my new assistant. She joined us last week and I thought this little trip would make a pleasant introduction to the company for her.'

Lethal swept her hair out of her eyes in the way that made you realise how achingly attractive she was. She was wearing a silk coat and dress in a colour that I thought might be cerise and a pert little cloche of a cerise hat. She might have been coming to the Arc for twenty years.

'Oh, we know each other. Dear Chauffeur,' she said, when it came to our turn to be introduced. And she embraced me with just the right degree of indifference, not quite an air kiss but not much closer.

'I didn't know you were a racing man, George.'

'One has to show one's face.' Then turning to Lethal, 'He's a rogue, this fellow.'

'Oh,' she said. 'I think he looks rather sweet.'

'No, he's a dangerous man, I tell you.'

Rowley went pink with pleasure as he protested his innocence. During this banter, Furcht maintained an unchanged expression, whether because deadpan was how he did banter or because he was incapable of making his face do anything else.

'To tell you the truth, Rowland, I do now have a modest investment in this business. We have brought a few two-year-olds over from Dubai. They're with Tommy Laforgue at Deauville. We hope to have some fun with them next year.'

'Well, the very best of luck. I hope you have better luck anyway than poor old Beaky is having with his racing.'

'Beaky Bentliff?'

'He got fed up with Tommy, you know, and took his best mares away to Chantilly, to Alfred Dunois, but they wouldn't settle, so Alf tried the old trick of putting a donkey in with them. Can't think why that should ever work – perhaps it's the size of his you-know-what – anyway it did the trick. So Alf asked Beaky over to look at his girls peacefully grazing and the donkey bit him in the arse so badly he had to go to hospital.'

George Furcht laughed, a rusty kind of laugh but one which conveyed genuine pleasure. Rowley was a master at serving up these

titbits. All they want is gossip, he told me once, they don't want to
hear your views on the future of the euro, they just want to know
that some business rival has got the clap from his girlfriend.

'I'm due at the paddock,' Furcht said. 'It has been a pleasure
meeting you, Rowland, as always.' He gave a salute like a policeman halting the traffic and turned away with a brusque movement
which suggested that we had interrupted his schedule almost beyond
endurance and only a superhuman effort of will had enabled him to
keep up his good humour. Lee Thorold followed, scurrying a little
to keep up with him. Furcht's stride seemed unnaturally stretched,
like the stride of a man leaping over a succession of medium-sized
puddles. She was still carrying his racecard and glasses.

'She looked like a real goer, that girl. Old friend of yours, is she?'

'Only an acquaintance really.'

'Worth making her acquaintance, I should think.'

'Rowley, that man Furcht. What exactly does he do?'

'What doesn't he do? To start with, he has what you might call the
South American mix — cattle, timber, soy, oil exploration too, that's
his latest — but timber's always been his big thing. They've got, Lord
knows, how many million acres, mostly in the Amazon basin and
further south, in the Mato Grosso, but a fair bit in the Texas panhan-
dle and the Midwest too, Kansas I think, no, I tell a lie, it's Iowa, I'm
pretty sure it's Iowa.'

'You mean,' I said slowly, 'he's a *logger.*'

'Keep your hair on, old boy. If you're going to raise cattle or soy,
somebody's got to cut the trees down first. Personally, I'm rather in
favour of feeding the famished millions. Anyway, isn't soy going to
be the biofuel of the future and replace all that nasty carbon?'

'He's a logger. He destroys the rainforest.'

'All right, he's a logger, but don't let it spoil your lunch. This is
supposed to be a day at the races, not the AGM of Greenpeace. I
expect you're just upset seeing your girlfriend with Another.'

'She's not my girlfriend, but, yes, I am a bit startled.'

'I don't blame you. I wouldn't want to see any of my loved ones
arm in arm with Georgie. He's not what you might call a nice
person.'

Rowley forgave my tetchy inquisition, as he forgave most
unpleasantnesses in life and as he expected to be forgiven for his

73

own strayings. His first two wives had had plenty of practice and only threw him out in the end from sheer exhaustion, retaining a baffled affection for him long after they had divorced. The present incumbent, not quite a wife yet I think, was sulking, so not present today, but Rowley told me he was confident she would come round. The first one was always the hardest to forgive, he said. First what, I asked. Oh, you know, he said.

'Does he run a hedge fund too?'

'Who? George? Not as far as I know, though of course a group as big as that has to be hedging currencies all the time, dealing in other futures too, I would imagine.'

'And arms, does he deal in arms?'

'Again, not as far as I know. Isn't his being a mega logger bad enough for you? Does he have to be a merchant of death as well? Oh, look, there's Hal.'

'Hal who?' I said, as Rowley waved at a plump man hurrying across the turf towards us.

'Hal Gombrich,' the man said as he shook hands. He was as pink as he was plump, and though out of breath he radiated bonhomie on a Rowley-like scale. 'A pleasure to meet you, sir.' He spoke in a rich and courtly American voice with something else in it, something earthier, perhaps ironical.

'Dickie Pentecost,' I said.

'Not D. K. Pentecost? I admire your work, sir. You speak with tongues of fire as befits your name.'

I record this flowery compliment only to say how startled I was by it. Nobody but nobody admires my work, scarcely anyone reads the paper, and as for taking in who writes the diplomatic stuff, forget it. As I say, these days even having a dip.corr on your staff is an anachronism, like still keeping a hatstand in the hall.

'Hal is the main man at Upstate First Bank.' Rowley likes you to be left in no doubt about these things.

'A mere figurehead, my friends, and one sadly in need of a lick of paint.'

'Do you have a horse running here?' I asked.

'Gracious, no. I know nothing of horses. I'm strictly a gambling man, a deplorable habit for which the Fates exact their due. *O lente, lente currite, noctis equi* – and I fear that for me they usually do.'

'Do what?'

'Run slowly, if not backwards. Tell me, Rowley, you haven't seen George Furcht by any chance? I had hoped to see him here.'

'We were talking five minutes ago. He just went off to the paddock.'

'Ah, I'll catch up with him there. What a pity to have to wrench myself away from you, Rowley old friend. And Dickie too, though I prefer to address you with due solemnity as D. K., it has been an honour which I hope will be repeated at the earliest possible opportunity. Until then, my best salaams to you both.'

He said goodbye with a warm embracing gesture to show how reluctant he was to leave us. Yet I could not help noticing that he really was in a hurry.

'Why's he so eager to catch up with George Furcht?'

'You'd be eager if he owed you somewhere north of a hundred million dollars.'

'So though King Log is ripping out the rainforest, he's also in deep doo-doo?'

'The shit does seem to be sticking to his shoes at the moment,' Rowley agreed with a seraphic smile. It was not in his nature to be downcast by the misfortunes of others.

'Why would Lee want to get mixed up with someone like that when he isn't even solvent?'

'Oh, solvency is a term of art, Dickie. One remains solvent until everyone agrees that one isn't. Besides, women like to help a chap.'

These brief encounters had my head whirling and it went on whirling as we went through the unvarying rituals under a bruised Paris sky: the trip to the surprising little paddock under the chestnut trees, the lobster salad and Veuve Clicquot in the cramped white box overlooking the finish, the whispered instructions to the boy taking our bets, the silken amble of the horses along the rails to the start, then the sudden palpitating drumming of their hooves as they came back to the hoarse wild cries from the stands and the cries dying in seconds from a roar to an anguished buzz. And all the time I was thinking, what's she doing with that man, or what's he doing with her? Are they really allies, or is she keeping tabs on him, or what?

'Another glass of the Widow?'

'No thanks, I'd better go and collect my winnings.'

'But I thought you were on Colibris.'

'No, I switched to Lady Roxanne at the last minute.'

Which I had not, but what I wanted was some air. I had thought I could swim through Rowley's world and not mind about it. But I had lost that strange blend of curiosity and tolerance which enables you to survive in alien waters when you are young.

The Gents had a picture of a jockey in the Aga Khan colours on the door. As I was coming out of it, I glanced at the long queue for the Ladies next to it. It was a queue of breathtaking elegance bending back on itself in a sinuous curve. The silken dresses and the feathered hats glistened in the fitful sun. All the same, there was a reduced, hushed note to the conversation that rippled along its length as though the women were acknowledging a shared embarrassment in answering nature's call so publicly. I tried not to stare at them, but before I looked away, I caught sight of the dazzling figure of Lethal near the front of the queue in her cerise frock, standing out even in that *soigné* crocodile.

I went closer to her and said: 'So what's all this about?'

'What is all what about?'

'What are you up to with George Furcht?'

'You heard, I'm his new assistant.'

'What exactly are you assisting him with?'

'I'm certainly not his girlfriend if that's what you're implying. I really can't believe you're being jealous on Luke's behalf.'

'That's not what I meant. What I want to know is how does he fit into the operation?'

She looked puzzled as if the question made no sense.

'How do you mean, fit into the operation? It's his operation. He's my boss.'

'So he owns Elcatron?'

'Elcatron?' she said with a studied vagueness, as though the word came from a foreign language she could not begin to identify. Then, with a slow, stagy dawning: 'Oh, that electronics firm Timbo told you about.'

'Told me about? Isn't Elks as you call it what your whole crazy plan is all about?'

'Yes,' she said reflectively, almost ruefully but not quite, 'he said he was sure you would believe him. Luke and I didn't think you would. We thought you would have more sense.'

'You mean, he made the whole thing up?'

'No, not the whole thing. Just the bit about Elks and the Brazilian Navy. I never believed it myself because I didn't know Brazil had a navy, not one we sold things to anyway.'

'But why?'

'He wanted to test you. Oh, look, it's my turn. I must go, I'm bursting.'

She followed a short woman in a tight turquoise dress up the little steps and through the door of the Ladies. I stared bewildered at the door which matched the jockey in the Aga colours with the figure of an elegant woman looking through comically oversized binoculars. Then I became aware that some of the women in the queue were staring crossly at me. Hanging around the door to importune her again was an indecent intrusion, and I moved away at a brisk pace, trying to look as if I had been called to some official duty.

I walked over to the pari-mutuel and, to steady my wits, placed a bet at random on the next race. I could have waited for Lee to emerge, but I was now too distracted to think straight. In what way could Timbo have been testing me? And how did he manage it? Hadn't I always thought of him as basically thick rather than devious? I suppose what I mostly thought of him was how odd he was, in a different category. To think of him as this artful person was to think of a completely different person, someone who, among other things, probably was not a healer at all but a cheap fraud. I began to think that he had not only misled my mind with his Elks story but he had also managed to fool my body too. The benefit I had experienced must be the result of a misplaced faith and not of his healing powers – worse still, a faith I had not even been aware I possessed. I was not the sharp sceptical journo I fancied myself as but a credulous sucker, scarcely fit to be allowed out by myself.

'Come on, old boy. You haven't had your summer pudding. They do it awfully well here.'

Rowley was jogging my elbow, disturbed by my absent stare, anxious to tug me back into the fun.

All the way back on the Eurostar, I fretted and puzzled over my half-knowledge. Of course what I minded most was swallowing a pathetic fantasy, but I also minded still only knowing half the story, if I knew even that much. Was Timbo really still in Brazil? Or was that part of the embroidery too, another mendacious flourish to enrich the deception? Perhaps he had travelled no further than Brent Cross or was holed up in Borehamwood. I ought to have waited for Lethal to come out of the Ladies and badgered her until I had wormed the whole truth out of her, but I had been sore about being suckered. I needed space to lick my wounds. In any case, she might not have told me any more, especially what exactly she was doing for or against George Furcht. And that was, after all, the new question: what she was doing carrying the race glasses for one of the biggest loggers in the Western hemisphere?

PART TWO

VI

Mrs Tallboys

I can remember exactly where I was standing when I heard – or rather saw – that Timbo was dead. Not difficult to remember really because I was in the foreign editor's pod watching CNN to see if they had the exit poll on the French elections yet. It was a small item running along the bottom of the screen and then repeated a few times before it was bumped by the exit poll and an air crash in Zambia: 'Briton found dead in Brazil hotel: Timothy Smith, aged 34, business consultant from London, was found strangled in a hotel in Manaus, Brazil.' That was all. There was no more detail on the agencies. The foreign desk got me the number of the British Consul in Manaus, which was all I could think of doing.

I have put all this down too brutally, as if I meant to shock. My excuse is that this was how I felt when I heard the news: startled, breathless and strangely numb, half-believing it was really Timbo, half-believing, and of course hoping, it might be someone else. It felt worse because I had nobody I could immediately turn to, nobody I knew who knew Timbo, except for Luke and Lethal, and I was not sure where to get hold of them, they were such birds of passage, virtually homeless as far as I knew. There was the mysterious Aurore, if she ever existed and if she really was Timbo's girlfriend, but I realised that I did not know her surname. One could scarcely call Médecins sans Frontières and ask to speak to 'Aurore in the Congo', even assuming she was still there. All I could do was ring the Consul in Manaus, who the FCO said was called Mrs Isolda Tallboys. She turned out to be a tough-sounding but helpful woman who spoke with a faint foreign accent, perhaps a Brazilian married to a Brit. Mrs Tallboys said she glad to hear from me because she was rather at a loss:

'Mr Smith was clearly a businessman of some standing but the curious thing is he had no business cards among his belongings and the next-of-kin details on his passport were blank. We put the news out on the wire in the hope of getting a response but you're the first person to call. You wouldn't be his executor by any chance?'

'No, I'm not, but I'm happy to stand in if you can't find one. It's true he didn't have much in the way of family apart from his aunt in New Zealand, but I'm not sure he was in touch with her and I'm afraid I don't have her married name, if she is married and I don't even know that.'

'Oh, dear, he seems to be rather an orphan of the storm, your Mr Smith. That was his real name, I suppose?'

'Oh, yes, Timothy Smith, always known as Timbo.'

'Timbo.' I could hear her reflecting on the sadness of it.

'How exactly ...'

'... did he die? Well, the hotel manager told us he had been found strangled in his room, and the police have confirmed that, so that's what we put out. It seems to have been a brutal business, I'm afraid. But that's all I can tell you until we've had the post-mortem. I'll let you have the full details as soon as I know them myself. Would you be thinking of a home burial? We would be happy to arrange that, but I must warn you that it works out rather expensive, what with the combination of the air freight and the hygiene regulations.'

I said that I would think about it and she said there was no hurry to decide. The idea of him lying friendless in an unmarked grave halfway up the Amazon was dismal, but then it was scarcely more cheering to picture a brief and sparsely attended send-off in a north London crem. Perhaps his ashes could be scattered over Beggar's Hill golf course, but it would probably take a meeting of the full club committee to secure permission. I began to cry and brought the conversation with Mrs Tallboys to an end as quickly as I could politely manage.

Then later on in the afternoon, I realised that obviously Lethal could be contacted through George Furcht's office. The name of his business had fled from my distracted brain, but Rowley reminded me what it was and gave me the number from his phone: 'The Maloca Group. I thought at first it was something to do with the evil eye, but then a Portuguese friend told me it was the word for a Brazilian longhouse where the natives live, though I expect George's maloca is a rather superior model, don't you? Well, best of luck with that fantastic girl. I knew you wouldn't be able to resist.'

It wasn't hard to get through to Lethal, but when I heard her hard, confident voice, I was even more uncertain how to break the news. I need not have worried, not on that score anyway.

'Yes, it is terrible news, Chauffeur, the very worst. Poor, poor Bimbo. I was going to phone you but I didn't have your mobile. The only person in the world who could have connected us was Bimbo and now he can't any more, isn't that a sad thought?'

'You heard already?'

'George's people in Manaus called him last night. They're on the case. It's all so ghastly.'

'Now can you tell me what he was up to?'

'Well, I could, but I don't suppose you'll believe me after—'

'No, I don't suppose I will, but tell me anyway.'

'At least now you'll believe it's serious, because I got the impression at the time that you weren't really taking any of it seriously, even though you said you did believe what we told you.'

'You're dead right I wasn't.'

'George is very distressed. He really is.'

'I'm glad to hear it.'

'He can't think who could possibly be responsible.'

'Has he tried looking in the mirror?'

'Look, what we told you about the mission was essentially true, except it wasn't anything to do with Elcatron or defence stuff. It was George's companies that were being shorted, or the ones that have shareholders anyway, and he needed to find out who was doing it because he couldn't raise any money from the shareholders and the banks weren't willing to lend. And he sent Bimbo to Brazil to find out who was shafting him over there.'

'So why did Timbo feed me all that bullshit about submarines?'

'Well, he needed a cover story to try you out with, to see if you would be interested in joining up with us. That way, if it was a no-no for you, you would not be burdened with the knowledge of what it was really all about. And besides …'

'Besides what?'

'He wasn't sure whether you would like the sound of George. He thought your first reaction might be, well, a bit hostile.'

'He wasn't wrong.'

'George is arranging the funeral. He'll make sure it's all done really nicely.'

'No, George is not arranging the funeral. I am arranging the funeral because I am the executor and Timbo is going to have a quiet service at Golders Green crem and then his old friends are going to scatter his ashes on the golf course where we first met.' In my fury I pulled on the executor's mantle without hesitation. The thought of the scattering at Beggar's Hill suddenly seemed elegiac and fitting. Just by the pond behind the thirteenth green would be the perfect spot.

'I am afraid that won't be possible, Chauffeur,' Lethal came back tartly, with something of the sting she had before she was dried out. 'George's agent has written agreement from the police that the body will be released into his custody as soon as the PM is complete, and he will be buried in the graveyard at San Salvador where apparently the Maloca Group has a sector reserved for its staff. George personally restored the church spire and the place has a special place in his heart.'

'I would guess that must be a difficult place to find. Look, Lethal, I don't want to pull rank, but it is the executor's duty to say what the funeral arrangements shall be.'

'You're too late. It's all taken care of.'

'The British Consul—'

'I don't want to shatter your illusions but I don't think anyone's going to take much notice of what some old Brit in a dirty panama tells them when they already have their orders from Furcht.'

'It's a woman actually, and I think she's Brazilian.'

'Look, Chauffeur, forget it. If you'd like to send flowers, I can arrange that for you. But otherwise there's nothing you can do. George's people will find out what happened and then they'll nail the bastard who did it, but—'

I realised that she was near tears too.

'I thought just behind the pond at the thirteenth.'

'No,' Garside said, 'that wouldn't do at all.' A look of horror crossed his face, muted because of the subject we were discussing, but horror none the less.

'Not the thirteenth? Well then, what about somewhere by the little clump of – are they sycamores – at the next hole?'

'No ashes anywhere on the course, that's the rule. We have had to take a firm line. My predecessor's widow had the same idea – only she wanted that little mound by the third tee in sight of the club-house. Now if it was a bench you were thinking of …'

'A bench?'

'The Committee looks kindly on a bench, and you can choose your own inscription of course. But ashes are a no-no. There are the hygiene regs, to start with.'

'That's very disappointing.'

'I'm sorry, but I'm bound by the Committee. We'll send a wreath of course. We always send a wreath for members of more than five years' standing.'

The ashes idea had come to me on a whim, but it seemed perfect for someone so elusive. I had not been thinking about a wreath, but Lethal said she would be able to arrange transport, so I asked Garside to send the wreath to my home address and I'd take it on.

'A wreath, for that ghastly man? Why on earth did you let them send it here? You're not his brother.'

'He hasn't got a brother, and his aunt's in New Zealand, if she's still alive.'

'That's no excuse.' Jane stood rigid with disdain, holding the large cellophane package which the DHL man had thrust into her hands. I had not expected much sympathy from her. She exhausts most of her sympathy in her work. What's left over is lavished on Flo and Lucy.

'I'll take it down to Furcht's office. They'll be able to ship it out to Brazil. It's the least they can do.'

'Furcht!' she snorted. She had read an article about the Maloca Group's activities in the *Sunday Times* colour magazine, and she was horrified when I revealed that I had met him. 'Get it out of here, please. It gives me the creeps. It was probably some gay thing anyway.'

'His death, you mean? I hadn't thought …'

'You can't have thought he was straight. Even you …'

She left the thought of my insensibility hanging in the muggy air. It was not for Jane with her impeccable liberal views to bring up the subject as if that meant his death didn't matter, but I kept the thought to myself. In her present mood, the main thing was to get the Beggar's Hill wreath out of the house. I had a briefing at the American Embassy at noon and Furcht's office was just round the corner, so I could drop it in on the way.

It's unnerving to carry a funeral wreath on the Tube with its waxy petals and fernery visibly through the shiny wrapping. People make way for you and you get a seat even in the rush hour. One or two passengers lowered their eyes, and an elderly Black matron muttered 'God rest his soul' to me, and I muttered 'Thank you' back. But some of the younger passengers looked affronted by being jostled by this emblem of mortality so early in the day, and on balance I wished I'd taken a taxi.

'Miss Thorold? I'm afraid she's not in yet.'

'Perhaps I could just drop it in Mr Furcht's office.'

'I'm afraid that won't be possible. They're all in a meeting.'

'Well, could I just send up a note.'

I sat in the hall while a crisp youth took up my scribble. It was an inconspicuous building off Grosvenor Square which still looked more like a large private house than a corporate HQ, like Ophion House in fact, except for the shoals of people coming and going.

'Mr Furcht will see you now, sir.' There was a flicker of surprise in the concierge's 'sir'. 'Fifth floor, I'll take you up.'

As we got out into the narrow hall, a gaggle of men in suits crossed our path. They seemed somehow hustled and discomfited. As the office they were coming from turned out to be Furcht's, I deduced that my coming must have interrupted their meeting.

The office looked too small to have fitted them all in, looked cramped in fact with only the man himself in it. I had hardly shut the door behind me when Lethal came in through a door on the far side. I wondered why the concierge had been told to say she wasn't in yet. You could hardly have missed her in her dove-grey shimmery shirt and flary skirt. Like Furcht, she looked a bit flustered. Perhaps there had been some hurried argument about whether to let me up.

'It is a pleasure to see you again,' George Furcht said in his rich effortful voice. 'That is a magnificent tribute you have there. Do put it on the table and sit down for a minute. Miss Thorold will pour us some coffee.'

The wreath seemed oppressively large as it lay between us on the table, almost as though it was standing in for Timbo's body. While Lethal was pouring, I looked round the room. One wall was filled with a finely detailed contour map, which I identified as the Eastern Seaboard of the US, although only a sliver of the Atlantic was shown along the right-hand edge. There was a thin blue tape pinned diagonally across the mountains in the middle of the map.

'Ah, yes,' said Furcht, following my gaze, 'yes, one of my favourite parts of the world. As a lad, I hiked over the Blue Mountains. I used to drink moonshine with the hillbillies. Terrible stuff. They were an amazing bunch of rogues.' For a reminiscence of youthful frolic, the words came out heavy with reluctance, as though these were things he had not wished to say. Once again, I had the impression that I'd come at an awkward time, but then a man with an oversized wreath from a golf club is probably never a welcome visitor.

'This is a terrible business,' he said. 'Terrible.'

'Yes, it is.'

'I feel very bad about it all. Your friend was engaged on a totally harmless mission on my behalf, pure research, nothing more. But Brazil is a very violent country, I have to admit that fact, although it is my native land. All I can promise you is that this superb wreath will be sent across as refrigerated cargo and laid with all due honour on your friend's grave, as soon as we are able to give him a decent burial. These wretched post-mortems always take an eternity. And now if you will forgive me, we have colleagues waiting on rather urgent business. Miss Thorold will guide you out, it is something of a rabbit warren, I fear.'

He rose. We all rose. As he went towards the door to show us out, he tapped the map with his big knuckles.

'Ah, yes, they were great fellows. We used to call them the flashers – they flashed these torches to warn the illicit stills that the Excise men were coming over the pass. Great days, great days.'

Lethal took me as far as the lift. She hissed at me as the door opened, 'He's lying, you know.'

'Lying about what?'

'I don't know yet. I'll make sure the wreath gets there.' She clutched me fiercely by the arm as though this was an acknowledged way of saying goodbye.

I waited until I was out in the street before I called Mrs Tallboys to tell her about the wreath. I wanted to handle this bit on my own, to make it clear, to myself at least, that this was the only part of the business which concerned me. Luke and Lethal might be up to their necks in it, but all I really cared about was seeing to it that Timbo was decently buried. I was surprised how much I cared about this, but I did.

'Yes, this is Isolda Mendoza Tallboys. Oh, I am so glad you called.' Her voice sounded softer than the first time we had talked. Now she sounded anxious, almost fluttery. I don't think she had used the Mendoza the first time. Her voice sounded more Brazilian too, perhaps because I had taken her by surprise. I pictured her sitting in a clean modern office in Manaus with a view of the river and a vase of sweet-smelling flowers on her desk. She would, I fancied, be handsome in a rather heavy way, especially in profile, with dark violet eyes, the faintest suspicion of hair on her upper lip and a lacy jabot at her throat, that too perhaps violet or some intense shade of blue.

'I have been calling you for the past four hours,' she said, 'but I think your mobile must have been switched off.'

'It was.' I had turned it off before I went into Furcht's office.

'I don't quite know how to start. The truth is that something extraordinary has come up and we are in a quandary, I mean we at the Consulate and the police too. We have spoken to the MD of G. Furcht and Co. over here because he had asked to be kept abreast of developments, but he was unable to help us because he had never actually met Mr Smith. He was expecting to, of course, as soon as Mr Smith reached Manaus, but the terrible event took place before there had been any contact with him. So you are our only hope.'

'Well, I'd obviously be glad to do anything I can to help. But from this distance—'

'You see, the medical side of the post-mortem is pretty much complete. I'll happily email you the details, though I fear they make grim reading especially for a close friend such as yourself. But what we now have is a problem of identification.'

'Identification?'

'I know it may sound peculiar at this late stage. That was a matter which seemed perfectly straightforward. The body was, after all, discovered with your friend's passport and a photo driving licence which tallied with the passport. There was even a name tape sewn inside the vest pocket of his suit. But then, well, the police began to have doubts. You see—'

'Doubts?' I broke in. 'You mean about whether it was actually him?'

'Yes. The first thing that raised concerns was that his suit didn't fit very well. It seemed very tight around the shoulders and under the arms, and it was a little odd that he should be wearing a three-piece suit in his hotel room. Most men take their jackets off, don't they?'

'None of that would surprise me. He was chaotic about clothes. He might well have taken a suit that had got too tight for him, and he could well forget to take his jacket off.'

'But then they looked again at the two photographs. Superficially they resembled the body, but when you looked closer, it seemed more like a Brazilian face. We wondered of course whether the photos were a reasonable likeness – they so often aren't. Would you mind if I jpegged them to you because you're the only person we know who could tell us?'

'Of course.' I gave her my mobile number and told her I'd be home in an hour or so and would call her straight back when I'd had a look.

'The body's blood type was one that is very common in Brazil, but it's common elsewhere too, I understand. They're doing a mitochondrial DNA test too but we have not had the results back yet. There is, however, one further matter which should be quite easy to resolve.'

She hesitated.

'Please, I'll do whatever I can.'

'Do you happen to know if your friend was in the habit of dyeing his hair?'

'Dyeing his hair?' I repeated numbly. It seemed a freakish suggestion and the more I thought about it the more absurd it sounded and I said so.

'Because the hair on the head of the body is definitely dyed. It's a reasonable match to the colour on the passport, but they forgot about the eyebrows which are heavy and dark, very much the Brazilian type. And when you look closely at them, even in death the eyes look more Brazilian too, the irises very dark brown. If he was doing the dyeing himself, I suppose he could have forgotten about the eyebrows.'

'I have absolutely no reason to think he dyed his hair and can't think why he would want to do so. It's true, it was an unusual colour, more the colour of rust or dried blood, but I never thought of it as being dyed.'

'You're right about it being the colour of dried blood. It took quite a time for the first pathologist to notice that he had been beaten over the head as well as being strangled because the blood on his scalp matched his hair colour so closely.'

'His red hair seemed very much part of him, especially because he was a healer, although he didn't make a big deal out of it.'

'A healer?'

'He could pass his hands down your back, without touching you, and cure your back problems. He was amazing. I went to him regularly. That's really how we met in fact.'

'That is most interesting,' she said. 'I'm probably being very stupid but what has that to do with the colour of his hair?'

'In our country, healing powers are often associated with redheads. It's probably just a myth.'

'I see. Unfortunately in Brazil we have so few redheads, so we must make do with healers who are brunettes. You do not think – I am only trying to exhaust every possibility – you do not think it possible that he might have dyed his hair red in order to convince his patients that his powers were genuine? I do not wish to appear cynical but surely there must be some element of autosuggestion even when the cure is quite genuine.'

'Well, I'm pretty cynical myself. I cannot tell you how little faith I had in Timbo when we started. But perhaps deep down, I did want to believe in him. It's hard to say.'

As I was speaking, a trickle of doubt about the whole healing thing had crept back into the corner of my mind. After all, Timbo had not always told me the truth about what he was up to. He had spun the cover story about the electronics firm with a puppyish enthusiasm which had totally suckered me. Why should he not have done precisely as Mrs Tallboys was suggesting, dyed his hair to reinforce his claim to have been born endowed with supernatural powers which were outside his control?

'The police have of course been through his luggage to see if he had any hair dye with him. They found nothing, but that is not conclusive. He might have been hoping to be home again before he needed another dip.'

'He could always have bought a fresh supply in Brazil.'

'For a man that might well be possible. A woman would, I think, like to be sure that she had her preferred brand with her.'

'Yes, I do see that.'

There was a silence. She had obviously said what she had to say, and I was still digesting this bizarre and puzzling news, uncertain what to think or feel about it. I could not help thinking, quite irrelevantly, of Mrs Tallboys's own hair coiled in a thick braid round her head, its dark lustre too perhaps fresh from the dye bottle.

'So if it isn't Timbo, Mr Smith, who is it?' I stammered after a bit. 'And where in heaven or earth is Mr Smith? Well, I cannot expect you to have any sort of answer to either of those questions, not at this stage anyway.'

'You're right, I don't. But there are two obvious lines for immediate enquiry. When we have the DNA information for the body, we can start matching it against the DNA of known missing persons. But this will be a huge task. So many people disappear without trace in our city, and even if their disappearance is reported, we may not always be able to find relatives who are willing to give DNA samples for matching. What would be helpful of course is if we could make certain that the body is definitely not that of your friend. For that we need a close relative to offer his or her DNA. You mentioned an aunt.'

'She's called Sarah-Caroline, and she lives in New Zealand but, as I think I said, I do not have her married name if she is married. In fact, I'm not even sure she's still alive.'

'We could ask our embassy there to put out an appeal. In a small country like New Zealand, someone is likely to come forward. As for where your friend is now, since he has not surfaced, there are several possibilities. One, I'm afraid, is that he too is dead. We must not assume that just because he is not in that hotel room he must therefore be alive and well somewhere else.'

'But if there are two dead bodies, why would whoever has done this have bothered to switch them round?'

'As we do not understand why there is one dead body, it is highly improbable that we should understand why there are two, if there are.' There was a note of irritation in Mrs Tallboys's voice. She sounded like a woman who did not care for mysteries, especially those she was responsible for clearing up. I was with her there.

'He could be in a hospital, I suppose, or have lost his memory.'

'Yes, he could, and we have already put out his picture to the regional hospital network which includes the psychiatric hospitals. But I do not wish to raise your hopes. Brazil is an enormous country and, I repeat, thousands of people disappear every year, including a surprising number of British citizens, although many of them are people who wish to disappear.'

We could go no further. I said that the best thing I could do now was go home and look at the jpegs.

To my surprise, in the prevailing fog, the one thing that was clear was Timbo's passport photograph. The focus was sharp and it must have been taken recently (Mrs Tallboys told me that the passport had been issued only eighteen months ago). It was a speaking likeness, for once the right phrase. Timbo's lips were parted as if he were about to ask the photographer a question. Apart from the crinkly dried-blood hair – the colour was spot on – his whole face had that in-your-face quality, the blundering forwardness which was the first thing you thought of when you thought of him.

'Yes, that's him. It's an excellent likeness. And so's the driving licence picture.'

'Good. Then I think that we can provisionally begin to assume that the body is not his. Since we spoke, they have emailed me the provisional DNA findings. They support, quite strongly I'm told, the assumption that the dead man is of Hispanic descent. Of course it is possible that Mr Smith had a Portuguese grandmother or something.'

'Nothing of the kind as far as I know. It's the sort of thing he would probably have told me if he had. He liked to talk about his family. Well, he liked to talk about most things.'

'I'm afraid that we must circulate the photographs to the morgues as well. At the same time, we'll be sending them our own photographs of the corpse, in case it might have been removed from one of their premises and its loss not reported or not yet discovered. There is much work to be done.'

I said I could see that, and I wished her well. As I put the telephone down, I felt so queasy I thought I would throw up. Then I texted Lethal, my fingers stubbing the keys as if I was a blind man.

VII

The Eureka Moment

It was a billowing Victorian flat at the top of Albert Hall Mansions. From the windows what you mostly saw was a sizeable segment of the dome of the Hall. It was like having your nose pressed up against an elephant's bottom, Lethal said.

She looked blooming as she opened the door to me, like an eighteen-year-old who has put on a swirly frock and a slash of lipstick to impress. She sat down on the squashy arm of the Conran sofa wiggling her bare feet into the fat linen cushions, and began sipping a Diet Coke through a straw. Luke had his trademark orange boots propped up on a big steel desk with three or four computer screens in front of him.

They seemed overjoyed to see me.

'Darling Chauffeur.'

'Salutations,' Luke said.

'So he could still be alive,' they both said almost simultaneously.

'Well, they seem to be pretty sure he's not the dead man with dyed red hair they picked up,' Luke said. 'But that's really all they know at the moment.'

'George is very pleased that Timbo isn't dead – if he isn't – but he's in a terrible state. He's taking it personally, says they're doing the whole thing to frighten him. He wants to see you again, straight away.'

'Me? Why me?'

'He keeps on saying you're the executor, and you're a hell of a smart guy, and you're the only man who can find out what's really happened.'

'I just brought the flowers from the golf club. And of course, I'm not an executor at all. I just said it to get access to the Consul.'

'No, he's really impressed.'

'Why can't he go and find out for himself?'

'He has to go to the States to sweet-talk the bankers.'

'Poor bugger,' Luke put in. 'We estimate that he has short-term finance with no less than seventy-three banks, most of it due to be rolled over within the next two months. So far he's only got seventeen signatures and half of those are contingent on everyone else signing. He claims that his total borrowings are in the region of $1.5 billion, but Anthony Wardle from Javits Thornton tells me that the true figure is nearer $2.5. He has to cajole and flatter every pompous little bank president from the Atlantic to the Rockies. Meanwhile the other guys are still shorting him like crazy.'

'They've been at it for months now,' Lethal said. 'Would you like a cappuccino from the lovely machine the last tenants left behind?'

I could not take my eyes off her as she busied herself, giving little clucks of amusement as she fiddled with the levers and frothed up the milk. All the fierce desperation she had flung at Timbo when we first met seemed to have vanished. She and Luke now seemed as frisky as a young married couple in a TV ad for sofas or coffee machines.

'So have you found out who the other guys are? Who's behind the whole conspiracy, if that's what it is?'

'Well, we started by looking at the more traditional operators, former bankers and stockbrokers who have left the old City behind and taken smart offices in Mayfair where they minister personally to the investment needs of high-net-worth individuals – what you and I would call the stinking rich. Take for example, Strang-Biggs Partners, started by the brothers George and Bertie Strang-Biggs, known as the String Bags. Pussy, George's wife, was one of the first friends Lethal made in her forays into this world.'

'Pussy's queen of the charity circuit and the friendliest soul you ever met. She gave me the run of her laptop almost the moment she let me in the door. Look at our mantelpiece. Half the stiffies come from Pussy.'

Stuck behind a Rubik's cube there was a sheaf of invitations. I went over and riffled through them. There seemed to be scarcely a benevolent organisation in London which wasn't throwing some do or other – a pashmina sale, a skating gala, a celebrity chef dinner, a fashion show, a dance in the grounds of the Royal Hospital, another at the Zoo, a clay pigeon shoot and barbecue somewhere in Essex, a sale of tapestry work by prison inmates, a quiz supper in a church crypt. The charitable wattage involved was frightening. But Luke was anxious to press on with his briefing.

'As an intellectual challenge, establishing the identities of the shorters turned out to be disappointing. In fact it was something of a pushover. Hedgies don't really worry much about security. This is not because the people who run them are incapable of installing deep encryption keys – many of them are computer nerds – but they are not that worried if some rival gets wind of what they are up to.'

'Why not? I should have thought that secrecy would be rather important to them.'

'Not really, if you think about it. Shorting is a momentum business. If you want the price of a share or a bond or a currency to fall faster, the more people who know you are shorting it, the more likely they are to imitate you and so accelerate the fall.'

'In most cases all we had to unpick was the standard security apparatus installed by the manufacturers – passwords, network keys and so on. These are meat and drink to the lowest phone hackers, the sort the *News of the World* employs. In some cases our targets had not even bothered to change the keys supplied – tapping in Welcome 123 did the trick. If that sort of thing didn't work, Lethal soon provided us with the information required to make an educated guess: mother's maiden name, first school, birthplace, or in the case of offices, name of office block and company or surname of head of IT. Once or twice, Lethal has had the luck to chum up with a disgruntled ex-employee who was only too pleased to hand us all the keys on a plate – mobiles, computers, back office, the lot.'

'So there was a bit of bribery involved too?'

'Not much. One chap who had been sacked did offer us a hard disk he had brought out with him, but he wanted too much money and in any case we already had the information we needed. The truth is that remote communication is a wonderful boon, but it is also a great destroyer of privacy. To overhear merchants whispering on the old Bourse in Amsterdam or London, you had to be standing behind the next pillar. The String Bags have the luxury of being able to do business from their beach houses in the Caymans – I haven't mentioned Flash Harry Falk who spends much of his time doing underwater archaeology in his submersible – but by the same token we evil interceptors can hear what they're up to, even if they're thousands of miles away or several hundred feet under water.'

'Did you manage to identify all the funds which were doing the shorting?'

'I wouldn't say all of them, but enough to constitute a critical mass that would enable us to discern a pattern, a purpose behind the market activity.'

'Even so, how could you possibly prove that there had been a conspiracy?'

'Date. That was the crucial criterion. We had to log the dates when each of the funds we had identified began to short Furcht. Were there any clusters of shorts at or around particular dates, and did they relate to bad news which would have led any rational observer to deduce that Furcht was on the slide? At moments I was so overwhelmed by the mounds of data, especially all the stuff Lethal brought in, that I began to despair of seeing my way through.'

'I sometimes felt like the little dog who comes panting in to lay yet another bone at her master's feet and gets a total brush-off.'

'But then when I had all the data arranged and set in date order, well, at the risk of sounding banal, I can only say Eureka. Here's the timeline chart I got up for George which he hasn't had time to look at yet.'

He had printed out the chart and now pinned it up to his clip-board with a pride he did not trouble to disguise.

'Look, there, you see, all through the first six months of the year, there is only a random scatter of unfavourable reports relating to Furcht, and the share price stays relatively stable. There is a small dip in May but that turns out to be temporary. Then at the beginning of July, the shorting begins. You see the cluster that spreads into the beginning of August. That is followed by a tail on the chart like a meteor tail and this carries on into the autumn. That would be consistent with a group of funds making a concerted raid over several weeks, with the follow-my-leaders coming in over the next two months as they get wind of the short and at the same time begin to read that the company is in difficulties.'

'So you have your conspirators,' I came back rather sharply, 'but what's their motive, apart obviously from trying to make money? If there's a ringleader, how did he or she persuade the others to come in? After all, for all they knew at the start, it might not work. Furcht is, as I understand it, a huge and powerful company. They had to want to bring him down badly to take the risk. What made them want to gang up together?'

As I was posing this question, I became aware of a strange quickening in my interest, as though a switch had been flicked somewhere in my head. Ever since Timbo had spun me that first dodgy yarn about Elks, the lack of interest I had shown in the whole rigmarole had been quite genuine. Now for some reason I could not immediately identify, I wanted to know everything. Luke was quick to spot my change of tone, and he smiled the half-stifled smile of the salesman who can see he has hooked his customer.

'You're quite right, Dickie. What was striking was not just the evidence of collusion but the levels of the bets and the uncharacteristic behaviour of some of the players. Flash, for example, came in at the beginning, not halfway through as he usually does, and he made an abnormally large bet for him, nine million instead of the usual three or four. Two other conspirators I haven't mentioned were surprises too. S. J. Schubart is a long-established investment house which normally sticks to bonds and currencies and has never been much of a player in equities. But there they were in for eight million bucks in New York and another five over here. And Clive Leonard Partners, who are rudely nicknamed the Hairdressers because that's what their name sounds like, are also cautious and infrequent players. Yet here they were in for nine mil. All this, and there was quite a bit more of it, seemed way beyond a coincidence. They all knew something or had been told something or had some inducement to act as they did. And it was possible too that they shared some motive for destroying George Furcht's business.

'It was quite possible that some or all of the conspirators had tangled with George in business at one time in his career. Furcht and Co. was a ruthless operator before it was renamed the Maloca Group. George did all the things that leave lasting scars: squeezed his suppliers when times were tough, bought companies at knockdown prices from distressed competitors, elbowed his rivals out of markets by predatory pricing. About the only thing you could say in his favour is that unlike Captain Robert Maxwell, say, he has been pretty honest. He pays his bills, in the end anyway, and he pays his taxes, even if he doesn't always pay them in the country he earned the money in. But it's not a crime yet to put up a brass plate in Guernsey or the Caymans.

'The extraordinary thing, though, is that not a single one of our suspected conspirators seems to have had any unfortunate dealings with Furcht, or none that we could trace. None of them appeared to have had the slightest personal motive for destroying George.

'We were baffled. We had expected to find it difficult, if not impossible, to establish the existence of a conspiracy and to identify the individual conspirators. That had turned out to be a laborious but not intellectually demanding task. But why did they do it? The motive for this elaborate and by no means risk-free operation remained as mysterious as the day we started work.

'So what could we do next? The obvious thing would have been for Lethal to keep worming her way into the affections of the hedge funders and their WAGs and then start asking a few provocative questions. What did they feel about George Furcht? When had they first thought he might be on the skids? Did they think he was finished? Had they personally bet against him? And so on. We gamed this one between ourselves, with Lethal asking the questions and me being Pussy, or Flash's latest squeeze, or whoever. We can show you the video we made of our hypothetical conversations. But as soon as we reviewed them, we could see the drawbacks of this route. Yes, we might elicit some useful material: our subject might tell an obvious lie about his or her involvement or unintentionally reveal some fresh detail of the operation. But the value of this info was unlikely to outweigh the downside, which was that we were almost certain to alert them. These are streetwise operators, some of them former barrow boys, and they would catch on in a flash that someone was on to the conspiracy. At the very least the order would go out to clam up. At worst, well, we have seen what happened to Timbo.

'So we decided that we had to rely on our own independent enqui-ries. Here too we soon began to feel we were delicately tiptoeing up a cul-de-sac. We came across no avenues that we had not already explored. We were on the point of going to Furcht and dumping our findings in his lap and telling him that we had achieved as much as we could hope to do and there was no point wasting any more of his money.'

Luke paused, swung his legs off the steel table and rose to his feet and stalked over to the window and stared out at the great grey backside of the Royal Albert Hall. With his back to us, in his orange boots with the cream chinos tucked into the top of them, he had a Napoleonic air. He swung on his heel with a theatrical suddenness which the Emperor might have applauded.

'And then ... You are, I'm sure, familiar with Edgar Allan Poe's story, "The Purloined Letter". It is one of my favourites.'

'Remind me,' I said nodding. I had only the faintest recollection of what it was about.

'The great amateur detective Auguste Dupin is invited by the Prefect of Police to find a missing letter which an unscrupulous Minister has stolen for the purposes of blackmail. The Prefect offers a huge reward, 50,000 francs, if Dupin can find the letter. The police have searched every inch of the Minister's hotel, checked under the carpet and inside the cushions, etc., but can find nothing. Dupin says that if the Prefect writes out the cheque now, he will give him the letter. The Prefect is astonished, but in deference to Dupin's reputation he writes out the cheque. Dupin instantly hands him the missing letter. Where has he found it? In a greasy letter rack dangling from the middle of the Minister's mantelpiece, in plain view, the one place the police had not thought of looking. The letter has been soiled and crumpled and resealed with a different seal to make it unrecognisable. It is a grotesquely implausible story. But I defy anyone to read it and not cherish the hope that one day he or she too might bring off just such a coup by seeing the obvious that everyone else is too blind to see.'

'Yes, I do remember thinking the plot improbable when I read it years ago, in my teens I should think, but I remember loving it too.'

'And yet you yourself, Monsieur le Chauffeur, have just riffled through a stack of cards, one of which does not so much conceal as blazon the answer to our mystery.'

'Blazon? How do you mean?'

'As proudly and conspicuously as a herald blazons a coat of arms to advertise the virtues of its owners.'

I went back over to the mantelpiece and took the sheaf of invites from behind the Rubik's cube. Again I looked through them, dumbly gazing at the engraved and sometimes raised and gilded lettering without any clue as to what I was supposed to be looking for: 'The Countess of Todmorden requests the pleasure of your company ...', 'Come to a Hoedown in aid of Cerebral Palsy ...', 'Get Your Skates On ...'

'There,' Luke said with a melodramatic pointing finger. 'Stop there, that one.' He spoke with the authority of a conjuror who can tell you, even when blindfolded, the card you have just picked out of the pack.

The card had a little green motif at the top, not unlike the new logo for the Conservative Party with the fuzzy green trees, but stretched out into an oblong. 'Green Hedges,' it said in unusually small print, probably no more than thirteen-point, 'invites you to a Celebrity Fashion Show at Mulvaine House, Berkeley Square, W1,' then the time and date, and RSVP details.

'What's Green Hedges?'

'No, we hadn't heard of it either. Lethal has since discovered, with some difficulty I might add, that it is a small and fiercely discreet club formed by a handful of hedge-fund managers who want, as they say, to put something back, in this case literally. Their activities are low profile, deliberately as close to invisible as possible. They don't even have a website. What they do semi-publicly is to support a range of environmental initiatives, like woodland trusts, ecological farming, restoring wetlands, in particular the revival of rare or extinct species. But they also do things on their own, and in total secrecy. They manage to avoid entirely the publicity that accompanied the reintroduction of the beaver in Scotland or the Great Bustard on Salisbury Plain. Nobody knows what they are up to. In places far removed from the official nesting sites, spotters have been startled to hear the boom of the bittern in the reed beds and to hear the call of the corn bunting in the fields, and to see large blue butterflies on the South Downs. The water vole which had declined to five per cent of its strength has been reappearing in abundance, first along the rivers of mid-Wales and now in the West Midlands. Up on the limestone pavements of Yorkshire and the North Pennines, botanists are finding plants that are normally found in the British Isles only on the Burren in County Clare: the spring gentian, the maidenhair fern, the hoary rockrose. Rarities like the bee orchid and the fly orchid are popping up in the most unexpected places.'

'It all sounds harmless enough, quite admirable in fact. But if they like doing good by stealth, why suddenly this fashion show?'

'Well,' Lethal said, 'I gathered from Pussy that there was quite a row about it. The hedgies themselves rather cherished their anonymity, as Luke says. The secrecy made the crusade all the more exciting, especially when they were doing things which wouldn't have been approved by English Nature or the planners, because hedgies love breaking rules. But Pussy and her sister-in-law Loopy, who's also her cousin, said, look, you're becoming just about the most hated people in Britain. Why don't you let the public know you're not all complete monsters and might even be capable of doing a tiny bit of good? In the end the appeal to their vanity wore them down, and they agreed to just one public fund-raising event, on condition that the identity of the members of Green Hedges remained strictly confidential. Pussy, who's a bit of a clothes horse despite being built like a towel rack, jumped at the idea of a fashion show as soon as I suggested one. It was she who told me all the splendid things that Green Hedges has been doing, though I'm sure she wasn't supposed to. Anyway, she was thrilled about me having done some modelling and started calling me the Supermodel and she was even more thrilled when I said I still had a few friends in the rag trade from when I was a fashion buyer for Selfridges – actually it was Primark, but I didn't want to put her off. So we were up and running and she said Beaky Bentliff would absolutely love to lend us Mulvaine House because he's just finished restoring it and the Adams room looked fantastic and he would adore to show it off.'

'Adam, my dear, not Adams.'

'I'm well aware of the difference, smartarse, I'm just talking Pussyspeak.'

Despite her amazing sobriety and her recovered marriage, Lee had not lost all her firepower.

'So we got Mutt to do the show. Mutt, as I had to explain to my dear husband who may know about eighteenth-century ceilings but has not a clue about anything modern, was the edgiest designer in town about five years ago, but he overextended like they all do and everything had to go – the shops in Beauchamp Place and South Molton Street, the prêt-à-porter contract with Burberry – and he was pretty well skint. So he leapt at the offer and he's knocked together a collection in no time. Most of the girls were really hot to do the modelling themselves, but we've mixed in a couple of TV announcers and a few actresses you might just have heard of, and I've been giving them some catwalk lessons which I must admit I rather enjoyed. But the really interesting thing is the comp list.'

'The comp list?'

'The tickets are five hundred quid a throw, a thousand for the premium seats next to the editors of *Vogue* and *Marie-Claire*. That's a stiff price but the hedgies can well afford it and it's all in a fantastic cause, etc., etc. This was the moment, though I say it myself, when I had a flash of inspiration. Pussy, I said, you know the inner circle who put up the initial twenty grand to get us off the ground, isn't it a bit unfair to make them pay twice? Wouldn't they really appreciate having complimentary tickets? You know how the rich like getting something for free and they'll make it up on the auction after the show. And she fell for it. "Gosh," she said, "you're so right"' – Lethal's imitation had an unexpected hooting quality rather than the upper-class bray you might have expected – '"and anyway there aren't that many of them, so it won't cripple us. And we'll do it jolly discreetly, so nobody else knows." And so the comp list was born.'

'And every name on the comp list had been an early and substantial participant in the conspiracy to short Furcht.' Luke took up the narrative with a ring of triumph in his voice. 'The saviours of the water vole are the destroyers of G. Furcht and Co. As soon as you understand that, the missing piece falls into place. You have the motive. At an undisclosed location in the Central Highlands of Scotland, they are replanting ancient forests of Caledonian pine to provide an extended habitat for that giant flying turkey, the capercaillie. Great, fantastic, but look what's happening in the rest of the world. At undisclosed locations all over the Amazon basin, the Maloca Group are cutting down the rainforests to raise cattle and plant soy. If Green Hedges can stop Furcht in the Amazon, that will dwarf anything they can achieve to restore the balance of nature in the Highlands. Furcht is much bigger game, the biggest there is.'

'But would they go as far as murder?'

'You must not think that in the heat of the chase we have forgotten Timbo. What happened to him has, I think, made us work far harder than if we had just been working for George, who we can admit between ourselves is a bit of an old bastard, though he too was deeply affected by Timbo's death, he really was, but he was frightened too. After all, who knows, he might be next.'

'Oh, I do miss Bimbo,' Lethal said. 'I can't think why really. He was such a prat in many ways but sweet somehow.'

'This is not strictly relevant,' Luke said, 'but you remember that the first time we met I explained how I didn't really believe in Narrative, the whole business about one's life being a developing story. And Timbo was rather shocked – you too I think, my dear Chauffeur – and he told me that he thought that everyone's life was indeed a story and that this was what was important and made loyalty the most important thing in life. And I said that this was just what I did not think, because your Self, or my Self at any rate, changed from moment to moment and so could not be expected to inherit the obligations and emotions of earlier Selves.'

'What a silly idea,' Lethal said. 'I remember you telling me all that stuff when we first went out together and I thought what a weirdo.'

'Anyway,' Luke continued, disregarding this intervention, 'I cannot help noticing that my feelings have changed. In strict philosophical theory I hold to my old position, but it seems to me now that each new Self does contain a selection of memories and affections from earlier selves, not so much inherited as chosen from the available store of such things. And so at the emotional level, I do feel a certain obligation to Timbo or his memory. Which is most peculiar, because as you will recall he only came to see me in the first place out of what he said was an obligation to the memory of my grandfather, a person he could never have met and of whom I myself could have no memory of whatsoever, since he was killed before I was born.'

His dry voice cracked and ceased to transmit. Lethal blew her nose. The room was silent and in the silence I found myself overcome too by this sense of, well, obligation was as good a word as any.

'But you are quite right to ask the question, would they go as far as murder?' Luke resumed, in control of himself again. 'It was not so difficult to imagine a group of this sort using legitimate means to halt what they regard as the destructive logging in the Amazon basin. There are, after all, quite a few other campaigning groups engaged on precisely this mission. But what would drive them to go a step further?

'I don't deny that they could be driven by fierce passions. The desire to save the environment is one of the strongest experienced by modern man. It is ironic that we should fall so hopelessly in love with Nature only after we have discovered how cruel she is and how utterly indifferent to our survival or the survival of any other species. The more callous she shows herself to be, the more we love her. We may have given up on God but we would do almost anything to save the vole. *Almost* anything. Can you imagine Flash or the Hairdressers actively conspiring to have a man strangled in that horrible fashion? There has to be a controlling intelligence, someone among them who is prepared to go the extra desperate mile, no doubt without letting his associates know the full reach of his intentions.

'We looked down the comp list. There are twelve individuals who qualified for complimentary tickets: the String Bags, the two Hairdressers, Flash Falk, Joseph Schubart of Schubart's and his cousin Alvin, and over in New York, Freddy and George Lewin, Ben Saturday, Fisher Wallbrook and Desmond Shea Jr. We have less reliable information on the Americans, but as far as we can tell they are fairly ordinary Wall Street players, and anyway we have the strong feeling that the driving force of the operation is over here. Now however hard we tried, we could not see any of the other seven on the list as a ruthless mastermind. Greedy, yes, that goes with the territory. Obsessed with the environment, certainly. But obsessed enough to start a punt of such big money in order to destroy Furcht? Fanatical enough to order a hit? I doubt it. There has to be a Prime Mover to set the wheels in motion.'

'But who? If you've ruled out all the names on your list …'

'I refer you back to the affair of the Purloined Letter.'

I was still holding the sheaf of invites and I looked again at the Green Hedges card, feeling the raised and gilded lettering with my thumb as I did so. The only unraised, ungilded line was right at the bottom in tiny type: 'by kind permission of the Bentliff Group'.

'Beaky Bentliff?'

'Sir Wilfrid Bentliff, KBE, KCVO, if you please. He's not on the comp list of course because he owns the place and doesn't need an invitation.'

'But from what you've told me, he isn't even part of the conspiracy.'

'Isn't he? You see, we've both been puzzled that the dirty dozen should be so ready to risk their fortunes for the sake of their ideals. These were not charitable donations. For several of the smaller players the bets were enormous. If the bet went wrong and Furcht shares recovered, they could lose all they had staked and more. It seemed plausible therefore that they had been comforted with some sort of inducement or reassurance. We wondered if there was any pattern of investment which could give us a clue. And this made us think of Beaky.

'He is, after all, just as famous for his environmental enthusiasms as for his total ruthlessness in business. All the time he was taking over those supermarkets and those steel mills and getting rid of half the staff and shipping the machinery out to China, he was replanting several of the Royal Forests at his own expense. He's inordinately proud of the KCVO he got to add to his bog-standard knighthood for contributions to party funds. Yet here is the greatest anti-logging coup you ever saw, and he doesn't appear to be playing any part in it.

'Then we started to look at the four investment funds which he uses to stash his loot and move it around the globe. Each fund is called after one of T. S. Eliot's *Four Quartets*. Beaky was doing a PhD on Eliot which he had to abandon when his father died and Beaky had to take over the mills, which he promptly sold just before the British textile industry went belly-up. Well, if you look at East Coker and Little Gidding over the past six months, you will detect a remarkably large movement out of equities and into hedge funds, somewhere between one and two billion pounds. And the funds which can boast of an impressive inflow all happen to be on the comp list. In other words, Beaky is staking them. He has poured zillions into their funds and assured them that they can't lose if they follow his lead. Everything points to him being our man.'

Of all the City names that Luke had been parading in front of my dazed eyes, the only one I had heard of was Beaky Bentliff. It was impossible not to have heard of him. Everyone knew the stories: how he had run away from school at the age of seventeen and won £100,000 playing chemmy at the Clermont Club and then lost it all again the next night; how he had been sent down from Oxford for screwing a debutante on the Fellows' Lawn, then hired an ace QC who proved that it never happened, although half the college had been hanging out of their windows with their eyes on stalks; how he had moved to France and shared a mistress with the Finance Minister and married her when the Minister was sent to jail for a fraud in which Beaky was thought to have had quite a hand. With Monique he had restored a chateau in the Auvergne which had belonged to Madame de Maintenon and transformed the old park into a wildlife domain so exquisite and so perilous that John Aspinall once was heard to murmur that 'it makes my own zoo look positively suburban'. It was when riding through this romantic *parc aux cerfs* that Monique was dragged from her white Mongolian pony by a pack of Beaky's wolves and so severely mauled that she never appeared in public again. Beaky was devastated, distraught, heartbroken, but he never thought of destroying the wolves (the pony was already dead) and his friends respected him for it. He still spent a month at the chateau every summer and they would sit together in her little turret boudoir and read Vigny and Verlaine together. His loyalty and patience were touching in a man who was so restless and itching to move on. Naturally a man of his dynamic appetites needed a fresh outlet, so he and Monique were amicably divorced and he married a White Russian princess known as Bric, whose father had done well in advertising but who never ceased dreaming of their long-lost summer palace in the Crimea. So of course Beaky bought it back in the Yeltsin fire sale and was also restoring it to its former sleepy splendour with its famous cypress avenue leading down to the Black Sea. This was not to mention his shooting lodge on the North Yorkshire moors, a daunting Gothic grange at the head of the valley which he had inherited from his father (both the grange and the valley), where the workers at his father's mill had picked daffodils on the first Sunday in April when he was a boy. In London there was Mulvaine House, which had cost more to restore than his other houses put together. The gold leaf and the Farrow & Ball paints had been slapped on without thought of expense. The pilasters in the music room, the coved ceiling in the Grand Saloon, the amazing flying staircase – all vandalised to the verge of destruction when the place had been a car showroom and then the headquarters of a giant insurance company – now shone as pristine as when the first Earl Mulvaine, the original Lord Scattercash, had been committed to the debtor's prison for failing to pay Robert Adam's bill. Doing up Mulvaine House was generally regarded as Beaky's finest achievement after the Royal Forests, and when he welcomed his guests there to some conference or charity do in his rich chuckly voice which still retained the gravel of the West Riding, he seemed utterly at home in his kingdom. Beetling over any party at six foot six with his enormous trademark broken nose, he looked like the Iron Duke on stilts. And like the Iron Duke, he was famous for never having lost a battle. He had skinned *Private Eye*, he had humiliated the Governor of the Bank of England and he had toyed with governments of both parties.

I stared at the two of them.

'Christ,' I said, 'you could hardly have chosen a tougher nut.'

'Oh, we don't intend to do the cracking ourselves. We are simply the humble burrowers and gatherers. And remember, though of course we don't have a hundredth of Beaky's firepower, we do have a couple of advantages. We have a pretty clear picture of the conspiracy now and who's in it and who's running it and Beaky doesn't know that we know. It's true that we have very little info so far about the South American end of the conspiracy, but if we are patient the threads of that too may begin to unravel. All we really have from Brazil is the one text that Timbo sent us. He probably sent it only a day or two before they got him, although the time lag between the message and the discovery of his supposed body was just over three days. We haven't told anyone else yet about the text because we didn't know what it meant and if we started off looking in the wrong place we might be alerting the wrong people. I certainly was not going to put it up on my computer after I'd decoded it. Here's what he sent. It's very short.'

Luke took out of his pocket a small folded sheet of paper on which he had written in his tiny donnish hand, so tiny that I had to hold the paper up to my eyes to read it:

am gd. cd u chek enida. x t

'It is clear, I think, that Timbo himself has very little idea what or who Enida is, whether it's a person or an acronym for some organisation or some slang word used by a gang or undercover fraternity of some sort, like Camorra or Cosa Nostra. It is also fair to deduce that its meaning cannot be that easy to discover because Timbo had been in Brazil for several weeks and didn't have a clue.'

'He could have only just heard the word, earlier that same day even, and it's because he now knows it that he has to be silenced,' I said.

'That is possible,' Luke conceded. 'But I would tend to deduce from the admittedly sparse evidence that it wasn't quite like that. The "am gd" suggests a less pressured mood. It's more as if "enida" has cropped up several times already in the course of his journey and the fact that he doesn't know what it means is needling him. He's not necessarily telling us that "enida" is the key to the whole mystery.'

'I don't think you can deduce anything at all from the "am gd". It's just the sort of idiotic thing Timbo would text while he was being murdered, if he was.'

'Yes,' I said, 'Lethal's right. It's so like Timbo.'

'And besides,' she persisted, 'it's the only text he sends us, which as he's such a chatterbox suggests that he's very nervous about breaking whatever you call radio silence these days. He doesn't want to give himself away, but at the very last moment he has to send this text because it's his only chance. Which suggests that Timbo at least thinks that Enida matters a lot.'

'This is certainly a plausible hypothesis,' Luke said.

'Which is as close as a philosopher ever comes to saying "you could be right and I could be wrong",' Lethal remarked gleefully.

'But it does not really advance our cause much. Either way, Enida is the only clue we have. And my instinct is that the only place we have much chance of picking up another one is in a month's time in Mutt's fashion show at Mulvaine House. Till then, I suggest we keep

Enida to ourselves and think rather than act, which as Nietzsche told us is the higher calling.'

'You told me that Nietzsche died barking mad of tertiary syphilis.'

'He didn't get everything right.'

They were still on a weird high, the two of them. Their mission had not only buoyed them up and brought them together, it seemed to have given them a sense of invulnerability, as though no one could touch them and they were bound to triumph in the end. I too was now gripped by the story, and wanted desperately to see how it all came out. But unlike the other two, I was loaded down with dark apprehensions and a sharp intimation that the odds were against us. I suppose that was the moment, though, that I realised, with a mixture of horror and excitement, that I was now part of the Us. By some invisible osmosis, I had crossed over from being merely a sympathetic listener to some sort of co-conspirator. Even after I thought it over later, I wasn't quite sure why. It wasn't just wanting to do something to help Timbo, if that was still remotely possible. And it certainly wasn't for love of George Furcht. Whatever side he was on, it could scarcely be described as the right side. No, there was in my mood switch another racier, by no means respectable motive, one that didn't come naturally to me. The thrill of the chase makes it sound attractive, but there was a sort of schoolboy prurience in there somewhere too.

Even so, the apprehension was real. I was well aware that Beaky Bentliff had avoided jail half a dozen times, he had sacked several hundred thousand men and women in three continents, his first company secretary had shot himself, he had harassed his troubled younger brother to an early grave. If Beaky had not personally had anyone killed before, it might be only because he had not needed to.

'Well, at least now you know who the enemy is, though I'm not sure that's much of a comfort in this case,' I said as I got ready to leave.

'Ye-es.'

'What do you mean, ye-es?'

'Shall we tell him?' Lethal looked at Luke.

'It will only confuse him.'

'Then let's tell him. I like when Chauffeur does his confused look.'

'At this preliminary stage in that particular enquiry ...'

'Oh, don't be so fucking pompous, Lukey. It's a mystery, and Chauffeur loves mysteries, don't you, Chauff?'

In fact, I prefer things out in the open, I feel much more at ease, but of course I said, yes, I loved mysteries.

'That map you saw in George's office when you came in with that obscene wreath, the map he gave us all that boyhood-rambles stuff about?'

'Yes.'

'Well, it hadn't been there the last time I was in the office the day before. I only saw it when he called me up to deal with you and the wreath. Then he was in meetings all day with I don't know who – his PA wouldn't say – and when I went in the next day to talk about the Newmarket sales, it wasn't there again.'

'So what? Probably someone sent it to him as a sort of souvenir and he had it hung up on the wall to see if he liked the look of it there and he decided he didn't, so he had it taken down again.'

'No, it's not like that at all, because if it had been, the PA and Sebby Lindt, he's the in-house Mr Fixit, would have known about it, and they'd have told me because we're all palsy, but they put on blank expressions when I asked, the sort you put on when you've been told to say nothing and it comes quite easily because actually you don't know anything.'

'But what makes you think it has anything to do with Beaky and the shorting?'

'Didn't say it had,' Lethal said tartly. 'It's just that George is up to something on his own account and he's not telling us, and we want to know what it is and why he's not telling us.'

'Well, for a start,' I said, 'the map was of the Eastern Seaboard of the States, wasn't it? And there was a piece of tape stuck across the mountains on the left, are they the Alleghenies?'

'They are indeed,' Luke said. 'And what do you think of when you think of the Alleghenies?'

'Hillbillies I suppose, if only because Furcht mentioned them, and isn't that where the coal mines are, or used to be? Couldn't he have discovered a new coal seam and not want to let anyone else in on it; that would be quite natural, wouldn't it?'

'It would.'

'Or,' I said, warming to the subject, 'his people could have found a lot of coal in a pit that was closed and he wants to open it up without letting the old owners in on the secret?'

'Ingenious,' said Luke, not meaning it. 'And what would the strip of tape be for?'

'I don't know,' I said. 'Perhaps it's to mark the line of a railway to take the coal out.'

'From what Lethal can remember, the tape covered a stretch of about 350 miles, from somewhere in northern New Jersey to somewhere above Pittsburgh. Rather long for a single seam, even a profitable one, don't you think?'

'Perhaps there are a lot of different seams,' I said weakly.

'The truth is that you don't know, and we don't know,' Luke said. 'But I strongly suspect that it has some connection to George's present predicament. And whatever it is, what we also don't know is whether Beaky knows. There is a dangerous amount of ignorance about, and bystanders could get hurt. Anyway, I'm sure you'll find out the answer.'

'Me?' I said, startled by this abrupt turn in the conversation.

'We told you, George is desperate to see you,' Lethal said.

'What for? I don't know anything except what the Consul told me.'

'No, but you're going to find out. George wants you to be his point man.'

'You mean, in Brazil?'

'All expenses paid, of course, plus a fair whack on top.'

'But I've never been there in my life, I don't speak—'

'You tell him. If you go across the Park to the Rose Garden, you'll see a familiar face who'll take you to Himself.'

'In the Park?'

'He thinks it's safer. He's obsessed about his office being bugged.'

'He seems to think I'm at his beck and call,' I said. 'Well, I'm fucking not.'

'Not even if it helps to get Timbo back? Anyway, you could at least go and see him, even if just to tell him you're not the right person for the job.'

'Go on, Chauffeur. For Timbo. It can't do any harm.'

'Yes, it can,' I said sourly, but ... 'the Rose Garden, you say.'

'You're a saint, Chauffeur.'

VIII

Hyde Park

It was a chill, blowy day and I felt the wind at my calves as I battled along Rotten Row trying to remember where the Rose Garden was exactly. I had only seen it once, from inside a taxi, and it turned out to be rather closer to Hyde Park Corner than I remembered, and it must have been half an hour before I finally found the place.

The last remaining roses were dangling from the bare thorny stems and rattling against the iron hoops of the arbours. As I hunted along the damp paths, one or two of the trailing stems lashed into my face, leaving the faintest dewy fragrance behind. There was nobody else about except an elderly couple in tracksuits who had taken the first available bench to recover from their morning run. The man was unpacking a thermos from his rucksack while the woman was fiddling with her camera.

I went on to the end of the curving alley. And to my astonishment round the corner, there was Rowley Beavan sitting on a bench with a fag in his mouth, reading the pink paper and looking, to me anyway, much as he must have done doing the same thing on the messenger boys' bench when he was fifteen.

'What the hell are you doing here?'

'You may remember George Furcht, I introduced you at the Arc.'

I did remember.

'And you may remember that I told you he was not a very nice person.'

I remembered that too.

'You may erase that latter thought from your database. George is an extremely nice person, one of the best. This I can officially confirm in my new capacity as his Head of Corporate Affairs.'

'You're working for Furcht?'

'I am indeed.'

'Why on earth ...'

'It's not a long story. We've got a few minutes yet before we're due to see George.'

The last thing Rowley Beavan wanted was a life-changing experience, he told me. He liked his life pretty much the way it was. What he liked especially were the limits of it. Within those limits he bounced around like the bubble in a spirit level. You might not be always able to locate him at a moment's notice – Ines, his bad-tempered half-Spanish secretary for years, often had the hell of a time tracking him down; it was one of her main reasons for being bad-tempered – but in truth there was only a limited number of places you were likely to find him: sharing two dozen oysters at Sweetings with a City friend, for example, or eating sausages and mash at the Savoy Grill with a rather grander City friend, until the Grill closed for refurb and he switched to Wiltons; in the summer he could be seen at Newmarket or Longchamp.

But his centre of operations was always No. 3 Bread Court, which had been the paper's City Office as far back as the sixties when he had joined the staff of the main paper as a messenger boy. He had been transferred to the financial pages after being spotted reading the *Financial Times* on the bench where the boys waited to be sent on errands. 'Well, old Dud thought it was the *FT*,' Rowley would explain when telling the story, 'but in fact it was the Pink 'Un, the special weekend football edition of the evening paper which they printed on pink paper too then, but poor Dud was too blind to tell the difference.'

Ever since, Number 3 had been Rowley's second home, sometimes his only home after one or other of his wives had chucked him out and he had to doss down on the little sofa in his office. 'No hardship for an old soldier,' he would say stoically, although his only experience of soldiering had been National Service in the Pay Corps. In fact I don't think any of us had ever been invited to any of his marital homes. Number 3, or the Bread Bin as he called it, was his real place.

So it was not surprising that he should have been distraught when dropping circulation and a rising new CEO between them decreed that the paper could no longer afford a separate and criminally expensive City Office. The lease on the Bread Bin was to be sold and the financial wizards would have to muck in with the common herd. Perhaps the horror that loomed largest in Rowley's anguished mind was the thought of being compelled to attend the morning editorial conference and having to laugh at the witless jests of whichever ignorant toady had been tipped into the Editor's chair for the time being. That really would be the end.

Rowley let it be known that he was open to offers. For the first few weeks nothing much came up. Rowley was a lovely man to lunch with, but the very loveliness of the lunches suggested that he might be an expensive pet to have around the house. Besides, he was getting on a bit. But then he got a call from George. And, well, any port in a storm.

'Congratulations.'

'I accept your congratulations gracefully. But as I can read your mind backwards, knowing that backwards is how it works, I can see that behind the tears of pleasure you are shedding at my advancement, a darker thought is forming. Why him? you are beginning to wonder. What would a great man like George dos Santos Furcht be doing hiring a broken-down City hack?'

I protested that no such thought had come to me. He swept this demurral aside.

'The answer, my friend, is that George is desperate and everyone knows he is desperate and he knows that everyone knows. These are not the best conditions in which to be raising fresh loans to pay off the borrowings which are falling due or being pulled by nervous bankers. And I can understand their being nervous. The net borrowings of Furcht and Co. are now approaching the two billion mark and rising. And now that the hedgies have shredded his shares, he has virtually no security to offer unless he starts pledging his private fortune which is usually the beginning of the end.'

'Should you be telling me all this?'

'Absolutely. When you're up shit creek there's no point pretending you're cruising in the Caribbean. You have to face the music and dance. You need to keep a spring in your step and wear a rose in your buttonhole. I'm the rose in George's buttonhole. Speaking of which, he's desperate to see you.'

'So everyone keeps on telling me, but ...'

'They are still having trouble with the post-mortem on your friend. And you're the only chap George thinks might be able to help him find him, dead or alive. The British Consul apparently told George's people that she needs to talk to you first, because you're the executor.'

'To be honest, I'm not really his executor. I just said—'

'Don't worry, George only wants to do the right thing. He's very angry but naturally he also feels guilty because if he hadn't sent your friend up the Amazon, he wouldn't be where he is now, which is God knows where. But it won't hurt him to wait a minute. Sit here a minute and get your breath back, old boy.'

'I see Furcht shares are up a couple of points this morning.'

'Only a dead-cat bounce, I'm afraid. By now most of the hedge funds will have covered their positions and taken their loot. Whatever conspiracy there was must be pretty much wound up, and very nicely it has worked out for them all too.'

'So we can't prove anything against them, even if we do find out who they are?'

'Trying to make a few quid by shorting a stock, well, that's part of the game and always has been. They were shorting tulips in Amsterdam in sixteen-whatever. It's a rough old world, my son.'

Rowley finished his cigarette and stamped it out on the crumbled bark of the all-weather path.

'This is probably a no-smoking rose garden,' he said. 'Let's go find George.'

We walked briskly under the dripping trees towards the Serpentine. Beyond the pavilion I could hear the shouts and splashes of the all-weather swimmers. Rowley led me off the path to a corner of the gardens that was unfamiliar to me. The area was strangely crowded, as though some accident had happened in this out-of-the-way place and people were scrambling to get a better view. The tourists were mostly Japanese, so it was not too hard to see over their heads, and what they were flocking towards was a curious-shaped pond with an undulating ribbon of flagstones bordering it and more tourists plodding gingerly in single file along the flagstones. Perhaps because of them being mostly Japanese and snapping each other,

I wondered whether this was the shrine of some ancient Eastern cult transplanted to Kensington Gardens to promote international peace and harmony. It was only when we came up close to the flagstones that I recognised the shape and realised that it was a shrine, but one dedicated to a new Western death cult. Rowley beckoned me to join the procession, which fittingly moved at the pace of a funeral cortège.

Almost immediately I saw George Furcht coming up on the gentle slope the far side of the water, carrying a large black umbrella. His head was bowed and his strange stretched gait seemed especially effortful as he negotiated the circuit. There was an air of penance about him as though he had been doomed to tread these slabs for some enormous length of time, possibly eternity.

He caught sight of us and acknowledged our arrival by giving that same gesture of a policeman holding up the traffic with which he had dismissed us at Longchamp. We came up alongside him, our town shoes sinking into the soft ground where the water had splashed over the rim stones.

'I thought this would be a good place to talk,' he said. 'The water will drown our voices. You remember how Western diplomats in Moscow used to talk in the bathroom with the shower taps on.'

Unfortunately we could only just hear what he was saying. Then we could not even hear the water any more, let alone Furcht, because two noisy parties of tourists were crowding around to get past us and onto the rim stones. The elderly couple I had seen in the Rose Garden were in the throng, jostling for position with the Japanese and their pretty coloured umbrellas. Furcht persisted for another half-circuit, then realised that none of us could hear each other. He stepped off the rim and with another policeman gesture led us away from the crowd back towards the dripping trees.

'That was not such a good idea,' he said grimly. 'We shall be able to talk better over here.'

We came to a halt under a large chestnut tree where the ground felt dry and our shoes crunched on the shards of old conkers. Furcht stood in silence under his large black umbrella, square and massive in his navy-blue raincoat, looking not unlike one of the substantial monuments that dotted the park.

'It is good,' he said at last, 'that the three of us are gathered here. We should begin, I think, by standing in silence for a moment in memory of our friend, whether he be dead or alive.'

I had no idea whether Rowley had actually met Timbo, but he was good at this kind of thing. I had seen him across the aisle at many a memorial service for some old Fleet Street rogue, his rosy features composed in a mask of grief, looking as sombre as an undertaker's assistant.

'Timothy committed himself wholeheartedly to our cause at a time when that cause was in great peril. I give you two promises here in this park this morning. We shall be victorious and our dear friend Timothy will be rescued or least avenged.'

'Amen,' Rowley said.

'Thank you, Rowland. It is very good to have you with us. And you too, sir, you are most welcome. Our plan of action is quite simple. We are Going West.'

He paused, allowing the phrase to resonate in the damp air, which also allowed me and, I think, Rowley time to compose ourselves. This was not the moment to point out that Going West had two meanings. When they were alone together, Rowley would no doubt advise him that it was not the happiest campaign mantra for someone in his position. That was the sort of thing you paid a Head of Corporate Affairs to tell you.

'We shall be following the example of my godfather and patron President Getúlio Vargas. He perceived that the solution to Brazil's problems lay to the West, in the vast Interior of the country. For my company too the answer lies in the Interior, but not the Interior of Brazil. My salvation lies in the place where I was raised and schooled, the Midwest of the United States of America. There I intend to rebuild my fortunes. I have given up on the bankers of the East Coast. They are effete blowhards who run away at the first whiff of grapeshot. Out West the bankers are made of sterner stuff. They will see a man through. I am not the first to take this road. A few years back when my friend Rupert Murdoch was running into difficulties, he found small succour from Wall Street. He flew a million miles to and fro across the States and patched his company together again with the help of banks you have never heard of in states you have only flown over. What Rupert did, we can do too.

'We shall be a small team, myself and Rowland here on the road and my brilliant friend Anthony from Javits Thornton and Mr Ekserdjian from our legal department who will pull the threads together in New York. We shall be taking the afternoon flight for Chicago. You will see us again in a month's time.

'Meanwhile it is my earnest hope that together we will be able to dispatch this wretched business of our friend Timothy. My CEO in Brazil, Arturo Nicols, is already on the case. He is a most brilliant man with impeccable contacts.'

He took a pace towards me, as though to talk to me more confidentially. 'You will find the people of the middle and upper Amazon are wonderful people, simple as you would expect, in many ways childlike, my dear Dickie, but good-humoured, charming, and given the right circumstances much harder workers than they are reputed. The right opportunities in this part of the world are tremendous. So far we are barely nibbling at the edges. Rubber of course is a thing of the past. Brazil today relies on imports for most of its latex needs. But the entire area is ideal for the cultivation of the new cross-bred soybean, the so-called tropical soy. You have only to consider the role that soy already plays in our daily diet, acting as oil or bulking material in something approaching 60 per cent of all processed foods. Sixty per cent, Dickie, think of that.'

Furcht paused and straightened his back, as though paying homage to this impressive statistic. He began to pace up and down the grass with his curious stretched gait, which made his presence even more oppressive.

'Not since man learnt how to bake bread at the dawn of the New Stone Age has nature granted such a boon. In my opinion, we are approaching the historical moment at which, if I may misquote the Good Book, Man Can Live By Soy Alone. But this is not the end of the possibilities. Far from it. By a happy synergy, two other great industries go hand in hand with the cultivation of the soybean. I speak of cattle and timber. When we clear-fell the land that is to be ranched or planted up, we provide ourselves with some very fine timber. We are blessed, as you know, with great rivers to float our product down to the Atlantic seaports. The Maloca Group has first-class manufacturing facilities in other quarters of the globe. But Brazil is where our heart is. Which is why I took the liberty of christening the new group after the traditional Brazilian longhouse that has provided shelter for my fellow Brazilians from time immemorial: Maloca. The word has a fine ring to it, do you not think?

'You know, I have always thought of the destiny of Brazil and my own personal destiny as interlinked. The Republic of Brazil was born under the same star sign as I was myself. And besides, I am a child of the President, in a manner of speaking. Did you know that? It is a strange story. If you have a moment, I would like to tell it to you. After the war, my father joined the Brazilian Navy. His experience of combat was invaluable in a service which, shall we say, had not had the opportunity to see much action. He soon found himself appointed assistant naval attaché to President Vargas. He even had quarters in the Presidential Palace which was in Rio then of course, the Palácio do Catete, and he saw the President almost every day. He was a great man, Vargas. Like all great men, he had his failings. He had girlfriends. And his favourite girlfriend was my mother, Sandra dos Santos. She was very beautiful. She lived at the end of the corridor. What could be more natural? I tell you, Dickie, you may not believe this, but I am proud of the connection. In a curious way, I think my father was proud too. And soon he had reason to be grateful also. Sandra did not want to be married to a naval attaché all her life. She persuaded my father to leave the navy and she persuaded Vargas to set him up with a bank loan and several thousand acres of scrub in the northern Mato Grosso. Dieter Furcht was to become one of the pioneers of the Estado Novo, the new Brazil. Alas, it turned out that Sandra did not want to be a rancher's wife either. She ran away to Palm Beach and never stopped running. I am not sure which of the Kennedys it was she first caught the eye of. Some say it was Jack, some say it was old Joe – they shared their women in that family. I could not blame them. She had such flashing eyes and such a figure.'

Furcht normally kept his hands still. But at the thought of his mother's curves, he sketched a clumsy outline in the air. It might just as well have been the outline of a car or a tall building.

'She dressed so beautifully. That was what she was most famous for in the United States, the way she dressed. Until she was well into her sixties she was regularly voted among the Top Ten Best Dressed Women in America by *Women's Wear Daily*. When she came to stay with us in the Mato Grosso, it took two station wagons to bring her luggage from the airport. They were such beautiful suitcases, matching soft dove-grey leather with green handles.'

'She did come to visit you then?'

'Once a year at first, later on less often. She never stayed long. In my innocence I thought she would stay longer because she had so much luggage. My father made a success of his ranching, enough to buy a couple of adjoining farms on the Iowa state line. I think he hoped that if we moved to the States, she might come back to us. But of course Sandra would no more want to live in the Midwest than in the Mato Grosso. Less so, if anything. The Mato Grosso was at least exotic. But Tyler, Iowa, was *tiefste Provinz*.

'Perhaps my father might have moved to the States anyway as a precaution. The generals were about to take over again, everyone could see it coming. Vargas was well aware that he was about to fall. He shot himself in the chest in the Catete Palace, whose corridors I had traversed as a child on my new roller skates. It was a great pity that he never came to see our farm. He had promised to come so often. I imagined myself saluting his car as it drove up the dusty track to our house. I was much moved by the news of his death – I was twelve years old at the time – and I would recite to myself the words of his famous farewell message to the Brazilian people, his *carta testamento*.'

George Furcht turned back towards the dripping fountain and intoned in his strong clanging voice, as though addressing the crowd gathered round it: "'Serenely I take my first step on the road to eternity and I leave life to enter history." Fine words, do you not think so, Mr Pentecost?'

'Very fine indeed,' I said, wondering why I had gone back to being Mr Pentecost. Perhaps the memory of the great President demanded a modicum of formality. But I wasn't really listening properly any more. Somewhere in the middle of his life story or the history of Brazil, which seemed to come to much the same thing, I had realised two things. First, that deep down Furcht didn't give a toss about what happened to Timbo – in fact it might suit him better if Timbo did turn out to have been martyred in the cause of saving Maloca. Well, that might seem obvious enough to anyone who had seen

George at work. But the second thing was more surprising, in fact stole upon me quite unexpectedly and against all my inclinations, viz. if Timbo was to come out alive from this ghastly struggle, someone was going to have to help get him out, and the only candidate on the horizon was me. I was startled to find myself even beginning to think anything so melodramatic, but somehow there it was.

Meanwhile, on he went: 'I went to high school in Tyler and then on to a small university in the state, a typical cow college, you would not have heard of it. But my father paid for me to go to business school in the East. It was almost the last thing he did for me; he was in failing health, though he was barely fifty. He never complained, my father. He had a philosophical turn of mind. Whenever anything bad happened, he would simply raise his eyebrows and murmur, "*So geht es, immer weiter*" – that's how it goes, on and on. When he died, I was still at Yale and the one thing I resolved was that I would never go back to Tyler. All through my teens I had dreamed of the Amazon. When I looked out over the dreary fields of Iowa, the jungle was calling me. And so I went back. My beginning again in Brazil was like a dream. Because of Vargas, because of my father, every door was open to me. In Manaus, in Santarém, the Governor and the Land Commissioner welcomed me with open arms. Land concessions and wayleaves were as easy to obtain as pizzas. Within five years Furcht and Co. had 24,000 hectares under cultivation or in cattle, mostly in the southern scrublands, but increasingly we looked north, to the valley of the Tapajós and to the Amazon itself.

'Soon we owned nearly half a million acres, but less than half of it was cleared land and we were still waiting for the necessary permits for most of the rest. Our credit lines were extended to their limit. I am sorry to say that bankers today lack the patience of the older generation. But we were still looking forward to the future with some confidence. We still believed that the destiny that Vargas had shown to us was ours to achieve. And then – smack!'

His great muscular hands met in a stately thunderclap.

'Suddenly everything changed. Just like that, overnight. The most reasonable requests for clearance permits or for wayleave to drive access roads through the bush were abruptly refused, even in cases where we had been assured in advance that there would be no problem. We offered generous commissions to the relevant officials, officially and not so officially. It made no difference. Overnight our diggers and cutters, our transportation fleets, our storage sheds and silos – all were brought to a standstill. We began haemorrhaging cash. Leave a Komatsu D275 idle for so much as a week and you are tearing up thousands of dollar bills. This is a business which has to go forward or it will go under. The worst of it was that we could not understand what had happened.

'Then the shorting started. We had done our best to keep the news of our difficulties as confidential as possible, but inevitably people began to see what was happening or rather not happening. We assured our bankers and investors that our difficulties were purely temporary. Our people did the rounds of the brokers explaining that we expected to find a way through very soon. We did expect the price of our publicly quoted companies to take a knock. We did not expect Furcht's share price to collapse as it did. Our brokers soon detected the unusual patterns of dealing which indicate a concerted shorting operation. The moderate fall we had braced ourselves for turned into a helter-skelter thing.

'Within two months, the price of the company's A shares had plummeted from 97 to 15. In no time the banks started bleating. They called in as many loans as they had the legal right to and refused to roll over the rest. We were heading for the precipice.

'Our people in Brazil are as bewildered as our financial team over here. The normal avenues of enquiry seem totally blocked. It is my belief, my very strong belief, that the campaign against my businesses and the ghastly fate of Mr Smith are intimately linked. If you manage to find out the answer to the second, you will have the answer to the first.'

'Well,' I said, 'I'm not at all sure that I am suited to this kind of thing ...'

'You're the only man, Mr Pentecost, our last and best hope.'

'But if I do go, I must make it absolutely clear that I am going entirely to find out what has happened to my friend. The fate of your businesses, even if I could have the slightest influence over it, is no concern of mine.'

'Understood, my dear sir, understood. The purity of your mission will be your best protection. I had almost forgotten this,' Furcht said, reaching into the leather bag slung over his shoulder and pulling out a fat envelope.

'Half in sterling, half in Brazilian reals. Miss Eaves will send you the tickets. She'll also organise a credit card for you at the office if you wouldn't mind filling in the details. We'll let you know if you're going over the limit, but don't stint yourself on hotels and so on.'

'You don't know what you're letting yourself in for.'

Furcht gave a wintry smile. I could see that he did not care for jokes about money. 'Our car is waiting. I have one last thing to tell you before we go.'

He came right up to me and seized the lapel of my coat with a fierce and sudden clutch. Now that his face was only inches from mine, the drizzly air no longer blurred his expression. It was one of terrifying anger and resentment.

'Do not believe for one second that our enemies will get away with this. Nobody murders or attempts to murder one of my men with impunity. They will wish that they had never heard of the Maloca Group or of George dos Santos Furcht. They will wish that with all their heart.'

He let my lapel go and took two steps back examining me as though to ascertain whether I had suffered any structural damage. Then he raised his hand in the policeman gesture and offered me what could only be described in his terms as a smile. And he was gone, springing over the soggy turf with that peculiar stretched gait and Rowley trotting after him like a spaniel being taken for a walk by an impatient master.

I stood there in the damp, dripping silence, looking after them as they disappeared back towards the bridge over the Serpentine. It was a relief to see them go. Even in the huge expanse of the Park the intensity of George Furcht's rage was hard to cope with. He left no breathing room for anyone else. I had no hope of explaining properly what I wanted to say, which was that his vendetta against the people who were three-quarters of the way to destroying his company was no business of mine. If I had a vote in the matter, I would be on their side rather than his, because whatever sort of people they were, his side was the wrong side.

Even so, I had to sit down on a nearby bench, still aghast that somewhere in the middle of George Furcht's rant, I had committed myself to something really crazy, reckless and almost certainly hopeless.

I needed a cover story, of course, in fact several cover stories, the first and most important one being for home consumption.

'They're really keen at the office for me to go out there.'

'Really?' Jane said with – well, it was hard to say whether scorn or disbelief was uppermost in her mind, both at maximum voltage.

'Gil thinks it would make a fantastic story.' Which was true enough, but only after I had primed him. 'So does the Editor. He says it would make a great series, like the Quest for Colonel Fawcett, looking for that chap who got lost in the jungle looking for the Lost City of Z.'

'And did he ever find it, this Lost City?'

'Well, no, not that we know of.'

'And this Colonel, did they ever find him either?'

'No, they didn't, in fact. But the explorer Peter Fleming wrote a wonderful book about it called *Brazilian Adventure*.'

'And what exactly makes you think you're qualified to be the next Peter Fleming?'

'Well, it won't be that sort of adventure. I expect it will be mostly assisting the police with their inquiries.'

'Isn't that what they say about prime suspects in murder cases? And how exactly would you be assisting them?'

To which there was no good answer, except that I was now committed. Miss Eaves was sending me the tickets, and I had had my jabs, none of them so painful as the jab in the ribs Jane gave me halfway through our worst row on the subject. Her anger at what she called my self-indulgent midlife crisis became so fierce that I was beginning to weaken, when Flo and Lucy came in from school, and she told them. To her unconcealed annoyance, they were hugely enthusiastic: 'Oh, Dad, that's so brilliant, you can write a book about it, or make a film.' 'Don't you see, Mum, it's like a Quest, or a Crusade.' Jane said, no, it wasn't, it was a wild goose chase, and totally irresponsible, but for once she was on the losing side. It wasn't any sort of crusade, but it was at least, what did the French call it, an *acte gratuit*, something I'd chosen to do of my own free will and not been nagged into by what people expected of me, certainly not the need to earn a crust. I hadn't really even been bullied into it by George Furcht. On the contrary, my hope, an earnest though only half-formed hope, was to rescue Timbo if he was still alive from Furcht and all Furcht's works no less than from his other enemies, and I found myself strangely looking forward to whatever it all turned out to be, even to the possibility, perhaps the odds–on chance of abject failure.

IX

Upriver

Timbo, we knew, had taken the steamer upriver from Belém. That much was clear. They had told him there was a direct flight to Manaus and the company had offered to book it for him – well, it was Lethal who had offered, for security reasons. But he had said no, apparently because he wanted to ease himself into the country and have a look around as an independent traveller, unattached, as inconspicuous as dust.

Nobody was to get in touch with him, not by email or text and certainly not by phone. He had to assume that the entire Furcht organisation had already been penetrated. He certainly had no intention of going anywhere near George's point man, Arturo Nicols. If Luke and Lethal had some material he needed to see, they were to go to an anonymous computer terminal – an internet café was good – and transfer the stuff to his purpose-built website Mothproof Associates. The security code on the site was a combination of a key which translated 1 to 9 into letters and a code bed on which the letters were then translated back into numbers. The key changed every month. The keys for the first three months were GRAPESHOT, UNSIGHTLY and MARKETING – GUM for those suffering from short-term memory loss. The code bed was IT IS A FAR FAR BETTER THING THAT I DO NOW THAN I HAVE EVER DONE (*A Tale of Two Cities* was Timbo's favourite book, not a title for which there was a lot of competition). You ignored the letters which weren't in the key, which made the resulting string of numbers vary in length. None of this was to be written down or tapped in anywhere else. Lethal loved the whole rigmarole.

My own approach was going to be quite different. No secret codes, in fact no secret stuff at all. I was travelling out simply to find out what had happened to him. So I needed to talk to as many people as possible, and I needed to advertise my presence. My visibility might also be something of a protection, at least so I hoped. It was possible that Timbo's elaborate secrecy had made him more vulnerable rather than less. The cover of darkness worked both ways.

I stood on the top deck of the big tourist boat, the *Papagaio Azul*. Behind me there was dance music playing in the bar, Latino dance music – was it a samba? I was not much of a dancer, but my heart could not help skipping with the beat as the carefree rhythm swung out through the open windows into the steamy evening and the huge waters.

'Is that a samba, Rapha?' I asked my interpreter Raphael Alvarez, who was standing at my side, flicking his cigarette ash over the rail.

'No, paso doble, I think, senhor, double step.'

'Dickie, please call me Dickie.'

'Dickee.' It sounded swingy the way Rapha said it. It could almost be the name of a dance, the Dickee.

It was well after nine in the evening now, but the sweat was still running down between my shoulder blades. The boat was due to leave at ten. Already the sailors were sauntering along to their launch stations and I could hear the thrum of the engines starting up. The sun had gone off the waters hours ago, but I had stayed out here watching the iridescence drain away from the oily swirls around the boat and dissolve in the dying shimmer of the great delta. I had squinched my eyes to try and detect the faintest fuzz of land along the horizon, but there was nothing except the unbroken water and I was pleased by the vastness of the spectacle. How far was the other side? Forty ks, Rapha said. But if I looked straight over to the left I might just descry the darker smudge that was the beginning of the Ilha de Marajó, Shark Island. 'Descry' was Rapha's word. His English vocabulary was a mixture of some old-fashioned dictionary and modern TV talk. He had shades pushed up onto his dark curls and he wore a Manchester United away-strip T-shirt. His white teeth flashed even when he was not smiling. That was one of the things the Conquistadors had brought to the New World, apart from syphilis and flu: big teeth. Rapha had met me at the barrier. I hadn't expected anyone, but he was carrying a little placard saying Sen. D. K. Pentecost, and he seemed to recognise me anyway – they must have sent on a mugshot – and he waved to me before I was past the barrier.

'I am accredited interpreter to the Maloca Group,' he said proudly as he introduced himself. Here, look my card.' I waved the card away and thanked him for coming along. I suppose I could have hired a guide of my own choosing, but George would be unable to resist keeping an eye on me anyway. And Rapha's big plus was that he told me he had interpreted for Timbo too and we could retrace the whole journey they had taken together.

In the bar the dance music had stopped and I could hear the sounds of the river above the steady hum of the ship's engines. There were big seagulls mewing overhead and the sound of hooters further along the quay. The boat began to move and the far bank of the river was easily visible now, no more than a mile away, perhaps less, and I could make out the trees and the pale sandy foreshore. There were white birds darting along the length of the ship and doubling back above it as if completing a low-level reconnaissance, and then turning out into the middle of the river and dive-bombing the water like crumpled handkerchiefs weighted with stones.

'So you really do think he may still be alive?' It was the first question I had asked him.

Rapha spread out his hands and bared his teeth in an unsettling smile, though it may have been meant to be reassuring.

'In this country, who knows? You see your best friend at supper, tomorrow he is gone. Timbo wanted to see the logging, well, he wanted to see the place where the bad guys were lousing up the logging operation. I told him it was dangerous. He looked at me and said, you think I am an idiot, Rapha? And I said, yes, I think you are an idiot. And we laugh. He laugh all the time, your friend, even when nobody says anything funny. But he's a funny guy, or was.'

'Or was,' I echoed. 'Yes, definitely a funny guy.' Perhaps Raphael was smarter than he seemed.

'And that red hair, like a clown,' Rapha added. Yes, I thought to myself, like a clown who wasn't really funny.

'So what do you think happened?'

'Me, I've no idea. I am just the interpreter. But if they want to kill him, why do they dress up the bum to look like him?'

'You really were the last person to see him alive, though?'

'Me and Luis Inacio, Mr Furcht's manager upriver. We put Mr Timbo to bed in the maloca. We expect he will sleep like a baby because of all the caipirinhas he has drunk. I admit we had a few too. In the morning his bed is empty, but the bedclothes are pulled aside like he has been torn out of them.'

That was really all he could tell me. I went to bed wondering whether my whole trip would be as big a waste of time as Jane had prophesied. Yet I slept well and climbed up on deck the next morning feeling unreasonably cheerful.

About a hundred metres from the boat some silvery fish started jumping, sprinkling ripples in the sluggish current. Further on, the river took a big bend to the left and the navigation channel leant in closer to the shore. I could see the roots of the mangroves branching out of the shallows like old varicose veins and their red and green leaves swaying in what little breeze there was. Above and behind the mangroves, the tall trees of the forest scarcely moved. A skittering of the grey-white birds came out of the trees and turned upstream ahead of them.

'On your own then, are you?'

'Yes, I am, just at the moment. My friend is playing table tennis with the purser.' I gestured over to the green awning behind us where I could hear the clack of the balls and Rapha swearing.

'I knew you were English. I said to my wife, he's English, that one. Oh, look, yellow-billed terns, they're the freshwater sort.'

The man at his side pointed at the birds making their abrupt little dives towards the far bank. He had a round pink face and shades pushed up over his silvery thatch to make room for the binoculars he was now squinting through.

'No, I'm wrong,' he said, putting down the bins. 'They're further away than I thought. This river plays tricks with your eyes because it's so big. These ones are the large-bills, you don't often see them this far upstream. Oh, sorry, I should have introduced myself. I'm Keith Rosewill, like the tennis player but with an "i" instead of an "a", and this is my wife Kay. They call us the KKs. We're from Norwich.'

He was wearing a beige bush shirt and long shorts to match and a floppy hat on a string hung on his back. His wife was kitted out almost exactly the same, except she had her floppy hat perched on her silver thatch and she had her shades on.

'K,' the woman said, sounding a little out of breath, 'there's a Great Black Hawk on that rock over there. Look, there.'

'He does all right for himself, that one, lives on frogs and baby alligators,' Rosewill said.

His wife was setting up a camera on a tripod. Suddenly a cloud of parrots came from behind them, screeching like a party of school-children, green parrots with orange wings, then red-and-yellow ones, then blue-and-yellow, and all blue, a dazzling hot blue, bluer than the steamy sky.

'Quick, K,' the man said. 'Oh, they've gone behind the trees. Here comes another lot, it's more of the orange-wings.' He turned to me. 'As I expect you can see, we're fanatical birders. Every year we take an autumn holiday somewhere nice and warm and see how many species we can clock up. We did Morocco last year, the Massa Lagoon. A bit disappointing, the Bald Ibis had gone. Of course on this river you're spoilt for choice. It's anybody's guess how many species there are out there, hundreds maybe.'

'With a whole lot more they haven't discovered yet,' his wife said. She was still fiddling with the height adjustment on the tripod.

'You on holiday then?'

'Yes,' I said, 'I've always wanted to see the Amazon.'

'And your friend, is he English too? He doesn't look English.'

'No, he's Brazilian actually. He's going to do a bit of interpreting for me.'

'That will come in handy upriver. K and I have only got a little kitchen Portuguese between us; there's a new Portuguese restaurant in Norwich near the cathedral and we've been practising on the waiters, but I always say if you can make friends you can make your-self understood. K makes friends just like that. You should see our sitting room at Christmas, cards from all over the world.'

'Oh, K. He does exaggerate, you know.' She took off her shades to shake hands with me. To my surprise, her eyes were a startling intense blue, the blue of the parrots' wings.

We had coffee together in the lounge. Keith was a loss adjuster. He had been looking forward to early retirement but after the floods there had been such a backlog of work that he couldn't see himself getting out from under for another couple of years. Kay had been a nursery teacher originally, then when the kids were young she gave up and started a business making fairy cakes which had done very nicely until the recession hit East Anglia. They had two children, a boy and a girl: Keith Junior known as Junior, and Karolyn with a 'k' and a 'y'. The funny thing was that they were both in Scotland now, although K and K didn't have a drop of Scottish blood between them. Junior was an accountant working for an oil company in Aberdeen and Karo was a nurse in Edinburgh.

Would I care to join them for lunch? They had a nice corner table and there was a spare seat, and it was well away from the noisy party who insisted on doing karaoke at all hours to the piped music. I ducked out of lunch. I could see that the Rosewills were good people, but I didn't fancy having every meal with them all the way to Manaus.

K and K were everywhere on the boat. It wasn't just the bird life they photographed. They took pictures of the Captain on his bridge, which the Captain said he was pleased about because not many people wanted a picture of the man who drove the boat. They snapped the purser and Rapha playing table tennis. Keith photographed the Captain's table too, the Captain waving at him as though at an old friend. They took pictures of a couple dancing the tango in the lounge after dinner – Rapha said they danced so badly they must be from Peru. They took quite a lot of pictures of me too. I had only to lean on the rail and watch the passing river traffic, and Kay would be setting up her tripod to get a good shot of me. She usually gave a talk to the Norvickies, the Norwich women's lunch club, after they got home, and she liked to include as many human-interest shots as possible because, to be honest, not all the girls were interested in birds.

It must have been the third morning after we left Belém, I woke up, had my porridge and honey and a cup of strong bitter coffee and wandered along the open deck. It was a glorious morning, the first really clear day, and the parrots were swarming from one side of the river to the other in a screeching, swooping rainbow. In the shallows a hundred metres away, several egrets were gently probing the water and then wading on in a patient, quizzical way. Swags of bright green moss hung from the lower branches of the trees like Christmas decorations. There was nobody else about (it turned out the boat was only half-full anyway), and particularly not about were K and K, which was the most blessed relief of all.

I half-closed my eyes, bathing in the delicious freshness of the morning sun, not thinking about anything much, certainly not about what I was going to do next. I had decided to retrace Timbo's footsteps as far as they could be traced and then see. It would be a total delusion to imagine that I could make anything resembling a plan. Nobody I asked on the boat had any recollection of an English guy with strange red hair, but Rapha was definite that it was the *Papagaio Azul* they had come upriver on.

I was still half-entranced when I became aware that the scene along the banks was changing, or rather the scene change forced me out of the trance, like the snap of a hypnotist's fingers.

Abruptly the tall trees and the tangle of creepers came to an end and the bank was lined instead with miserable shacks with rusty corrugated-iron roofs propped up on rickety stilts. In between the huts streams of mud and rubbish slithered over the banks into the river. In front of the shacks there were even more miserable shelters with a covering of old sacking or palm leaves insecurely held up by stunted poles. I could see Indians crouching in these wretched dwellings. They were the first Indians I had seen close up, and I stared in a daze at their emaciated limbs and pot bellies covered only with a ragged shawl or loincloth. Here and there a dismal bumpy track came down to a gimcrack jetty with the sewage, garbage, whatever it was, lapping at its filthy piles. The shanties went on for miles and seemed to stretch way back into the Interior under a vile smoky haze. Beyond them round the next bend were large industrial sheds with heavy lorries rumbling along the rutted lane between them. When the boat got closer, I realised how enormous the sheds were, dirty great structures of corrugated iron. As the boat finished the bend, I could begin to decipher from the end the big peeling letters painted on the biggest shed: CHT MILLS. Even as I began to wonder what CHT might stand for, I could see what it said in full: FURCHT MILLS.

I looked round quickly to see if K and K were anywhere in view because they would certainly be snapping this ghastly sight. Not that they could possibly know that I had any connection with the place, but they would want to talk about it, because they wanted to talk about everything. We do like a natter, Kay had confided.

But they were nowhere to be seen.

'Your friends?' Rapha said. 'Oh, they must have got off last night. There is a stop at Belvista for naturists.'

'Naturalists. Naturists are—'

'Oh, yes, I know, naked people. It is where the best trail starts to see the rare hummingbirds, best place except the zoo.' Rapha laughed. He had already made it clear that he had no interest in nature, except where it had commercial possibilities.

'Mrs Rosewill mentioned that they hoped to catch a glimpse of Spix's Macaw.'

'Ha,' said Rapha, 'they all hope to see a Spix's Macaw. Nobody has seen one for twenty years. And what is it anyway? Just another blue parrot. You can sit on the deck here and see a hundred blue parrots and drink a nice cold caipirinha at the same time.'

It was while we were drinking the second caipirinha that Raphael began his lament.

'I am the third-generation English interpreter, you know. My grandfather, my father and then me. Grandfather worked for the Americans when they first came in the 1920s to plant rubber trees. They needed rubber for their tyres and they did not trust the British. Your Winston Churchill, he told his colonies not to produce too much or they flood the market. So Henry Ford said he would grow his own damn rubber and he bought a vast stretch of land on the Tapajós – we come to the mouth of the Tapajós after Santarém. Ford's estate was as big as the state of Tennessee and he spent big money on it. The Companhia Ford built golf courses, tennis courts, dance halls for their workers, but the one thing they did not know how to do was plant rubber. Henry planted rubber trees like he made cars, close together, one after the other in rows, hundreds of them in the bare earth. So what happens? If it is dry the trees are burnt to death. If it rains and, boy, can it rain in the Tapajós, they are washed away. And if one tree gets the leaf blight, they all get the leaf blight. In the jungle the trees grow far apart, one or two per hectare. The bugs cannot reach the next tree, the roots of the other trees conserve the moisture in the soil, the forest protects them against the wind and the flood. But Ford's trees die, year after year. And every year the

Ford people tell my grandfather, this year Mr Ford will come to see his trees and you will interpret for him. But he never comes. I think he cannot bear to see that he has failed. So the Americans go home and then the anthropologists come. The Americans want to make the Amazon into a factory; the anthropologists want to make us into a fucking folk museum.'

Rapha was all fired up. I was not sure whether another caipirinha would calm him or add fuel to the flames but I liked the taste myself and decided to risk it.

'I will tell you something for free,' Rapha said, when he was well launched on the next one. 'You are wasting your time here. Your whole mission, it is a waste of time. You will not find Senhor Timbo, he is dead. I don't know who killed him, but he is dead for sure. You are wasting my time too, but I do not care because I am being paid. You have not a hope in hell of finding him. And the further we go upriver, the more dangerous it will be, every day it gets more dangerous. Five years ago it was the people who stood in the way who got hurt: small farmers, Indians who resisted, wildlife campaigners. Nobody is safe. Now it is the loggers who are being beaten up too, three were killed last month in Pará province alone. You had much better take some pictures of the parrots and then go home. But I can see you are an obstinate man and so I will take you to see Inspector Morales in Manaus, and he will tell you the same thing.'

The next morning I was woken at first light by Rapha knocking at the door of my cabin.

'We are here, Dickie. Senhor Morales says he'll see us at eight o'clock.'

I tumbled out on deck to find the ship slopping at the quayside and a straggle of passengers already disembarking. Beyond the port I could see cranes and tower blocks. The day before began to seem like a mirage, even the Furcht mills and the wretched huts.

We sat in the anteroom on the eighth floor of one of the new tower blocks. Inspector Morales was a slight, dark man with a pleasing melancholy look. The sharp bark of his voice came as a surprise.

'No, I need no interpreter.' He waved Rapha aside and relegated him to a little chair at the back of the room. His English was indeed pretty near flawless.

'I will make it plain from the start, Mr Pentecost, that we cannot really help you. I am only seeing you at all as a courtesy to Mr Furcht. We have no information as to the whereabouts of your friend. Nor have we any clue as to why this other man should be found dead dressed up in his clothes and with his ID in his jacket pocket. DNA enquiries are proceeding, but we have found no match as yet. So far all we are sure of so far is that the dead man is of Brazilian ancestry and so cannot possibly be your Mr Smith.'

'But why go to all that trouble?'

'We could only conclude at first that some sort of ransom demand might follow. "See, we have your friend in our power, and we will stop at nothing" – that sort of thing. But there has been no such demand. We have good contacts with the criminal gangs who specialise in that sort of operation, and there has been no whisper.'

'I wonder if the British Consul might—'

'Senhora Tallboys is a good friend of ours. She will tell you the same thing. We are in touch daily. She is not here at the moment, she is visiting with her son in Rio. And now if you will excuse me, Mr Pentecost …'

We took a taxi back to the harbour and strolled along the quay in the milky sunshine.

'There, you see, the meeting of the waters.'

I followed Rapha's pointing finger and saw that the great river was divided into two enormous placid streams of colour, the further one a pale cocoa, the nearer a brilliant, intense blue – ultramarine, I said to myself.

'Now you see how brown the Amazon is beside the Tapajós. It is the silt from the mountains. For many kilometres the two rivers run side by side without mingling, nobody knows why. You will love the Tapajós.'

'I loved the Amazon too.'

'The Tapajós is the true jungle. That is our boat over there. The tourist boat is faster, but it does not go beyond Alter do Chão.'

The *Vera Sotomayor* was a chubby old steamer converted to diesel. She kept her funnel for decoration and her decks had been spruced up in royal blue and white. I liked the look of her. She was the sort of boat adventures started from.

Rapha insisted on pointing out the more modern points of local interest.

'That is the new soybean terminal. It is built by Cargill. You know Cargill? It is the largest cocoa processor in the world. Now it will be just as big in soy.'

It was another two hours before the *Vera Sotomayor* was due to weigh anchor. Rapha took me to a café further along the quay. It was dark and thick with tobacco smoke. We ordered bean stew and a beer. Through the windows I could see the blue waters rippling.

'It will be hot upriver, even at night. It is best to sleep on the deck because there is no air con in the cabins. They will put up mosquito nets for you.'

Soon after we had cast off, pale brown bluffs reared up on either side of the river and the shadowed river took on a darker colour.

Rapha was still in an irritable mood after being snubbed by Inspector Morales. I was irritable too, and I couldn't help thinking that even if the Inspector had had a clue what had happened to Timbo, he would not have told me.

'Are there many trees in England?'

'Not a great many.'

'And why is that?'

I summoned up a cloudy recollection of the track record of Prehistoric Man. 'I think our ancestors cut them all down when they started herding animals and needed pasture for them.'

'So why should we not do the same and raise cattle to feed the world?'

'Good point.' I did not feel like arguing. I preferred to watch the freshwater terns making their last dives of the day into the dark blue water, their wings a ghostly white now that the light was slipping away behind the cliffs with a rapidity that seemed too rapid to be real, like the way night falls in a film.

Anyway, I liked listening to Rapha talk. It was easy to keep him going as long as you refilled his glass and kept asking him questions, the way Timbo used to. I was beginning to see that the thing was never to be frightened of asking the obvious, because most people enjoyed telling you about themselves or showing off on any subject they thought they knew something about. It was pleasant to lie on the deck under our nets in the black and velvet night and look at the stars swimming above the dark water, or perhaps it was my eyes that were swimming after all the beer.

The next morning was grey with a thin mist over the water. And the landscape had changed too. The cliffs had fallen away and on the right bank the forest had disappeared and there was a flat green prairie stretching to the horizon. On the left bank a straggle of ramshackle settlements came into view, the same miserable straw huts on crooked piles and the same Indians watching them go by with sullen, incurious stares. The huts were overlooked by a giant shed set back from the river with smashed windows and a grubby cement chimney behind it. Round about, I could make out other big sheds, too broken down to make a guess as to what they might once have been used for. The only building that was in any kind of shape was a little chapel standing close to the shore. It was built in the American Colonial style with a tiered tower topped by a tiny dome. This neat little doll's house only made the rest of the settlement seem more utterly desolate.

'That's Fordlandia,' Rapha said. 'The big shed was the powerhouse. They still use the church, I think. From here on is where the cattle country begins,' he said, stretching his arms and then rubbing the sleep out of his eyes. Sitting up in his sleeping bag, he looked like a schoolboy.

There was a Land Rover and driver waiting for us at the jetty. Rapha certainly knew how to organise things. As we watched the *Vera Sotomayor* steam on upriver, Rapha leant across from the back seat and brushed the dust off the shoulder of my shirt. It had crossed my mind before that Rapha might be gay, for all his talk of girls. But then I reflected that most young Brazilian men seemed to like touching one another. On the quayside they had walked arm in arm on their evening *passeio*. I rather envied that. We bumped along a rutted track across the prairie, scattering drowsy herds of cattle. In the back my suitcase hurtled to and fro on the deeper ruts. After half an hour we came to the edge of the forest. The cleared land stopped abruptly in a straight line which stretched to the horizon. The spindly trunks of the exposed forest looked naked and white. Rapha had told me that every hectare of forest might contain as much as five hundred different species of tree, but from the Land Rover they all looked much the same: feathery-leaved with these spindly white trunks. Only now and then could I make out a big tree spreading above the canopy – a fig tree or some sort of Brazil nut, Rapha said.

We drove on along the foresters' track at the edge of the forest, going no more than 20 mph, if that. In the distance, a noise began to grow: at first a dim rumble, then resolving itself into a harsher, splitting, screeching roar. The Land Rover bumped on over a little rise and we saw two huge bulldozers attacking the edge of the forest. They were like tanks, with enormous treads as tall as the men walking alongside and murderous cutting blades attached to the far side, relentlessly slashing at the frail tree trunks and throwing the felled wood off to the right. The blades each had a spiked end and every now and then the monster paused to allow its operator to stab and twist at a stubborn trunk until it came loose from the soil. The rear of the dozers had fearsome great ploughs fitted to chew up the ground as they passed. A hundred yards behind each dozer, a backhoe was passing to and fro over the cleared ground and shovelling the fallen timber and creepers and stones off to the side. Behind them two tractors tethered together by a heavy chain weighted down by a steel ball a good four feet in diameter were passing over the ground again, yanking out the root systems as they went. This cruel convoy was moving at less than walking pace, but it was fast enough to fell a rainforest.

'Those are Caterpillar D9s or maybe D11s. The Komatsu D275s are more powerful but they are not so reliable.'

Standing out in the prairie about a hundred yards apart from one another were two men in breeches with shotguns slung over their shoulders and cartridge belts round their waists. They were both wearing mufflers to protect their ears from the screech of the bulldozers. Further out in the field stood a large vehicle looking like some sort of armoured car. It was completely torched. The windows had melted and the engine compartment was a blackened shapeless heap.

'That's poor Humberto's Humvee. He used to be the biggest rancher for miles round. Bu he was scared all right. He had the

Humvee converted into a caravan so he could keep an eye on things. They firebombed it two nights after your friend disappeared. There wasn't much left of him when they pulled him out. He was a cussed bugger but he didn't deserve this. They killed two other ranchers last week.'

'And the men with guns, are they his, or policemen?'

'They're his, I think, trying to save what's left of his operation. But I reckon his people are finished in these parts. Now we go see Luis Inacio. I haven't spoken to him for a few days, so he may have heard something. I advise you to put on the maximum dose of jungle juice and hold on to your hat. The last stretch was a motorway compared to this. Senhor Timbo was nearly sick.'

About five miles further on there was a turning off the cleared land into the forest, a mucky deep-rutted track which had seen recent heavy traffic. The rumble of the dozers began to fade once we were in the forest and the air became damp and sticky. The trees were swathed in creepers which rattled and scraped against the roof and windows of the Land Rover, but the trees had been slashed back just enough for a big truck to pass. The cruel white scars on the trees were like a trail blazed by an angry giant.

'What happens if we meet something coming the other way?'

'Not very likely. The bad guys move mostly at night to avoid the cops, which suits the cops who aren't so eager to run into them either.'

Now and then the creepers exploded into bunches of flowers – deep pink and orange and purple. Once in a while the sun found a gap in the canopy and the forest around them became a blazing bright green until the branches and the dripping moss closed the light out again and the steaming midday twilight took hold again. We stopped to allow the driver to pour another can of petrol in the tank. I listened in a tense ecstasy to the muted clicking, whir-ring sounds of the forest. Even the distant cry of some unknown bird seemed somehow hushed. Perhaps this was how the animals had talked in the Garden of Eden, quietly, at ease in their unsullied paradise. In this part of the forest, the trees were so closely entangled they seemed to conspire, breathing together as they exchanged their saps and fungi and parasites, their trunks not yet tapped or ringed, the chainsaws still far away. I dropped into a dozy reverie which was close to sleep, despite the jolting of the Land Rover.

'We must be about ten minutes away now by my reckoning,' Rapha said.

'Closer,' said the driver. 'I can smell the smoke.'

As abruptly as it had begun, the forest came to an end and we were out in the open again.

The broad track went through the middle of a muddy wasteland spattered with tree stumps and piles of dirt and stones and roots. It was a scene of brutal devastation, like the photos of the battlefields of World War One, only here the smoke came not from the big guns but from bonfires smouldering every hundred yards or so. At the far end of the wasteland, a half-mile further on, I saw a couple of dirty old tractors dragging logs into heaps at the edge of the uncleared forest beyond. The driver switched off the Land Rover engine and I was deafened by the grating roar of chainsaws all round us. As my eyes got used to the woodsmoke, I could see the men, naked to the waist, most of them without safety helmets, working the saws along the forest and stepping back in a hurry as each tree began to heel and topple. Humberto's operation looked like high-tech demolition, this was low-tech savagery.

'It's poor-quality timber here, you see how skinny the trees are. Most of it's only good for charcoal. They float it down to the ovens and take it overland to the South where they use it to smelt the pig iron.'

'And what happens to the iron?'

'A lot of it goes to the States. The steel in your Ford saloon may have been made with charcoal from the Amazon. So part of Henry Ford's dream is being realised but not quite how he had it doped out. Ah there's Luis Inacio.'

A handsome young man with designer stubble came over to the Land Rover. He sauntered across the smouldering wasteland in a cocky, promenading way as though he was walking past a group of girls in a pavement café.

'Ah, so this is the great detective,' he said in English with a teasing smile.

'Nice to meet you.'

'Look at the trees, you can see how crappy they are. But it is great country for cattle and for soy. You have seen poor Humberto's *estância*? Five years ago it was forest just as bad as this and now he raises cattle to go all over the world. But we have to operate this way because we cannot obtain the licences, and because we cannot get the licences, the bankers won't lend us the money for the Caterpillars, and so we have to make do with these crappy tractors. Even here in the jungle there is one law for the rich and another for the peasant. You know, I was raised here in the Tapajós, I believe in this country. Even five years ago it was not so bad—'

'What's changed?'

'Enida. Without Enida we would be doing OK, not brilliant but OK. We would still be unrecognised but we would be able to operate. Before, we could get our timber into Santarém or Belvista and it would go in mixed with the other timber. You had only to change the numbers on the bills of lading at the port. There was a small commission to be paid, but everyone knew what was going on. It was a reasonable accommodation. But then Enida came in and began to inspect the Federal inspectors. And the Feds got scared, so we had to pay them twice as much and then they would not help at all. Why? Because Enida had begun putting in its own agents provocateurs to bring in timber to be laundered, and the officials could not be sure which was genuine illegal product and which was Enida product pretending to be illegal.'

'Enida? What is Enida?' I interrupted, startled to hear the name. Timbo too must have heard it mentioned in the guides' chatter and sent that hurried text to Luke and Lethal. I had to let them know that he had been on to something, though what exactly?

'What or who? Some say she is a crazy baroness living in Rio who loves trees more than people. Some say it is a front for the Communists. Me, I think it may be the CIA who are paid by the cattlemen in Texas. They do not seem to be open to persuasion' – Luis Inacio rubbed his finger and thumb together – 'so it cannot be the police either. These are slippery customers and they operate outside the usual criminal channels. None of our sources has a line on them.'

'So what do we do?'

'"We", Senhor Pentecost? We work together and we work higher up the river.'

'Which way would that be from here? I'm afraid I've rather lost my bearings.'

'I do not mean higher *literalmente* only, though that is true too. What we need to do is feed our product into the chain higher up before it is milled or burnt. Until now Enida does not come deep into the forest, because they do not need to. They can intercept the timber as it comes into the mill or goes overland to the charcoal ovens. But suppose our timber is mixed in with the legal stuff on site up here, so that its papers are already in order. And perhaps your legal logger is connected to a leasing company which has some spare bulldozers. Your mills need timber, we need Komatsus and an outlet for our product. You cannot get any more *licença*, we do not bother with them. We are a perfect alliance, no?'

'Sounds great,' I said.

I looked round the clearing. Here at last was the heart of the matter. We had come a long way, but in this blasted heath with the spluttering flames of the bonfires and the roar of the tractors going up and down and the shrill music of the chainsaws, here must lie the answer I had come to find. At any rate, that was what I was being told. But did Enida really exist? Was there really a crazy baroness in Rio behind it? Or was it an acronym for some organisation whose initials would probably sound quite innocuous if spelled out, like NATO or OPEC?

'Come on, it is time to eat. We have been driving since dawn and I am starving. There will be roast cayman for dinner in the village. It's only an hour on from here.'

'How on earth do you know that, about the cayman, I mean?'

Rapha waved his mobile phone merrily.

'You see, this is my jungle magic.'

'So let me get this straight,' I said. 'You get your mixed-up timber down to one of the legit concessions, say one of Mr Fur—'

'I don't think we need mention names, do we? The forest has ears, you know. It is amazing how the sound carries,' said Luis Inacio.

'Well, Mr X's concession then, and it goes down to his mill already clean. But won't Enida begin to investigate when there's a whole lot more legal timber being unloaded at the mill and no sign of any illegals at work?'

'Oh, there will still be plenty of illegals. I know half a dozen at work between here and the Tapajós alone. Our arrangement will be quite modest in terms of the total felling.'

'And how will you make the contacts?'

'Don't worry about that, Senhor Dickie. We know who to talk to.'

Rapha chivvied us into the Land Rover and we headed off down the track. The men with the chainsaws did not look up as we passed.

Inside the Land Rover we were cheerful, I was not sure why. It was like being on a coach with a football team that had just won three-nil away from home. As we bumped on through the forest, Rapha began to sing the old Boney M number 'Brown Girl in the Ring', and Luis Inacio joined him. I could not remember the words but joined in the chorus: 'Brown girl *in* the ring, tra la-la la-la.'

'It was only the B-side originally, did you know that? "By the Rivers of Babylon" was the A-side.'

Luis Inacio started to sing 'By the Rivers of Babylon' too. He had a seductive reedy tenor that made you want to sing along.

'It's a Rasta song.'

'It's a great song.'

I thought I would remember this moment for the rest of my life, the Land Rover bumping through the forest and the three of them singing.

After half an hour we stopped for a piss by a muddy stream. When the engine was turned off, the noise of the cicadas was as loud as a fire alarm. As the arcs of our piss cascaded into the leaves at the edge of the stream, something about a foot long slithered out from under the leaves and flopped in the stream.

'Hey, did you see that? A baby cayman.'

'He must have taken fright when he saw Rapha's *pinga*.'

'Don't talk so loud, or all the girls will come running.'

We drove on, quieter now. Luis Inacio and Rapha exchanged the odd remark in Portuguese without bothering to translate. They seemed to know each other quite well, without being friends exactly.

'See those yuccas, we're almost there.' The Land Rover brushed through the tall spiky plantation and we came into a sort of orchard. There were mango and orange and lemon trees planted in rows and behind them a row of tall coconut palms. Beyond was a neat semi-circle of mud and wattle huts with palm-thatched roofs. The whole place looked spotless. As we got out of the Land Rover, I could smell cooking.

'That's the cooking hut over there.'

The hut had no windows. Once inside the dark and smoky interior I could make out two girls tending a flat pan raised on stones over a fire. One of the girls was lifting pieces of meat with a stick out of an oil drum at her side and dropping them into the sizzling pan.

'That must be our cayman, or it might be tapir. No, it's the cayman, look.'

I jumped. Draped along the back wall of the hut was the skin of a huge croc, six foot long at least, the light from the fire shining on its horny knobs and wattles. The creature seemed not dead but dozing. Then the girl turned it over, and even in the darkness I could see the axe blows that had split open its white belly.

Another girl came into the hut and beckoned us to follow her. We went out into the village clearing and walked over to another, larger hut which had benches in it. We sat down and the girl brought us tin cups containing a dirty milky liquid.

'This is manioc beer. They cut the roots from the sweet cassava into thin slices, then they boil the slices and squeeze them and then – this is the important bit – the slices are partly chewed by young girls, before they heat the liquid again and leave it in jars to ferment.'

'Why young girls?'

'Their spit is sweeter. Drink up, you will find it refreshing after the journey, like buttermilk the Yankees say.'

It was refreshing and rather stronger than I had expected. The first two girls came in, carrying the pan with the sizzling strips of cayman. I wondered if it was their spit that had flavoured my beer and rather liked the thought that it might have been.

The cayman was chewy like a piece of fish that had been somehow impregnated with chewing gum. I needed several cups of beer to get it down without gagging. The strange thing about the beer was that the more I drank the stronger it tasted, whereas with most drinks it was the first drink that had the strongest kick and after that you hardly noticed.

'Now I show you the maloca,' Rapha said.

We walked to the far end of the village clearing, and there, half-hidden by the trees was an enormous building with a huge sloping penthouse roof of woven palm leaves coming almost down to the ground. The last light of evening gently gilded the feathery roof. Rapha was already pulling open the rough door of wooden palings woven together with vines.

'It is empty now, the Indians are all gone, except for the festival time. I offered Senhor Timbo a bed in one of the new huts, but he said he had to sleep in a maloca, it was a sacred place. We aren't really allowed in, because of Native Heritage laws, but I thought that just for one night …'

I stared into the immense gloom, the fading light gently gilded still playing through a hole in the roof high above us.

'It is like a cathedral,' I said.

'For the Indians it is their cathedral. This is where they perform their sacred songs and dances, but they sleep and eat here too. Since the logging started, they only come up the river two or three times a year.'

Now only for the first time, standing there half-woozy in the half-light, I realised what a liberty George Furcht had taken in naming his group.

'That is where we put down the Indian quilt for Timbo, in that corner, so he would see the dawn coming in through the window. But he never did. I came in to check on him when it was still dark, but he was already gone, with the bedclothes thrown aside, like that.' Rapha mimed a violent tearing-apart motion. 'Perhaps if we had stayed in here with him, we might have saved him, but he said he wanted to be alone.'

I stared up at the great whirligig roof, and my head began to spin. The whole vast empty hall smelled of neglect, and the palm leaves were coming loose from the beams. That was the moment when I knew for sure that I would never find Timbo.

PART THREE

X

Going West

There was a Jewish wedding going on in the Great Plains Hotel, Des Moines. Through the airy atrium, decorated with murals showing sturdy Midwesterners bringing in the harvest in about 1920, and then down the middle of the long lounge with its Versailles-style gilt mirrors, the men of the wedding danced, arms linked, black hats askew, ringlets flying, belting out the wedding song. George Furcht barely looked up as the dancers passed on up the main staircase and then along an open gallery above their heads.

'Double,' said Furcht, looking up now at Rowley with a defiant glare.

'Oh, you've made an error there, my dear sir. You'll wish you hadn't done that,' said Rowley, picking up the little leather box and rattling the dice above the backgammon board. Like many captains of industry in Rowley's experience, Furcht was not nearly as good at the game as he thought he was. Gambling with dice (and cards too) was a much more precise and unforgiving science. In the rough and tumble of the real world you could get away with some lousy bets.

Not that George's prospects in the real world were looking too hot at the moment. He had $750 million of short-term debt due for repayment in three weeks' time. If he failed to make the call, he would have to start selling assets, and then the holders of the medium-term debt would start getting jittery and the chances of them rolling over their tranches (which as of now totalled out at $1.3 billion according to Tony Wardle, although Furcht himself claimed it was less) would be minimal, verging on invisible.

They had been on the road now for twenty-three days without interruption, and they had barely half the signatures they needed and most of those were contingent on the other thirty-nine banks coming in on time. At the start, their hopes had soared when Hal Gombrich at Upstate First Bank had promised to ring round some major players, telling them that Furcht was too big to fail. Hal was not only President at Upstate, he was also the senior non-executive director on the board of Maloca. Upstate had been Furcht's banker ever since he first listed on the New York Stock Exchange, and it was Hal who had held his hand all that while. Perhaps it was because Hal had never wanted to be a banker in the first place that he was so good at it. He had majored in classics at Yale and then taught at a liberal arts college in upstate New York while he finished his master's on the Silver Latin poets. His long-term project had been to write something on the *Attic Nights* of Aulus Gellius, but then his father's real-estate business had gone belly-up and his father had done the same in the pond at the back of their farm outside White Plains, and Hal had had to earn a living to keep his mother, to whom he was greatly attached. Fragments of classical learning still clung to him like burrs. At tricky moments in business meetings he would murmur *pecunia non olet* or *festina lente*.

Every evening Rowley put in a call to Hal back in the East. Because of the time difference, Hal would already be home in Connecticut, in his *villino* as he called it, and he would have a full rundown on the day's events on Wall Street. So far the news stayed grim. Hal had only cobbled together half a dozen banks to sign up, most of them small fry who depended on Upstate to survive.

It was Hal who had originally ordered the two of them to get on the road: 'I tell you for nothing, Rowland, just as I tell my confrères, that if Furcht goes down it will be a tsunami, especially in the Midwest where a hell of a lot of his creditors are based. I know these small-time bank presidents, Rowley. That's why George has to get off his butt. They're cussed independent types. If George dos Santos Furcht thinks his business is so goddam important, he has to get down there and tell them why they need to bail him out. *Labor vincit omnia*, dear boy.'

Comfort was hard to come by in those gruelling days. The road-show was the same in each place: four hours of schmoozing bank high-ups in the morning, then a lunchtime presentation for brokers and investment analysts, and a further round of calls before catching the flight on to the next city.

'I thought today went well. Didn't you think so, Rowland?'

Rowley kept his eye on the board. He could scarcely bear to confront George's pleading gaze any more.

The truth was that today had not gone well. The President of Polk Premier had pleaded an unbreakable engagement (a golf tournament in aid of Lou Gehrig's disease) and had fielded his assistant for corporate affairs, i.e. a junior PR guy, to listen to Furcht's pitch. The Vice-President of Heartland Savings had listened to George courteously but had made it clear that in the prevailing climate they were looking to close positions rather than roll them. Personally of course he would be only too happy to oblige an old and valued client but his Board ... No, today had not gone well. Not as bad as the lunch in the Twin Cities when the senior analyst at Keillor Garrison, a scrawny punk with gel in his spiky hair, had got up and said that, in his considered view, Furcht and Co. was basically insolvent and he could see no good reason why it should be allowed to continue trading. No, not as bad as that. But bad.

Rowley's mobile phone rang and he fished it out of his pocket just as the wedding party came surging back along the gallery, singing rather louder and hanging on to their hats, with the bride and her attendants scampering down the lobby in a froth of tulle and lace. It was the President of Fillmore Bank saying how much he appreciated George coming by and how sorry he was that he hadn't been there to give him a real Des Moines welcome but his wife had been having a hysterectomy. At least that seemed to be the gist. It was hard to hear clearly until the jubilant wedding guests had passed on out of earshot.

'And *mazel tov* to you too,' Rowley said, clicking off the mobile. 'There's another one who'll come in if everyone else does. Talk about sheep.'

'I have a sense that the tide is turning in our favour,' Furcht said, chalking up another doubled game to Rowley on his little matching leather scorepad. The phrase sounded slightly familiar to Rowley. Had some famous person said it: Napoleon after the retreat from Moscow perhaps, or the Emperor of Japan just before Hiroshima?

'On to Tyler tomorrow. My old stamping ground. I'm looking forward to it. I think we will be able to make something of the support that we shall receive there.'

Rowley agreed, nodding his head vigorously, being too tired to think of the words to go with the nodding. He knew George well enough by now to be aware how much he was dreading his return to what was as near to being his home town as anywhere else in his wandering life.

Sleep was hard to come by. The brandy was not helping and they had gone to bed too early, because what else was there to do in Des Moines on a wet night in March? Rowley's watch said 1.45 a.m. He shook it drowsily but it still said 1.45.

The first noise from next door was a rhythmic knocking, like a percussion player idly tapping the rim of his drums as a warm-up routine. Then came a hoarse roaring noise, rhythmic too in a heavy way, like some kind of engine, now obsolete, possibly a steam engine which was not firing properly. The roaring stopped or died down anyway, and was followed by a long low groan which sounded as though it came from a different source. It was such a terrible sound that Rowley forgot about the other noises and assumed instantly that George was having a major heart attack. Afterwards he thought to himself how odd it was that he should have snatched at this explanation and not the other, because after all he was not without experience in the other department, fancied himself as something of an authority in fact. But the truth was that he had not thought of George Furcht and sex in the same breath. Although overpoweringly masculine, Furcht at the same time seemed somehow sexless. He emitted no signals of desire. Rowley did know of course that he had been divorced years ago. Perhaps there was some off-and-on mistress kept hanging in London or New York, but he had as yet seen no sign of her. True, it was possible that he was both romping, as Rowley liked to put it in his old tabloid style, *and* having a coronary, the other following the one. Which complicated the problem. If George was unwell, it was crucial to contain the story. Once the news got out that he had had any sort of heart attack, he would be dead meat and Furcht and Co. would be toast. On the other hand, if he was merely winding down after some heroic exertion for which he was obviously not in training, then he would be furious if Rowley put his head round the door. These were delicate circumstances but then Rowley delighted in delicate circumstances. He slipped on his dressing gown and with a gentle touch unlocked his door. There was an alcove a few yards down the passage with an armchair and an ashtray. He would sit there and smoke a cigarette on the pretext that he had booked a non-smoking room by mistake.

It was about ten minutes later that she came out. He was startled by how young and pretty she was, her pale head cocked to one side as she finished putting the elastic band on her ponytail. She looked at him with a delightful wry smile as though he had just said something quite amusing.

'Hi,' she said, 'you standing in line?'

'No,' he said. 'I couldn't sleep.'

'That don't surprise me,' she said.

He returned her wry smile.

'Well, so long,' she said. 'It's been nice meeting you. Another night perhaps.'

'I hope so. Take care.'

'You too.'

After she had gone, he tiptoed back to George's door and listened as hard as he could but he could hear only the sound of his own breathing.

They had to be up for breakfast at 6.30 if they were to catch the morning flight down to Tyler. Rowley expected to find his master full of himself, if he found him at all, and he was not wrong.

'We must have porridge for breakfast, Rowland, made with good Iowa oats. Do you have porridge, young man?'

'Yessir,' said the plump young Mexican serving them.

'And made from Iowa oats, I trust?'

'I no know where oats come from. I ask.'

He disappeared into the kitchen and returned with the news that the oats came from Minnesota.

'Minnesota oats are poor stuff. They are shrivelled by the winds from Canada. And your bacon, where does your bacon come from? There's nothing to beat bacon from Iowa hogs.'

The waiter was unable to say where the bacon came from. Rowley wondered whether Furcht was going to go on like this all day. He could not imagine that the Tyler bankers would warm to his master in this mood.

They flew over endless squares of fields, most of them a pale dun this early in the year, only a few showing the faintest green-gold. Now and then at the corner of the squares there would be a huddle of grain silos and a scattering of homes and gas stations at the junction with what must be the Interstate. Rowley felt the apprehension gather in his stomach.

At least the President of the First Tyler Bank had the courtesy to turn out to meet them for coffee and muffins at the motel next to the little airport. Dennis O'Rourke III had one of those sad ruddy Irish faces that looked close to tears even when he was warmly shaking your hand.

'Great to see you, George. Welcome back to Tyler. We were just tickled to hear you were going to visit with us. How long has it been now?'

'Since I was in Tyler? Oh, forty years at least. It's great to be back.' George went on pumping O'Rourke's hand as though attempting to extract something from a machine he was not familiar with.

It was clear from the light in O'Rourke's rheumy eyes that he knew George already, no doubt from way back. It was equally clear that George had completely failed to recognise O'Rourke and O'Rourke was going to have to remind him that they were old acquaintances. It was a rock-bottom start. Rowley was quick to notice such things and no slouch at sorting them out either.

'You two boys in school together then?'

'We certainly were, Saint Francis Xavier High. George was a coupla years ahead of me. Then he left for the East in his senior year, ain't that right, George?'

'Too damn right it is,' said George. 'Great to see you again, my friend.' Rowley could see that George had not only failed to recognise O'Rourke but in his flustered state had mislaid the briefing note with O'Rourke's name on it. So Rowley had to come to the rescue again.

'Rowley Beavan,' he said, putting out his hand in an enquiring manner.

'Denny O'Rourke. Swell to meet you, Rowley. Welcome to Tyler, Gateway to Nowhere in Particular, but we just love it.'

Rowley could see that O'Rourke had now spotted that George had not recognised him. This was not going swell at all.

'Remember old Skip Turner?'

'Skip, of course,' Furcht responded without conviction.

'Toughest football coach this side of the Rockies. Died last week. Ninety-three. Still took his dip at Cottonwood Hole every morning if they could manage to break the ice.'

'Skip was really something.'

'Of course you weren't much into sports, were you, George?'

'Well, no, I was not a gifted sportsman.'

There was a pause. Denny O'Rourke seemed to be waiting for something.

'But you yourself were quite a football star?' Rowley picked up the pass that Furcht had fumbled.

'Well, I made Iowa State. They were short on quarterbacks that year, but we had a damn decent squad, we whipped Kansas and only just lost out to the Twin Cities. Then I did my knee in and that was the end of that. Took up chasing a little white ball with a stick instead.'

While Denny was outlining his subsequent career on the golf course, George Furcht was laying out his papers on the table without pretending to take any real interest in what they were saying. As soon as O'Rourke ran out of gas, he began his spiel.

Rowley had heard it all a dozen times already: the solid forecasts for the timber business, the brilliant outlook for soy, the even more brilliant outlook for cattle prices following the drought in Texas, the hotel arm improving its occupancy rates each quarter, and of course the agricultural and biofuel interests across the Midwest were really the bedrock of the whole group and the prospects there were just fantastic, once this temporary cash constriction had been dealt with. They had twenty-seven signatures already in place, with a further thirty to come in as soon as the comprehensive agreement had been finalised. The whole thing might go fairly close to the wire because the Japanese banks had such cumbersome decision-making structures. But he was confident that everything would be settled by the 28th of the month, and he would count it as a great personal vote of confidence if Denny's signature was up there good and early because it was always nice to know that you had your home town right behind you.

During the early part of all this, Rowley was looking over Denny's shoulder out of the motel window, watching the little planes taking off into the milky Midwest haze. But as the spiel drew towards its close, he looked down directly into Denny's faintly bloodshot eyes. And what he saw there provoked a shudder which he had trouble to suppress.

For what he detected in the eyes of Dennis K. O'Rourke III was naked hatred. O'Rourke's lips were parted in a patient expectant sort of way which might have been the prelude to a smile. But the eyes – well, it was hard to say exactly how you could detect the loathing, something about the tightening round the eyelids perhaps, but there was no mistaking it.

'Wow, that presentation was just amazing, George. We don't get many folks down this way who can lay out their business as clear as a damn spreadsheet. And I want to thank you for being so frank with us because I know you would expect me to be just as frank with you.'

'That goes without saying, Denny.'

'And I have to say that we have our own, what was your word, George, constrictions, that's a fine word, well, we have our own constrictions down here. The truth is that First Tyler is just a mite exposed on too many fronts. Our Risk Committee is looking to call in pretty much every loan which isn't one hundred per cent secured. Naturally some of us have been arguing that we need to keep helping our good friends who have been with us for yonks. But Avery, who's Head of Risk and the hardest-headed guy you ever didn't want to bump into, says, no exceptions, you gotta give a lead on this one, Denny. Well, I'm only the President, I do what they tell me. This is a small bank in a small town and we have to live together. So the bottom line, George, is that as of now I'm not in a position to oblige you. If you'd come to me a month ago, I'd have signed like that, as quick as I sign my bar bill at the club, quicker in fact because I'm not famous as the quickest in that department. Come to me in a couple of months' time, again no problem. But now ...'

He shook his head, and Rowley looked closely at him again. The hatred had been replaced by an expression of barely suppressed joy. Denny was loving it.

'The timing is crucial, Denny. I don't have to tell you that.'
'No you don't, George. That's what makes me feel so bad.'

'Two million bucks. A fucking two million dollars, that's all he was in for. We don't need him. We need never have come to this pathetic small-minded town, except for the damn sentimental angle. And it was a pack of lies, all that stuff about being overexposed. First Tyler has the lowest gearing of any bank in the state. Almost all its borrowings are covered by its retail deposits. He could have let us have ten million without a second thought.'
'Did you remember him?'
'What? Oh, well, as he said, he was a couple of years younger than me.'
'But did you remember him?'
'I might have.'
'Because he remembered you and I don't think he liked you very much.'
'Well, that's not so surprising. A man who leaves his home town and makes a certain name in the world is bound to excite envy.'
'I don't think it was just that. I got the impression, I don't know why, that he had something against you.'
'Against me?'
'Dating back from you were at school together, that would be my guess.'
'That's absurd.'
'If you say so, George.' Rowley gave him one of his trademark quizzical smiles. He had discovered over the years that there were times when it was better not to push it. It was a couple of hours later and they were on the flight to Denver when George spoke.
'He's changed a lot of course, but I'm beginning to think he might have been one of the Irish boys at the swimming hole, Cottonwood Hole it was called, half a mile upstream on the Tyler River. At this distance in time, I can't remember their names, O'Reilly, O'Rourke, who knows? I never could tell them apart anyway, they all had these freckles and jug-ears and they used to come over in a gang from Irishtown, which was the other side of the tracks – literally, Tyler still had a railroad then. And they would come down Locust, past

our house and shout out Spick and things of that nature when they saw me. I still had quite a Latino accent in those days and I was also rather plump. I was an easy target.'

'Well, I can see why you might not care for them, but why the other way round?'

'Ah …' Furcht began and then paused for a moment as if uncertain whether he wanted to go any further.

'George, come on. It was fifty years ago.'

'We used to go skinny-dipping at the hole after school. I say "we" but I wasn't part of the gang and I only tagged along a couple of times with my friend, pretty much my only friend then, Chico Dallalio. He was a great guy, Chico, killed in a plane crash in his twenties, I often think of him. I didn't really want to go but I didn't want to appear a wimp in Chico's eyes – he looked like Chico Marx, the one who played the piano – so I went. And after we had all had a swim, which was fine because swimming was the only sport I was any good at, the guys went up into the trees and started fooling around. And I went up after them and I saw a couple of them, you know, and I knew you weren't supposed to do that.'

He stopped again. He was not enjoying the telling, but somehow he felt he had to get to the end of it.

'So?'

'Father Gerald had told us not to be shy about coming forward and letting him know of any impure activities that might be going on. We would not get much thanks for it at the time, he said, but God would thank us. I was a pious boy and I wanted to do the right thing. So I told Father Gerald what I had seen and he gave all the Irish boys a hell of a larruping and told the ringleaders he didn't want them in his school any more. Well, Francis Xavier was the best school for miles around, the others were little more than shacks on the prairie, and if you were flung out of it you hadn't a cat in hell's chance of getting to a decent college. So you can imagine I was not exactly popular after that.'

Furcht gave a short sea lion sort of bark which could have been loosely described as a laugh. Though Furcht had found it hard to retell the story after it had lain buried so long, there was also a hint of pride in the way he told it, as if unpopularity was a goal worth achieving, however you achieved it. His brusque way of talking had made the whole scene surprisingly vivid: the skinny, freckled boys playing with each other in the shade of the cottonwood trees, and the plump half-Latino boy, still dripping like an otter after his swim, lumbering up the sandy bank, at first not quite clear perhaps what the other boys were doing and then overcome with revulsion, slithering back down the bank again to find his clothes and hightail it back to the school and Father Gerald's confessional.

'Well, I'm not surprised you didn't want to go back to the town.'

'You know what they say, Rowland: you can't go home again. American cities don't stand still. I wouldn't recognise the business district. My old home's probably a used-car lot. No, we did well to make it a whistle-stop.'

All the same, there was a gloom hanging about him throughout the flight to Denver and it hadn't left him when they settled down to their evening game of bezique. Furcht liked bezique because it had been Winston Churchill's favourite card game, but he was no better at it than he was at backgammon.

The next morning there was the same business with the porridge. The oats in Denver came from Minnesota too. There was a story in the *Denver Post* business pages that the troubled billionaire George dos Santos Furcht had been revisiting his home town of Tyler, Iowa, for discussions with the President of First Tyler National Bank, Dennis O'Rourke III. Mr O'Rourke was quoted as saying: 'We are always glad to see George in Tyler and we are doing our best to assist him through his difficulties, but in the current business climate our first priority has to be to strengthen our balance sheet.'

'The little prick,' Furcht said, smacking the paper with the back of his hand.

'I told them no publicity. That's why we had the meet out at the airport.'

'For some people, Rowland, publicity is the best revenge.'

The bankers in Denver were a little better, not much. If everybody else signed, they would sign too, but they didn't want to be the first over the top. In the evening, there was a conference call from three big banks in Pittsburgh who wanted to make it clear, on legal advice they said, that their signatures had been provisional on a general agreement to roll over the entire $750 million. The small print had made this proviso, but they wanted to be sure that George understood their position. There had been a confusion of just this sort in the Murdoch negotiations a while back and they wanted to avoid a repeat.

'They signed, goddammit, the fucking finks are just trying to weasel out. It can scarcely be a coincidence that those banks in Pittsburgh and that jerk in Tyler are all spouting the same garbage on the same day.'

'Well, yes, it can, George. They're all just covering their arses.'

'Rowland, you are an innocent. You cannot imagine the evil of which human beings are capable. And coming after the terrible business of poor Timothy … By the way, what news of the admirable Mr Pentecost's rescue mission?'

'He drew a complete blank, I'm afraid. Went the whole way up river to the maloca where the poor chap disappeared but never had a sniff of him. Arturo Nicols too had nothing to report at all. The FBI in Manaus have a full-scale alert out for Timbo nationwide. Every police force has the passport photo. After all, he must stick out like a sore thumb in any Brazilian crowd. I can't believe we won't hear something soon.'

Furcht shook his head. 'I doubt whether we shall ever know. You do not know Brazil, my friend. Great evils lie buried there until long after they have been forgotten.'

'George, please. The only sensible thing we can do now is to try to get a decent night's sleep. We've got an early start in the morning.'

Furcht did not move. He continued to sit slumped in the big armchair, his fist clenching the brandy glass as though Rowley was about to wrench it from him.

'We may be on the back foot now, but we'll kick their asses in the ninth, I promise you that.'

'Sure we will, George, sure we will.'

As Rowley closed the door behind him, Furcht was glaring into space now as though some object suspended just below the ceiling had provoked his fury.

Rowley hated these brandy sessions. They guaranteed a pulsating, sleepless night. He lay on the bed, once more trying to dream of mornings on the gallops, watching the chestnut two-year-old quicken under a clear sky.

The groans from next door seemed to start almost immediately this time, but when he looked at his watch it was 1.45 a.m., just as it had been the night before in Des Moines. He took an empty glass from his bedside table and went over to the other side of the room and cupped it against the wall and listened. He had thought at first that the groans were much like they had been the night before, but then he thought, no, they weren't. They were sadder, slower this time, the urgency was not there, they had a drag to them. There was a saying, or was it a song, how alike are the groans of love to the groans of the dying. But it was not true, not if you heard them one after the other, on successive nights.

Rowley had the back bedroom in the suite he had booked for the two of them. There was a connecting door into the shared sitting room. He opened it with care, in case George was up and prowling. But he saw him as soon as he put his head round the door.

Furcht was lying toppled sideways on the floor in front of the sofa. He was in his shirt and underpants with the trousers lying in a tangle by his feet. It looked as if he had been taking off his socks, or trying to, when he collapsed. His breathing was quite low, stertorous, clanking, like an engine shunting in a distant yard.

This was what he had been dreading the night before, and it could mean curtains for George himself and, even if he recovered, for the whole Maloca Group, which depended so totally on him. At all costs, he had to get George to hospital without letting anyone know who he was.

Rowley called 911 on his mobile phone and asked them to send an ambulance to the underground car park and instruct the para-medics to come straight up in the lift to the suite and not waste time at reception. By the time the paramedics came up, he was dressed and he had managed to shroud George in his midnight-blue silk dressing gown. As they levered him on the trolley, he gave a huge heave and shudder and Rowley thought that this might be it. But he subsided onto the trolley and went back to the groaning and clanking.

They took him in the service lift down to the car park.

'It's just a minor incident,' Rowley had said to the night man who had unlocked the lift. 'He's had these things a dozen times before, but he doesn't like his family to know. I know I can rely on your absolute discretion.'

The night man took the hundred-dollar bill with a pleasant murmur.

Rowley thought he had done pretty well so far, but after helping the ambulance men to slide George's great frame into the back, he was flustered and out of breath and he was not properly prepared when the assistant paramedic took out his clipboard just as they were bumping up the ramp from the underground parking.

'The patient's name?'

'Name? Oh, Smith. Timothy Smith.'

He kicked himself as soon as he had said it.

At least Rowley could pay the fees himself up front on his own credit card. It turned out to have been a severe stroke, and they wanted to keep him in hospital for two weeks, a month would be better, they said. The paralysis down his right side was not so noticeable when he was in bed, but his face was badly lopsided and his speech was slurred to the point of being incomprehensible. But the aftershock was mostly in the mind. His speech had become hesitant, not only because he was now physically incapable of barking in his old curt, overbearing style but because he was not at all sure what he ought to say. The greatest loss was the loss of self-confidence. Dr Brokenhart told Rowley that this was one of the commonest, longest-lasting but least reported effects.

'It has a particularly marked impact on guys who are used to calling the shots, which I guess was the case with your Mr Smith.' Rowley jumped every time anyone in the hospital referred to George by any part of his alias – some of the nurses called him 'Timothy' or even 'Tim' – and he kicked himself all over again for having been panicked into it. There was a moment when they were transferring the patient from the Frank B. Olsen Memorial Hospital to the LonePine Hospital Suites, which was only on the next block, when he fancied he might be able to rechristen George again, but it really was not practical. Dr Brokenhart from Olsen Memorial had promised to drop by every couple of days to see how George was getting on. No, George was stuck with being Timothy.

As far as saving the company went, George was clearly out of it. He was no longer presentable. There could be no question of subjecting this hesitant, shuffling, suddenly old man to any sort of business meeting or seminar, let alone to a press conference. Even a video link would throw him into a total flap. He found it hard enough to answer properly when the waiter asked him where he should put the breakfast tray.

So Rowley was stuck in Suite 2301 as George's nurse and keeper. The former master of the universe spent most of the time watching daytime TV – PBS Kids mostly, he couldn't handle *The Simpsons* – and sometimes he played patience, very slowly. They had also started to play bezique again together, but Rowley had to keep reminding him of the rules.

There were moments when Rowley looked up from his airmail edition of the *FT* and watched George sitting mute and apparently rapt in front of *Clifford the Big Red Dog* when he wondered whether his devotion to duty was not misplaced, not to say a complete waste of time. Would keeping his employer hidden away like this really make it possible to save the company? Why wasn't he strolling down the King's Road arm in arm with Midge on the way to a quiet one at the Chelsea Potter?

To any impartial observer, George dos Santos Furcht was finished, fucked, kaput. Of the fifty-seven signatures he needed to complete the rollover, he had twenty-nine still to find and some of them the biggest holders of his debt. Rowley had done the sums a week ago and he reckoned the outstanding banks were in for $800 million-plus.

Tony Wardle rang him from New York every day to give him Javits Thornton's latest numbers. Rowley had not told Tony about George's stroke. He had not told anybody. George might be toast anyway, but if any outsider got a peek at the patient in Suite 2301, he was burnt toast. This had always been one man's company, and if that man was known to be a shambling wreck, then the company would be torn apart in a couple of days and the juicier pieces tossed to the circling vultures.

Rowley stared out at the Rockies and wished he was 10,000 miles away.

They watched the CBS early-evening news together. Not much seemed to be happening in the world and by the time the presenter got on to the financial report, Rowley had lost interest and began mixing himself a martini.

'Cotton,' came the plaintive voice. 'We grow cotton, you know. In Brazil. It's very good cotton.'

'What's that, George?'

Rowley went across to the figure slumped on the sofa and handed him his glass of elderflower cordial. George was forbidden alcohol, not that he had ever been a serious drinker, power being his preferred tipple.

On the screen a man in a bright blue shirt was standing in a muzzy white field.

'Here in West Texas there is anger and there is fear,' said the man in the bright blue shirt. 'The World Trade Organisation today handed down a judgement that the US administration's subsidies to producers of upland cotton are unfair. That means that the livelihood of cotton growers like Bob Staley here could be put at serious risk. Isn't that right, Bob?'

'Sure is,' said Bob, coming into shot beside the man in the bright blue shirt. Bob was dressed in full Texan gear, his cowboy boots riding high above the fledgling cotton and his big hat half-hiding his weathered ruddy face. 'We have a saying here in Texas that some fellow is all hat and no cattle. Waal, if the pointyheads in Washington DC go along with this WTO baloney, we'll be all hat and no cotton. You can kiss goodbye to the US as the world's number one cotton exporter. Them Brazilians are gonna walk all over us.'

'It was Brazil which launched the complaint against the United States,' the man in the bright blue shirt resumed, 'and it is Brazil and the other big emerging nations like India and China which stand to gain if the WTO panel verdict is accepted. Tonight the word in Washington is that the administration intends to fight this one all the way. This is Peter Bland in the South Plains, Texas, where cotton is king – for the time being.'

Rowley moved away from the sofa and walked slowly over to the panorama window, head bowed, hands in pockets, scuffing up the carpet with the toes of his loafers as he went, which he often did when mired in thought. He lifted his head and stared out at the light fading over the mountains.

Then something odd happened inside his head. He remembered the exact moment it happened – staring out at the mountains with George slumped on the sofa behind him – because it was so totally unexpected. Yes, Maloca was one man's company, but if that man should … Rowley had spent his working life as the bridesmaid, never the bride, reporting on the head honcho's latest move, occasionally cleaning up after him, never himself the main man, the one who took the decisions. But he knew how it was all done, he had seen inside the machine, he had witnessed a bold coup turn round a hopeless situation, one sudden switch of direction wrong-foot the markets. So why shouldn't he step in and try his luck at the big table?

'Yes,' he said to himself, 'it could just work.'

'What's that, Rowland?' George called out from the sofa, and Rowley realised that in his excitement he had spoken aloud.

At first he thought he would email Arturo Nicols in Manaus, but then he decided to call him directly about what he had in mind. The hell with security, this was going to be a straightforward business thing, up to a point.

'Arturo,' he said, 'you remember your Great Cotton Project?'

'How could I forget? After the chewing up Mr Furcht gave me, I felt like a squashed armadillo.'

'Well, we would really appreciate it if you could dig out the details and email us a copy of the outline business plan.'

'Tonight?'

'Yes, tonight.'

'But Mr Furcht said my plan was a total fantasy that ought to be buried in the mud of the Mato Grosso.'

'Not any more it isn't. It may well be the shape of the future.'

'Well, if you're sure, I'll get it up and send it across right away.'

'George will be most grateful, Arturo. Oh, by the way, any more news on poor Timbo Smith?'

'No, not a thing. I called the police again this morning and they haven't got the faintest smell of a lead. He seems to have disappeared off the face of the earth.'

'It's a terrible story. Well, I hope that the next time I call we shall both have better news.'

'Please give my regards to Mr Furcht. I hope he is in good health.'

'Never better, Arturo, never better.'

While he waited for the email, Rowley began to draft the statement on his yellow legal pad. He had never actually set eyes on the business plan himself. He had only heard Furcht cursing these imbeciles on the Amazon who wanted him to cover the whole of the Mato Grosso with cotton.

'But I thought you said that the MG was the finest place in the world to grow cotton – perfect mix of sunshine and rainfall, you said.'

'That is correct, Rowland, so I did. But with spot cotton at 35 cents a pound, it's financial suicide. I'd go bust in a week if I did what these jokers are telling me to do. Price before climate, that's the only way to survive.'

Rowley picked up the *FT* and rootled about for the commodity prices. Cotton was up to 56.24 cents and that was before the news of the WTO judgement. He reckoned that prices would probably double again within a year or eighteen months, now that the subsidies were under threat. Of course the US government would appeal and appeal again, and the next President would promise to keep on appealing. But the reality was that the subsidies were doomed to wither and the US government would find it next to impossible to revamp them. The Staleys of the South Plains would go belly-up or switch to other crops. The low-cost producers – and in the Western hemisphere that meant Brazil – would pour in to fill the gap, and they would make a bomb. Cotton would be the Next Big Thing one more time, but not anywhere in the US of A.

'The Maloca Group welcomes the judgement of the WTO panel,' he wrote.

We believe in a level playing field for all cotton producers. And we aim to be a major player on that field. The Mato Grosso offers the finest conditions for growing cotton anywhere in the world. The area has a perfect mix of sunshine and rainfall. Our subsidiary, G. Furcht and Co., already operates a cotton plantation of FILL IN FIGURE thousand acres which is highly profitable at current prices and without a dollar in subsidy. We also have a land bank in the area amounting to FIGURE thousand acres. If planted up with cotton, this acreage is expected to generate FIGURE million dollars in revenue per annum and FIGURE million in net profit. With cotton prices expected to rise following the WTO judgement, we foresee annual profits topping $500,000,000 (OR SOME SUCH FIG) within five years. As soon as the current refinancing exercise is completed at the end of the month, the Group intends to move forward with the implementation of its business plan (outline attached).

Rowley drained his martini and surveyed his handiwork. Not bad as a first shot, he thought. He was rather proud of 'refinancing exercise', as though the company had taken this decision quite voluntarily. But the narrative needed emoting up. Oh, and he had forgotten the most important bit. He began scribbling again.

This is a once-in-a-lifetime opportunity to bring lasting prosperity to one of the poorest regions in South America. In the Mato Grosso the average income is FIG but the rainfall is abundant and the soil full of nutrients and the sun shines FIG days a year. There is no need for costly irrigation projects which may do lasting damage to the environment. Cotton is a renewable and sustainable crop which enjoys the full approval of environmental campaigners and wildlife experts.

'Mmm,' Rowley purred as he read over his silky prose and made a few modest adjustments. He did not take the yellow pad over to George for him to glance at. George was presently discomforted by the written word, though he was beginning to manage the *Denver Post* in small doses. There would be time enough later to fill him in.

While he was waiting for Arturo's business plan to come in on the phone, he began to scroll through the photos in his archive. Yes, there was a nice one of George standing in what was undoubtedly a field of cotton. Further on, he found another pic of George shaking hands with the Governor of the Province. Admittedly the picture was two years old and the occasion was the opening of a somewhat controversial petrochemical plant, but no matter. They would do nicely to illustrate George's prominence in Brazil and his commitment to the land of his birth. Better still if there had been a shot of George with some Indians, but Indians always looked too small in photographs.

It was no more than ten minutes before Arturo's business plan surfaced as an email attachment, and Rowley filled in the missing figures, dialling down his poetic licence but telling much the same story. After reading the whole thing through – it was still no more than a couple of sheets – he emailed it to Tony Wardle for onward transmission to all those holdout bankers. But the first banker he needed to get to was Hal Gombrich at Upstate. If Hal thought it would fly, then he could get the momentum going and tow the smaller fry along in his wake.

Rowley attached a covering note:

Hal baby, here at the eleventh hour are two sheets of paper which can save us all. Cheers, Rowley

Half an hour later Hal came back:

Rowley, you Welsh wizard, this is a tectonic shift. Serendipity is the mother of invention. I'll harness up the huskies at first light.

Rowley fixed himself a second martini as a reward and sat down on the sofa with George who was watching a hospital soap.

'Is that the nurse who was in the car?'

'I don't know, George. I haven't been watching.'

It occurred to Rowley that he was committing the Maloca Group to grow cotton on several hundred thousand acres of Brazil without anyone's knowledge or approval, least of all that of the Group's Founder and Chief Executive Officer, who was now watching with some intentness an ad for mouse repellent.

Well, he said to himself, someone had to do something.

Because of the time difference, he expected some swift feedback from Tony and Hal. Even so, he was pleasantly surprised to get calls from both of them before 1 p.m. Mountain Time the next day.

'It's unbelievable,' Tony said. 'Within an hour of your release going out on PA, I had a couple of bank Presidents calling me, the top people, not the brush-off guys. Then another CEO wanted to give me his signature there and then. The office is going crazy. It's totally brilliant, one of George's masterstrokes.'

'Yes, indeed,' Rowley said, 'there's life in the old dog yet.'

Hal Gombrich was only a few minutes behind in offering his congratulations:

'The huskies are yoked. The sun is glinting on the snow. By night-fall I expect to have mustered the entire dog-train. *Jubilate Deo*, baby.'

Over the next couple of days the signatures began to trickle and then to flood in. The laggards and holdouts had digested the ecstatic comments of the financial columns. Rowley might have ghosted them all himself. The consensus was that, however long the US government dragged out its appeals, the future of cotton in the Western hemisphere lay in Brazil and the future of cotton prices was up, up, up, and it was G. Furcht and Co. that had the inside track. Only slugs and laggards were underweight in the fluffy stuff now. By the 26th the rollover had achieved critical mass. Those who had signed provisionally now went unconditional, and those who still refused to extend the credit, either because they had given up on George or because they needed the cash, well, there would be enough money in the kitty now to pay them off. Furcht was saved.

'All anyone needs is a narrative,' Rowley said to no one in partic-ular because George was watching TV.

It was time now to put George in the picture of what had been done in his name. During the past few thrilling days as news of the signatures came in, Rowley had gently lobbed his master the odd piece of good news – 'Santa Fe General has signed for five mil,' 'Miami Savings has said Yea,' and so on – but he had not attempted to convey the full glory of what they had achieved.

Now he sat down opposite George on the sofa and spoke to him slowly and clearly as if he was talking to a foreigner.

'You realise, George, that we now have signatures to roll for six hundred million dollars, and Hal expects sixty or seventy of the outstanding two hundred million to come in tomorrow, which is still a day short of the deadline. It's March 26th, George, and the company is safe.'

Furcht looked up and smiled that wan smile which Rowley had seen so often in the past three weeks.

'Six hundred million dollars is a lot of money,' he said.

'It is, George, it is.'

'And we are safe now? The Maloca Group is safe?'

'Yes, quite safe.'

'That is … wonderful.' The adjective dripped very slowly, like a drop of honey, from his tremulous lips, gilding the whole process with a sense of the miraculous.

'And the Tyler bank, that man I knew, has he signed?'

'Well, no, George, he's one of the few holdouts but he's only in for two or three million.'

'He didn't like me much, did he?'

'No, I don't think he did.'

'That thing at the swimming hole. I was only doing what I thought was right.'

'You were, George, you were.'

The landline on the little table next to George rang and he looked at the phone with a benign curiosity as if this ringing too was an interesting thing, just as interesting as the fact that seventy-odd banks had just agreed to lend him 600,000,000 bucks. Rowley rose from the sofa and picked up the phone.

'Is that Mr Smith, Mr Timothy Smith?'

'No, this is his assistant, Rowland Beavan. May I ask who's calling?'

'This is the Denver Police Department, sir. We would greatly appreciate a few words with Mr Smith, if that is possible. It's pretty much a routine thing.'

'Well, I'm afraid that won't be possible tonight. As you may or may not know, Mr Smith is recovering from a severe stroke and it is vital not to prejudice his recovery.'

'Yes, sir, we are well aware of Mr Smith's medical condition and are extremely sorry to have to disturb you both. Would it be convenient to you if we dropped by tomorrow some time?'

'Well, as long as it is only a couple of minutes, and I'm afraid I shall have to do most of the talking for him.'

'That's just fine by us, sir. Would 10.30 a.m. be convenient?'

'We'll see you then, Officer.'

Damn and fuck and double fuck. He had known the moment he did it that his moment of panic would come back to haunt them. He could not quite foretell how. He had imagined some trouble with paying the bill at the hospital, or his accidentally calling George by his true name in front of the doctor or the waiter, but this was worse, much worse. Even if the police stayed only five minutes as they had promised, the first thing they would want would be George's

passport and papers. So far they had survived by paying for everything on Rowley's Amex, but they were done for now. The general
alert for Timbo must have been passed on from Brazil to the FBI,
because where would an Englishman on the run from the Amazon
flee but the United States? And the first place to look for him was
among current or recent hospital patients (whether physical or
mental). Rowley walked towards the panorama window, scuffing his
toes into the carpet again, asking his brains for a miracle. This time
all he wanted was an escape route. He and George had to be out of
Denver by sunup and without leaving a vapour trail.

'George,' he said, 'would you like to play a game of patience while
I pop out for ten minutes?'

'Patience is a great game.'

Rowley brought the packs over and fixed George a glass of elderflower. Then he put on his overcoat – the evenings were still chilly
– and slipped out along the passage to the service lift. He rode down
to the basement and walked up the ramp behind a laundry truck
which happened to be leaving too. Then he walked half a dozen long
blocks down to a little park where he had briefly sunned himself on
bright Denver mornings, to get a breath after being shut up with
George in Suite 2301. He figured he was out of the hotel Wi-Fi
range here, and he was trusting to luck that the police did not yet
have his mobile phone number and so could not hack into his calls.

There was a flight out of Denver at ten minutes to midnight
which landed at JFK at 6.45 a.m. He booked two economy seats
in the names of Dick Francis and Rowland Francis. They could be
cousins, he thought, and Francis happened to be his second name.
Then he called Hal Gombrich.

'Hal, we need to talk face-to-face, *urgentissimo*.'

'That will be the most frabjous pleasure. Come stay the weekend
at Buckley's Landing. I can promise you *otium cum dignitate* and a
glass or two of tolerable Falernian.'

'We fly into JFK at a quarter of seven.'

'My chariot will await you.'

'Can your chauffeur make it to the runway? My friend is not a
well man.'

'The tarmacadam is Alberto's second home. He is a complete
stranger to Arrivals. *Salve atque vale*, my friend.'

Rowley walked back to the LonePine Suites, and took the service elevator up from the garage to 2301. George was only halfway through his patience.

He hustled George into his jacket and then looked for his overcoat because it was a chilly night, but George gripped him with his meaty hands and thrust his heavy flushed face close to Rowley's.

'Have you got it?'

'Got what?'

'The en-vel-ope.'

'What envelope?'

'Moon … shine … in desk.'

Rowley followed George's staring eyes to the faux-Chippendale bureau in the corner. It seemed quicker to humour him and he went over to the desk and to his surprise there in the top left drawer was a fat unmarked envelope. George must have been compos enough to bring it with him and then to stow it away, which showed how much whatever it was mattered to him. He put it in his pocket and gave George a reassuring smile.

'I'll look at it later, George, when we're in the plane.'

'Don't look … give me.' Seeing that he wasn't going to budge without the envelope, Rowley put it in his outstretched hands. Then he went back to the clumsy business of heaving him into his overcoat and taking him along the corridor.

When Rowley had asked Hertz to deliver the car to the LonePine, it was not for use as a getaway vehicle. He had hoped that he might be able to take George for the occasional afternoon spin in the mountains, but in the event he decided it was too risky to take him out at all. So the car had sat in the basement garage, which in present circumstances could not have been handier. The only problem was that to raise the exit barrier you needed to insert your room keycard, which alerted Reception to the fact that you were leaving the building, and without paying too. He was pondering this when he spotted the car valet polishing someone's bumper a few yards from the exit.

'Hey, Mike, you couldn't put your card in for me, could you? I left mine up in the room.'

'Sure thing, boss.'

Rowley flipped a five out of the window as the barrier rose and the valet saluted briskly and they drove up the ramp into the frosty night air.

When they were safely airborne, he helped George out of his overcoat again. He was about to give it to the stewardess to hang up when he felt the edge of the fat manila envelope in the pocket. Well, he thought, I am in loco parentis, I need to know what's going on, and he slipped the envelope into his own pocket.

He waited until George was sunk in snoring slumber. As the plane soared back East to meet the dawn, he began to read.

At first the only thing he could make sense of in the wad of papers was the reference on the top sheet – Moonshine HG/GdosSF. The rest was a jumble of technical data which only a computer geek like Furcht could hope to grapple with. At the end, there was a cover sheet signing off on the project, whatever it was, and the signature 'H de P Gombrich' and the date. As far as technical stuff went, all Rowley could manage was to look up the stock prices on his phone, and he was surprised that Hal, the old classicist dilettante, should apparently be so at home with the IT lingo and the engineering data mixed in with it. There was a small sheaf of technical drawings, what looked like cross sections of a pipeline and some sort of lifting gear. Some of the drawings bore place names – Wildcat Mountain, Dorothy's Crossing, Green Hollow – and there were one or two partial street maps, of places he'd never heard of – Carteret, NJ, Sunbury, PA. Rowley was never one to labour over things he couldn't immediately get the hang of, so he put the envelope back in George's pocket and went to sleep.

'Ah, yes,' Hal Gombrich said, not the least discomposed as he poured coffee out of a Colonial silver pot. Beyond the veranda, the lawn stretched down to the estuary where the first dinghies of the day were already racing. 'You'd better let me have that envelope. We don't want it getting into the wrong hands. I was rather opposed to George seeing the technical specs at all, but he's a devil for detail. By the way, would he care for some breakfast, do you think?'

'He'll sleep for hours yet,' Rowley said.

'After he procured us that drill from Brazil, he wouldn't stop badgering us about how it was all going.'

'He never told me a thing.'

'Quite right too, but *tempora mutantur nos et mutamur in illis.* You are now willy-nilly George's guardian. Nobody else has any idea of the state he is in. You and I hold the fate of this great enterprise in our hands. It is only fitting that I should enlighten you about Moonshine because our little plans are trembling in the balance. If you remained in ignorance, you might, quite inadvertently of course, spill the beans, and I cannot tell you how precious those beans are going to be.'

'Is it to do with Beaky Bentliff?'

'It has everything to do with Beaky and with Joey Schubart and my dear friends the String Bags and every other hedge funder you've ever heard of and quite a few you haven't. Only they don't know it yet. Because we're going to top-slice them as cleanly as a *jamón ibérico*, we're going to front-run them so fast they'll never know we were there until they look at the bottom line. This is payback time, my dear Rowland, and how sweet it is.'

XI

Downriver

When he woke, he had the worst thirst of his life. His throat was burning as though it was being raked with steel bristles. The hut was black, tar-black. He remembered there being a low door but he could not even see the outline of it. It must be night outside. Had he only slept a couple of hours? Hard to believe because what he could remember was that he had felt unutterably tired. He remembered too that he could not move even before they had tightened the ropes on his bare skin and he could not speak either. It was like that state at the beginning of an operation when the anaesthetic is taking hold and you cannot move or speak, but you can still see the doctors moving around in their green gowns and half-hear what they are saying to each other. Only it hadn't been doctors but that strange couple from the boat cooing to each other as they tightened the ropes. He thought he heard the woman say 'Timbo' but he couldn't answer, and then he thought what she – it was the woman – was saying was 'Bimbo', so she wasn't talking to him because the only person who called him Bimbo was Lethal who wasn't here and anyway the man was calling her Topsy, so it couldn't be the couple from the boat at all.

Timbo could feel the insects moving over his body and the terrible stinging they had left all across his lower abdomen and his groin. He tried to shift his hips to dislodge them and he felt a slithery mess under his buttocks. He must have fouled himself in his sleep, or had he half-woken and crapped and then gone off again without being aware of doing it? Or had a whole day passed, and the sun sliced in at the door and at the gaps in the wattle walls and then gone away again?

As he looked around him in the encircling gloom, he saw that he was no longer in the huge great maloca he had chosen to go to sleep in. They must have moved him to this much smaller hut, no more than six foot square, it looked. As he felt about him, he found that he was caged in a sort of rope cradle, which they must have carried him here in. They, who were they, that strange couple from the boat, and where were they now?

He tried to wriggle into a more comfortable position, but found his back grinding against the tight ropes. He lay still to get his breath back. As his breathing got easier again, his whole body was shaken by a shudder of terror. He could not stop shuddering for what seemed like several minutes. He felt pitifully weak and cornered and he began to sob and to shudder again as he sobbed. The crying consumed him so utterly that at first he did not notice the noise on the roof. To begin with, it was only a soft sound, like muffled drums. Then the drumming became harder and louder, and he realised that it was raining.

The drumming of the rain was so insistent now that he did not hear the two figures come into the hut until they were standing beside him: a man and a woman, but not the English couple from the boat; these were two Indians, both tiny, barely more than five feet tall, if that, as far as he could tell in the darkness of the hut. The woman had a damp cloth in her hand and she began to wipe his whole naked body, quite gently, so that he began to think she might be friendly, and he gestured as best he could with his tethered wrists to indicate that he wanted to be untied, but she shook her head and the man standing beside her made a gesture of disapproval. But then he stepped forward and handed Timbo a wooden bowl containing some sort of gluey mass. He raised it clumsily to his lips; it was sweet and warm, rather like potato soup but with an odd bitter aftertaste; and he slurped it down gratefully, then handed it back and again gestured that he wanted to be untied. The man shook his head, but quite mildly as though Timbo ought to know that this was a futile request. And then they were gone.

It must be daylight outside now, and little shards of dusty light came in through the chinks in the palm-leaf walls, not enough to dispel the gloom. He was desperately tired and wanted to sleep again, but the chafing of the ropes and the stings of the insects kept him awake. All the same, he must have drifted off somehow, because it was dark when he became conscious of his surroundings again, and it wasn't long before the two Indians came in once more, the man carrying the bowl of sweet potato mush, the woman with the damp cloth. Their return sank his spirits further still. These were clearly his jailers, and his stay would not be a short one. He tried sign language again despite his tethered wrists, pointing to the wattle door and then to himself. The man shook his head. Timbo put up a single finger, then two, then, three hoping to indicate that he wanted to know how long he would be kept here. The man shook his head.

That was the first day, and the second, and the third was much the same. First there was the boredom, the suffocating boredom and loneliness and sense of abandonment, but also the bewilderment as the third day began to fade. What were they keeping him alive for? Were they waiting for some headman to come and decide his future, perhaps to finish him off in person? Or were they waiting for orders from much higher up, the Enida bosses perhaps, who had not yet made up their minds? But the searing pain of the ropes and the insect bites prevented him from thinking too much, certainly from thinking coherently. He tried to mark off the days by scratching with his fingernail on the nearest thick bit of creeper, but the fingernail left no mark. Then again the dismal glimmering of the next day, and the silent visits of his captors who still did not respond to his gestures, though they did bring him water when he mimed thirst with his index finger and his open mouth.

He was managing to keep count of the days in his head, or thought he was, and it was the seventh morning when he woke from his tortured sleep and suddenly found that he could move his arms. There were no creepers binding them any more. Then he twisted his neck to look at his legs, which were still tied up, but now he had his hands free, he managed to work his legs free too, and then extricated his feet. He lay there exhausted by the effort, and very gingerly rolled over and rolled free. Still feeling unutterably weak, he did manage to sit up, and then he became aware that his hand was supporting itself on a piece of cloth, a garment of some kind loosely folded on the ground beside him. He recognised it as the sort of loose trousers the Indians wore, and underneath there was a ragged shirt and a cord belt. He staggered to his feet, but his legs were so shaky that he crumpled to the ground again. He looked round to see if there was anyone watching. Nothing but total silence, except for the metallic calls of the birds outside. Was it possible that they wanted him to go? Was it becoming too dangerous to keep him prisoner any longer? Ridiculous to dream of any prospect of rescue, but at least they might want to see the back of him. He managed to crawl the short distance across the hut, no more than four or five feet, and pushed very gently against the door. It opened.

He went back to put on the shirt and trousers, aching in every limb. Then he heard the rain begin again on the roof. This time when he stood up, he managed to stay standing and to hobble across to the door again and push it open.

Timbo went out into the black deluge and stood a few yards from the hut, letting the water sluice all over his body, washing away the bugs and the muck and relieving the pain of the bites. It was the most delicious shower he had ever taken. He raised his head to the early-morning sky and let the water splash over his face and down his burning throat. He gulped and gulped until he could take no more, then he paused because he was breathing heavily from the effort and began to gulp again. The noise of the storm in the trees and the unrelieved dark blotted out all other thoughts as he drank and drank.

There was only one path from his hut leading away from the maloca hut, and he followed it, walking stiff-legged with red-hot cramp running down his calves.

It was a little lighter now, and he could begin to make out the outlines of the coconut palms tossing in the storm, and then the grey glimmer of the village huts. There wasn't a soul about.

Better still, just in front of one of the huts there was a plastic bucket with a pile of bananas in it just visible in the half-light. Timbo stumbled on, munching one of the bananas as he went and cradling the rest of the bunch under his arm, then gulping more rainwater when he had finished the banana.

The rutted track back into the jungle was easy to pick up. As he came into the thick of the forest, he was aware of the dawn, grey and listless at first through the treetops, then shot with pink and peachy streaks as the storm died down, and the birds began singing their odd bell-like tweets and rattles.

He was ankle-deep in mud now and he moved off the track into the mossy undergrowth in search of firmer ground. The trees swung low under the weight of the drooping mosses and lichens which frolicked up their gnarled boughs. The opulent damp smell of the fungi was suffocating and the mosses were spongy under his bare feet. He tripped over a twisted root and found himself face down in the mushy forest floor. He lay there for several minutes in the emerald ooze, feeling utterly desolate. Then he suddenly remembered the same overpowering stink from a walk years ago in a sodden wood somewhere in the valley of the Upper Dart, with Moth behind him going on about the ancient wildwoods which he said this was a tiny fragment of, because the rest had been nibbled away over the centuries by the sheep grazing the moor. 'Sheepwrecked,' Moth had said in his thick frothy voice, and then repeated the joke because he was so pleased with it, though Timbo suspected it wasn't his own. Timbo had cried bitter tears then, aged ten or eleven, because he desperately wanted to be back home in the dry, watching TV, and he cried now, snuffling his sobs into the dripping mosses. But for some reason the thought of Moth braced him, and he started shaking off the shaggy green sludge and the queer orange fungus shaped like human fingers which stuck to his bare arms as though it wanted to grow on him too, and he eventually managed to stagger back to his feet.

He tried to work out how far it would be to the river station. The Land Rover had taken hours, four or five hours in total not counting stops, he reckoned. But most of the time it had been unable to bump along much above walking pace. It might be no more than a couple of days on foot at most, and you could live on bananas and rainwater for ever.

He walked on the crackly leaf mould at the side of the track. The bites still stung him, especially round his genitals, but the cramp had gone and the burning in his throat was not as bad as it had been. Then he caught sight of the sun shining on a little stream and he saw it was where they had stopped for a piss and Pablo the driver had spotted the baby cayman slithering under the leaves. That had been about twenty minutes from the village in the Land Rover and now it must have taken not much more than an hour to walk back to the spot. That was when he first heard about Enida. He had sent the text to Luke later when the others weren't looking. He wondered whether Luke had been able to make sense of his question.

He stopped to scoop water from the puddles the storm had left behind. In one or two places the rainwater had gathered in the hollow of a dead tree or in a cupped leaf of one of the giant bushes, which looked a bit like rhododendrons but could not be because Moth had grown rhodies at home and had taught him they came from the foothills of the Himalayas. After he had had enough rainwater, he munched another banana. It was quiet in the forest now that the sun had risen.

Presumably it was the Indian couple who had loosened the ropes and left the door unfastened. They must have had enough of him, and would not want trouble. It was hard to imagine worse trouble than a decomposing foreigner being discovered in one of their huts. Or was he eventually let go on instructions from higher up, from the Enida bosses? But surely they would have been content for him to moulder away until the maggots got him. Enida did not much care whether he lived or died, so long as he was eliminated from the game and his disappearance would be a warning to others. No, game was the wrong word. K and K hadn't come all the way from Norwich, or wherever they really came from, to play anything resembling a game. But then had it actually been them in the hut urging each other on to truss him up like a turkey, or had he already been in the first stages of delirium when he thought he heard them calling each other Bimbo and Topsy?

But perhaps the Indians had let him go on their own initiative, and Enida had never consented to his release. Or was it their plan to play cat and mouse with him, scooping him up again and then letting him go? Either way, he had to stay hidden. If Enida knew he was on the loose without their say-so – he had taken to assuming that his persecutors were part of Enida, though he knew no more who or what Enida was than what Rapha had told him and Rapha didn't seem to know much – they would finish him off without a moment's compunction if they needed to.

Whatever Enida was, it was now clear to him that Raphael Alvarez must be in with them. For it was Rapha who had brought him up the Tapajós and into the forest. It was academic whether it was he or the village girls who had spiked his drink. He had led Timbo into the trap and must have made sure that he was securely trussed up before he melted back into the forest. He was probably even now waiting to greet the next sucker who came upriver. All that stuff about his grandfather having been guide to Henry Ford's men. His grandfather had probably led the ignorant Yanks to the worst spot on the Amazon for growing rubber. They were all hereditary con artists waiting on the quayside to fool any idiot who fancied trying his luck in the forest.

Ahead of him the trees were thinning out and slivers of sunlight were slicing between the bare trunks. He must be somewhere near that desolate clearing in the forest where the men had been at work with their chainsaws.

Timbo stepped aside from the track and moved carefully from one tree to the next, trying not to let himself show through the gaps in the forest. It must have taken him a quarter of an hour to cover the last hundred yards before he could safely peer out at the clearing.

It was deserted. There was not a man or a vehicle anywhere. Nothing moved in the silent wasteland, except here and there a stutter of smoke from the bonfires which were still smouldering. The fresh tractor tracks on the road leading out of the clearing were the only evidence of recent occupation. For a moment Timbo thought that they might have finished work on the site, but then he saw that at the far end there was a jumble of felled trees which had not yet been stripped or trimmed. There was plenty of work still to be done here. The gang must have pulled out in a hurry, not stopping to put out the bonfires, despite the fire hazard. Something must have frightened them badly.

He crouched in the shade of the trees staring out at this sunlit wasteland, as though it would tell him what had happened if only he stared hard enough. The smell of the woodsmoke drifted across into the place where he was crouching and he began to feel drowsy. But he had to keep going. He stumbled on for an hour or more. His feet were giving him grief now, worse even than the insect bites, with the cuts and bruises from the thorns and broken branches he had trampled on. He lay down to rest on a drift of dry leaves and dozed off almost the moment he lay down.

As he woke, he shivered and shivered again. For a minute or so, he lost control and then he needed to empty himself. Crouching in the undergrowth with his ragged trousers down to his ankles, he felt that he had come to the end. He stood up again and pulled up his trousers. Suddenly there was a wild screeching overhead and a flock of blue and yellow macaws exploded out of the trees and into the prairie. Then they wheeled abruptly as though they did not fancy the open spaces and skeetered back into the trees above his head and were lost in the forest.

He began, very cautiously, to make his way down the slope, keeping a few yards inside the forest, here trimmed to a relentless straight edge by the bulldozers. The undergrowth was thinner lower down the hill and he was soon making ground at a fair rate. His hope was that there would be a stream or river he could follow down to where it met the Tapajós. It was probably nearly an hour before he reached a boundary fence and a thick swathe of trees beyond it. As he clambered awkwardly over the fence, he heard the sound of waters splashing over rocks and for the first time he dared to hope that he might get out alive.

He was so eager to reach the water that he tripped over two fallen branches and fell head first into the stream, bruised and tousled, and then lapping like a thirsty dog. The fall had knocked the last two bananas out of his grip but they snagged on the rocks next to him and he reached out and began to eat one. There was a narrow path beaten out on the far side of the water and he waded across the waist-high stream and began to follow it down in a battered daze. He must be going more or less parallel to the track that the Land Rover had followed from the jetty. With a bit of luck he might hit upon the landing before nightfall.

In fact the light was only just beginning to go as the stream widened and the trees began to clear and he could see the huddle of huts that straggled down to the quayside. At last things were going his way. True, he was on the wrong side of the stream, but that might not be such a bad thing. He could lie up for the night undercover and swim across in the morning.

There was no view of the big river from where he was, but as he was straining to catch a glimpse of it through the trees, he jumped at the sombre hoot of a ship's siren. The hooting seemed to come from very close by. He could not tell whether the boat was going up or down the river. All the same, it was an opportunity that might not come again soon.

Timbo slipped into the stream and half-swam, half-drifted with the current to the other side. He managed to grab hold of an exposed mangrove root and hauled himself up onto the muddy bank. Standing there dripping and panting, he could not imagine how they would possibly let him on the boat in his bedraggled state. His only hope was to sidle up to the quayside and pick a moment to slip aboard when no one was looking.

He was out onto a grassy spit of land now and it seemed better to amble across it in a nonchalant manner as if taking his *passeio* and then drop back into hiding again. As he came nearer the jetty, he saw the outline of a man sitting on the grass. He jumped when the man turned and said: 'No, I don't believe it, it's you. I never thought I'd see you alive again.'

'Pablo.' The little guy who drove the Land Rover and spent his spare moments with his head in a porn magazine.

'That rat Rapha said you were tired and they were taking you to a hut to sleep it off. Then he disappeared in the Land Rover and I had to walk back to the site. I slept in the van and the next morning we heard you'd gone missing. Hey, you wanna catch that boat? It's the *direto* to Manaus.'

'Yes, but I haven't got any money.'

'Don't worry, I know the Captain, we were in school together. Just sit here and I'll whistle when you can go aboard.'

Pablo embraced him. Timbo realised that he was a little drunk. They were companions in misfortune. Timbo felt like crying again.

He sat on the bench watching the lights of the boat come on as it angled across the middle of the great river towards the jetty.

A gaggle of passengers began to stagger aboard heaving their luggage along the narrow gangway. Timbo wondered if he had missed Pablo's whistle. His spirits went down as he saw the crew moving towards their casting-off stations. But then he heard the low whistle, like a nightbird in the dusk. And he ran across to the gangway.

Pablo was there in the shadow of the boat. He embraced him again. Timbo smelled the beer on his breath.

'Don't say a word. You're my cousin, who's in trouble with the police.'

At the top of the gangway there was a man in grubby white ducks who led him down silently to a bar on the lower deck and pulled a beer out of the fridge and handed it to him and pointed him into a little room behind the bar and then left him, still without saying a word. There was a tiny bunk in the room and when he finished the beer Timbo curled himself up into it and slept until the grey dawn began to fill the fogged porthole behind him.

He remembered the address of the Furcht office: No. 11, Avenida Vargas. And he remembered who to ask for: Furcht's general manager in Brazil, Arturo Nicols, who George had described as the most trustworthy man in South America. Not a lot of competition there. He had avoided contacting Arturo when he came through before, because he suspected that the entire Furcht operation had been penetrated, and he wanted to stay undercover as far as possible. Now he needed all the help he could get.

He limped up from the harbour through the scrubby low streets until he came to the broad high-rise avenues of the business district. He saw some boys jumping in and out of a fountain under the acacia trees, and when they had gone he had a splash himself and let the water cascade over his stubbly cheeks.

His feet were hurting badly now. But at least this was not a city in which an unshaven man going barefoot looked out of place. Even in the business district there were plenty of bums and derelicts on the street. All the same, he expected trouble at No. 11.

The tall commissionaire stood immovable in front of him, barring the way to the revolving doors.

'What is your business?'

'I have to see Senhor Arturo Nicols.'

'Does he know you are coming?'

'Yes, he does,' Timbo lied.

'Will you write your name down, please.'

'I have no pen.'

The doorman stared in silent contempt at this penless vagrant. Then he turned inside, returning with a pen and a notepad.

Timbo wrote his name. The commissionaire disappeared again. Timbo sat on the steps of the enormous glass building and examined the cuts and bruises on the soles of his feet. He was beginning to wonder whether Arturo Nicols had been such a good idea and whether he should try and think up some alternative next move when a blue Mercedes drove past and a man with a black moustache leant out of the driver's window.

'Get in the back, quick.'

Timbo jumped in and was about to sit down when the driver said in a rapid, low voice, 'No, lie down, under the blanket, and don't speak.'

The car drove on. He lay under the blanket inhaling a smell of old dog and still trembling from the speed of the pickup. The driver flicked some slow Latin American dance music on the stereo. One of the speakers was right by Timbo's head and the mournful, halting beat throbbed straight into his ear. He had heard music like this playing in the bar on the *Vera Sotomayor* the night he and Rapha had got drunk together. They must have driven for fifteen or twenty minutes before he felt the car swing hard left and then go slowly down a short steep incline. The car stopped, the door next to his head opened and the man with the black moustache gently removed the blanket from him.

'I apologise for the melodrama but we had to move off quickly. You were sitting outside the front of our office for a good half-hour. Plenty of time for them to be alerted.'

'I am sorry, I didn't know where else to go.'

'Absolutely, I quite understand. I can only say how overjoyed we are to see you alive. I was firmly convinced that we were destined never to meet in this world. Oh, by the way, Arturo Nicols.' He put out a big hairy hand. 'We had better get upstairs. This place is supposed to be secure but—' He shrugged his shoulders and ushered Timbo out of the car, across the underground car park and into the lift at the back. When they were in the elevator, Arturo Nicols clasped Timbo's hands warmly like a lover who has to wait to be in private before he can show his affection, and he smiled, a big open smile of relief and welcome, and Timbo was hard put not to burst into tears.

The elevator opened into a tiny private lobby, three or four floors up. Arturo unlocked his front door and led Timbo into an airy sitting room full of glass tables and low sofas. The venetian blinds were drawn and the morning sun was filtered gently through the slats.

'My wife Angelina.'

A dignified woman with braided hair rose from the sofa and shook his hand.

'Angelina, we need coffee and *rocambole*. Mr Smith is starving. Meanwhile I will find some clothes for you. We are about the same height but not, alas, the same width.' He patted his stomach with mock melancholy.

'I am sure you need a bath, senhor,' Angelina Nicols said. 'I do not mean—' She laughed.

'No, no, you are quite right, there is nothing in the world I would like more.'

'Except the *rocambole*,' Arturo added. 'It's the Brazilian cake with guava marmalade. For that it is almost worth getting lost in the jungle.'

She had put some fragrant creamy unguent in the bath she had run for him. He felt his cuts and stings and bruises yield to the delicious balm. His whole body sank into a unique and wonderful languor. There was a white fluffy gown on the back of the door and fluffy slippers to match.

'You look better already, my friend. There is nothing I would like more than to make you at home here and help you to relax after your ordeal. But I must not offer you false comfort. I cannot disguise from you that your position remains perilous in the extreme. But first please tell me quickly exactly what has happened to you.'

Timbo gulped down the coffee and began on the rich spicy cake which Senhora Nicols handed him. In between mouthfuls he told them the story of his days in the forest – how many days it had been he still had no clear idea.

'The interpreter? You keep talking about "your interpreter". I do not understand,' Arturo broke in.

'The interpreter you sent to meet me at the airport.'

'I sent no interpreter. After we had met, I would have gladly found an interpreter for you if you needed one, but I sent nobody to the airport.'

'You don't know Raphael Alvarez at all?'

'Never heard of him. Whoever he is, he should never have taken you so far upriver. It is too dangerous now. Enida has its people everywhere. There were three men killed in a fire at a logging station in the northern Mato Grosso last week at the edge of the forest. And it is not only the burning. A man was shot in a gun battle near Belvista a few days before that. There is no doubt that Enida is quite ruthless. They do not care how many people die in the course of their operations, so long as the logging stops. I do not deny that there have been many terrible incidents on the other side in the past, when the illegals have forced the Indians off their land at gunpoint, and some of those guns have gone off. But two blacks do not make a white, and who wants a civil war?'

'You mentioned Enida. It is the first time I have heard the word outside the forest.'

'We have heard whispers for months. Everyone has. But now the whispers are so loud that we are all talking about Enida, but even now none of us really knows what exactly we are talking about. I see no reason why we should not blame Enida also for the terrible things that have happened to you. But that is not the worst of it.'

'What do you mean?'

'I too have a story to tell about you.'

'About me?' Timbo wondered if Arturo had got his pronouns mixed up.

'Well, about someone who is both you and is not you.'

Timbo did not even need to open his mouth to signal his bemusement.

'Last week a body was found in the Hotel Júnior in the Avenida Rocha. The body was fully clothed, wearing a three-piece suit in fact, and carrying your documents – passport, credit cards and so on. He had red hair which has subsequently turned out to be dyed, and his face had enough of a resemblance to your passport photograph to pass for you, that is, until they had the DNA evidence.'

'How could they have any DNA evidence for me? I was lying tied up in a hut miles away.'

'Not DNA from you but from the body of some bum who had been strangled and then stolen from the morgue and transferred to the hotel, but not before the guys at the morgue had taken his DNA in case they could establish his identity. So now they know for sure that the body is not you.'

'What a weird thing to do, to tie me up and try to fool everyone into thinking I've been murdered.'

'It is horrible. And of course the police also have to start thinking, why should anyone do a crazy thing like that, and if it's not you, where are you? And one of the lines of inquiry the police are following now, quite naturally I must admit, is that you might have staged your own disappearance.'

'Why on earth would I want to do that?'

'Well, to start with, they couldn't think of a reason. But then the news of these atrocities began to come in, and so it's an easy leap from there to thinking that you disappeared in order to undertake this terrorist campaign without coming under suspicion for the very good reason that you're dead.'

'So they think that I am the terrorist, not Enida.'

'No, you still haven't quite got it yet. They think you *are* Enida or at any rate a leading agent of Enida.'

'Christ almighty.'

'They don't need to make their suspicions public yet, because there is already a nationwide alert out for you as a missing person. Officially, you might have been kidnapped or have lost your reason and gone wandering. But I have enough contacts in the police to be able to tell you this for sure: if you turn yourself in at any police station in Brazil, you will be immediately arrested and charged with arson and manslaughter and probably murder too. At the same time, your friends in Enida can sit back and watch you squirm. Any time they want to reel you in, they can hack into the police inquiries and nip in ahead of them to track you down and finish you off. The police would assume that your murder – your second murder if you like – was a revenge attack by a bunch of berserk loggers. And you would go to your grave earmarked as the British terrorist who ran amok in the jungle and the police would stop looking for anyone else in connection with these crimes. Is "earmarked" the right word exactly? Even after all these years I still have difficulties with my English.'

'"Earmarked" will do fine,' Timbo said glumly, 'though "tagged" would be better still, I think.'

'I'm putting all this as frankly as I can, because I don't want you to be under any illusion about how dangerous your situation is and how essential it is that your presence here remains secret. For the same reason, I do not intend to let Mr Furcht or his people here or in London know that you have turned up with us. I shall say nothing to anyone who comes looking for you. And I suggest that you observe the same silence, and that includes your friend the professor and his wife. I have no confidence that any of our communications networks is secure. In any case, ever since I became George's general manager I have despaired of his invariable tendency to come blundering into any delicate situation and make it far worse. Besides, he has enough on his plate just now, don't you think? There is a lot to be said anyway for leaving as many people as possible believing that you are still running around the forest, if indeed you are alive at all. So you stay disappeared — that is something we are quite good at in South America.'

'Fine, I won't tell anyone,' Timbo murmured weakly.

'I don't want you to start imagining either that you can simply slip out of this building and catch a taxi to the airport. I'd be happy to advance you money for the flight and more. Mr Furcht has already authorised me to let you have up to 20k sterling if you need it. But I just don't think you'd make it, now that half the population of Brazil has a pretty good idea what you look like.'

'Another piece of *rocambole*?' enquired Senhora Nicols, raising the silver cake-knife like a question mark.

'The truth is that if you go out of here looking like yourself you are dead meat. I can see only one way out, literally, and this brings me to the first bit of good luck you have enjoyed since you came to our country.'

'Luck?' Timbo queried vaguely, as though he had never heard the word before and needed to try it out.

'Let me tell you, Timothy, what this country is really famous for. You will say coffee, or the samba or the Amazon. But today what Brazil is really celebrated for is plastic surgery. People come here from all over the world to have their faces and their bodies reshaped and made even more beautiful than nature intended. You want a tummy tuck or a bum lift or a nose job, you come to Brazil. There are a dozen holiday companies offering vacation packages with comprehensive cosmetic surgery and luxurious aftercare included. Some people go to Peru, because it is cheaper, but the Peruvians are butchers. You will come back from Lima looking like that poor woman in Paris, the Bride of Wildenstein. Our Brazilian surgeons are artists. You will see on their brass plates "*Cirurgia Estética*" – aesthetic surgery. It is a beautiful phrase, and for us each operation is a work of art. When I first met my wife, she was the theatre nurse to her brother Jorge Paravicini. Jorge is one of the finest plastic surgeons in Brazil, which means he is one of the finest in the world. Today they are partners in his private clinic which is housed in the mezzanine of this building. She likes to keep her hand in now and then by helping him out in theatre.

'You see where I am drifting. I honestly believe that your best, in fact your only, chance of getting out of Manaus in one piece is to place yourself in the hands of Jorge – and of Angelina of course.'

Senhora Nicols gave Timbo an encouraging smile.

'I happen to know that Jorge is free for the rest of the day. I know this for the simple reason that we always play golf on Wednesdays. I have already suggested to him that we cancel our game for this afternoon and that he plays a round with you instead.'

'You really are sure it's the only way out?'

'Regrettably I fear that it is. Your distinctive red hair will have to be shaved off first of course and a pair of plain glasses will help too, but such obvious measures are unlikely to be enough. We are dealing with professionals. I do not know exactly what will be necessary, we must leave that to Jorge. You are booked in for 2 p.m. He thinks that a general anaesthetic would be best to give him more time and scope.'

'And afterwards, what happens after?'

'Ah, I am sorry, I forgot to mention that we also have a rather comfortable recuperative suite where you can repose until the bandages are removed and the scars have begun to heal, though with Jorge the scars will be minimal. A week or so should suffice. Do not worry. We shall look after you. Angelina is a wonderful cook as well as an excellent nurse. You shall have as many slices of *rocambole* as you can eat, though no more just now because of the anaesthetic or you might throw up. Mr Furcht will be happy to pay all the expenses. After all, he got you into this mess.'

Timbo did not feel like arguing. It seemed to be one of those bets that you could not afford not to take, although you had little idea what the real odds might be. If his passport photograph was on the wall of every police station in Brazil, the chances of being recognised as soon as he left the safety of the Nicolses' flat sounded prohibitively high.

'If you would care to come downstairs now, I could give you the shave and you could have a little rest before you see my brother.'

Senhora Nicols led him out to the elevator. They said nothing much as they rode down to the mezzanine, but her smile was cheering and her delicate scent filled his mind, that and the sheen of her hair. It was months since he had kissed a woman and that was an occasion he did not wish to think about.

She showed him into a sunny little room with a view of the garden at the back of the building. The room smelled of beeswax polish and something else, eucalyptus, was it? It was a quiet and soothing place.

'If you don't mind, we thought it would be best if you were shaved all over so that there is no trace anywhere of your lovely red hair.'

'Nobody has ever called my hair lovely before,' he said.

'Well, I think it is,' she laughed, and spread out a towel on the bed and left him to undress. When he was naked, she came back into the room wearing a white coat.

'Oh, you poor man, all those cuts and bruises. I'll try not to hurt.'

She rubbed some cream into his head and began gently shaving him. As he lay on the bed, the flap of her white coat brushed against his bare chest. Out of the corner of his eye he saw his rusty curls falling on the towel.

'Like Samson,' he said.

'What? Oh, yes. I don't think I'd make a very good Delilah.'

'I'm sure you would.'

'In fact,' she said, 'I seem to remember that it wasn't Delilah who did the shaving. She got a servant in to do the work.'

'This is much better.'

'Anyway, you need not worry that it is going to deprive you of your strength. After all, in the Bible Samson's hair grew again and he managed to pull down the pillars of the Temple.'

But he did begin to wonder about the healing. Had the hair really had something to do with it after all?

'It would be worse for you, though, wouldn't it, losing your hair?' he said, partly to cheer himself up.

'Yes, it would, I think. Much worse. When our sister had breast cancer and lost her hair after the chemo, she cried for a whole day. I've nearly finished. I won't show you in the mirror just yet. It might give you quite a shock.'

She had such a comforting way of talking that he was beginning to think that perhaps he didn't mind so much about the whole thing. His face had never been his fortune after all. When he first got to know Aurore, she said she was amazed she could fall in love with a man who was so ugly – in fact that had been the first time she said she loved him.

Angelina began to smear the cream over his body. As she slowly drew the razor to and fro, he felt as though he was in a luxury spa, which in a sense he was. At the end of it all, he felt strangely refreshed. The shaving was like being shriven of your sins.

'I hope your brother has as gentle a touch as you.'

'Oh, yes, we are very alike, you know. We are Italian by descent. Italians all have gentle hands. I'll bring you a cup of mint tea and then you must rest.'

Dr Paravicini did look very like his sister: the same dark eyes full of light and the sheen on his dark hair.

'Some of my older colleagues would have more experience than I in this particular line,' he said. 'After the war, you know, there were many people coming to this country who wanted to look different. These days people just wish to look better. I hope that we shall achieve both these things for you. It will require a certain amount of work, I think. Even without the hair yours is a rather distinctive face.'

Timbo sat in a dentist's chair with the light from the garden window flooding in on his face. Jorge Paravicini unhooked a stalk from the array of instruments on the silver gantry in front of the chair. He circled the tiny lens around Timbo's face, checking the angles against the images showing up on the little screen next to him.

'Yes,' he said, 'a decidedly distinctive face but not so difficult to reshape so that your mother would not recognise you.'

Timbo thought briefly of Mia and what a fluttery panic she would be in if she had known a quarter of what he had been through, or the pickle he was now in – pickle was her default term for any setback ranging from a missed bus to a mortal illness.

'I never really knew my mother, I'm afraid. I was mostly brought up by my grandfather and his second wife, my stepgran. And she's just died.'

'I am so sorry, but in this connection perhaps that is just as well. I have known mothers react rather violently when they see what I have done to their sons. I should add that wives tend to be less troubled by the results. A question, I suppose, of being or not being one's own flesh and blood.'

'Yes, I can see that.'

'What I would suggest is really quite modest, I might even say standard. I would first propose to raise the bridge of your nose perhaps three millimetres to give it an outline more towards the aquiline than the retroussé end of the scale. This will be done by making two small incisions inside the nostrils, quite invisible from the outside. In addition, I propose a further, quite inconspicuous external incision across the columella, that is, the end of the septum, just here, the bit that separates the nostrils. This technique is what is known as the Coronal Forehead Lift, or Open Rhinoplasty. Then we peel back the skin and soft tissues from the underlying base of the nose and take a small sliver of cartilage from the septum and relocate it along the bridge to create more of a ridge. Given the breadth of your nose, there should be plenty of cartilage to spare. After we have sutured the incisions, the whole nose is covered with tape to maintain the new shape and then held in place with a metal splint. For a few days you will look like Iron Man. Then we remove the splint and the tapes. There may be some slight residual bruising and a tiny scar across the columella. But otherwise you will have a fine aristocratic nose which will be not only more aquiline but somewhat narrower, by a couple of millimetres or so. The overall effect will be to pull the cheeks towards the nose, making your whole face appear less broad and flat and more angular. The work which I would like to do on your chin at the same time—'

'On my chin? What's wrong with my chin?'

'Nothing at all. But your new nasal outline will demand a corresponding new outline for the jaw. "Nose and chin go together like sex and sin", as Gordo Gordon, my old mentor at Boston General, used to say. By making the chin outline a fraction firmer, the face acquires a fresh balance. If we attend to the nose alone, there is a risk of it looking artificial, even stuck on, however flawless the operation may have been.'

'I see. I'm just worried about looking like Mr Punch.'

'I promise you, Senhor Smith, that the effect will be altogether more subtle. We regard ourselves as artists not puppeteers. Let me reassure you that the genioplasty, or chin augmentation, will be an even simpler procedure. We merely make a cut inside the mouth, again quite invisible to the outside eye, and create a pocket in front of the chin bone but under the muscles of the jaw, and we insert a small implant.'

'Implant? What sort of implant?'

'There are many different materials in use. Silicone and Teflon are perhaps the best known. Some of my colleagues in Rio use a material known commercially as Alloderm which is made from the skin of human cadavers, but I am not convinced that the risk of rejection has been entirely eliminated. My own preference is to use Gore-tex.'

'Gore-tex? You mean the stuff that keeps the rain off your boots?'

'Exactly so. Among its other virtues are that it is biocompatible and also porous, so that the soft tissue and the bone too will grow through the implant and anchor it beautifully.'

'So you'll give me a chin like a climbing boot. Well, I suppose it's better than corpse skin.'

'Then finally, again in the interests of rebalancing the face, I would suggest a very modest procedure to bring the lips forward. Here too there are many implant materials on the market, including Gore-tex. My preference is for a material called Radiance, which is a synthetic suspension of bone calcium in a gel. It is entirely safe and can last for anything up to five years.'

'Does it affect the feeling in your lips?'

'Not at all. If anything, sensation is heightened. And of course looking at it from the other person's point of view, you will be a great deal more kissable.'

Dr Paravicini laughed in a quiet charming way that suggested a good deal of experience in this line. Timbo suddenly thought that he really didn't like him at all.

I could get out of this chair now, Timbo thought, and take the elevator up to the lobby and be out in the street in two minutes. Then he thought he would look pretty silly if he got a bullet in his neck before he crossed the road. Better to be a physical freak than be dead. It was a quite simple equation. In fact it wasn't an equation at all.

So he settled back in the chair and pretended to look relaxed as Dr Paravicini handed him the consent form.

He took the pen and was about to write his name when he suddenly noticed that the form was made out in the name of Roger Bellville.

'This must be somebody else's form, I think.'

Dr Paravicini looked over his shoulder.

'No, it's – oh, I see, Arturo must have forgotten to tell you the name on your new passport. Would you like another piece of paper to practise your new signature on?'

Timbo practised signing Roger Bellville over and over again like a bored schoolboy, while Dr Paravicini wheeled up his portable X-ray and placed the cold little plate against Timbo's nose and then against his jaw.

'Don't worry about the consent form leaving a paper trail. I do need to keep it in case you sue for malpractice but it will be hidden where nobody on earth can find it.'

Typical doctors. Ultimately the only thing that really mattered was protecting their own backsides. Timbo signed the form 'Roger Bellville' with a flourish.

'Thank you, looks as if you've been doing it all your life. Well, we are ready to begin now. You know my anaesthetist already, I think.'

Silently Angelina Nicols had appeared on Timbo's other side, summoned by some imperceptible command, and with a half-whispered 'May I?' started to take his blood pressure.

It might all be a complete con. He had been deceived so often ever since he had landed at Belém: by Rapha first of all, and then by K and K if they were not figments of his drugged imagination, and by those charming-seeming girls in the village. How was he to know that the Nicolses and Dr Paravicini were not fakes too? What hard evidence did he have that the man who had picked him outside the Furcht Building really was Furcht's General Manager and not somebody from Enida who had blagged his way into the office? Even if Dr Paravicini really was an 'aesthetic surgeon', might he and his sister not be deliberately planning for the operation to go wrong? That sort of thing often happened, and doctors were dab hands at covering up for each other. When you read about a particularly gruesome case in the papers, you thought what a fool the woman was to risk her life to improve the tilt of her nose. Now here he was doing the same thing, the only difference being that a perfect stranger had scared him into thinking his life was at risk if he didn't do it. And the only trace of him would be a consent form signed with a false name.

'It will just be a little prick,' Senhora Nicols said.

When he woke again, it was dark and he thought for a moment that he was in the hut in the forest. Then he felt the cool linen sheet against his arm and the scoop neck of the hospital gown rubbing against his skin, and he remembered what had happened to him. His chin ached like hell, as though he had a slightly displaced toothache and the thought of it being crammed with waterproofing material did not seem the least bit funny. His lips were somehow numb and sore at the same time, but the worst pain was running along inside his nose with the weight of the iron clamp pressing down from outside.

Quite soon light began to edge round the venetian blind. The dawn stole very gently, as though it did not wish to wake him, and he had an unreasoning inkling that things might be turning his way. Then he dozed off again and began to dream a little: of learning to ride a bike staying with a schoolfriend outside Leatherhead, and of going to an archaeological museum with Moth, in Devizes perhaps, and thinking that the flint arrowheads were probably not knapped at all but had just broken off into that shape naturally. Knapped was an odd word. It didn't seem to be used for anything except splintering flints.

'Good morning. I hope you are well rested. You must have slept for almost fifteen hours. I have to take your blood pressure first and then you can have some mint tea, only tepid I'm afraid for the first forty-eight hours because of the very slight risk of haemorrhaging.'

He caught Angelina's scent as she bent across him to wrap the rubber strap round his upper arm. It was a jungle fragrance. He could imagine the waxy white petals glowing in the dim light of the forest. He was ashamed now that he had doubted her good faith.

Why should you worry about how your face was arranged? Unless you were the vain type who peered eagerly in every passing mirror, days might go by without catching a glimpse of yourself (he always shaved blind during his morning bath). And when you did accidentally catch sight of yourself in a shop window, you often had the feeling that you were looking at a slightly unnerving stranger or someone you did know a bit but could not quite place.

Senhora Nicols began to wash him down with a fleecy white flannel, very gently, as though he might break. And he thought that he would be in no hurry to find out what he looked like.

When Arturo had told him that he would need to convalesce for a week or so before they took off the bandages, Timbo worried that the time would pass too slowly. He thought of himself as an impatient person, someone who could not wait to get on with the next thing. But he slipped into the torpid rhythm of convalescence quite easily: the gradual progress from clear broth to chicken consommé and then to tomato soup with a little cream in it. In the evening Dr Paravicini would call in to look him over and say how pleased he was with his own work and with Timbo's progress. Jorge was a creep, but a creep who seemed to know his stuff. Next door to the recovery room there was a small exercise suite with a bike and a treadmill. After three days Angelina shooed him in there to get some exercise. There was a screen in front of the treadmill which automatically began to show a video of the Amazon as he started pedalling. After fiddling around with the control panel, he discovered how to turn off the video. He had had enough of the river.

On the sixth evening Jorge removed the bandages.

'It has all turned out even better than I expected. The facial balance is excellent. I insist that you take a look.'

He handed Timbo a wooden mirror of the sort barbers use to show you how the back of your head looks after they have finished.

He had resolved that he would not flinch. He would look on his new persona with a stoic indifference. A *persona* was just a mask after all. He remembered that much from his Classical Civilisation GCSE.

But in the event he could not stop himself recoiling in startled horror. This bald, beaky weirdo leering back at him was infinitely worse than he had imagined. He had intended to keep smiling, to show Jorge that he didn't care and was grateful. But the smile came out as the most hideous sex offender's, well, leer was the only word.

Dr Paravicini waited for Timbo to say something but no words came out, so Paravicini filled up the silence himself.

'You may notice that the lipline is fractionally oblique. This is the consequence of a very slight muscular reaction to the procedure. It is entirely normal and will pass off after a week or two, as the lips are gently exercised and the muscle returns to its normal path. The bruising along the nose will fade over approximately the same period.'

Timbo tried another smile. The effect was, if anything, even more horrific. The twisted mouth seemed incapable of any expression except a contemptuous sneer.

He handed the mirror back to Dr Paravicini and managed to stumble out a few words of thanks.

'Do not worry, my friend. It is natural to be a little self-conscious at first, but in a day or two you will forget the whole thing and carry on as if you had never looked any different.'

After Jorge had gone, Angelina came in and instructed him how to apply the makeup so the wounds didn't show. Then she took his photograph for the new passport and brought in a set of clothes which he was to wear straight away to get used to them. Better still if he spilt some coffee or tomato soup over them.

'All bought here in Manaus: chinos and a linen-cotton-mix jacket like any young businessman going to Europe would wear for the flight, and a baseball cap because every bald man wears one. You'll carry just this cabin bag so there's no hanging about at the carousel and your check-in is automatic so there's no wait there either. You're on the cheapo red-eye flight which only the students and migrant workers travel on. Spooks need their sleep like the rest of us, so the flight is less likely to be watched. And we suggest you walk the back way to the bus station in case they have the number of Arturo's car.'

Twenty-four hours later she came in with the new passport and a wallet containing $10,000 and an American Express card in the name of Roger Bellville. Then she gave him a quick kiss on the cheek and she was gone, though her fragrance wasn't. He sat on the bed and unzipped the bag she had left behind. It contained washing things, two pairs of socks, two casual shirts, two pairs of underpants, a blue

V-neck jersey and two old paperbacks by Elmore Leonard, obviously snatched from Arturo's shelves. He zipped it shut and waited on the bed for Arturo's call. He remembered how at the end of the holidays he used to sit on his bed at home beside his packed suitcase, waiting for Moth to call up from the hall to say it was time to go.

Arturo took him down the back stairs to the deliveries entrance and shook his hand and wished him better luck. Timbo could sense how desperately eager both of them were to be rid of him and how hard they were trying not to show it. He did not blame the Nicolses. But he himself was sorry to leave. The whole place had been a refuge, almost a home.

The bus station was no more than six hundred metres from their apartment. Even if Arturo had not carefully coached him on the route, he had only to follow the backpackers who were thronging the pavement. He fell in amongst them with relief, pulling the dark green baseball cap down over his bald skull. He liked being on the bus too, listening to the babble of the students and watching how the boys twisted over the back of the seats to chat up the girls.

He began to grow nervous, though, when they trooped out of the bus and into Departures and he saw the row of check-in desks and the armed policemen. Just as he was joining the queue for immigration control, he saw a youngish man standing by the railings where the Arrivals came out into the concourse. The man had shades pushed up over his curly black hair and one leg cocked on the lower rung of the railings, and a general air of insolence. Raphael Alvarez.

The two of them were no more than twenty metres apart when Rapha turned his head and with a gaze that was sleepy rather than vigilant began to survey the queue Timbo was in. He did not seem to be looking for anyone in particular. Then after ten seconds perhaps he turned back again to resume his watch on the Arrivals. Perhaps he was there to pick up a new client rather than to finger the client he had already betrayed. All the same, it was a relief to get to passport control.

'Have a pleasant flight, Senhor Bellville.'

XII

Mulvaine House

Everyone was very kind. Nobody could have done more, they all said. People in the office I hardly knew hugged me like treasured friends who had been thinking of me all the time – perhaps they had. The Editor congratulated me with a warmth I didn't know he had in him. He was thinking of a three-part centre spread, he said. I had to break it to him that I couldn't think of writing a word as long as Timbo was missing, and he seemed reconciled to that, muttering, 'Later perhaps, take your time.' At home, the girls hung around my neck like seaweed, and Jane; well, Jane melted in that startling way she had when we first got together, and I was touched to the depth of my being. Nobody mentioned that I had not succeeded in my mission – the journey, not the arrival, seemed to matter. Perhaps all the people who had gone out to find Colonel Fawcett had had the same welcome when they returned home empty-handed. I was only mildly miffed that George Furcht did not write himself but merely sent a message via Rowley that he was glad to see me back in one piece and was very grateful for my efforts. Nobody talked about Timbo at all. Speculation seemed indecent to everyone, except for a crass fellow on the subs' desk who emailed me a cutting about a tribe in the southern Mato Grosso who were allegedly still practising cannibals.

For my own part, I was mostly just dog-tired. Depressed too. I told myself that I had never really expected to find him, that from the start I had been prepared for failure. But as the images of the river and the rainforest began to haunt my waking hours as well as my dreams, I could not help feeling ashamed that I had not persisted longer, asked more questions, followed up more leads. The truth was, though, that everywhere I went I met the same resigned shrug and words to the effect that these things happened in Brazil. Even Arturo Nicols, who seemed like a decent man, gave the impression that he had never held out much hope of finding Timbo, certainly not of finding him alive.

But then as I brooded on Timbo's fate again, I could not repress a shudder of gratitude/guilt that I was still alive, and bewilderment too. I had been watched the whole time, obviously, and not just by Rapha, so why did they let me go? Because I was just a bit player, or so I could warn others off, or because they just liked playing cat and mouse?

'You have to come to Mutt's comeback show,' Lee pleaded over the phone.

'Mutt's show?'

'You must remember, Dickie. The charity fashion show that gave us the clue to Beaky. You must come, Mutt's such a laugh, like a crazy puppet, I'm not surprised he went bust.'

'It doesn't sound quite my thing.'

'Look, Dickie, nobody could possibly have done more to find Bimbo. But it's time now to move on to the next phase, Bimbo himself would have really wanted us to.'

'What's the next phase?' I queried feebly.

'Beaky. We can't give up now after what he's done to Timbo. The show is a precious chance for us to see the enemy close-up. It will take you out of yourself, too.'

And so I traipsed along to Mulvaine House and marvelled at the gilded ceilings and the extravagant boiseries, sitting next to Luke. Lethal was backstage somewhere. I hadn't seen her since I got back, so not for weeks.

Mutt was everywhere. To start with, he appeared on his own to welcome us, with the single spot playing on him as he walked down the catwalk, rather slowly and awkwardly like someone recovering their legs after an op. He looked frail in his skimpy glittery-blue jersey with nothing under it but his narrow hairy chest, and his stonewashed jeans and his trademark blue Doc Martens with silver laces which seemed much too big for him. His spiky hair glistened under the spotlight. He looked both shocked and lifeless like a picture in a comic of a boy who has been electrocuted. Then when he reached the end of the catwalk, he exploded into life. His stick-like limbs began to jig about and he gave little personal waves to the audience and pointed at real or imagined friends the way celebs do. His sad pale face was now flushed in laughing surprise as if it was completely amazing to see them all assembled there, although none of them could possibly have got in without an invitation.

I was surprised by how tight security was. 'We might be at a fuck-ing summit,' Luke muttered. He had more trouble getting into the show than I had because he was on his wife's invitation which she had in her handbag and she was already behind the scenes warming up the nervous amateur first-timers among the models.

'*Well*,' Mutt said finally after having excited the audience into a frenzy of happiness and self-love without needing to say a word. 'This is really awesome. I never thought you'd all make it.' He had a chirpy east London voice with a softening on the th's which came out more like v's and made him sound like a friendly little boy. 'Look, I really hope you're going to be a *nice* audience, yeah, I just know you are. Because, let's face it, vis show is sort of flung together. It's, like, let's do the show right here. So, you know, if you see a seam coming apart or someving that's off the shoulder when it ain't meant to be, then just turn a blind eye and vink of England, will you, just as a personal favour to me. Because it's all in an absolutely smashing cause and you're going to see some fabulous frocks and some abso-lutely fabulous ladies wearing them.'

He paused to let the applause flood across Lord Mulvaine's Grand Saloon which was so packed that the back rows were pressed up against the murals of Cupid and Psyche by G. Franchi (1782), their chattering heads bobbing in and out of the scenes of amorous dalliance.

'So, ladies and gents, what's going to be the magic word to get the show on the road this evening? I'll give you a tiny musical clue.'

Quietly to begin with, over the sound system came the tuh-ta-ta-tata of the percussion and then the sighing, meditative warble of the oboe. Someone cried out, perhaps rather louder than she meant to, 'Bolero!'

Mutt stretched out a hand into the back curtains and brought out a slender woman with short streaked hair wearing a tomato-coloured waistcoat over a tomato-spotted blouse and a black pencil skirt. She and Mutt glided along the catwalk, pushing their toes out to the side in a faux-skating motion, although their feet dragged a little on the unforgiving floor drape and the effect was more like guardsmen doing a slow march.

'Yes, you've guessed it. The magic word is Waistcoats. And Loopy is wearing a scrumptious matador's *chaleco* with Seville stitching and black silk flamenco trews and lovely Choo-Choo pumps.'

As Ravel's *Bolero* swelled over the saloon, another pseudo-skater sidled out of the blackness.

'Tish is wearing a shantung moiré gilet in muted jade with very gentlemanly lapels and a primrose puff skirt in frazzled cotton and Whoopee sneakers. Doesn't she look someving?'

A thin young man with shades and designer stubble stood up behind us and let out a yell of delight. 'Flash Falk,' Luke whispered.

'Pussy is wearing a head waiter's waistcoat in five-minutes-to-midnight-blue linen and a box-pleated cotton skirt in distressed slate.' I could see what Lethal meant about Pussy Strang-Biggs being shaped like a towel rail, but somehow her gawkiness combined with the imitation skating motion to give her performance a certain coltish allure. Further along our row two pale fortyish men who looked like qualified accountants rose and clapped as though it was expected of them.

Ravel exhausted his whirling orgasmic climax as the pseudo-skaters made the return trip along the catwalk, the resemblance to a funeral march rather more pronounced on the home straight.

'Not exactly Torvill and Dean,' I whispered to Luke.

'Not exactly who?' he whispered back, though I suspected he knew perfectly well.

The sound system was playing another Spanish-sounding tune now, which I didn't recognise until the next hedge funder's wife came on clutching a rose between her teeth.

'Dinah is wearing a Carmen bolero of studded appliqué leather with an organza-and-lace scoop-neck gipsy blouse and a ra-ra raspberry organza skirt.'

Dinah was followed by a bouncy girl with short blonde hair in what Mutt told us was a sawn-off biker's jacket. He asked us to welcome Patty from *What's That Supposed to Mean?*, a sitcom which Luke turned out to be a huge fan of, casting some doubt on his claim not to have heard of Torvill and Dean. He listened intently as Mutt asked Patty if she really was going to marry Brian after the way he had behaved at the pub quiz night.

After Bizet's *Bolero*, Mutt told us, we were going to have Borodin's *Bolero*, and on came Tish again, this time in a Caucasian lambskin waistcoat and matching tall white lambskin hat which she looked a bit warm in.

I thought we had seen enough waistcoats, but for an encore Mutt brought on all the girls in gorgeous embroidered silk numbers which he said he had borrowed from the African Waistcoat Company and they all danced together to some Cuban-African fusion beat, and the audience rose from their little gold chairs and jigged about in what space they had, and I could see that Mutt really had something.

My interest began to flag in the next section of the evening, which was all about handbags and what to wear with them or conversely what handbags to wear with what outfits. Then there was a selection of party frocks with a whole new lot of models, which gave the first shift time to change into their swimwear. I had been looking forward to the swimwear, but the cruel spotlight gave the exposed flesh an unexpected chilly quality that made me think of butcher's slabs. Only Leana from *Next Door*, a daytime soap we genuinely hadn't heard of, in a canary two-piece trimmed with white daisies, sent out any kind of erotic message, and that was more because of her come-on smile. Pussy would have done better to avoid the swimwear altogether. During the penultimate section – Office Wear Doesn't Have to Be Dull-Dull-Dull – I began to nod off. But I woke up again in time for what said Mutt was his Tiny Grand Finale: 'We're going to finish the show with the Seven Ages of Woman, well, actually to be pervickly honest wiv you, it's only four tonight, 'cos I've forgotten the other three.'

First on came Tish, Flash's latest squeeze apparently, as the Schoolgirl in a snazzy grey cotton blazer with a rose on the breast pocket. Next was a girl we hadn't seen before who Luke recognised as the co-host on a breakfast TV show. She was wearing a swirly floral-print shirtwaister and was canoodling arm in arm with Mutt and obviously represented the Age of Courtship. Then came Loopy, Pussy's rather slimmer sister-in-law, in a white wedding dress with puff sleeves and Mutt as a mischievous page holding up her train: ''cos you can't have a rock show wivaht a wedding dress, can you, girls?'

But what really made me sit up straight was the final figure in this foreshortened life cycle. Behind the other three models on came the mistress of ceremonies, Lethal herself, in a loose pink linen dress with scarlet ruches at the neck and sleeves and a decided, unmistakable bump of maternity.

Well, my first thought was, she's just padded up. Then I thought that, no, that wasn't something you did, not unless you were acting in a play which this wasn't quite. And I looked at Luke.

'Oh,' he said, seeing my surprise. 'Didn't you know?' And he went as pink as a sallow middle-aged philosopher who is not drinking is capable of going.

I had not thought of Lee and children in the same breath – I began to think of her as Lee again, her old nickname now seeming to belong to an earlier age (perhaps Mutt's Four Ages of Woman had helped put this thought into my head). Her former self had enough trouble coping with her own inner child. Getting pregnant might be a confirmation that her new start was going to last. For Luke too, this was a restart. He was old to be becoming a father for the first time, but not too old to dote. Rather late in the day, it seemed his life was becoming a narrative – something he had already confessed he was softening towards. At any rate I now understood why she had looked so blooming in Albert Hall Mansions. That drawn, sharp look which had been so thrilling had gone. Though she was still slender except for the bump, she was now lovely in a blowy, almost indulgent way.

'Well,' I said to her, as she paused in passing and took my hand, 'you might have told me.'

'Why? You're not my fucking GP, are you?' she said, as we clasped hands during her triumphal progress through the audience who were now stumbling out of their little gold chairs and swarming round the catwalk. I watched her taking the plaudits with Loopy ploughing along behind her, still holding her bridal bouquet of assorted freesias and looking more like the matron of honour than the bride.

There was a thunderous handclap, and towering above us on the catwalk was the huge figure of our host. At least a foot taller than the models we had been watching, and they were mostly tall girls, he transformed the modest black ramp into a dictator's podium.

'My friends,' he began, his hands still clasped above his chest from his thunderous clap, 'My name is Wilfrid Bentliff. Some people call me Beaky, I can't think why' – pause to allow a ripple of amusement to spread across the room, the ripple breaking out into laughter when it sounded too tepid. 'You are my guests here tonight, and I forbid you to start drinking without first bidding you the warmest possible welcome and extending to you my personal thanks for your unfailingly generous support.'

Despite its expansive and amicable wording, his welcome carried a note of command, even of menace. As his piercing blue eyes swept the room, the total effect was one less of greeting than of inquisition, like a headmaster checking that he had a full turnout and there was no one mucking about at the back. There was a smile on his wide, thin-lipped mouth, but when he stretched it to achieve the smile, the lips turned down in a mean crescent of disdain, so that he was really less unnerving when he stopped smiling. I had read a fanciful profile of him which described his smile as 'twinkly'. It was at best the twinkle of approaching gunfire.

'This has been a rare departure for our little movement. When we began operations barely four years ago, we resolved amongst ourselves that Green Hedges would maintain as low a profile as possible. We would keep our heads below the parapet. And so we have conducted ourselves, privately and quietly, not unlike an old-fashioned Swiss bank. But we had reckoned without the ladies. Not for the first time in history we mere men were tempted, in the most charming fashion I must add, and of course we succumbed. This evening (*forte*) we have eaten of the fruit of the tree, and (*fortissimo*) how sweet it has tasted.'

Hysterical applause. I looked round the audience and was taken aback by how rapt most of them were, their eyes turned upwards like saints in a baroque painting, although those closest to the catwalk would be able to see little more than the knees of Beaky Bentliff's dinner-jacket trousers. I could see how the voice would have enchanted them: the richness of its baritone and the chuckle in it, the sound of water flowing over the gravel of a stream in his native Brawldale as the same fanciful profiler had put it (in fact Beaky had mostly been brought up in Roundhay, the prosperous suburb of Leeds). And there was too an intoxicating suggestion of unused power. He was speaking to us now in a fairly confined space, but I could see that he could reach the furthest corner of a vast arena if he needed to.

'This evening's entertainment will remain an exception and we shall treasure it all the more for that reason. But in everything except its semi-public nature, this wonderful show conforms to our preferred method of operation: in its dash, its informality, its readiness to attempt the unorthodox. I like to think of Green Hedges as the SAS in the battle to save our planet. We are the undercover troops of the Green Revolution. We are silent, we are merciless and we take no prisoners. *Qui ose gagne. Wer wagt gewinnt.* Ladies and gentlemen, comrades, it is the same in every language: Who Dares Wins.

'Tonight, my friends, our little vessel breaks the surface for only a few minutes. But as I survey the scene from my conning tower, I cannot disguise from you my satisfaction at what I see. I can reveal to you this evening that the Governor of Pará Province, the central province in the Amazon basin, has today issued a decree that no more logging is to take place within the boundaries of his domain. That decree is effective forthwith. My friends, this is a great victory.'

A tsunami of whoops and cheers rolled across the Grand Saloon. Luke and I clapped until our hands stung. We were away fans in the home stands and we had to fit in.

'Much of what has been done to achieve this triumph must remain confidential until most of us are dead. The feats of brilliance and daring undertaken by our associates the world will never know. But this I can tell you, my friends, we are on our way.'

Now he was on continuous fortissimo and the mellow baritone had become a hoarse bellow. The menacing echoes bounced back from the mild frolics of nymphs and shepherds on the walls, ricocheting over the roars and yelps of the hedgies and their significant others.

Beaky Bentliff spread out his arms and silenced them with his huge down-spread palms.

'But before I leave you, there is another matter on which I must say a word or two. A matter of some urgency which may threaten your livelihoods and mine too. For our enemies never rest. We may protect our beloved planet from their cruel incursions, but we must not forget to protect ourselves. They are at their most dangerous when their flimsy empires are crumbling. They have not yet lost the power to retaliate. By now you are well aware that our honourable calling—'

'Honourable,' Luke snorted under his breath.

'—is assailed by a dastardly conspiracy which breaches all the laws and customs of commerce. My friends,' he roared, 'this is an interference up with which we shall not put, as Winston said. Tonight is not the night to go into detail about our plans. All I will tell you is that we shall fight back with every weapon at our disposal and with every fibre of our being. And we shall overcome. Goodnight and good hunting.'

'What was that bit at the end all about?' I whispered.

'That, I suspect, may be George Furcht's last secret. And I only wish I knew what it was, because it may kill him before we find out.'

Bentliff strode down the catwalk without a backward glance and disappeared into the curtains. The applause rumbled on for several minutes after he had gone and then morphed into a buzzing hubbub which was almost as loud.

'Thank God, the U-boat has dived,' said Luke, after we had escaped out into the music room where we could hear ourselves speak and where Luke had agreed to meet Lee.

'At least you know what you are up against.'

'A much overrated plus in this case as in others. Knowing what a terrifying fascist bully Beaky is doesn't really help.'

At that moment Lee came out of the little door at the back of the music room. She stood half-turned in the doorway, saying goodbye to one of the girls who had modelled. Above the door there was a graceful lunette of cherubs throwing flowers about, no doubt also by G. Franchi. As she turned and smiled at us, framed there in the eighteenth-century doorway, she seemed to be at a turning point in her fractured life, one that nobody had expected, least of all herself.

'You'll never guess,' she said.

'What?' said Luke.

'Beaky's asked us to stay.'

'In France?'

'No, at his place in Yorkshire. Something-Grange. Sounded like a place out of *Wuthering Heights*.'

'Christ,' said Luke. But he had the light of battle in his eyes.

She came over to me and we embraced now that we had room to. I sketched a vague gesture of amplitude.

'It's wonderful news,' I said.

'Yes, it is, Chauffeur,' she said. 'Wonderful.'

I stumbled out of Mulvaine House, dazed by what I had seen and heard, still clutching my North Face anorak which the flunkey in the Grecian Hall had handed back as reverently as if it were a valued part of the Bentliff collection going out on loan. It was a chilly evening with sharp drizzle swirling under the street lamps of Mulvaine Place. As I stood on the pavement shrugging on my coat, I saw a *Big Issue* seller crouched beside his pile of mags, sheltering from the rain with his head hunched under a grubby old anorak with the hood up. It was an odd site to choose, this empty little corner between St James's Street and Green Park – St James's itself would have been a far better pitch. Perhaps he had been tipped off that a bunch of hedge funders with open wallets would be passing through. As I passed him, he turned a little towards me and called out from under the anorak, '*Big Issue, Big Issue*.'

His voice had an edge, not of menace exactly, more of low-level resentment, suggesting that part of the blame for his predicament could be pinned on me. It was a middle-class voice too, not without a certain confidence in it. *Big Issue* sellers were often not what you might expect. But what struck me to the heart, so that I froze in mid-stride as I was passing behind him, was that his voice was familiar. I knew who it was instantly and only the sheer unlikelihood of it being him made me hesitate.

'Timbo?'

No response. I realised that in my anxiety I had failed to make any audible noise. So I said, louder and more pulled together this time: 'Timbo, is that you?'

The man poked his head out from under the anorak and I was struck dumb with fright and embarrassment. His head was entirely shaven and he had a broken nose which looked as if it had been bashed up quite recently and a prominent scarred chin. There seemed to be something wrong with his mouth too and when he turned his face towards me, holding out a copy of the paper in his hand, he gave me a terrifying, twisted smile. He could not have looked less like Timbo.

'Only two quid to you, mate.'

'I'm so sorry, I thought you were someone else.'

'That's all right, it's a dark night.'

I handed him two pound coins and took the magazine. He tugged the anorak back over his head and began chanting again, '*Big Issue, Big Issue.*'

I walked on more dazed than ever. The voice still sounded a lot like Timbo's but not quite so much as it had before, a bit less middle class. As I was about to turn the corner out of the little square in front of Mulvaine House, I turned to look back at him. But there were guests piling out of the pillared doorway now and he was lost to view in the middle of them.

The next morning was a Saturday and I pedalled off to Waitrose to fill up the gaps in the fridge. The drizzle had gone and it was a bright day, still just too chilly to feel like spring. There wasn't much on the list, but I had trouble tracking down the basil and the cork-screw pasta, and it must have been half an hour later when I came out and ambled round the back of the store to pick up the bike. The car park was crossed halfway down by a pedestrian path between two low brick walls leading to the market. By the entrance to the market there would sometimes be a down-at-heel minstrel sing-ing some ancient country song like 'Hang Down Your Head Tom Dooley'. If I was in a good mood, I would drop some silver into his open guitar case, scarcely bothering to notice whether it was the same songster as the time before. This morning, the performer had stationed himself not at the market entrance but right by the bollards you had to pass between to reach the far section of the car park, so it was impossible not to brush past him.

I could hear him singing from some way off. He had a loud, flat, hoarse voice that sounded embattled, as if he was battling a head-wind, though it was a dead still morning. He was singing the bit from the 'Green Green Grass of Home' about Mary with hair of gold and lips like cherries running down the road. He was a terrible singer, but there is a fascination about truly awful performance and I could not help glancing at him as I passed. At first I thought I was out of my head, but then I looked again and harder and it was the *Big Issue* seller of the night before, his dirty anorak now flung around his shoulders as a minstrel's cape and his bald skull raised to the calm blue sky while he murdered the chorus. His eyes were shut as his twisted mouth poured out the ghastly raucous sound and he gave only the barest nod of acknowledgement as I tossed a coin into his guitar case. Well, I could not stand around waiting for him to open his eyes, so I moved on, clutching my groceries more tightly as though they offered some purchase on reality.

That was the second sighting, and I said to myself, there's going to be a third. I was now as thoroughly spooked as a medieval peasant. As I pedalled home, I replayed in my head once more the scant material I had to go on: '*Big Issue, Big Issue* … only two quid to you, mate … that's all right, it's a dark night', and the chorus of 'Green Green Grass of Home' which was not much use because his rendering of it sounded indistinguishable from anyone in a pub doing a Tom Jones impression. As I revolved the uncertainty in my fretful brain, I became aware that I had taken to saying to myself 'sounding like' and not completing the phrase, as if reluctant to tempt fate by mentioning Timbo's name, even in my head. All the same, I felt curiously certain that I would see the man again, whoever he was, and wondered when it would be.

Two days later, in fact. He was on the forecourt at the Tube station standing in the lee of the coffee stall. He was holding out a sheaf of *Big Issue*s at the people rushing into the Tube. His appearance was so arresting, now that his face was fully visible in the morning sun, that quite a few of them slowed down to get a better look at him, and then, embarrassed by having stared, started fumbling in their pockets for coins. I stood about ten yards away, leaning against the faux-Tudor window of the pub, watching him quite unashamedly now. Suddenly I was determined to have it out and settle the business. His last customer, a squat woman in a rainhat, had found the right money, and he was on his own. I went over.

'Hi,' I said. 'How's it going this morning, Timbo?'

He looked at me and smiled a crooked impudent smile.

'You took your time, I must say,' he said, in a voice that was unmistakably Timbo's.

'So it really is you.'

'I'm sorry about the scars. They were supposed to have healed by now. But it was the voice, wasn't it, not the face?'

'Yes,' I said. 'It was the voice. I'd never have guessed from the face.'

'I was never much good at other people's voices. If I had had more time, I was going to have some voice coaching. It would have been good to get a convincing Scots accent. People believe a Scotsman, don't they?'

I was still gawping at him. This utterly familiar, rather annoying, but it had to be admitted somehow lovable, voice coming out of a face that was so strange and cruel and battered. And of course now that he had revealed himself, he began to talk in his old unstoppable way, a little plaintive always, running on wherever his mind took him, quite unaware, it seemed, of how freakish he looked.

'Is there somewhere round here we could go for a coffee?'

'There's a builders' café round the corner. They do a great all-day breakfast. I'm starving. I've been on this pitch since seven.'

We found a table in the corner of a little Greek place behind the motorbike shop which I had never noticed before although we had lived in the area for years. I had a cappuccino while Timbo ordered up the full works with baked beans and toast on the side. As he dug into the steaming plates, hoovering up the beans and toast in sync with the sausage, egg, bacon, tomato, mushroom and hash browns, I felt he was really back. It was a pleasure to watch him eat. The all-day breakfast was central to my earliest memories of him. He paused to take a slurp from his mug of milky tea.

'You are the only person I can speak to,' he said, 'because you are not part of the operation. I do not dare to speak to Lethal or Luke, because they are almost certainly bugged. Enida has people everywhere. So you must promise not to tell anyone you've seen me, not even Luke and Lethal. Because I've only got one card in my hand, which is that no one knows I'm alive.'

'All right,' I said, 'I promise. But tell me, how did you find out about Beaky?'

'You think Luke is the only codebreaker in town?' There was something close to a smirk on his enhanced lips.

'Do you want to tell me the whole story?'

'I warn you, it's a long story,' he said.

'I love long stories. I've got a few things to tell you too,' I said. 'You know I came out to look for you?'

'Really, all the way out to Manaus? I don't believe it.'

'Even further, to the maloca where you disappeared.'

At which he jumped to his feet and leant across the table and buried me in an awkward, intense hug. I hugged him back and we stayed in this clumsy embrace with the all-day breakfast steaming between us for a minute or two, and I felt all at once, I don't quite know what the word is, would 'redeemed' be too strong?

'God, how on earth did you find it?' he gasped as he sat down again.

'I had George's interpreter with me, Rapha, the one who took you upriver too, I understand?'

'I'm not surprised you didn't find me. So he had you fooled too. I can see you've still got a lot to learn. I've got to say it again. You mustn't tell a soul you've seen me, let alone what I look like now, not until this whole thing is over, especially not Luke and Lee. Their systems are fatally compromised. Telling them would be like putting the news on Twitter. If they ask whether you've heard anything about me, you can just say, oh, I'm sure old Timbo will turn up some time, but I've already been to the other side of the globe and drawn a blank, and I'm not going to waste any more of my life looking for the silly bugger.'

'But aren't we supposed to be some sort of a team?'

'In this business, the Colonel used to say, the most effective teams hunt separately. I'll be in there somewhere, don't you worry, and isn't it fantastic luck that I've got the best disguise in town?'

Then he told me the whole story.

PART FOUR

XIII

Brawley Grange

'I do wish you were coming with us, Chauffeur, you'd be such a comfort.' She was in the last months of her pregnancy now, and I knew I wasn't allowed to say she looked blooming, but she did.

'NFI,' I said. 'Beaky doesn't know me from Adam, at least I hope he doesn't.'

'But you can keep a close watch on us with this little darling,' Luke said. Out of his briefcase he scooped a flat dark green box the size and shape of a small laptop. 'It's an ERNX ultra-remote Eavesdropper, first developed by the US Defense Department for use in Afghanistan. It's been upgraded several times since, this is Mark V, but it's still known as the Rummy, in honour of Defense Secretary Donald Rumsfeld.'

'The Known Unknowns, and the Unknown Unknowns?'

'Exactly. Anyway the Rummy reduces the Known Unknowns to the bare minimum. The range is huge, the quality of the reception is superb and you can just hook it up to your phone. You can listen in on anyone anywhere. And it's so simple a child could work it.' He placed the dark green box in my hands with a certain reverence, plus a surprisingly slender manual.

'Well, do look after yourselves,' I said weakly, as I kissed Lethal goodbye.

'The most frightening thing will be driving all the way to Yorkshire. I'll probably pup before we pass Peterborough. My gynae says I shouldn't go, but I wouldn't miss it for worlds. And I can still drive, I'm not due for another month.'

I said goodbye to them with a mixture of guilt and foreboding. I was obediently following Timbo's strict instructions not to tell anyone, even them, that he was alive and well and somewhat altered. But it didn't seem right, and I wondered whether any good could possibly come of it. I knew that non-disclosure was supposed to be one of the core skills in this game, but I didn't care for it.

Luke Deverill did not drive. 'I don't drive,' he would say simply. Not can't drive, certainly not can't. Not-driving was an act of heroic abstinence, an assertion of the will, like not smoking. He refused to submit to the indignities of changing gear, of obeying the commands of street furniture, of accommodating himself to the vagaries of other motorists. To be a passenger was to belong to a higher order of existence, like being a Brahmin or a mandarin, a superior contemplative caste.

Lee, by contrast, was a born motorist. Her cars, usually red, always at the nippy end of the range, were an extension of herself. When she shot out of the bedroom at 2 a.m. after a lover's tiff, she would jump straight into her GTi and put her foot down, often reaching 4,000 revs before the end of the street. The only reason she was not tearing away from Dewdrop Cottage in her beat-up Golf when Timbo (as it turned out, also a total non-driver) first met her was that both she and the car were off the road; she for twelve months on the orders of Market Deeping Magistrates' Court, the car hovering between life and death in the workshop of Fenland Motors.

Now she was back on the road with a vengeance (the *mot juste* in the circumstances) at the wheel of the Fiesta, hired to be as anonymous as possible, as they snaked through the Dales approaches, passing through the villages of Combover, Snagglesby and Worple before they cut over the brow of Worple Bank and down into Brawldale, celebrated by Alfred Wainwright as 'the Dalesman's Dale, its fells unequalled in their stony grandeur'. The River Brawl chuckled alongside the road – Wainwright hazarded that it was this mischievous beck that had first provoked Yorkshiremen to talk of waters brawling.

Lee had *True Blue*, the third Madonna studio album, on the stereo and was singing along to it when the fancy took her. It was not so much the songs, more the idea of Madonna as a free spirit that appealed to her. She didn't really mind when Luke said he thought that the word caterwauling might have been invented to describe Madge. It was the rebel, not the melody that counted.

After he finally persuaded her to turn off the stereo, Professor Deverill began describing the text he had just been reading, which was the *Res Gestae Divi Augusti*. From having regarded Narrative as a pathetic delusion, Luke had now become obsessed by the subject. He lapped up life stories of every kind: biographies, autobiogs, diaries, letters, memoirs, pen portraits, showbiz anecdotes, mislit, criplit, memoirs of sporting heroes ghosted by disgruntled hacks. On his desk *The Confessions of St Augustine* jostled with *Jade: Fighting to the End* and *Graham Gooch: The Biography*. The autobiography of the Divine Augustus was a short work, which was just as well seeing that the Emperor had commanded the text to be engraved on bronze pillars all over the Empire, but he packed a lot into it.

'What is so amazing is that this is probably the first celebrity autobiography to have come down to us and already it has all the tricks of the genre, especially the false modesty. Listen to this: "The Senate decreed still more triumphs to me, all of which I declined. The consulship was also offered to me to be held each year for the rest of my life and I refused it." Oh, and this is the best: "I restored the Capitol and the Theatre of Pompey, both works at great expense, without inscribing my own name on either." He wants to have all his achievements *and* his reputation for incurable modesty splashed all over the Empire.'

'Perhaps he didn't write the book himself, perhaps he got some PR hack like Rowley to give him a write-up.'

'That seems unlikely. The autobiography is attached to his last will and testament. And it has the personal touch. Whoa back there.'

Lee hit the brakes as a flock of sheep spilled out onto the road, chivvied on by a grinning shepherd in a muddy 4x4.

'The thing is,' Luke resumed after the last sheep had crossed the road into the field on the other side and the shepherd had grinned some more at them, 'there are two sorts of life writing. There is the sort that dribbles out like blobs off a spoon and you're never quite sure how the author is going to behave or what he's going to think next, like Rousseau's *Confessions* or Barbellion's *Journal of a Disappointed Man*. The Self wobbles all over the place, the author doesn't seem to have a stable personality at all, he's not consistent in the way we expect persons to be consistent. That's my kind of Self and those are the life stories that I really like, because I think that's what human beings are really like and so I think they are much nearer the truth. And then there is the other sort.'

'What's the other sort?' Lee asked.

'The other sort is what I call the Little Old Me type. The author is always the same: he or she has a fixed set of qualities, basically pretty sterling qualities that shine through all the author's ups and downs. It's like one long karaoke session in which the only song ever played is "My Way". The Acts of the Divine Augustus is a Little Old Me Book, so is everything written by Winston Churchill, and so is *Beaky*. In fact *Beaky* is a classic of the genre. You have not yet read *Beaky: The Life and Times of Sir Wilfrid Bentliff, KCVO*?'

'Of course I haven't, you've been hogging it the whole week.'

'Our hero emerges from the womb the same courageous, self-deprecating, dynamic, humorous, sensitive human being that he is to remain for the next three hundred pages. His earliest memory is weeping at the age of four when he hears Kathleen Ferrier singing 'Blow the Wind Southerly' at Huddersfield Town Hall. His next is helping a young lad home who has broken his arm when a fulling machine malfunctions at his father's mill, and Beaky being deeply distressed when he sees the poverty the lad lives in down the Back Butts. And he sees the lad again when everyone from the works comes up to Brawley Grange on Daffodil Sunday to pick his father's daffodils, but the lad is too shy to speak to him and it is young Beaky, still barely six years of age, who goes up to the lad and asks him if his arm is better. Are you in tears yet?'

'Almost but not quite.'

'Beaky's father, you will be surprised to hear, is a hard man but a fair man, Prosper Mill pays the best wages in the West Riding – did you ever hear of a mill owner in a memoir who didn't pay his men well above the going rate? But it was his mother who gave him the decisive push to greatness and beat him with the flat of her silverback hairbrush when he couldn't do his seven times table. It was her proudest day when Beaky won his scholarship to the Queen's College, the first boy from Brawldale ever to go to Oxford. Are you sure you can take much more?'

'So what's the point of telling me all this?'

'The point, my darling, is that buried in this insufferable stream of self-serving, mendacious, sentimental effluent, there lies, almost invisible to the naked eye, the answer to our riddle.'

'And the answer is?'

'The answer is Bimbo and Topsy.'

'Not my Bimbo, I suppose, and who the fuck is Topsy?'

'Bimbo is a Siamese kitten, and Topsy is a fox terrier. Topsy is a playmate for Bimbo. She has a pretty black head and black tail and soft brown eyes. She is about five months old and she wags her tail a lot which is a signal that she wants to be friends. She eats biscuits and milk.'

'Why should I care what she eats? What are you on about, Lukey?'

'I may perhaps manage to spark your interest when I tell you that *Bimbo and Topsy* was Beaky's favourite book when he first learnt to read. In fact he taught himself to read with it when he was not yet five because Beaky always does everything before anyone else, e.g. virginity surrendered at the age of thirteen, first million made before he is nineteen.'

'So?'

'The opening chapter is entitled "The New Little Kitten". It begins as follows: "One day a little kitten arrived in a basket at a house called Green Hedges."'

'Ah.'

'And your agile brain will, I am sure, be at this moment jumping to the conclusion that the only person who could have penned that immortal line herself lived at a house called Green Hedges. And her name was E—'

'Oh, Enid Blyton.'

'Yes, and—'

'Enida?'

'Yes.'

'So it was a woman after all.'

'A woman whose name was taken in a playful conceit by Beaky as the undercover name for his campaign to stop the logging, a campaign which has to date claimed at least fifteen lives one way or another, probably including your Bimbo.'

'More than fifteen, probably nearer fifty. In his last email Arturo said that news of several fires and explosions in the north Amazon basin was just coming in. Several members of logging gangs previously unknown to the authorities had been killed and injured. The exact numbers are unknown and may never be known, Arturo says, because these are illegals who obviously don't keep records.'

'But what we do know now, at least to our own satisfaction, is that Beaky is the connecting link. Enida and the shorting are part of the same conspiracy and he is the driving force behind the whole thing.' Luke spread out his hands like a priest blessing his flock.

'Can we prove any of this?'

'If you mean, have we got any evidence that would stand up in court, I very much doubt it. We've already gone through how difficult it would be to make a charge of market abuse stick in the UK. Evidence of the crimes committed in Brazil would be even more elusive. In many cases, we don't even have the bodies. And even if we could find any reliable witnesses, they would be shit-scared. As for joining the two ends of the business together, that would be just about impossible seeing that the crimes were committed in two different continents. Whichever way you tried, there would be huge problems of extradition. Remember the trouble they had retrieving Ronnie Biggs from Rio and he was a convicted prisoner doing time. Besides, George Furcht might not make the most sympathetic witness for the prosecution.'

'So what the fuck are we doing here?'

'Well, for one thing he invited us and it would look rather odd to refuse.'

'But what are we going to do when we get there?'

'The only thing we can do, which is to confront him with the knowledge that we now have.'

'And he just laughs in our face.'

'Of course. But suppose we say, stop it now or else—'

'Or else what?'

'We don't say we'll go to the police. Because he will know that we don't have any hard evidence that would interest them. No, we say, we'll go to the newspapers, who have a rather less demanding standard of proof.'

'Oh, Lukey, you are an innocent, woolly old prof after all. Beaky has already destroyed several newspapers in court, not to mention giving *Private Eye* the fright of their lives. Can you imagine any Editor in his right mind saying, oh, fantastic, let's go out and whack Beaky Bentliff?'

'Do you know, that objection had already occurred to me. But I also thought, what have we got to lose? At the very least, when he knows just how much we know, he may be provoked into going too far and doing something silly.'

'I don't like the idea of being on the receiving end of Beaky's going too far.'

'Oh, I don't know, it might turn out to be quite fun. Anyway, we owe it to Timbo.'

'Poor Bimbo, he was sort of like a kitten in a way.'

She looked across her husband who had a tight little smile on his face. She had never thought of him as courageous. But there was no doubt about it, he was positively blithe.

'God, I hope I don't give birth in this ghastly spot.'

The wind-bitten hawthorns were leaning closer into the turf now, as though about to take off into the brooding sky. Storm clouds were massing to the north over the distant higher hills. The sheep were sparser on these stony uplands. Here and there a tumbledown shed in the corner of a field, half-sheltered by the equally tumbledown drystone walls. Nothing much else.

'Why would anyone want to live here?'

'Nowt so queer as folk. In fact getting away from folk was probably Meadow Bentliff's motive for buying the place. He sounds pretty grim from Beaky's description. Even on Daffodil Sunday there was a strict ration of a dozen daffs per family.'

'Meadow's a funny name, rather picturesque.'

'Nothing fancy about the Bentliffs. His mother, Beaky's grand-mother, was Susanna Meadow, a farmer's daughter from Brawldale which, now I come to think of it, was why he bought the Grange from another mill owner who had gone bankrupt.'

'The heights are really wuthering now.'

Quite suddenly the storm clouds were on top of them.

'I don't like the look of this,' Lee said, peering through the wind-screen as the rain began to come in, hard and heavy from the start, not looking like any sort of passing squall. 'You silly buggers,' she muttered as she had to swerve to get round two cyclists doggedly pedalling up the Dale on fold-up bikes, gnome-like and anonymous under their dark green capes.

'Think how much nicer it would be if we turned round and freewheeled down to that pub back there and got slaughtered in the snug,' she said.

223

'I never think about the poison now, well, not more than once every ten minutes,' he said.

'That's the nice thing about my delicate condition,' she said, 'I don't even have to not think about it.'

They drove on through the unrelenting rain. The road seemed to narrow. Through the sleeting downpour the head of the valley was just visible now.

'Oh, that must be the Grange. There in that little bunch of trees.'

They had come to the head of the dale. Through stabbing rain it was just possible to make out the turrets of a long building in a half-circle of firs half a mile ahead. Then, somehow too quickly, they were there, rattling over a cattle grid and up a short curly drive with the slate-hung gables (they turned out not to be turrets) beetling over them. Close up, the place looked like the surviving wing of some half-demolished Victorian institution, a mental hospital or home for fallen women perhaps.

Taken aback by being there quicker than she had expected, Lee braked awkwardly, sending a shower of gravel towards the man who had come out of a side door and was scurrying towards them with some empressement under a large golf umbrella.

'Welcome to the Grange, madam. I'm Keith, Sir Wilfrid's man.'

He had a thatch of silver on top of his round pink face and a general expression of grave cheerfulness. He took their bags out of the boot with careful deference as though it was a privilege to handle such luggage. Bentliff could obviously afford to employ the best.

'And this is my wife Kay, who's the housekeeper here.'

Except for her specs, the woman might have been her husband's twin: the same silver thatch and round rosy face. She shook hands with Lee and then Luke with the same careful deference as her husband had shown to their dusty old suitcases. Luke tried to remember whether Mrs Danvers shook hands with Rebecca when she arrived at Manderley – no, of course it wasn't Rebecca because she was dead, it was the narrator and you never discover her name.

'It's a real pleasure to have you with us,' the woman said. 'I'm sorry it's such a horrible night but no one ever came to Brawley Grange for the weather.'

'I suppose you must be used to it by now, the weather I mean.'

'Well, we're not local, you see. We're from down South, from Norwich in fact. Sir Wilfrid brought us up with him when he decided to open up the Grange again. It had been let for years, ever since Mr Meadow passed away. Oh, madam, let me help you with that. You must be quite near your time, Sir Wilfrid told us you were expecting. I do hope the journey hasn't been too much for you.'

Although she rattled on, Lee somehow got the impression that the talk did not come naturally to her. It was more that a proper house-keeper's welcome had to include a fair bit of friendly chatter and she was doing her bit. Also she smiled when you were not expecting it, as when recounting the circumstances of Meadow Bentliff's pass-ing: from a gunshot wound when trying to extricate his old King Charles spaniel from brambles just below the waterfall; the gun had caught in the brambles, and they couldn't get the ambulance nearer than half a mile away and he actually died when they were carry-ing him up the hill; and one of the ambulance men broke his ankle when Meadow collapsed on top of him; he was a heavy-built man by all accounts, eighteen stone or thereabouts. As it happened, Luke had just reached the passage in *Beaky* describing his father's death in less graphic, more emotive terms: 'He died on his beloved Brawley Edge with his adored King Charles spaniel Prospero at his side.'

'I have disappointing news for you, I'm afraid,' the housekeeper said when she was showing them their room, high on the attic floor, reached by a winding stair. 'Sir Wilfrid has just telephoned to say that sadly he won't be able to dine with you tonight. He has a late meet-ing in Newcastle and he will be staying over, but he looks forward greatly to meeting you and showing you around tomorrow.'

'Oh, that is sad,' Lee said.

'But Lady Bentliff will be very pleased to entertain you at dinner. She's upstairs in the belvedere; it's just a sitting room really but Mr Meadow called it the belvedere because he said it had the finest view in the Dales, though not today I'm afraid. The light is terrible in here.' The housekeeper was right about the light in the belvedere. The long windows were so dark it was impossible to tell whether night had already come. The only light in the room came from an overhead gasolier that cast an even dimness across the long room.

'Come closer, I can hardly see you.' The voice from the far end of the room called out in a plaintive foreign accent which Lee assumed was Russian. 'Beaky is so mean, he insists that the lighting must remain just as his father left it, but I say to him, Beaky, you hate your father, why do you keep his lights? Then of course he says, I didn't hate my father, we had our differences but I always respected him and I say, no, Beaky, you hated him, why can a foreigner see this when you can't see it yourself? Then we quarrel and we make love and we forget about the lights. Oh, you are so beautiful and so much *enceinte*. I adore pregnant women.'

Bric Bentliff rose from some complicated piece of furniture, all scrolls and buttoned velvet, and held out her hands to Lee. She was enormously tall and statuesque with long brass-blonde hair falling around her bare shoulders. Even to a professional eye like Lee's, the garment she was wearing was as hard to classify as the sofa. She thought it might perhaps be called a tea-gown, the sort of thing that Mrs Meadow Bentliff might have been wearing while reclining on the sofa in about 1910.

'You are so tall,' babbled Lee. 'You must be almost as tall as your husband.'

'I am a Circassian, all Circassians are tall. In our part of the Caucasus, Beaky would be only an average man.'

'Such a pity you could not make it to the fashion show. I would have loved it if you could have modelled something for us.'

'I had *la grippe* and anyway I am too fat. I always have *la grippe* in this dreadful climate. In my house in the Crimea the roses will be already blooming in our parterre and the gardeners will be laying the dust in the cypress avenue, or they would be if those horrible Russians had not confiscated it for their headquarters. Our people have all fled, it is so terrible. Here at least it is quiet, but oh, so dull, so dull.'

She flipped her wrist contemptuously in the direction of the murky windows.

'My husband is so rude not to be here. He is looking at shopping centres.'

'With a view to buying them?'

'No, he already owns them, I think. Perhaps he wants to sell them or to build more, I do not know. Why always Newcastle or Gateshead or Middlesborough? He never buys a store in Paris or even Odessa.'

'Is it Odessa you come from, Lady Bentliff?'

'Bric, you must call me Bric. It is short for Brigitte and in Russian or French it sounds so nice, Breek with a little breath on the "h", Breek-h, charming, no? Then I come to England and they pronounce it like the building material and I feel just like a brick.'

Lee could not make out whether Bric really was thick as, well, a brick or concealed a quick wit under her torrential talk. Or perhaps it didn't matter either way. What was clear was that she was accustomed to looking after herself, which included the ability to get other people on her side in the most unpromising circumstances.

'Do you have many friends up here?' Lee enquired, as they were sitting down to dinner in the equally uncheery dining room next door to the belvedere: tall Jacobean-style chairs, silver pheasants on the dark polished table, on the walls grimy pictures of ships capsizing.

'My dear, I am the toast of the county. Here comes Beaky's mad Russian wife, they say, and they expect me to behave like a crazy woman, throw the champagne glass over my shoulder and tear off all my clothes. So I behave in a very stately style, ask after their wives and their peasants – oh, I mean pheasants' – she clapped her hands over her face in a mimicry of embarrassment – 'and they think, oh, she is so charming and eccentric, she is a true Princess. Oh, Professor, you are not drinking. Your wife of course I can understand but I had expected better of you. Beaky left out the claret specially. What is it, Keith?'

'Margaux 1982, madam, in my opinion the best year since '61.'

'You see, we are not going to poison you. You will at least have a little more of the beef and Yorkshire pudding – it is *du pays*, after all. My husband says, when in Yorkshire, eat Yorkshire. It is one of his few sayings which is *sur le bouton*.'

'I didn't know the French had the same phrase as we have,' Luke interjected.

'They have now,' said Bric merrily. 'It is my privilege as a French Irish Circassian Serb. I make up the language as I go along.'

'You are Irish too?'

'Or Scottish. My grandmother was called MacMahon, she is cousin of General MacMahon who massacres the workers in the Commune and they name mayonnaise after him.'

Luke thought he would have some of the wine, after all, and beckoned the manservant, who whispered in his ear as he poured, 'Quite right, sir, you won't regret it.'

'One must always give in to temptation, don't you think? That is what it is there for, is it not?' Bric watched the slow dawning of bliss on Luke's face as he put down the glass and asked if he might have another.

Lee thought, yes, after all, this woman is sharp. She managed to hold back from saying something to Luke about the drinking because she did not wish to expose herself to Bric's contempt. She could have it out with him later.

'I am very simple person. I eat, I drink, I sleep, sometimes I fuck, not so much now I am so fat. I am happy in my body. I do not need books. I am a relief to Beaky after his first wife who thinks she is an intellectual. She sits in that gloomy house in the Auvergne and reads all day. She never goes out because she does not want people to see her scars. I think she must be very stupid woman. If I had an accident like that, I would wear a veil and go out hunting and everyone would say, there is Beaky's wife, she is so tragic, so romantic.'

'Isn't it quite romantic, though, becoming a recluse after you have been a great beauty?'

'Monique was never great beauty. She looks like a concierge who you have forgotten to tip. Like so.' Bric made a sour moue of disappointment.

'You knew her quite well then?'

'I never meet her, but I have seen photographs. Beaky is a sentimentalist. He keeps all photographs of his old loves. At first I want to burn the photos or at least put them in the attic. But then I think, no, one day he might want to put me in the attic, like Mrs Rochester. You see, I have read a book.'

'I expect you have really read a great number of books.'

'But of course. Pushkin, Lermontov, Gogol, I read them all. My great-grandfather won a lot of money off Tolstoy when they were Cossacks in the Caucasus. Ah, this is the famous 1945 Armagnac. Professor, you are very privileged. Beaky usually hides it away from his guests, but for you he makes a special pilgrimage to the cellar. You see, we drink it from ordinary glasses. Beaky cannot get his nose into those absurd *ballons*.'

Luke picked up the little latticed crystal glass and raised it to his nose. Immediately he felt himself transported to a land of lost content, his nostrils swimming in the peaty, plummy, greengagey, walnutty aroma. He was a small boy playing in a sunny orchard, miles and years away from this dim flickering dining room. He had never tasted anything like it. At his elbow Keith was already refilling his glass. Across the table Bric seemed to shimmer at him like a Rhinemaiden in a mist, no, not Rhinemaiden, Crimean maiden, Crimaiden.

'I think my husband is a little tired.'

'No, my dear.' Bric put her hand on Lee's. 'It is you who must be tired. Husbands are not allowed to be tired. But both of you run along now. It has been such a pleasure for me to see your bright faces. Up here there is nothing to look at but daffodils. My heart does not dance with the bloody daffodils. I dream of the roses and my dear cypress avenue leading down to that wonderful sea. Goodnight, my dears, goodnight, *dormez bien.*'

She shooed them down the passage and up the twisting stairs to the attic floor. They stumbled through the door of the bedroom together, knocking against the frame. Lee had meant to jump straight into her lecture. Not merely had Luke broken every vow in their mutual pact to give up the poison. He had chosen the worst possible moment to fall off the wagon, on the eve of their showdown with Bentliff, an encounter which promised to be as mentally testing as it was frightening.

But thirty seconds later after she had taken off her earrings, she turned round to find that Luke was asleep, flat out on the bed and snoring powerful Armagnac snores. So Lee, herself exhausted, undressed and crawled under the duvet that he lay rigid on top of. She lay there, rigid herself and apprehensive about the day ahead, but fatigue overcame her too and she paddled quietly into oblivion.

Luke had no idea what time it was when he woke up needing a piss. Still fuddled, he was not too fuddled to forget his fall from grace and certainly not brave enough to risk Lee's rage by turning on the light even if he could find it. It took him a minute or two to become aware that he had all his clothes on.

He rolled clumsily off the bed and began a slow experimental crouch-walk to where he thought the door might be. His hip struck a protruding knob and he switched direction by about forty-five degrees and his fumbling fingers found the edge of a half-open door.

Very slowly he edged out into the passage, still crouching as though he was in a low tunnel. The passage seemed to go on a long time, much longer than he remembered when they had come down it from the dining room, not that he could remember much about that. No sign of any door in the wall. He tried to recall what the housekeeper had said about the facilities when she showed them to their room. The passage turned at a shallow angle and then went down a slight incline, or was that the effect of his stumbling crouch? He felt he was now in a different wing of the house, the servants' wing perhaps, but there might be a servants' WC at the end of it and he crept on. On his right-hand side he came to a long uncurtained window, very low, only about eighteen inches high. He stopped and looked out of the window to the side of the hill behind the house. There was a faint glimmer from the night sky, just visible above the rim of the hill.

As he was peering through the small dusty panes, he became aware of a light moving erratically outside below the level of the window. He looked down and as his eyes got used to the dim, he could see that he was looking down into a yard, irregular-shaped like a 'C' or even a 'G', perhaps to fit the shape of the hill behind. On the far side of the yard, he could just see the outline of open stalls divided by wooden pillars. As the light skeetered about, he caught glimpses of vehicles parked in the stalls, a little car, then a much bigger car and beyond it an old Land Rover. It must be a torch, the light, that was obvious now from the way whoever was holding it was moving about in the yard. He was a big man, and as he crouched to fiddle with something at the back of the little car, he almost blotted it out. Beaky, it must be Beaky. But what the hell was he doing rummaging around in his own yard at five in the morning (there was just enough light through the low window now for Luke to see the time on his watch)? Newcastle could not be much more than two, two and a half hours' drive over the hills. Why had he come back so late? Nobody inspected shopping centres at 2 a.m. Whatever had gone wrong with the little car could surely wait till morning. Luke was turning to make a last desperate search for the toilet when his eye was caught by another figure coming out of a little door at the far side of the yard. The new arrival had a dark coat on over pale trousers, pyjamas perhaps, and he walked in a neat, unhurried way over to the big man fiddling with the car. This could only be Keith, the butler or whatever you called him. There was something about his calm, unhurried walk. He had obviously been summoned to help out, because Beaky now handed him the torch and walked off in a quick huffy way, as though annoyed that he had not managed to fix the exhaust or whatever it was.

But now Luke really had to go. He decided to return the way he had come and just before he reached their bedroom he saw a door he had missed in the darkness and it was what he hoped it would be. In his woozy relief he stopped thinking about what he had seen and crawled straight back onto the bed, still fully clothed, and slept.

His sleep was fretful, though, and he dreamed that he was walking up a lane between deep banks full of cow parsley and he saw some tall chimneys on top of a red roof behind green hedges. The hedges were high too, and he couldn't see over them, but he felt he would be warm and safe if he could get inside the house, but there was no gate in the green hedges and he could not get in, but somehow he could hear what they were saying inside the house, and there was a woman talking and what she was saying was, 'I thought he was a nice little boy but he isn't nice at all, he's really nasty and he's not coming in.' And then something awful happened to him in the lane, but he did not know what it was because that was where the dream stopped.

It was well after ten when he woke up and Lee had already left the room. Downstairs he found a cooked breakfast fresh on the hotplate, the scrambled eggs still runny and the kidneys winking, and Lee just finishing her toast while Keith was refilling her coffee cup. He looked unperturbed either by being called out into the yard in the small hours or by Luke coming down so late. His presence at any rate protected Luke from any telling-off from Lee for his lapse the night before.

'As I have already informed Mrs Deverill, sir, Sir Wilfrid apologises not being here to greet you this morning and hopes you will join him for a glass of Chambéry in the belvedere at 12.30. He is very partial to his Chambéry, is Sir Wilfrid. It's just a jumped-up vermouth if you ask me, but he claims it makes all the difference if you drink it out of silver goblets. They are a devil to clean, those goblets, but he will have them.'

Luke had a feeling as he had had with the wife that Keith was acting the old retainer's part, consciously overacting it even, and was enjoying his own performance. But then perhaps all old retainers tended to ham up their act after a bit, if only to keep themselves amused.

Keith, having completed his duties for the moment, was gazing out of the window. The rain had cleared and a watery sun was warming the blanched slopes of the Dale and the greener valley in the distance.

'It will be a fine morning for the daffodils, sir. Today is Daffodil Sunday, so there will be quite a crowd later on.'

'I didn't realise it was Sunday,' Luke muttered.

'There is morning service at Snagglesby at eleven, sir.'

'Thank you but no.'

'You could just make it if I drove you in the Bentley.'

'No thank you,' said Luke.

Keith nodded gravely and withdrew.

After breakfast Luke badly needed to clear his head. 'I'm feeling like death,' he said, as he opened the French windows and led Lee out on to the lawn.

'So am I,' said Lee. She looked ghost-pale, too tired even to reproach him.

'You don't think you're going to—'

'Christ, I hope not, but let's just walk round the house. I don't feel up to a tramp.'

They plodded across the lawn, their shoes sinking into the soggy moss. At the end of the grass they brushed between dripping trees and felt the cold drops on their necks. Beyond a disused-looking path led round the back of the house to a rusty kissing gate. Lee just managed to squeeze through it and they came into the yard that Luke had looked out on from the passage. There was a huge saloon which Luke assumed was the Bentley but his not-driving included, as a dependent principle, not knowing about cars. Beyond the Bentley there was an inconspicuous small car which must be the one they had been fiddling with, and beyond that the Land Rover. Luke could see nothing remarkable about any of them and in any case he felt too grotty to tell Lee the story of what he had seen in the night, such as it was.

They went back up to their attic room to take off their wet shoes. The walk had not cheered either of them.

'I don't fancy any of this.'

'Nor do I.'

'I mean, you really do have to ask yourself, why the hell did he ask us here? The welcome isn't exactly on the mat.'

They were up in the belvedere on the dot of 12.30. They had debated being deliberately early or deliberately late and decided against both, not wishing to seem either too eager or too casual.

Bentliff was already there, standing in front of the fire, enormous in a country suit with a faint mustard stripe on a peaty ground. He had looked so awesome on the catwalk that Luke had not quite taken in that he was also remarkably handsome. There was nothing fleshy or coarse about his face. If he had been a little younger, he could have been a stand-in for one of those stars who played in improbable romantic comedies in the late forties set in Park Lane or on Park Avenue. He did look a little American, though Luke could not pin down quite why, his unashamed zest perhaps – there was no fading about his elegance, although he did look just a trifle weary, the eyes fractionally baggy, the skin a little off-colour, but then being up at five in the morning never did anyone much good that day.

'Lee, my dear, and Professor – how very glad I am to see you both at last.'

'Luke, please, Luke.'

'... and Luke. I had been looking forward to our meeting so greatly and now I have been neglecting you abominably.' Luke now detected, as he had not fully from Beaky's harangue at Mulvaine House, that touch of Yorkshire gravel in the way he talked, the accent perhaps accentuated on home turf but recognisable as the trademark which sent profile writers into such rhapsodies. Something about the way he rumbled 'abominably' made you think of every Yorkshireman who had ever made a career out of speaking bluntly, although otherwise his voice was so fine and clear that you fancied his singing voice must be just as fine.

'As you no doubt know,' he began, 'Yorkshire people are famous, I might almost say notorious, for not beating about the bush. And so I hope you will forgive me if I come straight to the point. There is so much we have to talk about that it would be a pity to waste a minute in pleasantries. First then, let me pay you both a very sincere tribute. I cannot disguise from you that I have been following your operations with growing interest, and indeed admiration. I am well aware that this may come as something of a disappointment to you both. One always likes to feel that one is invisible, does one not? But alas, the modern world is something of a panopticon – it is so pleasant to be with people for whom one need not translate. As you said yourself, Professor, Luke I should say, may I quote you: "remote communication is a wonderful boon, but it is also a great destroyer of privacy". I particularly liked your illustration about having to hide behind a pillar to overhear the merchants whispering on the old bourses of London or Amsterdam, while these days the evil interceptors, as you call them, can listen in wherever the merchants happen to be dealing, perhaps thousands of miles away. I would venture only to add, if I may adapt that excellent question posed by the poet Juvenal: *quis intercipiet ipsos interceptores?* I hope I have the future tense correctly.'

Luke had gone sheet-white. He could think of nothing to say. Still, two could play at that game and were. He could feel the tiny Rummy mike in the watch pocket of his jacket. Lee had hers securely stapled inside her bra.

After a gulp of Chambéry, Bentliff resumed, immense in front of the fireplace, his legs spread like stanchions supporting some tower block: 'I would not wish to take any personal credit for the remarkable achievements of our information and surveillance network, except to claim a little Yorkshire gumption for recognising talent when I see it. When I first bumped into Keith Rosewill in the mid eighties, he was station officer for MI6 in Cyprus at a rather tricky juncture in our relations with the Middle East. I had a modest interest in supplying matériel to certain parties, nothing very offensive, you understand, mostly trucks and spare parts. The British government's policy towards the regime in question was in the process of changing but nothing had yet been officially announced. It was a delicate moment and considerable finesse was required to get matters under way while sanctions were still in place, with the risk that if we were too slow, nimbler rivals, notably the French, would be in there first and slam the door in our face, and if we were too quick, we might all end up in jail. Keith was a total star. In the event, we never actually sent them so much as a sparking plug and I was relieved that we had not, but I never forgot Keith or his girlfriend, later his wife, Kay, who was a brilliant cipher clerk on the station. It was my great good fortune that he then fell out with his masters and left the service, I will not say under a cloud but with a certain amount of resentment at the way he had been treated.'

'Keith? You mean the man who has been looking after us?'

'The same. He told me this morning how much he was enjoying his new role. When he and Kay finally retire, they are thinking of taking it up professionally, buttling in Miami perhaps or managing a country-house hotel in the Lake District – no, not the Lake District, Kay tells me she cannot abide the climate up here.'

'So he was bugging us all the time we—'

'There was a meeting, I think in the Rose Garden in Hyde Park.'

'Not with us.'

'No, no, with that friend of yours, the journalist whose name we need not mention. First he saw you both in that apartment with the fine view of the Albert Hall. Then he went on to meet his old friend, Mr Beavan, Rowley I believe you call him, and later they both met George Furcht at the Diana Fountain.'

'How did—'

'Your friend had a little something sewn into the lining of his coat. I must hasten to reassure you, he was quite unaware of this. It was a simple matter of switching coats in that Italian restaurant he frequents. I cannot tell you what pleasure it gave us to sit in, as it were, on your discussions. A little more Chambéry, Luke? It has such a bracing effect, don't you find, at this hour? And, Lee, I do hope the elderflower agrees with you?'

'It's very good, thank you,' Lee said in a trance.

'You look pale, my dear.'

'I have felt better.'

'A little walk after lunch to see the daffodils will restore you, I'm sure. You cannot come to Brawldale today of all days and not see the daffodils.'

'Can we get on with it?' Luke said.

'I could not agree with you more. Well, as I say, we found ourselves following each move of yours with increasing fascination and not a little admiration. The way you won the confidence of those ladies, Lee. The childlike trust they showed when they gave you their pass-words, in some cases their husbands' passwords too. Well, we took our hats off, did we not, Keith?'

'We did indeed, Sir Wilfrid.'

Luke and Lee whipped round in unison to see the manservant standing respectfully behind them with his wife at his side.

'Keith in his various guises of heating engineer, relief doorman, passing jogger, computer repairman and I don't know what else had as much as he could do to keep up with you. The Silk Road – what a charming phrase to describe such a charming deception, the phrase was quite new to me. And your guess that the complimentary guest list for the fashion show might yield the decisive clue to the identity of our associates, that was a masterstroke. I have read somewhere that it is one of the greatest pleasures in life to watch a cast of competent actors perform a play that you have yourself written. So it was with me as I sat enthralled in the best seat in the house. I can only say that you read your lines impeccably.

'I admired too the grace with which you acknowledged that your efforts were ultimately futile, since none of us had broken any law. The only crime that we could be accused of was that of being some-what more perceptive than other players in the market. This is not yet a crime until stupidity becomes enforceable at law, which, I fear, may soon be the case. I think it was your Mr Beavan who observed that any one of us could say, "I was merely taking a legitimate view of Furcht's prospects and as usual I turned out to be right, which is why I've got a private jet and you have not." though personally I would deplore the possession of a private jet as the criterion of success – a rather vulgar bauble, I have always thought.'

'You bloody well know that isn't the point. You were able to destroy Furcht's business only because you were running a campaign of terror in Brazil.'

'Campaign of terror? That's strong language, Luke, actionable language I rather fancy, not that I would dream of suing someone I so esteem and would like to think of as a friend. I have, as they say, form when it comes to libel suits, rather hot form, as you undoubtedly know. But I have no intention of resorting to Messrs Sue, Grabbitt and Run, unless you positively compel me to do so. I would much rather attempt to dissuade you from using such emotive language. What, after all, have we witnessed going on in the Amazon basin? An entirely honourable campaign to save the richest habitat remaining on this planet from the depredations of greedy and short-sighted thugs. The success of that campaign which I announced to you all the other evening at Mulvaine was one of the proudest moments of my life. I felt privileged and, yes, humbled to have played some small part in the business.'

'Were arson and murder honourable? At least twenty men dead, probably twice as many, billions of dollars of property and equipment destroyed, whole villages terrorised, public officials suborned and blackmailed. The rightness of the cause cannot possibly justify the methods. What makes Enida any different from Al Qaeda or Mossad or ETA?'

'Enida, ah, yes. That moment too gave us a little throb of pleasure when you spotted that giveaway passage in my poor memoirs, a rather trumpery publication I now think, although some of the critics were kind enough to say otherwise. I was so glad that Keith had had the foresight to nip down to the Hertz office in Leeds and personally select your hire car. Otherwise we might not have shared another of your Eureka moments as you call them. The least I can do is to give you a copy, not of course of my own work but of that little masterpiece which brightened my lonely childhood. Not a first edition, I'm afraid, but the cover does have a certain period charm.'

He handed Lee a small pink book with a picture on the cover of a Siamese kitten pouring some yellow liquid out of a blue-and-white jug onto the lolling tongue of a fox terrier.

'So far as I can recall, it's custard he's pouring,' Bentliff remarked, peering over Lee's shoulder. 'Would you like me to inscribe the book for you? Or perhaps it would be more appropriate that Bimbo and Topsy should sign it themselves.'

'I think it would be better coming from you, Sir Wilfrid,' the woman interjected.

'As you wish, Topsy. It remains our impression that you never managed to hack into our own internal communications – though we could be wrong about that, one never knows with these things – but had you done so, unless you had also stumbled upon what one might call the Green Hedges Connection, you might well have been puzzled by the constant references to Bimbo and Topsy and sometimes by extension to "the Kitten" and "the Terrier". I am afraid the whole thing was deplorably English, combining as it does two of our abiding national weaknesses: for children's literature and for secret codes.'

'Look,' said Luke, 'I don't give a bugger about your fucking codes. All I care about is Timbo and the other people you murdered or kidnapped.'

'Timbo, ah yes. At first we found it difficult to take seriously a person who insisted on such a ludicrous nickname. It seemed to me one more indication that George Furcht was running out of road that he should have chosen such a person to seek out the cause of his difficulties. We only began to take proper cognisance of Timbo when he showed the unexpected good sense to recruit you two to his team. There was something so out-of-left-field, almost off-the-wall about his choice that we began to suspect that there might be more to young Timbo than we had thought. In retrospect, I am not sure that there was. My final judgement would be that he belongs – or belonged – to a not unfamiliar type: that of the Englishman who plays the silly ass but who is in fact a silly ass, his only redeeming feature being that he knows what he is and resolves to play down to his image. Or is that unfair? At all events, rightly or wrongly, we began to regard him as a potential nuisance who might, if only by his blundering, derail our plans in some way that we could not foresee. So when Furcht sent him to Brazil, we came to the conclusion that he had to be stopped in his tracks. We reached this conclusion with some reluctance because the stopping itself carried certain risks. That business in the longhouse, which you may or may not know about, was in essence something of a compromise, a rather violent prank, one might call it, but we judged it a sufficient deterrent to any further inconvenient activities on his part, at least after he had had time to cool down in that dear little hut we hired for him.

'It was a piece of good fortune for us that the authorities out there should have deduced that it was he who was responsible for those appalling fires on the Tapajós. But who could blame them for thinking this? They had after all received photographs of Timbo carousing with a notorious illegal logger – it may be assumed in celebration of some unlawful contract he had signed on his master's behalf. What could be more likely than that they had then between them started a series of fires to put rival operators out of business? We did not suggest to the police that he had intended to burn Senhor Humberto alive, but they would certainly have been justified in bringing charges of culpable homicide against him. A horrible way to die, do you not think? But then horrible things happen in that part of the world. I do hope that your friend survived to tell the tale, though I doubt that many would have believed his version of events. I'm afraid that for once our information systems have failed us on this point. We have no knowledge of your friend Timbo's present whereabouts, none at all. Yes, Keith?'

Luke swung round again to see that the manservant stood alone behind them. The woman must have left as noiselessly as she had come.

'My wife says that lunch is ready, sir.'

'Ah, I think I can promise you that this will be a treat. The Daffodil Sunday lunch at Brawley has been a tradition since my father's day, but like many good old British traditions it has had to be revived. Topsy has been burrowing away in some of the old books and she has come up with what I am sure you will find a splendid simulacrum of the lunch that Meadow Bentliff would have served circa 1930.'

Lee was about to say something, Luke could not guess what, but he squeezed her hand in a gesture not only of affection but of warning. The thing to do, he thought, was to let Bentliff keep on talking.

Bric was already sitting at the table in the dining room. She had a plate of assorted meats piled high in front of her.

'You must excuse me. I overslept and missed breakfast. You have led me into terrible ways, Professor. Normally I expire in a ladylike fashion at the mere sight of a brandy glass, but last night I drank like a peasant.'

Bentliff stooped to drop a kiss on her golden braids, then led his guests to the hotplate which was crammed with a bubbling array of dishes, pots and pans.

'This, I fancy, is rump of hogget – halfway between lamb and mutton. You will excuse the accompanying lentils which are scarcely local but the ravigote makes a gradely combination. Now in this dish here we have sweetbreads, blanched and then deep-fried. Sweetbreads? Only a southerner would ask. Sweetbreads are the pancreas of lambs or calves or piglets, doesn't matter which but the animal must be less than one year old. Here of course is black pudding in a special honey sauce which I like to think I invented. And tripe and onions – a Yorkshire lunch would not be complete without tripe and onions. The ox's stomach is best; this one comes from the beast we slaughtered last week down the road at the home farm. Oh, I also see some chitterlings in broth, pig's intestines as opposed to stomach, often regarded in the States as typical soul food but you can find them in English cookbooks as far back as the eighteenth century. Chitterlings is, after all, a medieval English word.

'Now if you prefer the cold table, we have brawn, jellied pig's head to you benighted people, and delicious smoked eel, from the River Humber; the eels are rather scarcer up here than they used to be, alas, but every bit as good as ever. Now what's this? Rillette of duck, I think, there must be a Yorkshire word for rillette but I can't think what it is. And this, I happen to know, is a terrine of pig's trotters and ham hock which for my money is better than any terrine you could buy in Paris or Lyons. For potatoes I have chosen my favourite first earlies, Home Guard, lifted this morning from the kitchen garden, and as the ideal accompaniment our own beetroot in a sour cream sauce.

'We shall wash it all down with a flagon of Brawldale vintage cider. It is a little-known paradox that the harder the climate the more delicious the cider. Those wind-blown little apple trees you will have passed on the way up here make the best cider in the world.'

Luke and Lee obediently piled their plates. Bric had already demolished her personal food mountain and was coming back for seconds.

'My father always ate his Sunday lunch in silence. He claimed that it was a tradition in the North Riding. Ours is not a county famous for the quality of its conversation. I doubt whether there has been much good talk in Yorkshire since Dr Sterne was rector over at Sutton-on-the-Forest and he was an Irishman. But I am unlike my father in this as in many other ways and I cannot abide a silent table. So if you will forgive me, after I have eaten, I would like to add a little more to what I have already said. No,' he put up a great paw, seeing that Luke was about to speak, 'you would do much better to eat up, Professor. Moral indignation is bad for the digestion.'

Bentliff paused to make an opening assault on the mounds of offal in front of him. He ate with a Napoleonic impatience. Yet he was somehow not gross. His eating speed came naturally to him, as it might have come naturally to an ostrich or a giraffe.

'You will say,' he began, putting down his knife and fork for the moment, 'that those men in the rainforest did not deserve to die. But do any of us actually deserve to die? Yet we all do die. That is the appointed end of the programme. What is not appointed, what is not included in the software, is that we should *die out*. That is a serious business, the extinction of a species, would you not agree? The most serious business there is. Compared with the total disappearance of a genus, whether a few individuals die a few years sooner or later than the average is a trivial matter. Extinction is a final and irreversible thing. Evolution does not have second thoughts. Nature does not come back to pick up stragglers. There is no species she has a soft spot for. You remember your Tennyson: "She cries, 'A thousand types are gone: I care for nothing, all shall go.'"'

'"Nature red in tooth and claw",' Luke threw in. 'But of course those lines occur in a poem several hundred pages long, a poem which is a lament for a single individual.'

'It is indeed a lament and a damn fine one, in its own way as fine as this hogget here. But does it matter ultimately that Arthur Hallam should have died at the age of what? – twenty-one, of the flu I think – any more than it matters that this hogget should have died when it was one and a half years old. Alfred, Lord Tennyson laments, so does the ewe who has lost her child. Yet in both cases the species survives and flourishes. But if the species goes, there are no more Hallams, no more hoggets and no one to lament their passing. It is a funeral with no mourners.

'As you well know, there have been many victims in the struggle to save the rainforests, mostly Indians beaten to death or forced off their land to starve or drink themselves to death in the shanty towns. Some of the loggers fought their way into the forest with pickaxes and shotguns. I do not see why they should not get a taste of their own medicine. There came a point when retaliation was the only way. If George Furcht and his wretched company have gone to the wall, it is an insignificant matter in the scale of things. And the same goes for his miserable agents. And there I cannot exclude your friend Timbo. He meddled, he paid the price. There is no more to be said. This has been a just war and we are winning it. It would be the sheerest humbug to be sentimental about its casualties.'

Kay, or Topsy, as neither Luke nor Lee felt inclined to call her, was now moving in her normal soundless style to slide their plates away, murmuring as she did so, 'The desserts are on the lazy Susan.'

'Let me talk you through the puddings,' Bentliff said, rising from his chair to preside over the revolving table in the corner of the room. 'This part of the world is famous for its hearty desserts, more famous even, I would assert, than for its fabulous offal. If you open up a dead Yorkshireman, you will find "Afters" written on his heart. We have chosen only a modest selection for you today in view of the heroic efforts already demanded of you on the first course. Nearest to you on the lazy Susan, there is a Yorkshire curd tart with its subtle and, I fancy, unique scent of rosewater. Next to it you will find an excellent rhubarb crumble. Our own rhubarb is not ready yet, but we have no shame in buying from one of the best growers in the famous Yorkshire Rhubarb Triangle which lies roughly between Wakefield, Morley and Rothwell. Nowhere else in the world is early rhubarb still forced by candlelight. I cannot imagine precisely why candlelight should be so efficacious but there is no arguing with the results. And finally on the other side, from just over the Derbyshire border, we have the legendary Bakewell Pudding, not to be confused with the inferior and overcommercialised Bakewell Tart. Like many great dishes the pudding was invented by a happy mistake. The land-lady of the White Hart Inn in Bakewell forgot to blend her eggs and almond paste in with the pastry mixture and left them on top of the raspberry jam, or strawberry if you prefer, with the ambrosial results you are about to experience. Topsy, is the pudding made with raspberry or strawberry today?'

'Strawberry, Sir Wilfrid.'

'So you believe in the law of the jungle?' Luke had declined the puddings and was itching to return to the attack.

'There is no need to put on that sour voice, Professor. The law of the jungle, as you call it, is a far more humane regime than many of those devised by supposedly civilised human beings. In fact, it is only in the jungle that human beings have learnt to live in co-operation with nature, in the same way as other species, both animal and vege-table, they share the planet with.'

'But isn't your picture of the forest equally sentimental? In those green depths there are species going quietly to their extinction every day, often without our even being aware of it. Some of these unlucky creatures were hunted out of existence by your environmentally sensitive Indians who happen to be just about the tallest animals left standing in your precious rainforest. And then there are the great extinctions of the prehistoric world in which we had no part. Indeed we had not arrived before they had disappeared. We never knew those victims.'

'Yes, but we mourn them to this day. If you already had children, Professor, you would know that almost the first thing about the world that a child learns to wonder at is that there are no more dinosaurs in it. Would you wish our grandchildren to be left wondering that there are no more elephants or tigers or crocodiles? We are in a unique position, Luke, one that no generation has occupied before. We alone have the knowledge of what might happen and the technological capacity to stop it happening. We can choose whether to save as much as possible of the world we inherited or to let it go, indeed to help destroy it ourselves. It is for us to draw up a new mission statement, to improve on the one handed to us by that bad-tempered old Jehovah of the Jews. What did he tell Adam? Be fruitful and multiply and replenish the earth and subdue it and have dominion over every living thing that moveth upon the earth. Dangerous instructions to give to a novice, Mrs Deverill. And the long-term outcomes were calamitous. We need to rewrite the whole thing: this time, no dominion, no subduing and certainly no more multiplying. Respect and protect: that is our new mission.'

'Does your mission justify you in murdering as many—' Lee rose from her chair, flushed with anger. Then she sat down.

'Oh, God, fuck,' she said. 'I feel terrible. I think I'm starting.'

The men round the table were gripped by a mutual and paralysing consternation. This was an unwarranted intrusion. One did not start going into labour at a lunch like this one. As Lee crouched on her chair, gasping and holding her stomach, it was Bric and Mrs Rosewill who were swiftly at her side.

'Are you having contractions, dear?'

'You must go straight to hospital. It may be a false alarm but even so.'

'The cottage hospital at Grimwade is the nearest, they haven't closed the maternity wing yet.'

'Keith, could you get the Bentley out of the stables?' Bentliff came to life.

'I'm certainly not going anywhere with you, or him,' gasped Lee, nodding and glaring at Mr Rosewill.

'Well then, I'll explain the route to the Professor.'

'I'm going up to pack. Come on, Lukey.'

She waddled stiff-legged out of the room with Luke scurrying after her like a bridesmaid who has lost hold of the bride's train. After they had climbed the winding stairs to their bedroom, she sat on their bed, still gasping and swearing rather quietly when she wasn't gasping. Then she went along the passage into the bathroom while Luke shovelled their few belongings into the two squashy bags. He could hear the noisy ringtone of Lee's mobile down the passage. While Luke was zipping up the bags and then opening the drawers to see if they had left anything (he was punctilious in that way as in others), he could hear her talking in a strange, high, excited way. 'No, no-o, I don't believe it,' he thought he heard her say. When she came back to the room with the water she had splashed over her face still dripping down her flushed cheeks, she had a look of triumph. Luke thought, even in this frantic moment, not a moment for dwelling in, that he had never seen her look lovelier.

'Who was—'

'You'll have to wait. I want Beaky to be the first to know.'

Down in the hall, they were all waiting. Mrs Rosewill gave them the directions to the hospital: 'You go through Snagglesby, and turn left at the Spar supermarket in Combover and then it's signposted. They've got a bed ready for you.'

'The very best of luck, my darling. We shall all be thinking of you.' Bric came forward and flung her plump arms around her. Lee wondered how much she really knew about her husband and then she inhaled the wine on her breath and thought that she was probably past caring.

'Are you sure we can't give you a lift? Keith is a wonderful driver among his many other virtues.'

'I wouldn't take a lift off any of you unless I was drugged and handcuffed.'

'Have it your own way, my dear. We shall be thinking of you all the same. It is a personal sadness to me that you can't stay any longer. The daffodils are better than ever this year.'

'Fuck the daffodils and fuck you too,' Lee responded briskly.

At this Bentliff suddenly seized her roughly by the shoulder and brought his face close up to hers, so that his great nose was poking into her hair.

'Just one word of friendly warning to you both before you go. I would counsel you very strongly not to attempt any further action against me or any of my interests. You are well aware that there is not one scintilla of evidence to link me with any of the unfortunate events that have unfolded in the Amazon basin, nor will you be able to prove any unlawful behaviour by myself or any member of the Bentliff Group. Any effort to suggest the contrary will be contested with the utmost vigour. Writs for libel, slander, invasion of privacy and criminal conspiracy are already drawn up in draft and will be issued the moment we have any cause. It will be so much better if we part as friends and consign these difficult past few months to a merciful oblivion.'

'You don't know yet, do you? You really don't know. I thought you mega-business types were in touch with events round the world 24/7.'

'I don't know what you're talking about.'

'Well then, let me break it to you gently. It isn't George Furcht who's finished. It's you.'

'What on earth do you mean?'

'We have just heard that George has rolled over all his debt and Maloca shares have doubled over the past twenty-four hours. Anyone who hasn't closed out the short, which I understand includes quite a few greedy pigs, stands to lose billions. I'm sure that with that super-brain of yours you can calculate the exact figure in no time.'

'That is all arrant nonsense.'

'George is going to be King Cotton. Rowley says he's going to cover the whole of the bloody Mato Grosso with the stuff now that the US cotton industry is fucked.'

'Rowley? You mean that clapped-out City hack?'

'That clapped-out City hack has just been nominated CEO-designate of G. Furcht and Co. There is a lot more I could tell you, but I'm rather busy just now, as you know, and I'm sure you'll enjoy finding out the details for yourself. Thanks so much for having us. I don't think we'll be coming again any time soon. Byee.'

She skipped through the front door as though she had quite forgotten she was about to give birth and swung herself into the driving seat of the Fiesta with dazzling agility, considering her shape, and had fired up the engine almost before Luke got into his seat. The tyres sent up gay spurts of gravel as the car slung round the tricky curves below the house. They did not look back.

After the first cattle grid, the hillside was alive with daffodils and members of the public picking them. By the second cattle grid, there was a stall selling cream teas and the trail of cars thickened to a standstill as children clambered in and out of them and adults carrying bunches in one hand tried to find the money for the tea with the other.

'I always hated daffodils, even as a child. Those rude trumpets and such a horrible yellow, not golden really, sort of sickly. That was the nice thing about Bric, she hates daffs too,' said Lee.

'Do you think she's really a princess?'

'All White Russians are princesses. That's why there was a revolution. Come *on*. I don't want little Derek to be born on Beaky's blasted heath.'

'I thought you said you didn't like the name Derek,' Luke said, struggling to make himself heard over the noise of Lee's hooting.

'I don't really, but we have to, don't we? In memory of dead Grandad.'

'I never thought—' But unusually he did not complete his sentence, because he was suddenly choked by the recognition of how much everything had changed for him, and so late on too, long after he had cast a cold eye over his life to date and concluded that any fool could see this was how the rest of it would be: a bottle of vodka a day, sometimes a little more, not often less; the occasional paper published in *Mind* or *The Cryptographer* if he was still up to it. His long-mulled work on Montaigne and Modern Consciousness might one day slip out of some academic press and plop into the murky waters, making no bigger splash than a frog. But that would be it. As for company, he and Lethal had fought each other to a standstill. Nothing more to be hoped for there, certainly nothing of what there had been between them at the start.

But now here he was bowling down the Dales with his glorious wife back at his side and about to give birth, and both of them cold sober (apart from his one-off lapse).

Lee had spotted a gap in the family hatchbacks and charged through it, bumping off-piste and erasing several nodding daffodils before returning to the road. As he jostled around at her side, Luke thought that he had no cause to be ashamed of the show he had put up against Bentliff, although there had been something stagy and pompous about the argument between them. What the man really needed was a punch in his big snoot, a disabling volley of abuse, a blinding flash of contempt. All these Lethal had supplied in her old manner, and there she was glowing and gravid at his side. 'Prima gravida' seemed to him a beautiful phrase, even if coupled, as her doctor coupled it, with 'senile' – Lethal was going to be thirty-nine in September but pregnancy had taken ten years off her. It was in fact she who had first suggested that the boy – they knew it was going to be a boy – should be called Derek, a name which he liked no more than she did. But as soon as she suggested it, he felt a tug inside him to say yes to the idea, and he realised that Timbo had won. Narrative had crept up on him and taken control. When he and Lethal had first gone into what he called Drunk School, one of the therapists had counselled him to take one day at a time – advice which he ruefully reflected was just what he himself used to teach: every day a fresh start and a new Self. The shrinks endorsed as he did the Reverend Sydney Smith's cure for depression: take short views. But now he thought that if life was to be worth living, the long view had to be attempted too, not to justify your past or gild your future – there was little enough hope of either – but simply to listen to the full score of the symphony. Deprived of nostalgia on the one hand or hope on the other, life could be no more than a timid tiptoeing, a succession of dainty sips.

It was not just giving up the drink, it was giving up the women. For a time, it had been a source of reassurance to him, his reputation in that department. He had to admit that he could not resist a secret smirk when now and then he had caught a whisper of that reputation: no research student was safe with Professor Deverill, to opt for Medieval and Renaissance Philosophy was to kiss goodbye to your virginity, that kind of thing. And they were so touching when he touched them, like being given a mark they were not sure that they deserved. He remembered them all as individuals – Joy and Alison and Angharad and Tina – he was not that heartless. But his fierce satisfaction, the way he finished off each time, that was not kind, and afterwards it was troubling. He was glad to be rid of it all.

And who had taught him all this but Timbo, not actually taught him of course because Timbo did not really possess what you could call a mind, not even a second-rate one, but taught him by example, by his sentimental delvings into his family's past no less than by his frenetic plotting for the future. He was so intricately engaged in time, not least literally. Luke remembered how they had listened amazed and bewildered as Timbo described his plans for his wedding to Aurore. There was a lovely little Norman church in the village where Moth had been stationed just before he came out of the army and though they didn't live in the village any more, they could get a special licence to be married there. The village was only a stone's throw from the runway at Manston Airport. Timbo had started flying lessons so that when he had his wings he could fly Aurore straight from the church after the wedding in a light aircraft across the Channel to Aurore's family home in the Beauce which was also within shouting distance of a runway, and they would have a banquet that same evening on her parents' terrace and then a civil ceremony in the Mairie the next day. What did Aurore think of all this? Well, it was all going to be a secret up to the last moment. In any case, he had to pop the question about getting married first though they were already kind of engaged, and then they probably ought to live together for a bit to make sure that they were sexually compatible. Besides, she wasn't due back for several months from Sierra Leone where she just been transferred from Rwanda. Which would all give him plenty of time to get his wings. And now it seemed that wings, of the earthly sort anyway, would elude him for ever.

'You look sad. I'm supposed to be the broody one.'

'I was thinking of Timbo.'

'I think of him every five minutes, the poor silly sod,' she said.

He placed his hand gently on her belly and thought how he would once have despised anyone who did that sort of thing.

'Do you suppose we'll ever see him again?'

'Less and less,' he said.

'Me too. So we'll never be able to bollock him for getting us into all this.'

'Do you regret it then?'

'You know I don't,' she said.

'Nor I. I'm not sure quite how he did it, though. Turned us into who we are now, I mean.'

'If you don't know, I certainly don't,' she said.

'Perhaps it was, somewhat paradoxically, because he didn't actually try to reform us. The point was, he wasn't like some ghastly smarmy therapist who's paid to cure you and who trots out his well-worn trick questions and basically doesn't give a toss about you. Timbo got furious with both of us, genuinely furious, and then he would get bored and fly off at a tangent, and, God, how boring his tangents could be, but that somehow took the pressure off you so you didn't think you were being got at. He swept you up into something which I suppose could be called real life, for want of a better word. I was entangled by him and, looking back, entangling was what I needed instead of careering off on my own desperate solitary road. What I mean, I think, is that he was entirely natural because he was incapable of being anything else. It was like being healed by falling into a patch of nettles. Oh, Christ, that's the Spar, you've missed the turning.'

She slammed on the brakes, screeched into reverse and backed the car to within inches of the supermarket's windows before zooming forwards at right angles.

'Only five miles to Grimwade according to the sign.'

'Thank God. Derek's very stroppy. He'll be taking over the steering wheel any moment.'

They were down in the vale now, winding through pretty little villages of honey-coloured stone with mossy slate roofs.

'It's a pity George Furcht's such a shit,' he said suddenly. 'It would be nice to have rescued someone who deserved rescuing.'

'He's the last person who deserves a second chance. But don't worry, he's had his comeuppance all right. I wasn't going to give

Beaky the satisfaction of telling him because Rowley told me not to say, but everyone will know soon enough. G. dos Santos Furcht has had a serious stroke and will be retiring from active management. Actually he's in a wheelchair – can you hear me, Keith?' she yelled, suddenly remembering that the Fiesta was bugged and nuzzling her head down towards the glove compartment as if that was where the bug might be planted.

'And is Rowley really going to be in charge?'

'Well, the new President of the company will be that New York banker who talks in Latin the whole time, Hal something. He's looking after George at the moment at his gracious home in Connecticut. But the clapped-out City hack will indeed be the new CEO.'

'But Rowley's never run anything in his life. He told me so himself.'

'Well, he seems to have saved the company, which is a good start. So perhaps there's more to him than the carnation in his buttonhole. Oh, look here we are. That must be the cottage hospital down that lane. Wish me luck, darling.'

They missed the entrance to the hospital car park and she had to back violently again, brushing the wing mirror of a departing ambulance. She heaved herself out of the car and stood waiting to take his arm while he hoicked her bag out of the boot. As they limped across the tarmac, he wondered if they would think he was her father. There was ten years between them but he thought it looked more now.

He waited behind the screen while she undressed and put on her hospital gown. Out of the window he could see forget-me-nots and grape hyacinths in the little garden.

'Nursie says there's a nice day room at the end of the corridor where you can wait, or you could go into downtown Grimwade and see the sights. Or you might prefer to amuse yourself with the Rummy.'

He kissed her and told her she was wonderful and wished her luck again. Then he trotted off down the passage, carrying his miniaturised surveillance kit and his copy of *Montaigne and Feminism* as a fallback, in case there was nothing to listen to on the Rummy.

The day room was empty and had a view from a different angle of the little garden. There was a blackbird scratching about on the patch of lawn. Luke felt himself trembling as he sat down.

The reception was amazing, even bell-like, as though it had been recorded for a radio play. Every now and then it faded, presumably when whoever was speaking moved to the other end of the room or turned their back on the bug, which he had squeezed down into a corner of the brocade upholstery of the armchair he had been sitting in.

At first there was nobody speaking, just the sound of crockery being piled up. There would be some massive washing-up to be done after that lunch. Luke felt he would never need to eat again. He wondered who was clearing the table, Mrs Rosewill presumably (he did not wish to think of her as Kay, certainly not as Topsy). The odd thing, now he came to think of it, was that during their stay he had seen no other servants apart from the Rosewills. He would have imagined that Bentliff would not go anywhere without an army of servants. There was something impermanent about the whole establishment, as if the whole show had been put on for their benefit.

Now there was someone humming. A woman, he thought. The sort of humming people make when they are performing some chore they are not enjoying. There was not much tune to it – oh, yes, there was, it was 'Somewhere Over the Rainbow'. Then more clanking of plates and knives and forks and the squeak of wheels across the floor, the lazy Susan being put to the side perhaps or a trolley being taken to the kitchen. How gripping these ordinary noises were when you were listening to them covertly. Then a door slamming.

Then all of a sudden, there was the unmistakable voice: gravelly, rich, but at this particular moment tetchy or anxious or both, not the confident baritone of lunchtime.

'I don't believe it, Keith, seventy-five, you say?'

'Well, Beaky, there's only Hong Kong open at the moment because of it being Sunday. But they expect it to reach ninety or a hundred when London opens tomorrow.' Rosewill sounded anxious too, and badly badgered.

'Have you closed the positions yet?'

'I can't reach any of the prime brokers at the moment.'

There was a commotion which Luke could not identify, then an odd low burbling. He was not sure which of them it was coming from.

'Christ, at ninety we're nearly eight hundred million down,' said Beaky.

'I didn't know we had so many positions open.'

'We? Don't try to softsoap me, Keith. It was my decision. I take the decisions, including the bad ones. Fuck, fuck, fuck. How could that heap of shit rise from the dead? He couldn't not go down, he was dead in the water. *Yes?*'

Then the burbling began again. No, it wasn't burbling, it was snoring. Bric, it must be Bric sleeping off her lunch on that chaise longue at the end of the room she liked to stretch herself out on. Unfortunately it seemed the bug was too near the chaise longue because now the burble was drowning the conversation.

For the next few minutes he could not make out anything coherent, and he wondered whether he ought to switch off and go and see how Lethal was getting on. But she promised him the nurse would fetch him if anything started happening and she said she didn't want him moping over her with his droopy face anyway.

He began fiddling with the controls, with not much idea of what he was doing, and suddenly the voices came through with unnerving clarity again, so that he jumped as if they were just about to come into the day room and catch him listening in.

'No, I said I was too busy to see them. Can't they leave a message?'

'They said it was urgent and they had to speak to you personally.'

'Ask them to come back in the morning.'

'I've already suggested that, Beaky. They said they have to see you now.' Rosewill sounded agitated. Luke noticed that when they were alone together, there was none of the Sir Wilfrid business. The Rosewills were co-conspirators not servants. The old retainers had just been one more role-play for them.

More mumbling sounds and then a creak or cracking noise, then a woman's voice, not Mrs Rosewill's, sounding a little peevish or upset but not decipherable. Bric, woken, perhaps forcibly, from her teatime nap and not happy about it. Then footsteps, and, quite clearly, a door slamming.

And now for the first time low or lowered voices, too low for the machine to pick up even with the volume at max. So low now that he could not be sure whether they were still talking at all.

Several minutes now of silence. Time, he thought, for the visitors to be let in and led up the two flights of stairs to the belvedere. Luke took the opportunity to switch off and walk briskly down to the ward to ask the duty nurse if anything was happening. The nurse said that there wasn't and that it was best not to go into Mrs Deverill just now because she was having a rest. He went back to the day room and switched on again.

'... see you alone, sir.'

An official voice, someone on duty, respectful but confident.

'What is all this about? Kay, would you excuse us? Keith, if you wouldn't mind.'

A silence, then very faintly a door closing. The soundless Rosewills leaving the room.

'So, Officer?'

'I'm afraid we have tragic news for you, sir. Your wife has been found dead.'

'My wife? There must be some mistake. My wife has just been having a nap on that chaise longue there. She has now gone to her room. You might even have passed her on the stairs.'

'I'm afraid there is no mistake, sir. Your wife Madame Monique Bentliff was found dead this morning in her sitting room at her chateau. I regret to have to tell you that there is worse, sir. The French police inform us that she was strangled, with her own scarf, it seems. They incline to the view that she surprised an intruder, though of course their inquiries are at a very early stage. The French windows had been forced and several items of the jewellery she always wore had been ripped off her.'

'Oh, this is terrible, terrible, I cannot believe that such a dreadful thing could have happened. It is such a peaceful part of the world, Inspector, though I suppose these things can happen anywhere.'

'The French have asked us to make a few background inquiries to fill in the picture. May I ask when you last saw Madame Monique?'

'Of course. But first I must make clear something rather difficult and personally embarrassing. And I would ask most earnestly for your discretion in so far as this is compatible with your professional duties.'

'I am not sure what you mean, sir.'

'Well, I said just now that my wife was here with me, my second wife, Princess Brigitte Bentliff. But while it is true that we have been living together as man and wife for a number of years now, you are quite right. In strict legal terms I am still married to my first wife, poor Monique. I won't go into the reasons why this is the case. I can only say that Brigitte would be very distressed if the fact were made public, and I must say that from the point of view of your inquiries, and those of the French police too of course, I cannot see why it should be relevant. It would be of no interest to the intruder or intruders.'

'I cannot promise anything. Things do have a way of coming out in an investigation of this nature. But it is certainly not our intention to cause unnecessary distress.'

'I am most grateful to you. Well, to answer your question, I have not seen Monique for several months now. I was hoping to pay her a visit very soon. I like to spend a week with her three or four times a year. She sees so few people. I am sure you have been told about her ghastly accident.'

'We have, sir. A horrible business. So you have not been to France at all in the past few weeks?'

'No, I've been up here for the past four days and before that in London and before that, oh, my PA will give you the details more reliably than I can. This is so awful. I'll drive down to London and catch a flight tonight.'

'We would rather you stayed put here just for the time being, Sir Wilfrid, if you don't mind, until we have a full list of the questions our French colleagues would like us to ...'

'Get Murdo, please, this one's a quickie.' Luke hurriedly took off his earphones, as he heard the nurse calling down the passage, and the noise of a trolley being pushed at speed.

'Mr Deverill, Mr Deverill, we think your wife is just going into labour.'

He caught up with her at the doors to the little operating theatre, and he held open the flappy door to let her trolley pass. Her hair was tucked up under a blue-chequered hospital cap.

'You look like Joan of Arc,' he said.

'You look quite funny too,' she said and gave him a woozy little wave.

XIV

Prosper Mill

'Do you think they saw us?'

'Not a chance,' Timbo said, with a return of his old plonking confidence. 'We had our capes over our heads and nobody notices cyclists.'

'That's true,' I said, wondering whether it was really true about cyclists.

Timbo had continued to insist that his resurrection must remain a secret as long as Beaky was still active. His being a non-person, and an unrecognisable non-person at that, was his biggest asset. This, he said, would be his final mission. I did not care for the sound of that, and I liked it even less when he added, 'And of course you're coming with me.'

'Not a chance,' I said, trying to echo his own plonking confidence. 'I've wasted enough of my life trying to clean up after you.'

'You can ride a bike, can't you?'

'More or less.'

'So what we'll do is sneak in behind the house, at the back of the stables, while Luke and Lee are keeping him amused.'

'How on earth do you know the layout?'

'There's a virtual tour on Dream Yorkshire.' I had only told him the day before about Luke and Lee going up to stay with Beaky, and already he had a plan of campaign.

'And what exactly are we going to do then?'

'We wait and see. When you're dealing with unknown unknowns, you can't make a precise plan. Talking of which, I need you to work the Rummy. I sense that things are coming up to the boil nicely.'

'I really do think that we should let Luke and Lee know we're coming. After all, we're on the same team.'

'It's not a bloody team game. Remember what I said about hunting separately. We mustn't cramp their style.'

I looked at him in undimmed amazement. After all that had happened to him, he still seemed to retain a serene belief that things would come out all right in the end, a proposition for which there seemed to be rather less evidence than for the existence of life on Mars.

At the same time, though, some other feeling crept over me, which I found hard to pin down and which I resisted in vain. Not pity for Timbo, though there might have been a smidgen, not even exasperation, though there was plenty of that, but rather a ghastly sensation of complicity. I had been dragged so far down this weird track that if I refused to travel any further with him, I would be responsible, to some degree, for whatever was going to happen to him. It was, after all, not impossible that, even at this late stage, I could help him to swerve. Not impossible but staggeringly unlikely. God alone knows why, but I had to go with him.

'It's only for a couple of days max.'

The ease with which I slipped away gave me false encouragement. Dr Watson never had so little trouble closing his surgery. Jane happened to be working nights that week, and Flo and Lucy were off on school trips. Nobody paid any attention to my faux-casual falsehood about a conference at Ditchley. It was another chapter in the life of a superfluous man.

So there we were toiling up the long slope through the daffodil fields, hidden under our sage-green cycle capes. I hadn't had a twinge from my back, though. Timbo said that cycling never did any harm to backs, or to knees for that matter. We got off the bikes when we reached the shelter of the trees, just after the last cattle grid below the house. Timbo had already taught me how to fold up the bike – he could do it in four and a half seconds now, just as the instructions claimed – and slung it over his shoulder. Then we began crawling through the trees round the house, aiming to approach from the back. There were thick clumps of rhododendrons under the trees and we had to shoulder away the dripping branches to get through. Quite soon we were high up behind the house. Through the bushes

I could see lighted windows on the top floor, roughly on the same level as we were. Below us was a stable yard and a set of open stalls. There was an empty space, a big car, a Bentley or a Rolls, the sort of car Beaky would insist on for showing off, then next to it an old Land Rover and a couple of empty berths beyond. Opposite I could see a back door to the house and another door at right angles to the first.

'Perfect view, perfect cover,' Timbo muttered, as he passed me my share of the sandwiches we had bought at Thirsk station and the Lindt 70 per cent chocolate bar, and gave me a swig from the whisky flask. So we began to wait, with the fold-up bikes out of sight behind us. I was determined to stay awake, but the exhaustion after the long ride up from Thirsk was too much for me.

We woke, quite gently, more or less at the same time, to the sound of a car engine. It was still pitch-dark and dripping dank in the trees now. We peered down between the rhododendrons and saw a small car coming into the yard, softly and slowly as though the driver was trying not to disturb the people in the house. The car edged into the first vacant stall next to the Bentley/Rolls, and the driver levered himself out of it. Even in the darkness of the stall, I could see how huge the man was. Unmistakably Bentliff. I looked at my watch. 4.45 a.m. Where the hell had the man been? Now Bentliff came round to the boot and I expected to see the boot lid fly up as he took out his luggage. But it stayed down. Instead, Bentliff was bending low over the back of the car and then squatting on his haunches, as though examining the exhaust or the rear lights. He stayed in this position for quite a time. It was impossible to be sure what he was doing, but he seemed to be tugging at something. He pulled several times, then stopped. He paused, then stood up straight and walked rapidly over to the further of the two back doors and went inside and came straight back out. A few minutes later, the same door opened and a much slighter man came out. He was wearing a dressing gown or a light coat and carrying something in his hands. He went over to the little car and began fiddling at the back as Bentliff had done. But he was standing more sideways on than Beaky was now, and so I could see that what he was doing was fiddling with the number plate. It was not long before he had unfastened it and laid it on the ground. Then he went round to the front of the car, presumably to repeat the process with the other plate, though he was now hidden from our view by the roof of the stalls.

There was a little more light in the yard now because of the first pale glimmer of dawn over the hill, not enough to decipher the number on the plate lying on the ground but enough to identify the narrow, compressed lettering: French plates.

'Keith Rosewill, it has to be, the man in the dressing gown, that constipated walk. You remember him too from the Amazon, Dickie, don't you?'

'Of course I remember him,' I said, 'but why's he switching the plates?'

Then both men disappeared inside the back of the house, and the place was quiet. I think we must have both have half-dozed off again, because it was bright morning when we came round. Through the rhododendrons we could see beyond the smoke from the chimneys of the house and on over the road down into the broadening dale and the watery green shimmer of the flat country beyond. I was tired to my bones, and now my back was really aching from the awkward way I had slept with one shoulder rubbing against the folded bike. I looked down into the yard again and there was the little car beside the Bentley. It was a Peugeot 207 and I could almost read the plates that were now on the back of it – GsomethingDWR – sturdy Yorkshire plates spattered with Yorkshire mud. Then I noticed that the Land Rover had no plates on it.

'What do we do now?' I whispered.

'We wait. Don't worry. It's all coming good. When you're faced with Unknown Unknowns, it's fatal to go looking for them, because you can't possibly know where to start. Talking of which, I think it's time for you to fire up the Rummy. They must be waking up in the house by now.'

I booted up the dark green flatpack, it was every bit as simple as Luke had claimed. Soon the mild breathy crackle from the Rummy mingled with the morning coos of the wood pigeons.

'Nothing so far.'

'Don't fret. In this game you have to be patient. I once listened for three days on the trot in Haywards Heath, staking out an insurance racketeer. Turned out he'd already fled to Belize.'

As the morning wore on, rich cooking smells began to waft up to us from the kitchen. I imagined huge Yorkshire roasts and pies the size of bollards.

It must have been well after midday when, without warning, the Rummy burst into life, and the rich gravelly tones – unmistakable though I had heard them only once before – crackled across the hillside.

'Turn it down, for Christ's sake,' Timbo hissed.

Even at normal volume, the resonance made the rhododendrons shiver. I turned the volume down again and Timbo crept closer to me, putting his arm round my shoulders to hear better.

At Mulvaine House there had been a certain gaiety about Bentliff's way of speaking, menace too in plenty as he seized his theme, but he did seem light on his feet. Now he sounded grim, his ironies heavier, as he described to Luke and Lee how he had managed to keep tabs on us every step of the way. I was surprised, though, to see Timbo nodding with something like approbation as Beaky recounted the relentless ingenuity of the Rosewills in their various disguises. He appeared to share none of my dismay and sense of humiliation at the exposure of our naïveté. When Beaky recounted the childish origins of Enida, Timbo again nodded sagely as though this was stuff he had known for ages.

When Beaky confessed that, despite his best efforts, he had no knowledge of Timbo's present whereabouts or even whether he was still alive, something like rapture spread over Timbo's features, his profile outlined against the midday sky now rivalling Bentliff's in the beaky department. Here was an accolade to be treasured from a master of the dark crafts.

Timbo's attention began to wander – so did mine – when the lunch came in and Bentliff took his guests through the menu. His voice was becoming hypnotic – and not in a good way.

Then, almost seamlessly to my ears, he launched into his prolonged polemic against the loggers, which seemed pretty cogent to me. But Timbo nodded his vigorous approval when Luke ventured on a spirited counter-attack, which only made me realise, not for the first time, how my loyalties, such as they were, remained hopelessly divided. Curiously, or not so curiously, what Bentliff reminded me of now, and powerfully so, was George Furcht, as though self-belief ended up sounding much the same whichever side you were on; the grinding certainty of the speaker erasing the exact nature of what he was trying to get across.

Suddenly this elevated debate was cut short by repeated cries of distress, from Lee obviously. There was a sound of chairs bumping and plates clattering as people went to help her. The tone of the talk changed – hurried, jerky, uncertain – as we heard arrangements being made to rush her to the cottage hospital. Then just as abruptly as it had opened up, the Rummy went dead.

'We must get down to the hospital,' I said, struggling to get to my feet on the steep hillside.

'What can we do? You're not a midwife. Anyway this really isn't the time to break cover. We need to hang on here. I'm sure there's more to come.'

The coldness of Timbo's response repelled me, but I could see his point, although I felt desperately anxious for Lee giving birth in a godforsaken cottage hospital miles from anywhere. As it turned out, there was an interval of only about fifteen minutes and then the Rummy came alive again, the sound rather more muffled now as though the transmitter had been shifted to a more remote or somehow shrouded site. At first only disjointed fragments of speech, barely decipherable, then sounds of lunch being cleared, instructions being given by a woman, drowsy, with some sort of foreign accent.

'Don't worry,' Timbo said, in a rather more human voice – he even patted my shoulder. 'I'm sure she'll be in good hands.'

We finished the chocolate and I had a gulp of the whisky – Timbo said he'd stick to the water, he had such a weak head. Everything was quiet in the yard now, and my gaze strayed to the sheep moving slowly across the bare hill on the far side of the valley. The sun had already gone down behind us and it was beginning to get chilly when there were sounds of more talk on the Rummy, indistinct at first as though the speaker was at the far end of the room or the other side of an open door. Then Bentliff again, sounding tetchy now, no, positively anxious. There was somebody at the front door he didn't want to see. But after a bit it seemed that Rosewill – I'm pretty sure it was him – apparently had no alternative but to let the man in.

The man was a police officer. And what he had come to say was that Bentliff's wife had been found dead. Bentliff said this wasn't possible, he had just been having lunch with her. And the policeman, an Inspector, said no, he meant Sir Wilfrid's first wife. She had been murdered, strangled at her chateau in France. Could Sir Wilfrid say when he had last seen her?

As Bentliff slowly set out his version of events (his voice now a gravelly crawl), I looked across at Timbo. He wore an expression of extreme gravity which masked another expression that wasn't grave at all.

'The plates,' he said.

'Yes,' I said.

'We stay put.'

'Yes.'

To our annoyance, the Rummy shut down again while they were still talking. Perhaps there was a time switch, or just a technical fault.

The light was thickening now. The watery sun had long gone behind the hill and there was a mist coming up from the valley. I began to shiver, dreading the thought of a second night in these dripping bushes. It was black dark when I heard a door opening down below in the yard and Beaky Bentliff came out, shrugging on a raincoat as he lumbered over to the stalls and jumped into the little car with the new plates. He reversed out of the stall, then, to my surprise, instead of curling round the side of the house to reach the road back down to the valley, he turned the car up a track behind the stable yard. From where we were crouching, it looked as if it led nowhere but into the depths of the wood.

Timbo beckoned me urgently to my feet, and we stumbled hurriedly through the bushes behind the back range of the outhouses, lugging the bikes which seemed to weigh a ton. When we reached the track we unfolded the bikes and jumped on and rode up into the wood. I could just see Bentliff's tail lights as the track took a sharp left-hander.

It was quiet in the wood. The track was covered with old pine needles and the only sound was the jolting of our little wheels as they hopped over a big root or a fallen branch. I could scarcely hear the Peugeot, which must be at least three hundred yards ahead. Once or twice a pigeon startled from its roost came flapping back over my head. Otherwise we and Beaky were alone in the wood together. The track took an abrupt turn uphill and then came out onto a tarmac road. It was a single track leading up higher onto the open moor, not much used by the look of it. The overgrown gorse bushes flicked at our calves and I caught the coconut smell and drank in the cool night air. It was hard pedalling up over two false summits, but there seemed little danger of losing the Peugeot. As we crested each brow, we could see the little car crawling along ahead, much the same distance ahead of us as it had been. Eventually there we were on the true top, panting hard and looking down over a huge black expanse and beyond the moor the lights of a town spread out over the valley and the opposing hillside. The town looked enormous in the night.

Now we were freewheeling, and once or twice we had to brake in order not to get too close. Then it struck me, for the first time, just how slowly the car was travelling over the moor, a beetle's pace through the heather. Beaky had seemed to be in a hurry when he jumped into the car, and he must be familiar with the way. But there was, undeniably, a certain hesitation or effort about his progress, rather as though the car was not working properly. 'I think he must be pissed,' Timbo said as he drew level with me.

We were almost down in the valley now and we saw the car stop abruptly at a junction, though there was no traffic visible in either direction. Beaky made a slow, clumsy curve left onto the main road. And now we were sure. No fugitive in history had ever driven his getaway car so slowly. The huge man whose every movement radiated a titanic impatience was driving like a little old lady. Beaky was drunk.

Even on the main road, it was easy enough to keep him in our sights, especially now that we were rolling down the side of a gentle hill into the suburbs of the town, past sleeping stucco villas and shuttered small shops and pubs with a couple of lights still on. At the bottom of the hill there was a little humpbacked bridge, and without warning Beaky swung hard right off the main road, but so late that he almost hit the parapet of the bridge.

I could see the glimmer of water from a lone street lamp, and warehouses on the far side of the water. We must be going along an old canal. The lane had potholes and puddles in it and my little bike bucked and swerved as badly as it had back up in the wood. In my mouth I had the smell of ancient coal dust and putrid water and I could sense the desolation all around us.

About a quarter of a mile ahead, I saw the Peugeot's brake lights come on. The canal lane was so straight that it was hard to be sure, but it looked as if the car had stopped.

We got off our bikes and wheeled them quietly up the lane until we were a hundred yards short of the parked car. Behind the car there was a hulking mill or warehouse on the canal with its windows giving directly on the black water. Now we could see the big bulky figure scurrying along the back of the building, in an ungainly way, as if unused to moving so quickly.

We stowed the bikes out of sight in a gap in the brambles at the side of the lane and crept towards the building. By the time we got there, we could see no sign of Bentliff, but there was a black door swinging open at the far end.

Inside the great brick hall there was a glimmer of grey light from somewhere above and I saw a wooden staircase with broad treads leading up out of the echoing empty space. Timbo approached the stairs at a stealthy crouch, making shushing gestures to me, no doubt fearing that Beaky might have heard him and be waiting, though I could see no place to hide in the huge twilit hall. The wooden treads creaked modestly as he climbed, with me a few rungs behind him. Anyone on a higher floor could not fail to hear us coming now. The floor above had long windows with small panes and hooped heads, and we could look down out of them on the still waters of the canal. There was a narrower stairway in the corner, a clanging winding metal stair, and Timbo went up it without a second thought. He gestured to me to stay at the bottom of the second stair, but I ventured up a couple of steps, enough to see the long high attic running the full length of the mill. The ceiling was all glass and iron ribs, soaring like the roof of an old railway station. Through the glass came the grey light, soft and ghostly, bleaching the life out of the broken machinery and battered boxes which lay about the dusty floor.

'Who are you?'

It was the same as the voice we had heard on the receiver, but all the more potent now it came to us directly in this great echoing attic. Even though we knew what to expect, it was still awesome, the rich Yorkshire gravel which was somehow grating and melodious at the same time.

'Oh,' said Timbo, startled, 'nobody you'd know.'

'You might be surprised. I know a lot of people.'

'My name's Smith. Timothy Smith.'

'Ahh.' There was a curious drunken contentment in the voice, as though this was the culminating moment in a long-worked-out plan. 'Timbo, the famous Timbo. So you got here in the end. I thought you would. Bimbo and Topsy said we would never see you again, but I had faith in your ...' – he paused for the right word – 'in your stamina.'

From my vantage point, it was hard to identify exactly where the voice was coming from. My tired eyes strained to pick out the shape of a man from the piles of stuff along the walls and in the corners, all covered with dust and ghostly grey light.

'They were hard on you, Bimbo and Topsy. They exceeded their instructions. Under that façade of bourgeois gentility they are quite merciless. That is both their strength and their limitation. One must always know when to stop. Never squeeze the last drop, my father used to say and he was accounted a hard man. If my other associates had also learnt that lesson, we would not all be in such a pickle.' In his boozy languor, he dragged out the word 'pickle' and made it sound homely, as though losing close on a billion dollars was like losing a pair of spectacles.

'Are you on your own?'

'Yes, yes, I am,' Timbo lied.

'I'm glad of that. I have had enough of the police for one day.'

Timbo had moved a couple of feet away from the iron staircase, and squatted on the floor to one side of it, so that I too could see Beaky, a huge figure sitting on a pile of sacking with his back propped against a thick iron stanchion anchored to the floor with hefty bolts.

Bentliff was quiet now. I began to think that he might have dozed off. Then he began to speak again, but in such a drowsy murmur that it was hard to make out what he was saying.

'Let me look at you.'

'I'm nothing much to look at.'

'They tell me you have the most amazing red hair.'

'Had, not have. Anyway you wouldn't be able to see it in this light.'

'I would like to see you all the same. My spies tell me that your face has undergone certain interesting changes.'

'Your spies seem to tell you a lot.'

'Information is power, Timbo. A cliché but a true one.'

'Why have you come here?'

'This is our old mill, Prosper Mill. In its heyday, three hundred men and women worked here. It was the biggest in the Dale, by some margin. This top floor was where they sorted the fleeces because the light was so good. The women tossed them into wicker baskets and let them down out of that long window there, on the gantry. I used to come and watch them as a lad. The women were so quick. The fleeces seemed to fly through their white arms as they graded them. They were kind to me, the lasses, not just because I was the boss's son. They were warm people.'

'And your parents, were they warm people?'

'No, not warm. I remember my mother's white arms too, but they were embracing Brahms and Mendelssohn, not me. And my father? Well, Meadow was a great man in his way, but no, you could not call him warm. Why do you ask? Do you fancy yourself as some sort of twopenny shrink?'

'No, I was just curious.'

'You're a curious fellow, Timbo, too curious for your own good. That's your trouble. But you are surprisingly ingenious, I will give you that. I could have used you. Too late now, though, much too late.' His voice fell away, reflective, melancholy.

'Can I ask you something?'

'I can't stop you. But I don't promise to give you an answer.'

'Why were you so keen to make it clear to the police that you were still married to Monique?'

'Because I am, and anyway it would come out sooner or later.'

'But Bric is always described in the media as your second wife. You never made it clear until now that you were not married to her. And I just wondered why.'

'You *are* curious. In fact you are bloody impertinent. And how the hell do you know what I told the police? Well, sauce for the goose, I suppose. There is no more privacy anywhere. I think you had better go now. I have business to do here.'

Timbo paid no attention to this command. He might not be a genius, but he stuck at things.

'You see,' he persisted, 'when I used to read about you in the newspapers, I thought that was so interesting, that you had this horribly mutilated wife, or ex-wife as we all thought then, and you still went to spend time with her, quality time, not just a flying visit for the sake of appearances, and that seemed such a nice quality, especially in someone who had a reputation for, well, being rather ruthless.'

'I could have just been fond of her still, you know. Such things do happen.'

'Yes, you could, but it was interesting anyway and it stuck in my head. And when your name first came up in our investigations, I thought to myself – I'll use her first name if you don't mind, to save confusion with your current partner – I wonder if Monique has any connection with the case. And so I got a friend in Paris to do some research for me. It wasn't easy because of the French holdings being mostly in nominee accounts. But he did eventually manage to find out that in the late eighties, some time before that horrible accident, you had transferred almost all your interests in France into Monique's name, to save tax I imagine, because, before Mitterrand got in, French tax rates were so much lower for the super-rich than they were in the UK. So obviously if you two had got divorced, she would have kept the lot. And it was a lot, because it was your French holdings which really took off over the following ten or fifteen years. They were all in solid triple-A companies which went on growing: big pharma, medical equipment, agricultural machinery, high-end ceramics, software. By comparison, after the property crash, your UK operation was more like a mega-casino, with all those hedge funds placing your bets.'

'You're an impudent liar and an ignorant one, too.'

'So that is why you had to keep Monique sweet,' Timbo continued, again paying no attention. 'If you didn't spend all those weeks reading poetry together in the chateau, there was always the threat that she might divorce you. Really though, I don't suppose it was much of a threat because she still loved you and was obsessed by you and wanted to hang on to you, but the only way she could be sure of doing that was to hang on to the money. You were handcuffed to each other. Not very romantic, I suppose, but then Frenchwomen are famous for being realists, aren't they?'

'I don't know why I'm letting you ramble on, but I'll give you two more minutes and then I'm going to kick your arse down those stairs. It's quite easy to break your neck on them. One of our mill-hands did it, a lad not much older than I was then, and he never walked again.'

'And then we started looking at the other parts of your empire. And, rather to our surprise, we began to pick up whispers that things weren't going too well. The Bentliff Group had taken a bath in the property crash, we knew that, but we didn't know quite how caught up you were in the worst Lloyd's syndicates and how much you had punted on the dotcom bubble, which you pretended at the time you had steered clear of, but again we found a trail through certain nominee accounts. And just like George Furcht, you were beginning to have trouble with your bank covenants and the rollovers were coming too thick and fast for comfort. And then you saw a golden opportunity to get home free. By destroying George Furcht, you would save the rainforests and save yourself at the same time. It wasn't just a high-minded conspiracy, it was a desperate last throw.'

'Nonsense, it was a perfectly rational business opportunity which happened to accord with my deepest convictions. Is there any way of stopping your interminable babble?'

'But to make it really work, to really squeeze the last drop out of the big short, you had to hang on until the last possible moment and that's what you told all your mates to do and they did what you told them because Beaky knows best, although as you just said squeezing the last drop is always the worst policy. And I think you could see the crash coming, though you pretended not to. And that was when you had to go to France and see Monique and plead with her to bail you out – with a monster bridging loan, by pledging her fortune as security for the unsecured debt, whatever it was you needed. If she loved you, really loved you, she had to save you.'

'This is your craziest notion yet. I haven't been to France or seen Monique since last autumn.'

'I saw you change the plates, you know. Or rather I saw Keith change them after you couldn't manage it. And I saw where he hid the French plates too, under the straw in the stall next to the cars. I should imagine the police have found them by now, if they got my message.'

There was a silence.

'Of course I don't know exactly what happened in France, nobody knows except you, but it's not hard to make a reasonable guess. She was overjoyed to see you, all the more so because she was not expecting you. And you had an idyllic candlelit dinner together, her face in shadow as always, to keep up the illusion that everything was just as it had been in the old days.'

'My God, you have a vulgar imagination.'

'And then, very slowly and gently, you brought up the subject. And she flew into a rage, a tearful rage, when she discovered that the only reason for your visit was to plead with her to hand you back half her fortune. And of course she refused. She was too sensible, too French to throw good money after bad. Why should she bail out her husband when she knew that, if ever he got back what he still regarded as his money, he would be over the hills and far away and she would never see him again? So then – well, as I say, I don't know exactly what happened, but we know what the outcome was.'

'No, you don't. You don't know anything. You don't understand any of it.' Bentliff spoke in a low choking voice. I felt no pity for him, and I wondered what Timbo was feeling. He must have dreamed of a moment like this, when he finally had all the cards in his hand and he could play them out one by one. But perhaps at such moments all you felt was not exultation but total exhaustion. Certainly I did. The backs of my legs ached from the pedalling, not to mention my back from the crouching there in this ghost place with my mouth full of dust. I wondered what Bentliff would do next but I was not really afraid, because with the exhaustion came a weird sense of detachment.

For some time, neither of them moved, I could not tell how long for, probably less than a couple of minutes. Then I heard rather than saw Bentliff shuffle to his feet. When he was upright, he stood there for a few seconds in the grey light, huge and looming, and from my vantage point halfway up the metal staircase I could see that he was covered with dust. He had become an anonymous hulk like a shambling giant in a children's story, those giants who were always so sad.

Then Bentliff began to walk towards Timbo, and I saw that he had a rope in his hands, a length of thick fresh rope. And Timbo scrambled to his feet and began to run towards the staircase. I was already clattering down the stairs ahead of him.

'You're running.' The gravelly voice was painfully slow and dragged now. 'They always run in the end. They talk a big game and then they run.'

Timbo clattered down the iron staircase and fell flat into my arms. And we ran together across the floor below and on down the wooden stairs at the far end of it. After he clanged the door of the mill behind him, we paused for a second. But I could hear nothing, only the thump of my heart. When we found our bikes, we stopped and listened again, but heard nothing, not a sound.

It is the early-morning joggers who are the first to witness the horrors now, and this time it was a fair-haired radiographer who always did her Five K along the towpath at first light before catching the train into Wakefield. She was three hundred yards from Prosper Mill when she saw the thing swinging from the iron gantry high above her. It was twisting gently in the morning breeze along the canal. At first she thought it was a bale of cloth, part of the new exhibition that had just opened at the mill. She was still a few yards off when she realised that it was a man's body and it was only when she came level with the great gaunt building that she saw how big he was. His clothes were tumbled about him which was what made him look like a bale of wool off-ends. There was nothing she could do on her own, so she called 999 on her mobile, and they said, thank you, they had already had a tip-off and a car was on its way and they knew where the mill was because there had been an application to develop it as a conference centre and they had been out there to check the premises for access and traffic implications.

'He had the length of rope tied round his neck when he jumped. He also carried a revolver in his pocket, a subcompact Beretta, what we call a ladies' gun, and he had an envelope too, containing three pills which we believe to be cyanide. In fact he had a regular Cluedo kit about his person. I wonder if you can shed any light, madam?'

'Oh, yes,' Bric said. 'Beaky was fascinated by suicide. He was convinced that his father had killed himself, though the inquest said he hadn't, and he would often bring up the subject, especially when he was having a good time. We would be at York races or having dinner at the Caprice and he would suddenly imagine his body swinging. The first book he ever told me to read when I came to England was *Oliver Twist*, because of the way the burglar dies at the end. Beaky liked it not being clear whether he had hanged himself on purpose or whether he was still trying to escape but the rope had slipped. But he wasn't sure whether he would ever have the courage to do it himself. That's probably why he took all those things with him so if he couldn't face using one he could use another. He always liked to be well provided.'

'Well, he made a good job of it, if you'll pardon the expression. I hope I won't be distressing you further if I ask whether you knew he was still legally married to his first wife.'

'Oh, heavens, yes. It was all a great game. I was to play his wife and I had to be a princess because otherwise the Yorkshire people would look down on me. Monique was so aristocratic, you see, or said she was, and it would be a comedown for him to marry a pharmacist's daughter from Odessa.'

'You mean you're not a princess?'

'No, of course not, but we lived very close to the Dolgoruky Palace and the Villa Efrussi was at the end of the avenue, and they all came to Papa's shop for their stomach pills and their eye drops, so I knew how to behave. Beaky loved my Russian Princess Act. He was such fun, always such fun.'

XV

Grimwade Cottage Hospital

He was a good baby, an excellent baby. Eight pounds three ounces at birth and regained his birthweight in no time. Lee was getting five or six hours' sleep now that he was skipping the 2 a.m. feed. Most of the time he lay gurgling in her arms. He had just developed a touch of jaundice, which made him look less of a ginger. At birth, his little aureole of frizz had been a pure auburn.

'All my mother's family had that hair,' Lee said. 'My mother was actually disappointed when I turned out mouse.'

'I don't know what colour hair my parents had originally,' Luke said. 'My mother had gone grey by the time I was conscious and Derek Senior, well, you know what a blank he is to me.'

'I don't think Derek Junior is going to be a blank.'

'That does seem highly improbable,' Luke said, looking down at the baby with a severe sort of fondness.

'He's a really lovely baby,' I said.

Events in the outside world came to her dimly in her drowsy torpor, she said. Nothing was anywhere near as sharp to her as the progress of Dekko's jaundice – he had been Dekko from Day Two – or his occasional flinching from her breast. She had been told the whole story, of course, almost as soon as she had come round: about Timbo first of all – now that Beaky was dead, he could surface at last; and about how George Furcht was still comatose in a wheelchair in Connecticut and would never be the same again, which Luke said acidly could be counted as a plus. Cotton had touched 200 and Furcht and Co. were over 120, and the hedgies were running very bad headaches. Nearly a dozen funds had been wound up and it was rumoured that the String Bags were selling their Greek island.

271

Only Flash Falk was in clover, having disregarded the advice from on high and remained faithful to his scummy motto of 'last in, first out'. Rowley was riding high, and was generally agreed to be giving a plausible imitation of a CEO, having learnt the patter at a hundred briefings and AGMs over the years. He was still in two minds about marrying Midge, even though Midge on hearing the news of his elevation had jumped over the wall of Chelsea Cloisters and taken an apartment in the Village and it was generally thought, not least by Rowley himself, that he was cornered. Not that he minded much. As always, he took things as they came.

There was a collective gasp when the size of Monique's fortune was revealed. All Beaky's early brilliance had gone into his French investments. The estate netted out at 5.4 billion euros. After a few bequests to cousins and the local nunnery, the residue went, as was only right and proper to her estranged but still beloved and lawfully wedded husband Sir Wilfrid Bentliff, now deceased. Beaky would have been well aware of this, as they had drawn up their wills together in happier days and they continued to share the same *avocat* in the avenue Montaigne.

As he tightened his huge hands round Monique's throat (her scarf had merely become entangled in the strangling, she was not stran- gled with it), while they were sitting in the little pavilion with its unrivalled view of the green volcanic hills of the Auvergne, what exactly had been in his mind? Was he ablaze with uncontrollable rage at her obstinate refusal to bail him out, or did he hope to inherit her fortune just in time for one of the biggest individual bailout operations in history? If the latter, he would have had to get away with the murder first, because like every civilised country France has a 'slayer statute' which prevents a murderer from inheriting from his victim. If he had been put on trial, let alone been convicted, the Bentliff Group would surely have imploded in the most spectacular fashion. But had he really expected the police to fall for the story of the intruder surprised?

'In my experience, they all think we're idiots,' said the Inspector when the ward sister let him in to see Lee for five minutes. 'Despite every other case they've ever read about, they still fondly imagine that the husband is the last person we are going to suspect when of course he's the first. It's funny really, they seem to think that killing your wife is such an awful thing to do, although they've just done it, that they can't imagine anyone else would guess. The whole time we're following another lead, or pretending to, we never stop watching the husband. I don't mind telling you, Mrs Deverill, this one was a piece of cake. As soon as we had the Peugeot plates, we picked up his trail from the Eurotunnel log. The French police also have his fresh prints on the French windows. Yet right up to the last he was still hoping to get away with it. That is why he was so anxious that there should be no doubt about his still being married to Monique. There were probably other relatives he feared might contest the will saying he wasn't. Amazing that such a brilliant man should—'

'Yes, it is, isn't it?' Lee said dreamily. 'And the money, what happens to the money?'

'Oh, a fair bit goes to the Princess and then the residue to the Brawldale Wildlife Trust, which will very likely include Monique's fortune too, because he died before we could nail him, although I'm sure that her relatives will put up a struggle in the French courts. So the otters will be eating salmon twice a day.'

'Well, I'm not much of a nature-lover,' Lee said, 'but I don't begrudge the otters, or the voles come to that. In fact, I can't think of a more harmless destination for Beaky's ill-gotten billions.'

The Inspector took his leave, and when the coast was clear, I brought in Timbo from the day room at the back of the hospital.

'No, I don't believe it, it really is you,' she said, holding out her arms to him.

'How could you tell? Nobody else has recognised me.'

'It's the way you come into the room, charging in defiantly as if you expect someone's going to throw you out. But oh, your poor bald head.'

'What about my nose, though, and my chin?'

'Your nose I like, yes, I definitely like your nose. It's a lot more aristocratic than the old one. And the chin has to go with the nose, I suppose. It's like a matching set, you have to have both.'

'Yes, that's what they told me. I felt I was going to look like Mr Punch. I still don't look in the mirror.'

'No, not like Mr Punch, or well, perhaps a little like but only in the nicest possible way. My poor Bimbo. What you went through, and all for nothing, really.'

'It didn't seem like nothing at the time,' Timbo said.

'No, I do know that. Arturo told us there was a killing frenzy on. He really didn't think you'd get out alive, otherwise he would not have recommended such a drastic operation. He wonders now whether he was right. But anyway if you really mind, darling, you can always get his brother-in-law to reverse the whole thing. I'm sure Furcht and Co. would be happy to pay after all you've done for them.'

'And my hair will grow again of course.'

She did not respond for a moment. Then she said: 'Yes, yes, of course it *could*. Just wait a moment, darling.'

She reached up behind her and pressed the bell.

'Oh, Della, has Livvy finished giving Dekko his bath yet?'

'I think so, Mrs Deverill. I'll just fetch him.'

In a couple of minutes, Dekko was in her arms, rosy and chubby, the jaundice more or less gone now, and his hair still wet from his bath which made it the colour of dried blood.

'Oh,' said Timbo. 'Yes. I hadn't expected that.'

'Nor had I, darling. It's the luck of the draw.'

'Oh, God,' he said.

'I told Lukey that all my mother's family had hair like that. It's best not to jog his memory of what yours used to be like, don't you think, darling, especially when Dekko gets more of a thatch.'

'Oh, God,' he said again. 'Yes, I suppose you're right.'

It had happened the evening he was clearing up Dilkusha before they moved out, Timbo told me later. Lethal had stayed on to give him a hand, while Luke had taken the Tube down to South Ken to supervise the unpacking at the new flat, the one behind the Albert Hall. There wasn't much to shift because Timbo had taken the place furnished. Lethal's little red car was loaded up and he was just looking round to make sure he hadn't missed anything. Lethal was resting on the bed, smoking a Silk Cut and gazing out of the window at the darkening city below. She turned and watched him putting the empty waste-paper basket back under the desk and she was overcome by a spasm of affection or gratitude or both.

'Bimbo,' she said, 'come here a minute.'

Even before he had kissed her, she had begun to tug up her skirt. They were together for two or three minutes, he thought, scarcely more, as brief as birds coupling. But it was wonderful, more wonderful really because it was so quick, so intense, so easy. He had never known anything like it. He could not help thinking of his long nights with Aurore but it was unfair to compare. This was something different. It would never happen again, but that didn't matter, that was part of it. He knew how little it would mean to her. She would know how much it meant to him. That was why nothing would come of it, except of course that something now had.

'Thank you,' he had said because he could not think of anything else to say.

'Thank you, Bimbo, thank you for everything,' she had said and he could see her smiling in the twilight.

XVI

Beggar's Hill Revisited

Timbo had warned me about the electric gate. He said that I could expect to see a few other changes too. All the same, as I tapped in the code, I couldn't help being startled by the ribbon of gleaming tarmac beyond and the bright fresh-painted railings, and then the new sign fixed to the tiled clubhouse roof (now cleared of its comforting old moss), showing a hunched beggar climbing a green hill. Underneath the beggar, there was a motto inscribed in gold – I never knew the club had a motto – *ardor et labor.*

'What do you think of it? Quite a good motto for a golf club, don't you think?'

'It's all amazing,' I said, staring at Timbo. He was a scarcely less amazing sight himself, in his green golfing jacket made of some puppyish material with the same beggar climbing the hill embossed on his left nipple and a green baseball cap with matching beggar. Below the beggar on the jacket, it said in modest but unmissable gold lettering: 'Captain'.

I could only point to the word, unable to think what to say.

'Oh, yes, that. Well, strictly speaking, I'm Managing Director, but we thought Captain had more of a sporting ring to it.'

'You …'

'What happened was that the Club's finances were in such a parlous state, there was talk of closing down and selling the whole place for development. You only needed planning permission for a tiny corner and you'd be laughing. Some of the members were looking forward to cashing in. Anyway, I happened to mention the whole sorry story to Rowley.'

'Rowley Beavan?'

'The very same. Well, for some reason he seemed to think they owed me one, so he said, why didn't they help us turn the old club into a limited company. I said, it wasn't for me to say, I wasn't even on the committee, and anyway who's going to lend a bean to a crummy old club like ours with an overdraft of two hundred thousand quid. Golf courses are closing down all over the country. But Rowley says, hang on a minute, and he puts the idea to Hal Gombrich, and Hal says, how much do they need, would three do, or no, probably they'd need four million to do a proper upgrade, pounds not dollars. So I jumped at it of course, and so did most of the members, though there were half a dozen holdouts who were still hankering after a bumper payday. So here we are, Beggar's Hill plc, and really motoring. There's even a waiting list, which is unheard of. It was Hal who suggested the motto, by the way, though he's not a golfer himself.'

'You mean Rowley and Hal have sort of bought the whole club for you?'

'Invested in it, though I am a major shareholder, along with Rowley and Hal and Upstate First of course.'

I gazed out over the rolling fairways, the little copses of sycamore and ash and the reed-girt pond at the short fifth and marvelled that this should all now be Timbo's personal domain.

'I do hope you'll join,' Timbo, taking off his cap to scratch his shaven head. His eyebrows were somehow more expressive now. His beaky nose, though you couldn't call it elegant, had a certain forcefulness. He had lost that blundering look which had first endeared him to me.

'That would be lovely,' I said, not meaning it. The whole business was too peculiar to get involved in all over again. 'Do you do a special membership package with back treatment thrown in?'

'I'm no good to you now for that,' he said. 'I've given up healing. I've lost the power.'

'You could always let your hair grow back. That might do the trick.'

'I can't do that,' he said.

'Why not?'

'Think,' he said.

'Oh, I see,' I said, then wishing to get off that topic, I added, 'Are you sure you can't do it any more, the healing, I mean?'

'I can see you don't believe me. Look, I'll show you. Sit sideways on that chair.'

I swivelled round and sat in the old position, trunk straight but angled forward a little and waited, despite what he had said, for the old warm feeling to creep down my spine. I felt his breath on my ear, but otherwise nothing. There were some pigeons cooing in the brooding sycamore at the end of the terrace, as if to say 'see, he told you'.

'There,' he said as he moved away, 'what did I tell you?'

'You could be not trying, or wilfully preventing the power from flowing through your fingers.'

'It was never a question of willpower. I couldn't turn it on or off. It just came and now it's gone. No reason why it should last for ever.'

'You must miss it, though, that feeling of power.'

'Do I?' he said reflectively – he seemed generally more reflective now, and somehow a little bitter. 'I don't think so, just like I don't miss my old face.'

'Or your old trade?'

'Oh, that I don't miss at all. I don't think I was ever really cut out for it. You know that Luke and Lee are setting up in the business, Deverill Risk Mitigation? They've already hired a surveillance whizz who used to work at Krolls. Rowley's put quite a bit of Furcht money behind them, which is the least they can do. Anyway, Furcht need some help in that department. George would never have come so close to going belly-up if he had had some early warning systems in place.'

'But what about your old colleagues? Surely they will miss your cheery face, even if it's not quite the same face any more – in fact that might be a plus in the trade, having a whole new identity as Roger Bellville.'

'What?' He had been gazing out at a foursome lumbering off down the first fairway. Throughout our talk so far, he had seemed distanced, not unfriendly but gone-away, as though I belonged to a part of his life which was finished and I had just happened to bump into him when he was already absorbed with his new life. But now suddenly he came alive and turned to look at me straight on, with his eyes bright, and I had an eerie sense that I could, just for that moment, see through the cosmetic mask into his old face, that eager blundering face which I had known so well.

'Jonty and your broker, what was he called, Ades, and the Colonel of course. They're bound to miss you.'

'You don't get it, you still really don't get it, do you?' He was still staring at me and I began to feel uncomfortable and a little resentful.

'What do you mean, don't get it?'

'You still think it was all kosher, Ophion House and all that.'

'Well, yes. Peculiar, it did all seem peculiar to me, I admit. But yes, I did think it was … genuine, if that's the right word.'

'Listen,' he said. 'A friend of mine got me a six-month fag-end lease on the place dirt cheap. I had my cards printed up at Kall Kwik and I had the brass plate engraved at a shoe repair shop in Clerkenwell which has a sideline in metalwork. Jonty is an actor friend who's mostly resting and needed a place to stay. We took his character from an old Le Carré novel. Adrian used to work in a bank but he had been made redundant and was between jobs, as you might say. When the lease ran out, the same friend who got us O.H. fixed us up with Dilkusha for another three months, not such a good address for meeting clients but we were still doing half a million quid's worth of business last year.'

'And the Colonel?'

'Ah, that's a longer story.' He stopped. I thought he might be wondering whether it was a story he really wanted to tell. But perhaps he was only gathering his thoughts.

'You see, when I left school, I didn't know what I wanted to do, so Moth got me a job in a bank. I don't know why. He wasn't the least bit interested in banking himself, in fact he regarded all bankers as villains, the way everyone does now. Anyway I took the job, and I hated it, couldn't get the hang of it at all. And I must have shown it too. Ades worked in the same bank actually, he did well, to start with anyway. But not me. As the years went by, I developed a bit of a reputation as a maverick, not a team player at all. In the end, they said it would be better if I looked for a fresh challenge. So there I was, out on my ear. I took it very hard and thought the only thing was to leave the country and start again. I didn't want to tell Moth what had happened, so I told him that I had decided on a change of direction and was going to hotel school in Switzerland to learn how to become a hotel manager. In fact what I did was to get a job as a waiter at the Augsburg Hotel in St Moritz, which happens to be where this club of world leaders meets every year – the Augsburg Club. Well, I turned out to be quite good at waiting and I enjoyed hovering at the elbow of these VIPs and listening to them showing off as I handed them their drinks. And that's when I got the idea.'

While Timbo was describing his failure at the bank, his beaky profile had gone into a doleful droop. But now that he was embarking on this fresh chapter, his whole expression perked up. Even with a refurb face he was incapable of concealing how he was feeling.

'This elderly gent was talking to me in the room where they had these big receptions three times a day during the Club meeting. He was one of those people who like to establish a personal relationship with staff, so he said to me, Tim – we all had name badges – every time I come into this room, I want you to be at my elbow with a vodka and tonic with a twist of lemon. Two fingers of vodka, no more, no less. And we got chatting because he was one of the first to arrive and anyway I think he was a little bit gay. And so I said, just to amuse myself really, of course I'm also here to keep an eye on things. And he said, what do you mean, Tim? And I told him I was really part of the security team to make sure that all the Club's discussions remained strictly confidential and that there were no intruders and nobody bugging them or hacking into their texts and emails. And he was most impressed and he said, now how did all that come about? And I said that our firm had been recommended by Colonel Kerrigan who was a famous war hero turned industrialist and who was on the Club's organising committee, and I nodded at this silver-haired much older gent at the far end of the room. And later on, I made sure to have a word with Colonel Kerrigan when the first chap was looking in my direction. The first chap was called Weston Brown and he used to be an American ambassador and now he was President of a Washington think tank. And Weston introduced me to George Furcht and a couple of other moguls, explaining who I really was. Then in my afternoon break I went down into the town and had some cards printed. I thought of the Ophites because I was reading an SF novel which had these snakeheads called Ophites in it. Then the next day I thought of a few add-on functions that we could offer – cryptography, industrial intelligence, risk mitigation

– all the stuff I'd read about in the newspapers, and they lapped it up. Oh, and my real bit of luck was that the Colonel turned out to have gone a bit gaga and he loved it when I suggested that he should be our honorary president. In fact, he was quite easily persuaded that he already was our President and he didn't want to make a fool of himself by revealing that he had forgotten being appointed. Anyway, by the end of the conference, I had a corporate brand and half a dozen potential clients. The fact that the initial contact had been made at the Augsburg Club really gave it cast-iron credibility in their eyes, especially because the contact had been made through an agent posing as a waiter. That was irresistible.'

'Then the Colonel did actually exist.'

'Yes, just about, but he scarcely ever appeared, which was great because I could always use him as an excuse, or as a source of authority: oh, I don't think the Colonel would approve of that, or the Colonel always says, and so on. And when I thought of a good idea or saw some useful rule for operations in a self-help book or management magazine, I would always attribute it to the Colonel to give it more weight. I mean, that's only what professors do, isn't it, quote some other professor to make you believe what they're saying. He's gone into a home now, the Colonel, so he can't even come to the Christmas drinks, though I try to pop in and see him whenever I'm in the area.'

'So the whole set-up was really just a façade.'

'Well, you could say that,' Timbo said, looking quite jaunty now, 'but there's nothing wrong with a façade. Business isn't really like architecture, you know. You don't start with the foundations, you start with the façade, then you build backwards.'

'Ah,' I said.

'That's what we did anyway and it seemed to work.'

It was this twang of complacency that snapped what was left of my patience.

'Don't you ever get tired of making things up?'

'You have to use a bit of creative imagination to get anywhere in this life.'

'It's what most people call lying.'

'Look,' said Timbo, 'I sense that you are getting angry and I'm really sad about this because I wanted this to be a special reunion.

Not just for you and me, but I also arranged that Aurore should meet us here. She's just back from Afghanistan, and she's off to South Sudan next week. And we've decided to use this window to get married. She's so keen to meet you.'

I had long ago forgotten about Timbo's supposed fiancée. From the start I had regarded her as semi-mythical. If she existed at all, she was probably just a person he knew slightly and fantasised about getting off with. As events unwound and the full range of his myth-making capacities was revealed, she seemed even more unlikely to exist. For someone who could conjure an entire counter-intelligence network out of a waiter's napkin, a shadowy fiancée in Afghanistan was no more than a grace note. It was typical somehow that she should turn out to be the only real person in the whole saga.

'Look, here she is now,' he said.

I turned to follow the direction of his pointing finger and round the corner of the clubhouse came a small, square-ish woman pushing a bike. She had short, streaked fair hair under her bike helmet.

'I'm so pleased to meet you,' she said, as she propped her bike against the parapet of the terrace. 'T has told me so much about you.'

She had a nose that was nearly but not quite snub and she had freckles on her cheeks, quite pleasant if you liked that sort of face. I could not detect the trace of a French accent in her voice. She could not have looked or sounded less like the female Médecins sans Frontières as seen on TV, with their long dark hair falling over their white coats and their luminous eyes and seductive French vowels.

'Oh,' she said when I complimented her on her English, 'I was brought up in South Ken. My father worked at the Institute. But T says he can still tell from the way I say 'my r's.'

There was something exotic, even alluring, about the way she called him T, as though he was the mysterious anonymous hero in an intellectual novel or involved in a delicate divorce case the details of which had to be kept secret. Perhaps it really suited Timbo better than any of the other names people called him by.

'When she gets back from the Sudan, Aurore's going to convert the old members' snug into a gastropub. She used to be a sous-chef at the Brasserie Lipp before she qualified.'

'Yes, my travelling days are over,' she said with a laugh. 'We're calling it Le Repos des Clochards, the Beggars' Rest. We will serve specialities from the Auvergne, the ones my mother taught me.'

'We all deserve a bit of rest, I think,' Timbo said.

'Yes, we do,' I said, and meant it. She looked like a really nice girl. And perhaps they really were going to get married – that at least seemed genuine. But for my own part, I had a sudden violent feeling that what I really needed was a rest from Timbo and his world. And I had had enough of Beggar's Hill too. I preferred the club the way it had been when it wasn't trying to impress, because it knew it couldn't.

I had been touched by Timbo when we first met and for a long time afterwards. He seemed so old-fashioned, so solid. His belief in loyalty, his devotion to his father's memory, the care he had taken with Luke and Lee when they were at rock bottom – all these things had moved me, apart from the energy he poured into healing my back. But now it seemed that Timbo, Timothy, Bimbo, Timmy, Tim, T, whatever you called him, was not solid at all. On the contrary, he was as sinuous and evanescent as a streak of oil on a pond. And this was the ultimate disconcerting thing, far more disconcerting than if you had been misled by someone who was obviously one jump ahead.

The truth was no more creditable to me than it was to him. For mostly what I was sore about was being suckered from first to last by a person of inferior intelligence. The only lesson I could take from the whole humiliating experience was that you did not need to be clever to be a good liar. I had attributed Timbo's healing powers to his simplicity of soul. Now it turned out that his soul was not simple at all. His healing powers were gone (if they ever existed anywhere except in my own mind), and it was time I was gone too.

As Aurore passed Timbo's chair on the way to the bar, she bent down and kissed him. When she had gone off – to the Congo, was it? – the man she must have kissed had a blubbery face and hair the colour of dried blood. Now she was kissing a bald eagle with lips like a film star's. To these people, material things like that didn't seem to matter.

'I'm afraid I have to be getting along,' I said, and I said it with an ill grace.

'Do stay for a coffee,' he said. 'It comes free with the couscous.'

But I got up and walked off along the path to the car park. The pigeons were still cooing in the big sycamore. As I ducked under the lower branches, a white spatter kissed my left shoulder. At least you could rely on the pigeons.

On my way, I passed by the little Dutch-style clubhouse porch, which sheltered the airjet machine for blasting mud off golf shoes. And I remembered Timbo bending forward to offer first one shoe, then the other to the hissing nozzle like a carthorse waiting to be shod, and how I had been overcome by an unaccountable feeling that the first couple of hours I had spent with him – my first experience of his healing hands – had been a sort of holiday from time. Well, so it had been, but what I realised now was how much I needed the holiday and how I had really made the booking myself. I had believed because I needed to believe, and it was too late to ask for my money back.

XVII

The Amp House

Hal Gombrich looked just as cherubic as the day I had first met him, hastening across the turf at Longchamp on Arc Day.

'Aha, the rushing mighty wind of Pentecost,' he hallooed as he caught sight of me.

On the manicured lawns of Longchamp he had been an urbane boulevardier. Here in his straw hat and two-tone shoes among the rougher punters under the old grandstand at Monmouth Park, New Jersey, he had the air of a chancer out of Damon Runyon, not unlike Nicely-Nicely Johnson in *Guys and Dolls*. Despite his extravagant personality, or perhaps because of it, he fitted in anywhere.

'Welcome to our bucolic pastures,' he said, waving a hand at the other Runyon types marking their racecards or staring at the odds on the big screen.

I don't often get foreign jaunts these days, but the PM was going to Washington and then on to the UN and the political editor was halfway through chemo, so I got the slot and Rowley persuaded me to tack on a couple of days to go racing with him.

'Hal's going to be there too and he's very keen to see you again.'

'Me? I only met him briefly, that one time at the Arc.'

'He wants to hear the full Timbo story. After all, you were the only one who was there at the beginning. Then besides, he thought you would like in return to know about Moonshine. You were the one who noticed the map on the wall.'

'Yes, but I hadn't a clue what it meant.'

'Well, now you shall. Hal's awfully proud of it, you know, and I must say I do take my hat off to the old boy.'

Rowley was right about that. I could see how anxious Hal was to show me whatever it was. We had only watched a couple of races before he looked at his watch and said, 'I think we'd better make a move if we're to get there before dark.'

He scuttled on ahead of us to the space behind the paddock where the owners' planes and helicopters were parked.

'It's only twenty minutes,' he said as he buckled himself in. 'So I'll make it snappy. You know what front-running is?'

'It's when a horse makes a habit of taking the lead right from the start.'

'That's in racing, yes. On Wall Street, it means getting in ahead of the other guy of the basis of information you have but he hasn't.'

'Isn't that called insider dealing?'

'That is the generic term which covers a multitude of sins. What we're interested in here is something a good deal more specific. Suppose some big investor, a pension fund let's say, wants to buy 100,000 shares of Coca-Cola. His buy will send the price up a couple of cents or more, so if you can get advance warning, you can buy the shares at the current price and pocket the hike when you sell them on. On large trades that kind of adds up, pretty soon you're talking millions, tens or hundreds of millions on really big deals. So how do you get the jump on the guy who's buying? What you do is offer a small packet of the shares, say 100, and when they get snapped up you know there's a big order in the wind and you buy 100,000 before the price has a chance to move. All you need is to be a couple of milliseconds quicker than the other guy, that's about the tenth of the blink of an eye.

'Now the fibre cables we use today are darned quick, but every time they have to go round a corner, it slows 'em up. Long distances slow 'em up too, like the distance between the New York Exchange in Carteret, New Jersey, and the NASDAQ Exchange in Chicago which is about eight hundred miles away. Every extra mile makes a difference, which is why you see brokers who are actually inside the Exchanges angling to get their desks closer to the big server or in a straight line with it.'

'Really?' I queried. 'Just for the sake of a few yards?'

'Bet your bottom dollar, and they do bet their bottom dollar. You wouldn't believe the kickbacks the guys managing the Exchanges get offered. Distance equals time equals money – the one equation Einstein never thought of.' Hal smiled benignly at the thought and continued with brio: 'So imagine, just imagine if you could get your cable running dead straight all the way to Chicago. Ah, here we are. Can you put us down in that field, Ed, the one with the brown stubble?'

The chopper landed on the place he was pointing to and we ran at a feral crouch from the declining whirr of its blades.

We stood to get our breath back, the three of us, in a desolate flat landscape. I could see cabbage fields beyond the stubble and beyond the cabbage fields there were scrubby bushes under a sullen sky. In front of us there was a forbidding concrete blockhouse about thirty foot square. A narrow blacktop ran off past the blockhouse dead straight all the way to the horizon.

'Look,' Hal said. 'There.'

He was pointing to a thin strip of fresh tarmac laid along the left-hand side of the old blacktop.

'That's our baby, runs fifty miles from here to the Delaware. Most valuable thing to cross the river since George Washington. Mark you, the Delaware's not as wide as the Susquehanna, that's two miles across and the only drill in the world with a reach that long was the one George had some place down on the Amazon. But then it turned out there was a bridge near enough not to damage the line and all we had to do was to pay a couple of guys a few bucks for the wayleave.'

'Have I got this right?' I said. 'You're digging a cable the whole way to Chicago just to shave a millisecond off the time it takes the computer to place an order?'

'Sure we are. And George's little service company, you won't know its name and you don't need to know it, was getting fifteen million dollars rental from every bank and broker we sold space on it. And because they were putting their clients' money through their dark pools where no deals are registered on the Exchanges, none of the clients – for example, the mutuals who invest the little guys' savings – had a clue what was happening. But, and here's the cream of the jest, the hedge funds didn't have a clue either, and they were the ones who were really losing margin, and they were sore as hell but they didn't know what was causing it. This is supposed to be an

information society, yet all parties were in a state of perfect ignorance, except of course the prime brokers who had signed up with
us, but even they didn't know which of the other guys was high on
the Moonshine too.'

'So this was the threat that Beaky was denouncing at the fashion
show.'

'We prefer to think of it more as an opportunity.' Hal could scarcely
contain his mirth. 'Of course this wasn't what put them out of business. That was due to their betting against George to the bitter end,
which turned out to be their bitter end. But Moonshine sure gave
them a haircut to remember. Come and look at the Amp House.'

Hal led them over the stubble to the big white blockhouse. He
gazed at the unlovely building, its fresh concrete still gleaming in the
dying afternoon light, as reverently as if he were looking at the Taj
Mahal or the Wailing Wall.

'This is where it's at, Dickie,' he said as he rapped the blank
wall.

'What is it exactly?'

'These little babies amplify the fibre optic signal. There's one to
restore the fade every fifty miles from here to the Windy City.'

He stepped gingerly across the prickly ground, his brown-and-
cream shoes picking their way like dainty ferrets.

'Where do you think you're going, mister?'

A tubby man in a fur hunting cap and cowboy boots came round
the side of the bunker. He was carrying an automatic weapon in a
fashion that looked both aggressive and uneasy.

'We're from Hyperconnect, I've got my ID somewhere,' Hal said,
looking gratified rather than discomfited.

'I don't care where the fuck you're from. I take my orders from
Maxsec.'

'We just wanted to have a look round.'

'This ain't no tourist attraction, buddy. You better get back to that
chopper of yours, because I've just radioed for backup.'

We retreated, Hal bleating the while how pleased he was at the
standard of vigilance.

'We have had bomb threats,' he chortled. 'And there've been a
couple of cases of sabotage on the Cleveland stretch, but it's child's
play to repair the line.'

'Hardly surprising, is it?' I said. 'You screw the hedge funds, you screw the other bankers who haven't signed up to Moonshine, and worst of all, you screw all the people who've entrusted their savings to Wall Street. I'm only surprised that every one of these block-houses hasn't been blasted to buggery.'

'Harsh words, Dickie, harsh words. It is sad but true that all advances in communication are liable to be met with incomprehension and suspicion at first. But consider the facts. Since the coming of computers, commissions on every stock exchange have been shaved from a hunk of dollars to a matter of cents. We all benefit, including the little guys, and we should not repine if some of us benefit more than others. It is a natural human instinct, and a laudable one, Dickie, to want to get the news first. Mercury is the messenger of the gods, after all. You remember Pheidippides?'

'The man who ran the twenty-six miles from Marathon to Athens to bring the news of the victory in the battle and then dropped dead.'

'I knew you would not fail me. What you may not know was that Pheidippides was not just a patriotic young man, he was a professional messenger, a day-runner or *hemerodromos*, employed by the banking community of Athens to bring them the latest intelligence. I had thought of christening this cable after him, but it is a cumbersome name and George was wedded to Moonshine for sentimental reasons.

'Yes, of course there are always winners and losers, that's what makes it a game. You no doubt also remember how Nathan Rothschild had carrier pigeons bring him advance news of the Allied victory at Waterloo. But you may not be aware of exactly what he did when he got that news. He went into the market and *sold* large blocks of shares. So everyone thought, old Nattie always knows, we must have lost the battle, and hurried to sell too. Shares fell off the proverbial cliff. Only then did Rothschild wade into the market and start buying on a colossal scale. Yet to this day Rothschild is the most respected name in the City of London, and who sheds a tear for those lesser mortals who got taken?

'Information is king, Dickie, and always will be, because everything is always changing, and nothing stays the same. *Panta rei, ouden menei*. Heraclitus had it right first time: go with the flow and get there before the other fellow if you can.

'And, my dear Dickie, you may console yourself with the thought that, if you've missed this bus, there's always another bus coming up behind. My friends tell me that fibre optic is already *vieux jeu*. Microwave is apparently fearsomely quick now. There will come a time, soon enough, when the Moonshine line and this splendid Amp House will be as obsolete as the sedan chair. Comfort yourself with that thought, Dickie.'

I wanted to tell him what I thought, but Hal had already signalled for the chopper to restart its engine and was teetering back across the stubble. Rowley followed him. They were both about to board when Rowley turned round to check that I was following.

I wasn't. Rowley advanced a few steps towards me, beckoning me with both hands. But I spread out my own hands, palms downwards, in a gesture of negation, dismissal, I don't know what, like someone smoothing down a bedspread. It wasn't just that I didn't want to go in that helicopter. What I wanted was to be anywhere on the planet where there was no prospect of ever seeing Hal Gombrich again.

I walked off across the stubble towards the blacktop road. I had the whole of New Jersey before me, without a banker in sight. I never felt so happy in my life.

Thanks and Goodbye

I cannot leave the scene without thanking, in the warmest possible terms, some of my guides along the way: Dr Redmond O'Hanlon, who led me up the Amazon in his irresistible fashion; Professor Greg Grandin, whose *Fordlandia* is an unmatched exploration of human dreams and follies; and Mr Ashley Silverton of Brewin Dolphin and Mr Graeme Stephen, formerly of the Man Group in Zurich, whose machetes hacked a path for me through the trackless jungles of the City; alert readers will also have spotted the profound debt I owe to Mr Michael Lewis for *The Big Short* and *Flash Boys*. I am extremely grateful also to Majors A. D. Parsons MC, D. L. M. Robbins MC and D. C. Gilson MC, authors of *The Maroon Square*, the history of the 4th Battalion, the Wiltshire Regiment, in Northern Europe 1942–5. I have learnt much too from Steven Levy's remarkable book, *Crypto*.

Few stories ever end, they are merely broken off. As I write, fresh logging has more or less slowed to a halt in Amazonia, officially anyway, and mild fields of cotton blow over the Mato Grosso. But in fifty years' time, who knows? Those cotton growers may become a tribe as forlorn as the rubber tappers of the Amazon, their warehouses as derelict as Fordlandia or Prosper Mill. And Hal Gombrich was right. His Amp Houses are already obsolete. To save a few nanoseconds, High Frequency Traders are now booking slots on Elon Musk's satellites instead. Everything flows, nothing stays and the wind bloweth where it listeth. *So geht es, immer weiter*, as Captain Dieter Furcht, late of the Kriegsmarine and retired naval attaché to the President of

Brazil, used to say. I owe so much to the encouragement and acute advice of Paul Baggaley and the brilliant editing of Gillian Stern at Bloomsbury, and, as ever, to the patience and diligence of my agent Matt Turner.

A Note on the Author

Ferdinand Mount is a novelist, essayist and former editor of the *Times Literary Supplement* from 1991 to 2002. As a political figure, he was head of the Number Ten Policy Unit. As a journalist, he has contributed regular columns to the *Spectator*, the *Daily Telegraph* and the *Sunday Times*. His novel *Of Love And Asthma*, part of a six-volume series, *A Chronicle of Modern Twilight*, won the Hawthornden Prize in 1992. He lives in North London with his family.

A Note on the Type

The text of this book is set in Bembo, which was first used in 1495 by the Venetian printer Aldus Manutius for Cardinal Bembo's *De Aetna*. The original types were cut for Manutius by Francesco Griffo. Bembo was one of the types used by Claude Garamond (1480–1561) as a model for his Romain de l'Université, and so it was a forerunner of what became the standard European type for the following two centuries. Its modern form follows the original types and was designed for Monotype in 1929.